DOUBLE CROSS

Patrick Woodrow was born in 1971. He was educated at
Cambridge and began writing after a ten year career as a
management consultant in London, Singapore and
Seattle. A dedicated sun-worshipper, he spends as much
time as possible diving in the tropics. He lives in
London. *Double Cross* is his first novel.

For my parents

DOUBLE CROSS

Patrick Woodrow

arrow books

Published by Arrow in 2005

1 3 5 7 9 10 8 6 4 2

Arrow Books
The Random House Group Limited
20 Vauxhall Bridge Road, London SW1V 2SA

Random House Australia (Pty) Limited
20 Alfred Street, Milsons Point, Sydney
New South Wales 2061, Australia

Random House New Zealand Limited
18 Poland Road, Glenfield,
Auckland 10, New Zealand

Random House (Pty) Limited
Endulini, 5a Jubilee Road, Parktown 2193, South Africa

The Random House Group Limited Reg. No 954009

www.randomhouse.co.uk

A CIP catalogue record for this book is available from the British Library

Papers used by Random House are natural, recyclable products made from wood
grown in sustainable forests. The manufacturing processes conform to the
environmental regulations of the country of origin

ISBN 0 09 947859 5

Typeset by SX Composing DTP, Rayleigh, Essex
Printed and bound in Great Britain by
Bookmarque Ltd, Croydon, Surrey

PART I

Ride a cock horse to Banbury Cross
To see a fine lady upon a white horse;
Rings on her fingers and bells on her toes,
And she shall have music wherever she goes.

Two rings on her left hand, one bell on her right,
She sits on her saddle at just the right height.
One bell on her right foot, one ring on her left,
She sits on her saddle with just the right heft.

Ride a cock horse to Banbury Cross
To see a fine lady upon a white horse;
Rings on her fingers and bells on her toes,
And she shall have music wherever she goes.

(Traditional nursery rhyme, adapted)

The mirror saved his life.

Ed Strachan never meant to look, but it was at the bottom of the stairs and he had to pass it to reach the bar. Dinner was going well. They'd almost finished their second bottle of wine so maybe that was what prompted it. No movement of the head. No break of the stride. Just a flick of the eyes to check himself out.

He was tanned and freckled after six days in the Curaçao sun. Although he'd taken a shower his hair was stiff with salt from the day's last dive. Stubble speckled his cheeks and chin, and his shirt hung from his shoulders like new. He wasn't vain but his mouth tightened in the faintest of smiles. He had to admit it: he looked pretty good.

He was halfway up the stairs when he realised what else he'd seen.

It was too late for a second glance but his mind had taken the shot. He took the steps two at a time as he processed the image. It was a side-on view of the table. There in the background, deep in the mirror's reflection: Christine Molyneux spiking his drink.

She was leaning forward in her chair, squirting something into his wine with a pipette. She'd attempted to hide the glass behind a menu and if it hadn't been for the mirror he'd never have known. Alarm surged in his stomach. What the hell was she doing? Drugging him?

He reached the bar and bought a packet of Camels. He lit one and drew on it, hard. *Drugging him.* Yes, that was exactly what she was doing. She'd told him about her penchant for Ecstasy over the aperitif. After the starter, her foot was in his lap, and she suggested that he should try some of the stuff. Her theory was simple: sex was better on E because it heightened and prolonged the pleasure.

Strachan didn't take drugs, so he'd laughed her off. Irritation had flashed in Christine's face, and he'd excused himself to go and buy cigarettes. Now he was amazed at her audacity. She was someone who couldn't take no for an answer.

He was heading back to London the next day with the films for the underwater calendar that he'd been shooting for *National Geographic*, and he'd been hoping to see her again when she returned from her holiday later that week. After catching the reflection, he wasn't so sure. Her stunt with the Ecstasy pissed him off. It was already obvious why they were here: at twenty-nine he was plenty old enough to know that when a pretty woman caressed his groin with her foot it wasn't to improve his circulation.

He took another hit on the Camel. The decision to switch glasses was made in a heartbeat. If she wanted to get high that was fine; she could do it on her own. He paid for the cigarettes and headed back down. Somewhere in the distance a band played calypso.

The Lobster Pot was the best restaurant in Willemstad. It was built from wood and wicker, and sat right on the waterfront. Their table was towards the rear. On his way back Strachan spotted a shoal of yellowtails, flashing like glass shards as they patrolled the water for scraps. The raffia blinds were up and a gust of wind caused the candle flames to shiver.

Christine had pulled her cardigan over her shoulders. She was exquisite. Her teeth were white and straight so that when she smiled she radiated health. She was fit and strong with cover-girl looks. The way the skin at the corners of her eyes wrinkled into crow's-feet reminded him of someone, but whoever it was the link was too distant to matter now. The waiter had cleared their plates and the drug in Strachan's glass had mixed without trace. He sat down and stubbed out the cigarette.

'Isn't that a bit stupid for someone who spends all his time diving?' Her accent: unmistakably East End London.

'I guess.' She favoured the athletic look so there was no lipstick on her glass, and both were filled to the same level. They wouldn't stay that way for long, though.

Strachan pulled a breadstick from the basket and broke it into four pieces. He tossed the bread over her head, and the yellowtails were on it in seconds. Christine turned to watch the frenzy unfurl in the water. Strachan shot out his hands and switched their glasses. Fast and steady. It only took a second. He had his new glass raised by the time it was over.

'To the fish,' he said, chinking his glass against hers. He rolled the wine round his mouth like a connoisseur before knocking it back in a single gulp. He would have preferred a beer.

'To the fish,' Christine echoed. If he overplayed the part, she didn't notice. She drained her glass, so that Sancerre and Ecstasy slipped down together. There was no gagging or clutching of the throat. Just a shimmer of those brilliant blue eyes, and a smile that said *Let's go*.

Dinner was over. Urgency consumed them. Strachan offered to make a contribution to the bill, knowing that

5

he couldn't afford it, but she told him to stop being a fool: this was *her* treat, and did he want to go back to his place or hers? They'd already discussed their respective accommodation. He was camping; she had a room at the San Marco hotel. It was a rhetorical question.

She settled the bill and they ran from the restaurant hand in hand.

Christine's room was small and had kitsch Caribbean decor. The stool by the desk and the armchair in the corner were bamboo. The prints on the wall were of skiffs, palm trees, and tropical fruit. A pair of jeans lay crumpled on the floor. A pink bikini dried on the windowsill. Strachan inspected the prints disapprovingly while she fetched him a beer from the minibar.

Christine giggled. She slurred her words as she ordered him out of his clothes. She was breathless as she disappeared into the bathroom, promising to return in something more comfortable. Something more comfortable turned out to be nothing at all, and when the door opened again he was waiting for her in a similar state on the bed.

'I said *completely* naked.' Christine shook her black hair loose so that it fell on her shoulders.

'I *am* completely naked.' Strachan's heart pounded inside his chest like a golf ball on a short length of elastic.

'Uh-uh. Take the cuff link off too.' She pointed to his neck, where he wore a solid silver cuff link on a chain like a pendant. The words tumbled out, heavy and awkward.

For the first time Strachan felt uneasy. Had she taken something herself before spiking his drink? If so, she might be in danger of an overdose. 'The cuff link stays on.' His voice wavered: the beginnings of doubt. The cuff link was a family heirloom. The only times he'd removed it in the last eleven years had been to pass through airport metal detectors. It had originally been one of a pair made by his grandfather, but the other had been stolen the night his parents died.

Christine's forehead creased as though she was searching for the answer to a puzzle. She said 'Never mind', and began crawling up the bed towards him.

'Chrissie, there's something I need to tell you.'

But she wasn't listening. She stiffened her fingers like claws, scrunching the sheets with every move forward. Strachan saw the tan mark of her G-string like a paper dart. He flinched as her breasts brushed against him. Her eyes were glazed now; earlier they'd burned. She was woozier with every movement. He tried to sit up, telling her that he'd changed his mind, but she continued crawling. She settled on his sternum, pinning him down.

'Chrissie, let's do this another time. You're not well. I switched our glasses.' Something was wrong. She was struggling for breath. 'Chrissie?'

There was a flash of comprehension in her eyes. It was the last thing Strachan noticed before Christine convulsed, clutched her hand to her chest, and fell to the floor with a thump.

Christine lay on her back. Her lips turned blue as the blood drained from them. Her eyeballs rolled back until they were as blind and white as boiled eggs. Strachan dropped to the floor and knelt beside her, pulling the phone down from the bedside table.

He dialled 912 for the ambulance service. His index finger skidded off the keys. He got a wrong number tone and was forced to redial. This time he stabbed the keys slowly and was instantly connected to the operator.

'My friend has collapsed.' Strachan was caught in that no man's land between reality and make-believe. He was absurdly aware of his own voice. It was as if he was playing a role in a performance that would later be judged. He wasn't panicking but he wanted to convey the urgency of the situation. 'I think she's had a heart attack.'

'Where are you, sir?'

'The San Marco hotel. Room 43.'

'Is your friend conscious?'

'No,' he replied. 'She's out.'

'Is she breathing?'

'No. She's not breathing.'

'How long has she been like that?'

'About ten seconds.'

'Does she have—?'

'Lady,' Strachan said, 'just send the ambulance.' And

then he hung up. They didn't have time to chat. Christine didn't look good. He wasn't sure if the paramedics would get there in time.

Strachan had never called on his medical training in eleven years of diving but it came back to him now, along with a flood of adrenalin. The responsibility of saving a life. He checked Christine's wrist for a pulse: nothing. He moved his fingers to her jugular: nothing. He pulled down her jaw and checked that her tongue wasn't blocking her trachea. It wasn't, so he began CPR, trying to ignore the irony that at last they were mouth-to-mouth.

After three minutes Christine showed no sign of response. He began again, counting the rhythm out loud. His compressions became increasingly violent as his desperation to revive her increased.

Still no response.

Within another two minutes the compressions had become blows of frustration.

Strachan slumped against the bed, staring at the ceiling. The ambulance crew could switch off their flashing blue lights. They could kill the siren and take their time.

Christine Molyneux was dead.

Strachan's vision blurred. His adrenal rush was so strong that he thought he was going to be sick. He didn't know what he felt. It was as if something had hatched inside him. Panic, fear, remorse, regret, curiosity, all buzzing chaotically round his stomach like wasps trapped in a jar.

He took his clothes into the bathroom. He couldn't look at Christine. He dressed quickly, then drank some water to settle his nausea. He returned to the bedroom, stripped the sheet from the bed, and used it to cover her body. He wasn't sure if it was for his benefit or hers. He wasn't sure if it was because she was naked or because she was dead. It just felt like the right thing to do.

Strachan cursed himself for not thinking things through at the restaurant. If he'd used his brain she might still be alive. He remembered now that Ecstasy usually came in pill form, which meant that it had probably been something else in that pipette. Come to think of it, he didn't know of any recreational drugs that people carried around in pipettes. Pipettes belonged in laboratories, not in restaurants. But the benefits of hindsight didn't really matter. It was still his fault.

He lit a cigarette. Something slithered through the back of his mind as he recalled the look in Christine's eyes when he'd told her that he'd swapped glasses. Recognition, comprehension, acknowledgement. As if it made sense; as though she wasn't surprised at what was happening to her; as though she was conceding victory. She'd had considerable experience of drugs so she would have known how much was safe and how much was dangerous. The pipette had been two inches long. It had been a big dose. If he hadn't switched glasses, it might have been him lying there with the blue lips and the egg-white eyes. It was a slim possibility but it hit Strachan like a demolition ball: *she was trying to kill me*. The sex games had just been an act.

Whatever Christine had been up to, her plan had backfired thanks to a glimpse in a mirror and a simple distraction and switch. The oldest trick in the book. She'd fallen for it, and now she'd paid the price. Out loud so that it sounded eerie in the small room, Strachan said 'Shit', and wondered what to do next.

It wasn't an easy decision. He knew what he *should* do. He should pick up the phone and make a second call to the police. With no hope of reviving Christine, this was a situation for two emergency services rather than one. But the police weren't just going to zip her up in a body bag and tell Strachan to go home. They would want to know what had happened. His prints were all over her naked body.

They would arrest him. It would take weeks to clear up, and even then he might never prove his innocence. Hell, he didn't even know if he *was* innocent. And to make matters worse he had a career-defining deadline to meet. If he didn't get those films to *National Geographic* on time he might as well go to prison anyway. He didn't trust anyone else to handle them and he sure as hell wasn't going to stick them in the mail. It was a sizeable contract. If his editor liked the photographs for the calendar, it would lead to an annual retainer. The next flight out after the one he was booked on wasn't until the following evening, by which time he would have lost a day and all hope of meeting his deadline. The cover shot, the money, the retainer and the prestige would go to somebody else. Someone who didn't need or deserve the break like he did. Someone with less talent. Someone like Bill Tanner. He *had* to catch that plane.

A flash of blue in the window told Strachan that the ambulance had arrived in the forecourt. He stole a look at the alarm clock. 12.08 a.m. His flight left in a little over six hours and with a bit of luck he just might make it. He would go to the police in London once he'd developed the films and sent them to Washington.

He didn't feel good running away. He didn't feel good turning his back on Christine. But when he weighed up the facts, he felt as though he had little choice. There was no way that he was going to stick around and wait for the paramedics. There was no way that he was going to be accused of murder. There was no way that he was going to sacrifice his career for someone who'd tried to kill him. And once the deadline was out of the way, he swore that he *would* find out why she'd wanted him dead. The decision was made. Right now his priority was to get the hell out of Curaçao.

Without looking back, Strachan slipped into his trainers and then into the anonymity of the hotel corridor. The lift was on its way up. The paramedics would be here in seconds. He hurried to the end of the corridor and took the stairs.

Once on the ground floor, he avoided the lobby and made for a side exit. He increased his pace, breaking into a run as he left the hotel. The revolving door flung him into the street like a pebble from a slingshot.

Strachan's tent was back at Piet and Maggie's dive school, six miles outside Willemstad in St Michiel's Bay. He set off down the street at a fast trot. He was glad to be exercising and used the tension to drive his legs. He stuck to the back alleys, only joining Breedestraat to cross the Queen Emma swing-bridge over St Anna's Bay. Away to his right the pipes of the Shell refinery coiled round dark fractionating columns. Behind them a stack burned off excess gas, its orange flame flapping like a windsock. Once over the bridge he turned left and followed the coast road past the Holiday Beach hotel until he found a track that took him down to the water's edge. He kicked off his trainers and paused for breath.

Had he murdered her? Strachan didn't know. It would come down to a legal technicality. He'd switched drinks knowing that there was something in the suspect glass – but how could he have known it was lethal? If he could prove that she'd tried to do the same to him, any charges should be reduced to manslaughter. *Manslaughter*? That didn't sound much better. Doubt reappeared. It settled on the edge of his mind, black and impudent. He tried to shoo it off. Whatever he had done to Christine, she had tried to do the same to him. It would be a hard line to sell to the police but it eased his conscience.

The crash of the surf gave him a rhythm to run to and he began to relax. He hadn't murdered her. It had been an accident. There was a way out of this, and it was going to be okay. He'd made a terrible mistake not confronting her about the pipette, but he'd done everything he could to help her. He *might* make it back to London, in which case he could walk into his local police station in just over seventeen hours and set the record straight.

Strachan arrived at the dive school thirty-five minutes later. He was breathing hard.

Back in Willemstad, the second floor of the San Marco hotel had become a hive of activity. Guests peered from their doors like prairie gophers, keen to see what was going on but ready to beat a hasty retreat if it looked like trouble. The Duty Manager bustled back and forth, reassuring them that there was nothing to worry about.

In Room 43 a third shock of defibrillation had failed to revive Christine Molyneux. The paramedics would continue on their way back to St Elisabeth's Hospital but the looks on their faces said their efforts wouldn't yield any results. The senior paramedic called the dispatcher to tell him they were on their way.

'How's the guy who made the call?' the dispatcher asked.

'What guy?' the paramedic replied.

And within another three minutes a squad car was pulling out of the Punda police station.

3

The Coral Kraal dive school was set in a cluster of three other buildings on a small beachhead. It was simple and spacious, a white concrete block with a blue corrugated-iron roof. The door was padlocked and the shutters drawn across the windows. Breaking in would have made Piet and Maggie mad, so Strachan was thankful that he'd removed his equipment before leaving for the restaurant.

The Zeemans were Strachan's only friends, not just in Curaçao but pretty much anywhere. Piet had spent six years with a naval unit of the Dutch Special Forces before a gunshot wound to the hip had forced him out early and he'd returned to the Caribbean to start a new life as a dive instructor. Strachan had met him five years ago on a reef off Bonaire. Piet's foot had been trapped under a rock. When Strachan had arrived with his cameras Piet had been sawing through his ankle with a knife. Between them they'd been able to shift the rock before he'd cut too far. Strachan had brought Piet to the surface as the air in his cylinder ran out. If he'd turned up five minutes later the very best that Piet could have hoped for would have been to lose a foot.

Strachan shook his head as he remembered the incident. He walked round the veranda to the side of the building. His tent was erected where he could enjoy a view of the sea. He collapsed it quickly, breaking the poles and rolling the mainsheet into its cover. He clipped the tent and sleeping bag onto the bottom of his rucksack, which was already packed. Next he retrieved his cameras, lenses, strobes and films from one of the lockers lining the school's rear wall. He'd had plenty of experience at leaving countries in a hurry, and he was ready to go in less than ten minutes.

Maggie Zeeman had been going to run Strachan to the airport at four-thirty. After what had happened he didn't want to wait that long before setting off. There was no way he could sleep after an evening like that. He wanted to keep busy, and he wanted to get going. He wanted to be alone. He wanted to put as much distance between himself and Curaçao as he possibly could. *Poor Christine*. She might have been trying to kill him, but he was still shaken by her death. The words were pathetically inadequate but however hard he tried they were the only ones that he could find.

The dive school's jeep was parked on the boat ramp. It was only ever used to ferry cylinders to dive sites around the island. In the five years that he'd been coming here, Strachan had never seen Piet leave the keys anywhere other than the sun-visor pocket. Piet and Maggie lived in a bungalow two miles further down the coast and no one heard the engine's bronchial rattle as it spluttered into life.

Strachan tried to drive at a speed that wouldn't attract attention. He guessed he was on the slow side because he was overtaken by a police car at the exit to Julianadorp. He arrived at Hato airport at half-past two. The sweat ran down his back.

His flight didn't leave until six-thirty. Check-in wasn't yet open. He had time to kill so he borrowed some paper from a security guard and sat down to write. He owed Piet and Maggie an explanation – and not just for his use of their jeep. Plenty of people on the island knew that he hung out at The Coral Kraal, and the police would be round to interview the Zeemans sooner or later. He would rather that his friends heard it from him than that they were left to form their own conclusions.

Strachan could trust the Zeemans, and he felt instantly better telling someone what had happened. Piet and Maggie would understand. They knew what this trip meant to him. They knew he had waited nine years for a break like this with *National Geographic*.

He scribbled manically. He told them about the mirror. He told them about the pipette. He told them that he'd switched glasses. He told them about Christine's invitation to go to her room. About her death, his call to the ambulance service, and his attempts to revive her. He told them that he hadn't called the police but was going to turn himself in once he'd established Christine's motives for attempting to drug him. He told them that he'd had no choice: he had had to catch that plane. He signed off with a promise to e-mail them soon and told them that he'd left the keys in the usual place.

Thirty minutes later Strachan stretched his legs with a circuit of the ticket hall. It buzzed with preparation for the day's work ahead. A cleaner in a straw hat pushed a humming floor-polisher over the tiles. It left a shining snail's-trail behind it. Two girls in blue uniforms were opening the KLM check-in desk. One slid a placard with the flight number into a bracket above the counter. Strachan was six feet and two inches tall. Transatlantic flights were a lot more comfortable in an exit-row seat. He waited until they were ready, then he checked in early.

The girl behind the desk was an Arawak beauty. She was tall, with a mane of auburn hair that tumbled down her back. Her face was heavily made-up. Eyelashes as thick as thorns protected truffle eyes, while maroon lipstick accentuated the fullness of her mouth. It was a good choice. It showed off her milk-chocolate skin and blue lapels. On any other day Strachan would have flirted with her and tried to score an upgrade. But not today. He wasn't in the mood. Accidentally killing someone tends to put a brake on that kind of stuff.

'Do you have an envelope?' he asked her.

'Sure.' She called to a colleague who produced one from an adjacent desk.

'Thanks. Anywhere I can buy stamps?' He folded his note and ran his tongue along the gum of the envelope.

'Not at this time of day.' The check-in girl smiled at him and then tilted her head to one side. 'But I'd be happy to post it for you in my lunch break if you leave me the change.'

'I'd appreciate that. Thank you.' Customer service Caribbean-style. Strachan handed her the sealed envelope and watched as his rucksack and dive-bag were checked through to London. He kept his cameras back as hand luggage. The rolls of undeveloped film bulged in the pockets of his photographer's jacket. He kept them with him at all times. They were his lifeblood, his currency, his future. He didn't trust baggage-handlers.

'You okay?' the KLM girl asked him.

'Late night, early start.'

She nodded knowingly and flashed Strachan a farewell with her big brown eyes. He scooped up his passport and boarding card and made straight for the Departures lounge.

4

The flight was full. Strachan found himself next to a Dutch couple, intent on conversation. The what-do-you-do-for-a-living-? and do-you-come-to-Curaçao-often-? kind. He told them that he was an underwater photographer, and learnt that the husband was an account executive for Hewlett-Packard while the wife was a teacher.

Strachan was in no mood for small talk. Christine's death had killed his natural civility. Mentioning his profession was a mistake: it would only encourage his neighbours to talk all the way to Holland. Any second now the wife would ask him which was his favourite dive site and her husband would follow by demanding to hear about his closest encounter with a shark. Not caring if he caused offence, Strachan terminated the conversation by pulling down the blind. Crippled with fatigue, he closed his eyes. Not for the first time he wondered who Christine Molyneux had been and what she'd wanted with him.

There were three possibilities why she might have tried to drug him. She'd wanted him high; she'd wanted him unconscious; or she'd wanted him dead. He tackled them in reverse order. Most serious first, most probable last. It was possible he was being hasty in assuming that she'd tried to kill him.

Despite the lethal size of the dose, murder was still the

long shot. Strachan didn't steal. He didn't gamble. He didn't visit brothels or loan sharks, and the only debts he had were to MasterCard. These days the fights he got into were over nothing more serious than a spilled pint of Guinness or a wink at another man's girl. Ten years ago he'd spent time on the other side of the world and the wrong side of the law; but the chances of Christine Molyneux being linked to his days of running bootleg jewels round South-East Asia were simply too remote.

If it *had* been her intention to kill him, she'd gone about it in a very personal way. Why bother with the fancy dinner and seduction? Why allow them to be seen together by so many people? Did she know how long it would take for the overdose to work? Strachan calculated that it had been a full twenty minutes from the time she'd drunk the wine to the time when she'd died, and it would've taken longer to work on a big guy like him. What if he'd wanted to stay in the restaurant? What if he'd turned down the invitation to go to her room? It didn't make sense. Aside from the practical problems, there was simply no motive. To assume Christine was an assassin was ridiculous. She was just another city slicker who liked her sex somewhere on the wild side of safe. And until she'd died that had been fine by him.

Unconscious, then. Why? To rob him? If *that* had been her motive, she'd picked the wrong guy. Strachan's bank balance wasn't worth the paper it was written on. He had less than eighty guilders in his wallet. Rape was also out of the question. How had he been supposed to perform if he was out for the count?

So, she'd wanted to get him high to improve their sex: exactly as she'd spelled out over chargrilled snapper and couscous. Maybe she'd been turned on by the power of manipulating him? It was certainly more credible than the two alternatives. She'd been fooling about but had messed up the dose, and that was all there was to it.

This conclusion didn't help. It made the fact that he'd killed her harder to take.

Six hours later Strachan was still wide awake. He tried watching the in-flight movie but his mind was too busy. It was running a reel of its own, replaying his dive and dinner with Christine, over and over. Past the Azores and east-north-east into Portuguese airspace. Trying to come to terms with what he'd done; trying to assuage his guilt. On into northern France, and still no respite. He couldn't get her out of his head.

It had all started with a conversation. Piet Zeeman slapping Strachan on the back as they finished their lunch. 'Do me a favour, Ed?'

'Sure.'

'I've got a student who finished her Open Water course this morning. I want you to take her with you this afternoon when you dive Knife Point.'

Strachan had shaken his head. He'd been on the rum the night before. Tuesday's deadline loomed like a circling vulture. 'Not on your life. Sorry, Piet, but this is the most important shoot of the week. The last thing I need is some amateur floozy struggling with her buoyancy, stirring the silt and scaring the fish.'

Piet's hand returned to his shoulder. 'She won't be a nuisance. I think you might like her.'

'If she's the one with the pink bikini, I already do.'

'So you'll take her?'

'Nope.'

'Ed, you're taking her. Maggie and I have got classes to teach and I promised her a decent dive. Besides, she's talking about making a significant contribution to the turtle rehabilitation programme, and right now we could use the cash.'

'How significant?'

'Couple of hundred dollars.'

'Uh-uh. Sorry, mate.'

Thirty years after leaving the Dutch Special Forces Piet Zeeman was still a hard bastard, and they'd argued with the passion of drunks. Strachan had said no, Piet had said yes, and when the hand on his shoulder had coiled in a fist, Strachan had said okay, she could come along, provided she kept out of his way.

Christine Molyneux turned out to be a lousy diver.

Strachan had to waste precious air while he adjusted her equipment. More while she struggled to keep up. In the end, though, it didn't matter. They found the barracuda after twenty minutes. It was basking in a shaft of sunlight on the edge of the reef, exactly where Piet had said it would be. Barracuda have the sharpest teeth in the ocean and this one was five feet long. Christine maintained a respectful distance, holding Strachan's spare camera. He shot two films while it hung in the water, grinning at the lens, daring him to come any closer. Two rolls of film. Seventy-two shots. Only one of which would be used. Such were the odds that governed his life.

Back at the dive school Christine had insisted on buying him dinner as a thank-you for letting her tag along. He was calmer now, his hangover had cleared, and she was deliciously easy on the eye. Maggie had been filling tanks from the compressor and had flipped him a wink from the shadows as Christine had suggested The Lobster Pot at ten.

They'd started flirting the moment they arrived. Conversation was easy. She was treating herself to a holiday after splitting with her boyfriend of the last four years. She bragged that she earned big money, and he figured she had fought tooth-and-nail to make her own luck. She knew what she wanted from life and was prepared to go out and take it. Live fast; die young.

Strachan wiped a hand over his face. She'd certainly done the latter.

The plane landed at Schiphol on time. It taxied to the gate, and the Captain made an announcement in Dutch, which Strachan didn't understand. Despite his regular visits to Curaçao, he'd made no effort to learn more than the basics. Piet and Maggie's English was as good as his, and English was as widely spoken as Dutch and Papiamento.

It was dark outside but Strachan could still see streaks of rain like scratches on the Boeing's windows. When the announcement was repeated in English he knew exactly what it meant. It meant that his films wouldn't be developed in time. It meant he was going to miss his deadline. It meant he could kiss goodbye to a five-figure cheque and an annual retainer from *National Geographic*.

It meant he was screwed.

5

'Good evening, ladies and gentlemen. This is the Captain speaking. As you have just heard, the local time is 20:46. I trust you enjoyed the flight and managed to get some rest. We are approaching the gate now, and I have to ask you to remain in your seats after the plane has come to a halt. There is a small police matter to attend to. We should not be delayed for more than five minutes. The police will be boarding the aircraft shortly. There is absolutely no need to be alarmed. Thank you for your cooperation, and have a pleasant onward journey.'

No need to be alarmed? Strachan's stomach leaped like a trout. He realised that he'd been naïve. He was never going to make it back to London. He should have known better. It was now over nine hours since he'd left Curaçao and fifteen since he'd left the hotel. That was plenty of time for the police to have traced Christine's movements back to the restaurant. The receipt in her purse would have been all that they needed. It was plenty of time, too, for the waiter to have given a description of her companion, and plenty of time for the authorities at Hato airport to have matched it. Manhunts didn't come much easier.

The plane lurched to a halt. Strachan closed his eyes and waited for them to come. It didn't take long. The Dutch accent was strong. 'Banbury Edward Strachan?'

Banbury. It had been a long time since anyone had called Strachan by his full given name. Usually it meant he was in trouble and this was another fine example to prove the rule. He opened his eyes to see two plain-clothes policemen in dark suits and white shirts standing in the aisle. There was a buzz of excitement right through the plane. Passengers as far as five rows forward turned in their seats, straining their necks over the headrests to watch the drama unfold.

'Yes.'

'I am Inspector Rutger Verhoeven of Interpol. This is Agent Ronald Groote of the Schiphol police. Would you follow us, please, sir?'

Verhoeven was tall and angular. He had a square jaw and thin ashen lips. His black hair was flecked with grey. He wore it in a widow's peak. He was strong-boned and carried himself with pride and purpose. Strachan put him at thirty-five. Groote was shorter, older, and overweight. He'd long since crossed the border between plump and fat, and had to shuffle sideways down the aisle to avoid jamming himself between the armrests of the economy-class cabin. He looked affable enough, though. Even slightly embarrassed to be standing up in front of so many people. He played nervously with the security pass that hung round his neck. Strachan guessed that he would play good cop before going home to a late supper of Grolsch and cheese with his equally corpulent wife.

Strachan undid his seat belt. He retrieved his cameras from the overhead locker and followed the policemen up the aisle, ignoring the stares and whispers that they left in their wake. Once out of the aircraft the policemen paused. Groote took up a position in front of him in case he decided to run. Strachan was wearing a short-sleeved shirt under his jacket. The change in temperature brought a rash of goose bumps to his arms.

'Passport.' Now that there were no passengers to overhear, Verhoeven dispensed with the pleasantries.

Strachan knew his type: a constabulary zealot with all the charm of a razor-wire fence. He searched through his pockets and handed over his passport. Verhoeven confirmed that he was being arrested on suspicion of murder. Groote read him his rights.

'Hands.'

'What?'

'Your hands. Show them to me.' Verhoeven barked the command, raising his voice for the first time.

Strachan did as he was told. He cupped them palms-up in front of his chest as though begging for food. The handcuffs were cold and hard. They clasped his wrists like claws. He wasn't panicking but a swarm of butterflies cavorted in his stomach. Right now silence was the best option. Silence couldn't be misinterpreted.

'Cheer up!' Verhoeven slapped him on the back and then walked through the gate to the terminal. Strachan followed with Groote close behind.

They took him to a holding room somewhere deep within the terminal. It was far away down a complex warren of scuffed linoleum, strip lighting and double doors. They were immediately joined by a uniformed policeman who went through Strachan's pockets. With the removal of his cameras, wallet, keys, and films, he felt vulnerable and exposed. Even his shoelaces were confiscated.

'And the thing round his neck.' Groote was sitting on the edge of a table. He indicated Strachan's cuff link with a nod of his head.

Strachan jerked his head back. The policeman frisking him was somewhere in his late forties with neat grey hair and a perfectly straight moustache. His blue uniform was starched and crisp as chicory. Wrinkle lines around his eyes suggested that he laughed a lot despite the seriousness of his work. His name was embroidered on his left breast pocket: RUISDAEL. He was within perfect butting range. He was also only doing his job. Strachan relaxed his neck. With his hands cuffed there was no way he could stop the chain from being lifted over his head.

On the other side of the room, Inspector Verhoeven noticed Strachan's reaction and it piqued his curiosity. 'Let me see that.' He held out his hand and Ruisdael passed the cuff link over. Verhoeven held it up and read the inscription out loud. 'What is that, a map reference?'

Strachan nodded. That was exactly what it was: $01° \ 17'$ $43'' \ N$. A latitudinal map reference, as engraved in his memory as in the metal itself.

'Where is it? In England?' Verhoeven was intrigued but he was also working. If he dug deeper, this trinket might provide an insight into his suspect's character. Pushing personal buttons was one of the best ways to build a profile.

'I don't know,' Strachan replied truthfully.

'Why not?'

'One degree and seventeen minutes of latitude cuts through sixteen different countries. You need longitudinal coordinates to narrow the list down.' He didn't add that the longitudinal coordinates were engraved on the second cuff link, the one that had been stolen. Nor did he mention that, together, the cuff links pinpointed his inheritance: a bloodline secret passed down from his grandfather to his father. The secret would in due course have come to him, but his father had died before he'd had a chance to disclose it. As a result Strachan had no idea *what* let alone *where* his inheritance was.

'Which countries?'

Strachan paused. There was little harm in telling. Besides, if he was *that* interested, Verhoeven could simply look it up. 'Somalia, Kenya, Uganda, Zaire,

Congo, Gabon, Equatorial Guinea, Brazil, Guyana, Colombia, Ecuador, Micronesia, Indonesia, Malaysia, Singapore, and the Maldives.' He rattled them off. He'd studied the atlas a thousand times and knew the places by heart.

Verhoeven was impressed. 'Why do you wear it round your neck? Most people wear them in their shirts.'

'I've only got one. The other one was stolen a long time ago.' Strachan was tired and worried. He didn't want to talk about the cuff links, but he wanted to co-operate. He was up to his eyes in something that didn't smell good.

'That was unfortunate.' Verhoeven grinned. 'What happened?'

'It's a long story.'

'Trust me; you have plenty of time. Is it valuable?'

Strachan looked away. The second cuff link had been hidden in a sheet of old newspaper and had been taken from his parents' safe the night they died. He had been eight at the time and his parents had left him with a babysitter while they went out for dinner to celebrate their anniversary. The usual babysitter was away, and the agency stand-in was mean-looking and tough. She'd even slapped him when he'd refused to go to bed.

His godfather, Adrian Hamilton, had discovered the theft a week later. Hamilton was his father's cousin and an executor of Strachan's parents' will. The will included instructions that Hamilton should become Strachan's legal guardian in the event of his parents dying before he reached the age of eighteen. Another clause, contingent on the first, was that Hamilton should present him with the cuff links on his eighteenth birthday along with the message that '*Ed will see their real value.*' The will included the combination to the family safe and when Hamilton

27

found only one cuff link, his suspicion immediately fell on the babysitter.

She'd been nervous and over-eager to leave when Hamilton had arrived at the house to break the bad news to his godson. Later he'd noticed a dimple in the carpet, suggesting that the safe had been moved. When he tried to track the babysitter down a few days later, he discovered that she'd registered under a false name with the agency. It was the final proof he needed and he'd reported the incident to the police. Unfortunately the police weren't interested. Nothing else had been removed from the safe, and a solitary missing silver cuff link didn't warrant any manpower. They'd made a token gesture at finding the babysitter but had called the investigation off after a couple of days. Hamilton had subsequently tried to track her down himself but had given up after several fruitless years.

Strachan wasn't going to tell all that to Verhoeven, so he answered the second half of the question instead. 'No,' he said. 'It has sentimental value but that's all.'

'How nice.' His curiosity temporarily sated, Verhoeven tossed the cuff link back to Ruisdael. The sergeant caught it and placed it in the plastic wallet along with Strachan's other belongings. Then he sat down at the table and began writing an inventory of the contents.

'You'll look after my films, won't you?' It was as much a warning as a question. Verhoeven looked capable of sabotage.

'Don't worry about your films, Banbury. Get some rest. You have a long night ahead of you.' Verhoeven smiled and the three policemen left the room. The key turned in the door. Their shoes squeaked on the lino.

They hadn't removed the cuffs. Strachan's wrists were swollen and sore. Verhoeven had set them as tight as possible, as though he'd already decided that his suspect was guilty. There were no windows, and the room was stuffy. Strachan started to sweat. He put his head on the table. His exhaustion was so complete that it felt like an illness. Thoughts of Christine Molyneux trickled through his consciousness as he drifted in and out of oblivion.

6

Hours later Strachan was woken by the rasp of the key in the lock. Groote stood in the doorway, holding a polystyrene cup of coffee. 'You are permitted a phone call. Would you like to make one?'

Strachan nodded.

Groote nodded back. 'Let's go.'

Strachan stood up. He blinked as his eyes adjusted to the fluorescent light in the corridor. How long had he been asleep? He quickened his pace so that he could read Groote's wristwatch. It was 2.05 a.m. They'd held him for five hours. Strachan reckoned he'd been dozing on and off for three. It felt more like three minutes and it hadn't made any difference. Jet lag still fogged his senses like an anaesthetic.

'Why is Interpol involved? I'm flattered.'

'Don't be. You crossed a border. You are English, the deceased is English but the crime is happening in the Netherlands Antilles. It is legally complicated. We are helping our friends in Curaçao. They do not always have resources available for this sort of thing.'

'I thought those guys spent their time looking for stolen paintings.' *Those guys*. Strachan was looking for an ally.

'Inspector Verhoeven spends his time on lots of things. Terrorism, drugs, counterfeiting, human trafficking, serious fraud. Even murder and date rape.'

'*Date rape?*'

'Date rape.'

That changed things completely. Strachan felt like he'd just been punched. *Date rape?* The words alone were sickening. Either the Dutch police were jumping to conclusions or Groote was trying to scare him. Strachan didn't push it. He knew when to shut up.

Once they were in his office Groote unlocked the cuffs. The blood raced into Strachan's blanched hands. He rubbed them to get the circulation going. It took a while for the numbness to fade. He sipped the coffee that Groote gave him. It was strong, black and sweet. Right then he thought it was the best coffee he'd ever drunk. Had this been England it would have been cheap and rancid, swimming in grime from a vending machine that hadn't been serviced in years.

Groote handed him a laminated card. It was an A4 sheet with a long list of telephone numbers. He told him to dial 9 for an outside line. Most of the numbers belonged to embassies and consulates. They were listed by continent in alphabetical order. Towards the bottom of the page was a list of other useful numbers: four lawyers, the Samaritans, and Western Union's main branch in Amsterdam.

Strachan handed it back. He knew who he was going to call, and he didn't need the card.

It was now Monday morning. The deadline was Tuesday evening. He should have been in the lab on Lupus Street, developing his stills so that he could air-express them to *National Geographic* in Washington. The editorial staff had seen his pictures of sea otters off the Vancouver coast in *Scuba Times* towards the end of last year. Suitably impressed, they'd offered him the cover shot and seven of the twelve months for next year's underwater calendar, covering his expenses for expeditions to Scotland, the Galapagos – and Curaçao.

Strachan dialled the number. McCauley Gilchrist's long Virginia drawl on the other end greeted him.

'Hi this is McCauley Gilchrist. Thank you for calling National Geographic. *I'm either on the phone or away from my desk, but if you leave your name and number, I'll be sure to call you back as soon I can. Have a nice day, and remember to take care of your planet.'*

This was another blow. Strachan had forgotten the time difference. Fatigue had doped him. It was eight o'clock in the evening in Washington, and Gilchrist would have left the office long ago.

Strachan had never met Gilchrist but they'd spoken on numerous occasions to confirm the brief for the calendar and the small print for his possible retainer. He'd formed a favourable impression of the gentle American, and envisaged a paternalistic editor in his early sixties. Gilchrist would have grey hair and a neat close-cropped beard, like Sean Connery in *Indiana Jones and the Last Crusade*. He'd wear jeans, cowboy boots, and checked lumberjack shirts in heavy drill cotton. Outside, he'd have a large Jeep Cherokee 4x4. On the passenger's seat there'd be a black baseball cap with *National Geographic* embroidered across its peak. He would live in the country. His wife would be called Mary.

'McCauley, hi, this is Ed Strachan. I've run into some bad luck. My flight back from Curaçao was delayed by twenty-four hours. You won't get the pictures until Wednesday. I'm really sorry. There's nothing I can do.'

Strachan glanced at Groote who was leaning against the wall, his hands in his pockets. The policeman made no attempt to hide the fact that he was listening. He made an exaggerated sniffing noise. He twitched his nose like a bear tasting the air, signalling that he could smell the lie.

'The shots are fantastic. You'll see my recommendation for the cover. It's one of my best. You have to trust me. I know the printers are booked, but please do everything you can to delay them.' At this stage there was no way of telling how the pictures would turn out, but he was confident that at least one of the seventy-two would be a strong candidate.

Strachan tried to remain calm. He didn't want to appear desperate. Gilchrist had explained it to him three or four times. Because of the high quality of the images and the larger than normal paper size, it was necessary for the printers to book a three-day slot to run the calendar off. The presses needed to be specially geared and the finished copies needed to go straight to distribution so that they'd be in the shops for Christmas. If the calendar was late it would have a knock-on effect, and the December issue of the magazine would be jeopardised. The deadline was set in stone.

'Don't make any decisions until you've seen the pictures from Curaçao. You won't regret it.' There wasn't much else he could say. Gilchrist had seen the images from Scotland and the Galapagos and expressed his admiration. The trip to Scotland had produced a magnificent shot of a fur seal chasing an eight-pound Atlantic salmon. Curaçao would provide three of the remaining seven shots: the cover, and two more pictures of life on the reef. The chances of stopping the presses were slim but it felt better to be pleading his case. Even if it was to a machine.

Strachan hung up. Groote led him down more corridors. They passed the turning to the cells and carried straight on. Now that Strachan had made his phone call, it was time for both men to find out what the hell was going on.

★

33

Inspector Verhoeven was waiting for them, leaning against the far wall of the interview room. His arms were folded on his chest and he looked as if he'd been stood-up on a date. He seemed really pissed off. So did Groote. They exchanged a few words and glanced in Strachan's direction. Strachan wondered if that meant a change of plan. Perhaps it would be bad cop, *worse* cop now that Groote had missed out on his Gouda and Grolsch.

Verhoeven walked over and kicked the door shut with his heel. Strachan took in his new surroundings. There was a black table in the middle of the room. Orange plastic chairs were placed around it like mooring buoys. On the right-hand wall he saw a calendar that doubled as a shift roster. There was a monitor and videoconferencing machine on a black trolley at the far end of the room. A security poster about unattended baggage was pinned to the back of the door. As with the holding room, there were no windows.

They all sat down at the table: Strachan on one side, the cops on the other. Verhoeven and Groote adopted the same pose, leaning forward with their elbows on the table, their hands clasped as though in prayer. Strachan immediately lolled back in his chair. He didn't want any symmetry in their body language.

'You did not call a lawyer, Banbury. That was foolish, perhaps. You are entitled to one. We can have one here in twenty minutes. Do you want one?' Verhoeven finally broke the silence.

Strachan shrugged. 'Does he speak English?'

'Of course.'

'Are you going to record this?'

'Yes. I would not want anyone to think we misunder-stood each other.'

'Then the lawyer can wait.' What was the point? The lawyer would sit there in silence, wishing that he was in

34

bed. He might object to a couple of questions but Strachan planned on doing that himself.

'If you wish, we are also obliged to inform a member of your family or household that you are in custody.'

Strachan shook his head. He had no close family and he lived alone. He wasn't planning on letting Hamilton know he was in trouble either. 'How long can you hold me?'

'Normally six hours. Then I have to charge you or release you.'

'It's already been five.'

'I know.' Verhoeven winked at him, and smiled. Then he stretched out a wiry arm and pressed RECORD on the video machine.

7

'The time is 2.16 a.m., Monday the eighteenth of October. Room 13, Schiphol International Airport Police Headquarters. Present are Inspector Rutger Verhoeven of Interpol, Agent Ronald Groote of the Schiphol Airport Police, and Banbury Edward Strachan of 27a Tachbrook Street, London. This conversation is being recorded.' Verhoeven paused to look at his captive. Strachan nodded confirmation.

'Mr Strachan.' Verhoeven pronounced the *ch* as in *church,* and not as a *k.* He hadn't made the same mistake on the plane, Strachan noted. He had an accent, but his English was good. The bastard was already playing games. 'Do you understand why you are here?'

Strachan nodded.

'Please speak for the benefit of the tape.'

'Yes, Inspector Verhoeven. I understand why I'm here.' Strachan spoke softly. There was something about authority that really pissed him off.

'Do you understand that you have been arrested on suspicion of murder and attempted rape?'

'Yes.'

'Good. Our interview will be conducted in the presence of Hoofd-Inspecteur Dirk Koopmans, who will be joining us via video link from Willemstad in Curaçao.' Pause. 'Do you understand?'

'Yes,' Strachan replied. Of course he bloody

understood. What was this guy's problem?

That was Groote's cue. He punched the remote with his thumb. The monitor screen burst into life with a soft electronic pop, and Strachan was confronted with a grainy picture of the Caribbean Chief Inspector.

Koopmans was sitting at his desk. He wore a white short-sleeved shirt. A row of cotton braids flashed like tropical fish on his breast pocket: colourful insignia identifying him as one of the island's highest-ranking policemen. He wore his hair in a buzz-cut, and the shades on his head said he spent more time outside than he did in his office. Strachan recognised his face from a drink-drive poster campaign. It was lean but hard. Cracks ran up his tanned cheeks like fault lines in a sandstone cliff.

'*Goedenavond*, Dirk.' Verhoeven was trying to be informal, perhaps unnerved by the broad-shouldered islander with the cold grey eyes.

'You can call me "sir", Inspector.' It was 9.00 p.m. in Willemstad. Koopmans wasn't still at work to shoot the breeze. Strachan filed that away as good news. Verhoeven would have to watch his step.

Koopmans began to speak, the words reaching Amsterdam two or three seconds before they saw his mouth move. It was old technology. The connection wasn't real-time. His hand movements were robotic. 'Mr Strachan. As you are no doubt aware, the body of a young woman was found in the San Marco hotel early this morning, following a 912 call made from her room. She had suffered a heart attack from ingestion of toxins, found in her stomach by our forensic pathologist this afternoon. The time of death is estimated to have been between eleven and twelve last night. You were seen dining with the woman at The Lobster Pot and are presumed to be the person who called 912 at 23:59. A

37

hotel employee has testified that a man matching your description was seen leaving the hotel in a tremendous hurry at approximately 00:10. Your behaviour is suspicious. Tell me about it. Please.'

Strachan shifted in his chair to make himself more comfortable. A camera eyed him from its perch on the monitor. He liked Koopmans's calm authority. There was no hard-cop talk. No melodrama. His sheer bulk and wolfish eyes provided presence enough. Strachan figured that he might be able to build a relationship with him if he kept it short and straight. Koopmans would appreciate that. Besides, like all good cops, he'd have a keen nose for bullshit.

Strachan drew a deep breath and began. 'I was with Christine Molyneux when she died . . .' He paused. Apparently he'd already said something interesting. Verhoeven and Groote were whispering together in Dutch. On the screen Koopmans was making notes. Either he'd forgotten to press 'record' on his video or – more likely – he didn't trust the technology.

Strachan started again. 'I was with Christine Molyneux when she died, but I didn't kill her. I wrote a note at the airport to my friend Pieter Zeeman, explaining my involvement in her death, and my reasons for leaving the country. Check with KLM. One of their ground staff agreed to post the letter for me. It should arrive with Piet tomorrow.' He held his voice steady. Calm and confident, letting them know that he was innocent.

Groote cleared his throat. 'What is the name of the member of KLM staff?'

'Yolanda.'

'Yolanda what?'

'I don't know,' Strachan replied. 'Her badge only gave her first name.'

Groote stroked his chin, chewing the information as if it was sufficiently important to blow the case wide open. Verhoeven saw its irrelevance, and launched his first attack. 'Never mind KLM. Who is Pieter Zeeman, and what exactly was the reason for you leaving Curaçao?'

'Zeeman runs a dive school on the south coast. Best instructor on the island.' Koopmans's voice was deep and mellow as he answered on Strachan's behalf. It also had edge. An edge that said Zeeman's status was a matter of fact, not of personal opinion. As though Verhoeven's temerity at asking the question was an insult to Curaçao itself.

Strachan looked at the screen. His expression was as surprised as Verhoeven's. If Koopmans knew Zeeman then Strachan was in with a shout. Zeeman would vouch for him.

'Keep going,' said Verhoeven.

'I was introduced to Christine Molyneux by Pieter Zeeman, a dive instructor at The Coral Kraal in St Michiel's Bay. She joined me on my last dive on Saturday afternoon. I'm an underwater photographer, and I wanted to shoot the big barracuda off Knife Point.'

'I've seen it,' Koopmans said. 'It's quite a fish. Must be at least thirty pounds.'

'Yeah, at least. Nearer forty, I'd say.' Strachan noticed Verhoeven staring at the monitor with an incredulous look on his face. 'She invited me for dinner. Maggie Zeeman drove me to The Lobster Pot at ten o'clock. Halfway through dinner I went to buy cigarettes, and caught a glimpse of Christine squirting something into my wineglass with a pipette.' Cigarettes. He could have killed for one now. He hadn't had one since Curaçao.

'Describe the pipette,' said Groote.

'It was difficult to see. I was several metres away. I

39

guess it was two inches long. Plastic rather than glass and with a flesh-coloured teat.' *Teat*. Was that the right word? It was a long time since he'd done any chemistry.

'What was inside?'

'I've no idea. A clear liquid of some sort.'

'Then what happened?' Verhoeven rejoined the assault.

'When I got back from the bar, I distracted her attention while I switched our glasses.'

'Why did you do that?'

'Excuse me?' Strachan looked at the screen, from where the question had come.

'Why did you switch glasses?' Koopmans sounded like he really didn't get it.

'I thought it was a drug of some sort. She'd been telling me all night how she and her boyfriend took Ecstasy before they screwed. I didn't want any.'

'She had a boyfriend?' Koopmans asked.

'Not any more. That's why she was in Curaçao. On holiday, to get over the break-up.'

'Sounds like she was doing a good job.' Koopmans allowed himself a chuckle.

'That's what I thought. Anyway, she'd been telling me I had to try it, and when I told her I didn't do drugs she decided I didn't know what was good for me. I guess she took matters into her own hands.'

'Only you saw her do it?' Verhoeven wanted back in. Koopmans was stealing his show.

'Exactly. In a mirror. I was lucky.'

'Why didn't you ask her what she was doing, and confront her?'

Strachan paused. He'd been anticipating that question from the moment when they'd arrived on the plane to arrest him. Five hours later he still didn't have a satisfactory response. What was he supposed to say?

That he thought the liquid would turn her into a sexual world champion? That he was hoping for the biggest bang since the creation of the universe? That he'd been thinking with his prick? That he was disappointed a girl like Christine was only interested in a one-night stand?

'I don't know. Curiosity I suppose. I wanted to see what effect it would have on her. It was pretty obvious that we were going to sleep together. I figured I could test her theory without taking the drug myself. She said she was a frequent user, so I didn't think it would be dangerous. I guess I thought she deserved a taste of her own medicine.'

'Medicine. This is an unfortunate choice of words, don't you agree?' Groote seemed pleased with his knowledge of English idiom. Strachan didn't bother to reply. Groote's was a bit part. It was Koopmans who mattered.

'Then you went back to her hotel for the purpose of having sex with her?'

Strachan winced. Verhoeven had stripped the situation down to its starkest level: crude but correct. Strachan sure as hell hadn't gone to Christine's room to read her a bedtime story. 'She invited me back to the hotel. We undressed, but she died before anything happened.' He was thankful for that at least. Evidence of intercourse would only have strengthened the case against him. He noted a look of intense disappointment on Verhoeven's face – as though the whole point of his staying up this late had been destroyed by that single remark. 'I called the ambulance, and then I tried to revive her. I'm a qualified first-aid medic but CPR proved useless.'

'Is it possible that you didn't do it correctly?' Koopmans asked.

'Is it possible you are lying?' Verhoeven added.

'Is it possible you were panicking and left her on the floor to die?' Groote's turn. The questions were coming thick and fast. They were tightening the vice, exploiting his fatigue, pressuring him into a mistake. Strachan didn't have time to answer before Verhoeven asked his next question.

'Why did you go to the bathroom? Did you want to whack off?' The words dripped from the Dutchman's mouth in a canine sneer.

'I felt sick. I needed water.' Strachan looked Verhoeven in the eye, speaking slowly as though explaining something to a child for the third time.

'You are lying, Banbury.' Verhoeven said it so matter-of-factly that Strachan almost believed him.

'No.'

'I will tell you again: you are lying.'

'No.'

'What was in the pipette, Banbury?'

'I have no idea.'

'You are lying. What was in the pipette?'

'Why do you think I'm lying?'

'We'll ask the questions, Banbury. You keep digging.' Verhoeven was onto him in a flash. The tone was changing. This was no longer an interview: it was now an interrogation. 'Did the woman say anything about dancing before you killed her?'

Strachan spotted the trap. Answering the question could be interpreted as acknowledgement that he *had* actually killed Christine. He said nothing. He kept his expression blank. He had the right to remain silent, and now was a good time to exercise that right. He was beginning to regret not having the lawyer present. He was heavily outnumbered by the policemen. There were three of them and only one of him. They did this sort of thing every day. They could easily snare him. He would soon be out of his depth.

'Okay,' Verhoeven said, conceding that the question had been unfair. 'I will rephrase that. Did the woman mention that she wanted to go dancing at any time?'

'Dancing? No, not that I recall. Why?' Strachan couldn't help asking another question. Given the chance he would have asked a thousand.

'The pathologist has concluded that she died from a substantial overdose of GHB, traces of which were found in a pipette in her handbag.'

'GHB? What the hell is that?'

'GHB is *gamma hydroxybutyrate*. In your country its slang name is Grievous Bodily Harm. In America they call it Georgia Home Boy. It is a sedative-hypnotic used by two types of people.'

'Which two types?'

'Nightclubbers,' Groote said.

'And rapists,' added Verhoeven. 'Date-rapists, to be precise. It produces a feeling of euphoria but anything more than a teaspoonful can lead to temporary coma, and there was certainly more than a teaspoonful in that pipette. It is a nasty little drug – extremely dangerous if mixed with alcohol. It can lead to all sorts of respiratory problems.' He left his words to hang in the air before he continued. 'So you see the problem: if she wanted to go dancing it might explain why she had a pipette of GHB in her handbag. But since she did not, it leads me to believe that the drug was yours and that you intended to rape her.'

Strachan looked away. He didn't speak.

'Why did you leave without notifying the police or waiting for the ambulance to arrive?' Koopmans glanced at his watch. He was speeding things up, taking control again.

43

'It's in the note I wrote to Piet. I had to get back to London to get my pictures developed. The films from my week in Curaçao are the final batch of a series I'm shooting for *National Geographic*. The contract is worth a lot to me. They're strict as hell with deadlines. If I miss it, I get nothing. They'll use someone else's pictures.'

'So you thought the death of a young woman was less important than your pay-cheque?' Koopmans sounded genuinely disappointed. Strachan didn't like that. It threatened what little rapport they'd developed.

'It's not just the money. If they like the shots for the calendar, there's an annual retainer on offer. I'm twenty-nine years old; the most I've made in a year until now is fifteen grand.' That wasn't strictly true, but it would do for now. Before becoming a photographer Strachan had spent two years running smuggled emeralds in Malaysia. He'd gone there on his gap year and been sucked into acting as a courier only to discover that he had a real talent for it. Right now, however, that particular boast was best kept to himself.

'So?'

'So, I've been peddling my photographs round the dive magazines for nine years, making a hundred bucks here and there when one of them gets published. I have to supplement my income by working in a warehouse. I've waited my whole life for this kind of break. *National Geographic* is the top of the tree. My whole career has been about this moment. I didn't see why someone who tried to drug me should take it away.' Strachan was ranting. He'd lost his poise, and cursed himself for it.

'But your flight didn't leave until 6.30 a.m., and yet you left the hotel some time after midnight. There was plenty of time for you to wait for the ambulance, and still catch your plane. Why didn't you wait? Don't tell me you had six hours of packing to do?'

'No,' Strachan replied. 'If I'd stuck around I wouldn't have made the flight. You know that as well as I do. You wouldn't have let me go.'

'Why not?' There was no rapport whatsoever now. Koopmans had Strachan on the ropes. He was moving in for the big finish. This was a trap. The sudden change in tempo, and the switch from friend to foe were probably both on page one of the interrogation manual. Strachan knew what was happening. Koopmans wanted him to acknowledge that his behaviour was suspicious. He wanted him to acknowledge that his decision to flee the hotel was evidence of guilt. 'I asked you a question.' Koopmans was thousands of miles away across the Atlantic. As he leaned forward on the monitor, it was as though he was in the same room.

Again Strachan said nothing. Even a response as innocuous as 'No comment' would give Koopmans an opening. If Strachan gave him an inch, Koopmans would take a mile. He was better at this than Strachan was.

'Banbury has lost his tongue,' said Verhoeven. 'What kind of a bastard name is that anyway? Banbury?'

Strachan narrowed his eyes. It had taken them a while but they'd finally found the trigger.

8

Strachan was instantly riled. Riled is a bad state to be in during a police interview. Perhaps if he knew the answer it might have been easier, but the fact of the matter was that he still had no idea why his parents had christened him Banbury.

He'd been born in a military hospital in Germany. He'd only ever driven through Banbury on his way to somewhere else. Originally the family was from Scotland, not Oxfordshire. The only connection he could find was in the God-awful nursery rhyme that his father used to recite while he bounced him on his knee as a kid. *Ride a cock horse to Banbury Cross*. Strachan got it every day for six years. It was always accompanied by a volley of painful thumps, and then a reminder never to repeat it to anyone. The biggest bounces came at the end of each line, and there was no special emphasis on *Banbury*. Besides, the rhyme was about a fine lady rather than the strapping young lad he took himself to be; so on his seventh birthday Strachan had announced to the world that from now on he was to be known as Edward or, better still, as Ed. Happily for him it had stuck. Until now.

Strachan told himself to chill. It didn't work. He was losing composure fast. He ignored the original question. 'If I drugged her, what was the pipette doing in her handbag?'

'You planted it there.' Verhoeven made it sound obvious. 'Once you realised you'd killed her, you made sure her fingerprints were on the pipette and placed it back in her handbag.'

Strachan felt the flush of anger seeping up his neck. His only defence was that Christine had tried to drug him first. It didn't make sense. His position stank and he knew it. 'Listen, she tried to drug me. I'm sorry for what happened, but I'm not responsible for her death.'

'Oh but you are, Banbury, you are. You see, even if we believed that she spiked your drink it was still your decision to switch those glasses. You fed her an illegal drug, and that is a naughty thing to do.'

Strachan was losing confidence now as well as composure. It had never occurred to him that switching glasses would kill Christine. Now he was going to prison. 'If I hadn't switched glasses,' he said, 'it might be *my* body lying there in the morgue.'

'And if you were confronting her, it would be no one's body,' Groote interjected.

'I'm not a killer. I didn't kill her.' Strachan's anger strained at its leash.

'Maybe,' Koopmans said. 'What about the theft of Pieter Zeeman's jeep?'

'Piet won't mind. It wasn't theft. Ask him if he thinks I killed her.'

'I already did. And he said next time he saw you, he was going to tie your ankles with weight-belts, and throw you to the sharks. He was supposed to be teaching a wreck course at the *Superior Producer* today, and couldn't get the tanks there because the jeep had gone.'

'Shit.'

'Shit is right. Want to know what else he said?'

'Not really.'

There was a long silence. Strachan could hear his own breathing.

'You are lying, Banbury.' Verhoeven looked at him with black eyes, unblinking, like a snake. It was becoming his catchphrase: a drum he could beat all night.

Strachan glared back. 'If I wanted to rape her, why would I leave fingerprints all over her room? Why would I call an ambulance unless I was deeply concerned for her? I don't know why she wanted to drug me. I haven't worked it out. That's your job.' He looked Verhoeven in the eye. 'So go figure.'

'Mr Strachan?' There was no mistaking the warning in Koopmans's voice. 'Don't be a tough guy. I don't like tough guys.'

'Banbury isn't a tough guy. Banbury is a coward. That is why he drugged a young girl. In case she resisted while he raped her. Isn't that right, Banbury?'

Strachan boiled with anger and frustration. He wanted to leap across the table and shut Verhoeven up. He knew then that he would fight him. Maybe not here, maybe not now, but soon enough. The two of them sorting out their differences the old-fashioned way.

'Do you know what a pubic comb-off is?' Verhoeven was relishing this.

'I can guess.'

'Do you want one? I can arrange it quickly. It's standard procedure in rape cases. Do you want a genital wash-off at the same time? The doctor's not so gentle, but maybe you prefer things rough?'

If Strachan spoke, he would be in danger of saying something that would harm his defence. He said nothing.

'That is what we are dealing with here, isn't it? Date rape gone wrong. You took her out for dinner. You drugged her, but you gave her too strong a dose and she died before you could have your fun. Banbury, people like you make me sick. It is people like you we have to protect our wives and daughters from.' Verhoeven stood up and leaned over the table. Their faces were inches apart.

Strachan didn't believe for a minute that Verhoeven had a wife or daughter. The inspector's breath was hot and smoky. It hit him like pollution as Verhoeven called him a rapist. Under the table Strachan bunched his right fist, extending the first two fingers in a V. His hand was a pitchfork. Verhoeven's eyes were less than a foot away.

'Thank you, Inspector, that's enough.' Despite being halfway round the world, Koopmans interceded, saving Verhoeven from serious injury. Strachan relaxed his hand. 'Mr Strachan, you and I will talk again tomorrow. You have given us plenty to think about and I suggest we all get some rest.'

'Wait,' Strachan said. He should have been glad that the interview was drawing to a close but he still felt under pressure. There was a long way to go before he was clear. 'Have you interviewed the staff at The Lobster Pot? Or checked the reservation list for the tables next to ours? Maybe someone else saw her spiking my glass.' It was a long shot, but he needed all the help he could get. 'Does the restaurant have CCTV?'

'You let us worry about that. In the meantime I suggest you calm down. You are in enough trouble without making an enemy of Inspector Verhoeven.'

Strachan nodded. The case against him was straight-forward. He could see why. All the evidence pointed towards date rape. They had a dead girl and they were looking for someone to hang. His adrenalin had kept him going but now that things were drawing to a close he suddenly became aware of his exhaustion again. This was going to run and run. Koopmans was right about his attitude, too. It wasn't helping his cause. Strachan watched as Koopmans's enormous frame filled the screen. His white shirt blocked out the room behind as he approached the monitor. The screen in Room 13 went blank as Groote hit the remote.

'Do you know Hoofd-Inspecteur Koopmans?' Verhoeven asked.

'Not personally. I know of him.'

Verhoeven grunted, not entirely satisfied with Strachan's reply. The Dutchman was still suspicious, perhaps even jealous as he looked his suspect over. As though Strachan's tan gave him some sort of bond with the island's Chief Inspector.

'Think about what you have told us. Sleep on it. Consider if you would like to revise your answers. We will go through it again tomorrow. The time now is 2:48 a.m. Inspector Rutger Verhoeven is terminating the interview.' He pressed STOP and the tape spooled to a halt. They were off the record.

'2:48 a.m.? Am I right in thinking you haven't actually charged me with anything yet?'

Verhoeven smiled and nodded. 'Correct.'

'And you can only hold me for six hours?' Strachan had spotted the lifeline and he lunged for it with both hands.

'Correct.'

'So any minute now, you have to let me go, right?'

'Wrong.'

'Why?'

'Didn't I tell you?' Verhoeven eyeballed him. An unspoken promise that they'd soon have a heart-to-heart conversation in a room without witnesses. 'The hours between 12:00 a.m. and 9:00 a.m. don't count.'

9

Strachan was led down the corridor, through a set of steel gates, and into the cells. A drunk was being ushered into one of them. His baggy clothes and matted hair marked him out as a career vagrant. Even from fifteen yards away, Strachan could still detect the acrid reek of the man's piss.

Strachan was shown to his cell by Ruisdael, the policeman who had taken the inventory of his belongings. The door closed behind him with a clang. There was an iron bed with a thin beige mattress pushed against the far wall. He collapsed onto it. At least they hadn't cuffed him again. And at least they hadn't charged him and flown him back to Curaçao. With his deadline inching inexorably closer, he had higher priorities than making friends with Colombian coke smugglers in the Bon Futuro prison.

The cell was small but clean. About twelve feet by sixteen. A temporary holding pen rather than a permanent lock-up. A single fluorescent strip ensured that even with no windows the room was flooded with light. A wooden table and chair were placed against a wall next to a plastic basin with plastic taps. In the corner behind the door was a grey partition screen and behind that a toilet. Graffiti had been scratched on the screen. Shielded from view, several inmates had used plastic cutlery to express their contempt of Dutch law.

The writing was large and childish – not unlike his own.

Under normal circumstances Strachan would have found it impossible to sleep in a place like this. There was glaring light, and a constant percussion of banging doors, roaring jets and barking dogs. But these weren't normal circumstances. In the last twenty-four hours he had taken a nine-hour flight, been arrested, been interrogated, had his only source of income confiscated, and watched someone die from a lethal drug. He was asleep in minutes.

At first Strachan was too tired to dream but then, later in the night, he recognised the large brain coral marking the start of the reef at Knife Point. Visibility was good. About twenty metres. A shoal of angelfish, rotating in the current like a child's mobile, hovered over algae-coated rocks. To his right a hawksbill turtle snapped a branch of dead coral with its prehistoric-looking beak. On his left the reef sloped away sharply, disappearing into the blue-grey void of the open sea. The bubbles of his spent air burbled in his ears.

A banging noise above told him that Piet was following his progress in a rowboat. He was sending a message via its steel hull. It was Morse code, telling Strachan to get out of there. Piet had seen Verhoeven enter the water with a harpoon, and the policeman was closing fast. Strachan kicked hard, his fins propelling him towards the cover of the boulders. The angelfish scattered like flashes from a welder's torch as he drove through them. He wasn't prepared for what he saw behind the rocks, and the regulator fell from his mouth.

Christine Molyneux hung suspended in the current. At first Strachan thought she was dead because she wasn't moving, and her naked body appeared stiff with rigor mortis. But then he saw a trickle of bubbles escaping the corner of her mouth. He swam to help her. He reached for his spare regulator. He was about to force it into her mouth but when he tested it he found that he was out of air. He tapped his pressure gauge. The needle stayed in the red. He sucked hard. Nothing. He sucked again. He heard the muffled tap of the valve as rubber closed on rubber. His tank was empty.

He couldn't bolt for the surface without risking the bends. Christine was his only chance of survival. Strachan clasped her head in his hands and clamped his mouth against hers to fill his lungs with the air that she exhaled. He made the seal as tight as possible. Her breath tasted bitter and had the texture of chalk. Instantly nauseated, he pushed her away. Her eyes rolled in her head.

When he looked at her now, her face had the olive hue of a zombie's. Her shoulders felt slimy as algae laid an early claim to her corpse. Her hair spewed behind her, waving in the current like a black flag. He could see fish working on her toes. Small cleaner wrasse nibbling at the skin so her blood oozed like green ink.

With his brain screaming for oxygen, Strachan looked closer at the bubbles escaping from Christine's mouth. They weren't air bubbles at all. They were drops of clear liquid. Poisonous liquid. At that moment she came alive. Out of nowhere she grabbed his head in her hands just as he had done to her only moments before. The move took him by surprise and he tried to recoil, but her fingers pressed his temples like the jaws of a vice. She was whispering something. He tried to wrestle free but her grip was too strong. His ear was against her lips. He could hear her clearly now: *'Let's dance!'*

Instantly awake, Strachan swung off the bed and rubbed his face. He felt the talons of a headache squeezing his brain. Someone had entered the cell while he was asleep and a breakfast of bread, jam and water had been left on the table. He ate it fast, and although it was thin fare it gave his system some much-needed sugar.

Strachan had lost track of the time again but it must still have been mid-morning when Agent Groote returned to the cell. The policeman opened the door and stood in its frame with his hands on his hips. He was trying to stare Strachan down. 'I am surprised, Banbury. You are in too much trouble to sit so calmly.' He sounded cheerful. The guttural cadence of his speech was more sing-song than before. Perhaps he'd finally had his carbs.

Strachan held his gaze. He was damned if he was going to be intimidated.

'It's time,' Groote said, looking down. 'Come with me.'

Strachan was ushered back to the video conferencing room. It was awash with the rancid flotsam of a night's police work. Polystyrene cups doubled as ashtrays. Stale smoke hung in the air as thick and noxious as industrial smog. His lungs craved a smoke. This was the longest he'd gone without one since he could remember. He looked at Groote, who looked at Verhoeven. Verhoeven shook his head.

'Come on, Rutger. Lighten up, will you? Gimme a cigarette.'

'Shut up and sit down.'

Only then did Strachan notice that the video machine was already on. Chief Inspector Koopmans was waiting for them to be quiet. He also appeared to have been working all night. Strachan could see blue sky through the window in Koopmans's office, and his yearning to be back in Curaçao made him forget his need for a cigarette.

Five thousand miles away Koopmans's camera picked

up movement in the room at Schiphol. 'Good morning, Mr Strachan. I have some interesting news for you.'

Strachan nodded.

'Inspector Verhoeven will be charging you shortly.'

10

'That's interesting news?' Strachan was crushed. It looked like Koopmans was playing games. Perhaps he'd misread him.

'Yes. For the time being we're going with wilful misconduct. We can't prove that you committed an offence, but your own statement admits an infringement of the law.'

'What's the difference?' Strachan tried to keep the relief from his voice. They weren't charging him with murder and that was all that mattered. Yesterday he'd been their man. The evidence against him had been overwhelming. Something had come up in the night. Something good.

'With an infringement, guilt in the sense of blame is assumed to be present and does not need to be proven. Your only admissible defence is for you to claim you were devoid of *all* blame, but after what you've told us, I wouldn't go down that route if I were you.'

'Great. Am I free to go?'

'You will be soon. But I have to warn you that we haven't ruled you out of our investigation altogether. We may yet find enough for *dood door schuld*.'

'Dead door what? What the hell is that?' If they were going to discuss his fate, Strachan would much rather they did it in a language he understood.

'*Dood door schuld*. Literally, it means death through

blame. It means you killed the girl, and are to blame for her death, even if you didn't intend it. Call it reckless manslaughter if it makes you feel better.'

It didn't. *Dood door schuld* sounded much less serious, so Strachan told Koopmans no thanks.

'You are to remain in daily contact with Interpol until this mess is cleared up. One false step and you'll be hauled back in faster than you can fart. Inspector Verhoeven will be your liaison officer.'

'Of course he will.' Strachan flashed Verhoeven a look that said their communication would be short but not sweet. His confidence had returned. 'Yesterday you all assumed I was guilty. What changed your mind?'

'There were some interesting developments in the night,' said Koopmans. 'The pathologist confirmed that the deceased hadn't been interfered with sexually and . . .'

'God!' Strachan said, 'What do you think I am?'

'Secondly, we took your advice about closed-circuit TV cameras in the restaurant. There weren't any inside, but they have one installed in the car park. It showed the deceased arriving on the night she died. The tape shows that she was nervous. She was fumbling for something in her handbag, and dropped it in the camera's field of vision. The tape isn't clear enough to be conclusive but the object appears to have been a plastic pipette, matching the description you gave yesterday. If what you told us is true, you can consider yourself lucky that you switched those glasses. The dose in a pipette that size would have been enough to floor a rhino.'

'Bloody hell,' Strachan said. Right then he couldn't think of anything else to say. So she *had* been trying to kill him, after all. This was information overload, and he could process it later. 'Anything else?'

'Yes. As a matter of fact. The girl's name wasn't Christine Molyneux.'

This time Strachan said '*Shit*'. Then he remembered the flurry of note-taking when he'd mentioned her name yesterday. That explained the quizzical looks and whispering in Dutch. A made-up name. It worked in his favour. They'd known all along.

'Shit is right,' replied Koopmans with a grin.

'So? What was her real name?'

'That doesn't concern you, Mr Strachan. What does . . .'

'Doesn't concern me? Are you kidding? She tried to kill me.'

'I'm not kidding. Why would I joke about something as serious as a potential homicide? What *does* concern you is the penalty for the offence that you *did* commit.'

Strachan's heart sank. The last few minutes had been great. He had a feeling that the next few would be ones that he could live without.

'We could fly you back to Curaçao and send the case to trial. You'd plead guilty to wilful misconduct and get twenty days in jail plus a small fine.'

Again Strachan said nothing, mesmerised by the word *could*.

'But I don't want the expense of flying you back or incarcerating you. For some strange reason I believe your story. I think you're thick as horse shit, but I don't think you meant to kill her. So I'm going to fine you and ban you from returning to Curaçao until the investigation is closed and your innocence is proven beyond all reasonable doubt. In the meantime I don't have room for people like you in my jails.'

Strachan knew why: the drugs trade. The South American mainland was only sixty miles away, and Curaçao was a staging post for the main smuggling routes into Europe. Seizures had tripled in each of the last three years as the cartels expanded their networks. The local papers were full of it. 'How much is the fine?' he asked.

'A thousand dollars should do it.'

'A thousand dollars?' Strachan drew in his breath. That was going to hurt. 'When do I have to pay?'

'Ask Piet Zeeman. He's the one you owe.'

Strachan flushed hot, then cold. Now he understood the '*strange reason*' why Koopmans believed his story. Perhaps the policeman owed Piet a favour? It didn't really matter. Piet had worked a little bit of magic, and now Strachan was going to walk. They had video evidence, and a false name, but it was the old-boy network that had saved him from prison. It was an opportunity too good to miss so he smiled at Verhoeven and gave him a wink. The Dutchman glared back, the skin of his neck livid with rage.

Koopmans continued. 'If you set foot in my country again, I will arrest you. Do I make myself clear?'

'Crystal,' Strachan replied. He had no doubt that when Koopmans described Curaçao as 'his country', he meant it. The thought of not seeing The Coral Kraal again was a heavy blow, but even with a thousand-dollar fine he was still getting off lightly. He hoped to God that Verhoeven would prove his innocence unequivocally over the next few days, but somehow he suspected that wasn't going to happen.

'Good. Agent Groote will put you on the next plane back to London.'

'Thank you, Chief. One last thing.'

'What is it?'

'What else did Piet Zeeman say when you spoke to him yesterday?'

'He said you were a hell of a good kid, and there was no way you could have killed the girl. For what it's worth I believe him. Piet's a good friend of mine. We've been playing cards together for twenty years. As a matter of fact I'm seeing him again tonight.' Koopmans relaxed and leaned back in his chair. As far as he was concerned this thing was a wrap. Interpol was taking over to tie up the loose ends, while he and his team got back to some real police work. With only fourteen narcotics officers in a staff of two hundred, he was rushed off his feet. 'Goodbye, Mr Strachan.'

The screen went black.

Back in the cell reception area there was a brief administrative interlude. Strachan had to sign release papers while Verhoeven ran through the protocol of the daily phone call and handed over his card. It had an office and mobile number printed in a simple black font. Strachan was to call him once every twenty-four hours to let him know where he was.

Strachan signed for his belongings. It took him a second to realise that the films had gone. He took a step towards Verhoeven, who was grinning at him like a basking croc. 'Where are they?'

'I am sorry. They appear to have been lost. We have a very careless member of staff who often mistakes personal belongings for rubbish.'

Strachan aimed the punch at Verhoeven's lip. He locked his wrist and let fly with all his strength. He imagined the point of impact as the back of Verhoeven's head rather than the front. That way he would punch right through the cop's face. He wanted to inflict maximum damage.

The blow glanced off Verhoeven's temple. Out of nowhere, Groote had lunged for Strachan's arm and pushed it up. Strachan was thrown off balance but still caught the look of surprise on Verhoeven's face. Surprise turned to relish as Groote held Strachan in a full nelson, exposing his stomach.

Strachan had been hit by bigger men than Verhoeven, but none of them had punched so accurately. The fact that he locked his abs was irrelevant. Verhoeven's knuckles drove into his solar plexus so that his nerves jangled like wind-chimes in a gale. Strachan doubled over, unable to breathe. Then Groote twisted him away.

Verhoeven straightened his sleeves and adjusted his tie. His face was flushed. 'You and I will be seeing each other again, Banbury.'

'I look forward to it.' Strachan spoke through gritted teeth. It felt like a nail bomb had exploded in his chest.

'Screw you.'

'Only in your dreams, Verhoeven. Screw yourself.'

Groote released Strachan and collected a padded A4 envelope from behind the desk. He spun Strachan round with his spare hand, pushing him in the small of the back. Strachan stumbled down the corridor towards the terminal. Groote said 'That is enough,' and handed him a boarding card. Then he told him that his luggage had been checked in already and they set off to find the plane.

The pain in Strachan's chest had eased by the time they reached the gate. Now dejection took its place. He was returning to England without his films. He'd wriggled out of the tightest hole he'd ever been in but the price had been high. His credibility with *National Geographic* would soon be in tatters. The prospect of a long winter in Hamilton's warehouse dragged on his mind like an anchor. The trip to Curaçao had been wasted. At his age, he might not get another shake of the dice. A drug-user and a sadistic cop had stolen the opportunity from him. In the space of thirty hours he'd been consigned to the scrap heap of failed artists. A has-been who never was.

The flight was boarding. Groote accompanied

Strachan all the way to the plane's door, flashing his security pass at the ground staff. Despite his reluctance to return to a wet and cold London, Strachan couldn't leave Schiphol fast enough but as he crossed the threshold Groote called him back.

'I found these in the refuse last night.' He tossed Strachan the envelope. 'Please. Send me a copy of the barracuda.' He handed over his card. 'My kids, they will love it. If you have one of a shark also.' He was embarrassed again. Apologetic. His jowls reddened as the blush blossomed in his cheeks. 'My boy is only eight. He loves sharks.'

Strachan shook the envelope. His films rattled like treasure. He held out his hand and Groote clasped it in the doorway.

'*Dank je zeer*, Agent,' Strachan said with a broad grin. 'I'll see what I can do.'

The rain lashed Strachan like an overseer whipping a galley slave as he heaved his luggage through the door of his Pimlico flat. It slanted sideways down the street and stung his cheeks.

He lived in a one-bedroom flat above a curry house. It wasn't much but he didn't have to worry about the opinion of family or friends. It was modestly furnished with second-hand stuff from car-boot sales and with the dregs from Hamilton's warehouse. After he'd paid the rent and bought his films and air tickets, there was never much left over for cars or fancy furniture – let alone pensions and other savings. But Strachan didn't care about any of that. Until this morning all he'd wanted was enough to build a modest shack behind The Coral Kraal, and a boat big enough to make the trips to Aruba and Bonaire where he planned to run the best underwater safari south of St Lucia.

The Zeemans were going to employ him long enough for him to swing a work permit. Once he had money coming in he could then apply for residency. Immigration law was notoriously lax. If six hundred Colombians could get residency each year then Strachan reckoned he had a fair shout. Curaçao was a poor man's version of the Caymans: they'd accept anyone with a sniff of cash. The diving was good enough for him to be able to charge premium rates and it wouldn't take long before they allowed him to stay. Until this morning he'd had it all planned out. Now he was barred indefinitely. Worse, he'd gone and struck the one man who could reopen the door. Christine Molyneux had a lot to answer for, whoever she really was.

Strachan had a quick shower, made coffee, and sat down to his first cigarette in forty-eight hours. It felt good but it wasn't enough. A second followed. Then a third. At last he felt the caffeine and nicotine seeping into his blood, twin stimulants giving him stamina for the night ahead. He looked at his living-room walls and felt the familiar surge of excitement that preceded a trip to the lab.

The walls were covered with photographs from his expeditions around the world. So much blue. So many fish. The room was like an aquarium. Some of the better pictures were mounted in glass clip-frames but glass clip-frames were an expensive luxury and the majority were stuck up with Blu-Tack. The photographs gave Strachan a sense of identity. He had no money, no job and no girlfriend but how many people had seen the things he had? A Mimic Octopus, for example? The damned thing had only been discovered a few years ago, and he'd been one of the first to capture it on film. Now there it was, darting towards the TV. *Underwater World* had paid good money for that series.

He glanced at his watch. Seven o'clock. Two o'clock in Washington. He reached for the phone.

'This is McCauley.' Gilchrist's soft, unassuming voice answered on the first ring.

'McCauley. It's Ed Strachan.'

'Ed. How you doing?'

'Fine. Did you get my message?'

'Sure did.'

'And?'

'No can do, my friend. Unless the pictures are here this time tomorrow, we're gonna give the whole lot to Bill Tanner.' Bill Tanner was a Canadian; a veteran who, now that David Doubilet had retired, was the only underwater Photographer-in-Residence on *National Geographic*'s books. He was good, but Strachan was better. Tanner was still taking wildlife photographs; Strachan's shots were art.

'Come on, McCauley, you know what I can do. These shots from Curaçao, they're the best I've done.'

'In which case we might use them next year. I'm sorry, Ed. Really I am. I know how hard you try, but I can't cancel the printers. You get the negs here by lunchtime, and we can still drop them in. The templates are all set and it'll only take an hour to choose the ones I want. You shouldn't have left it until the last minute. Shit, you've had months to do this.' There was a pause while Gilchrist told his secretary to hold a call on the other line. His voice softened again. 'You get them on the first plane outta Heathrow tomorrow morning and you should still have plenty of time. Time difference works in your favour.'

Strachan smiled to himself. This job would be a whole lot easier once he could afford a decent digital camera. Then he could simply download the images onto a PC and send them to the States by e-mail. In the meantime Gilchrist was right. There was still a chance he could make it.

'Ed?'

'Yes?'

'You do realise something, don't you?'

'What's that?'

'I can't pay your expenses if I don't get my shots.'

'Yeah, I know. I wanted to talk to you about . . .'

'Ed?'

'Yes, I'm still here.'

'What the hell for? You ain't got time to be talking to me, son. Get outta here and we'll talk again tomorrow.'

'Thanks, McCauley.'

Strachan grabbed his films and was gone.

12

The clock was ticking. The urge to go straight to the lab was strong but Strachan was still shaken by his experience in Curaçao and the need to see a friendly face was stronger. Hamilton's place in St George's Square was on the way. He'd only stop for a few minutes to let his godfather know he was back. He wasn't going to tell him the trouble he was in, but since Hamilton had raised him after his parents' deaths the least he could do was say hello.

Hamilton was a bachelor and lived in a three-bedroom flat on the west side of the square. It was a classic Regency building, designed by Thomas Cubitt in the first half of the nineteenth century. The flat occupied the first and second floors of a five-storey house. Like all the others it was stucco-fronted with white columns, tall bay windows, and a graceful balcony overlooking the communal gardens.

The bells of St Saviour's were ringing out from the top end of the square as Strachan passed. It was a quintessentially English sound, he realised. Other countries tolled their bells but the English made theirs sing, the chimes tumbling over each other as clear as snow-melt cascading down the bed of a mountain stream. He smiled wistfully. London wasn't all bad, and he knew he was fortunate to have grown up in such a well-heeled part of town.

Each of Strachan's parents had been an only child so there had been no aunts or uncles to foster him after their deaths. His paternal grandmother and maternal grandfather were both still alive at the time of the accident but the old lady lived in Scotland and his grandfather no longer drove, so between them they'd decided that he was better off living with his godfather. He continued to see his grandparents during the school holidays but for ten years Hamilton's flat had been his home too.

Now, standing outside, Strachan experienced a mael-strom of conflicting emotions. It was the same whenever he stepped through the door. It was like coming home – only it wasn't *home* because his memories of what *home* was like were so vague that he was no longer sure they were real. St George's Square reminded him how lucky he'd been to have Hamilton, but also how unlucky he'd been to need him in the first place. From the age of eight to eighteen the room on the second floor had served as his playroom, his den, his study, his gym, and his bedroom. It was a place where he had laughed and cried; where he had sat for hours calmly watching the turgid flow of the Thames – and then had beaten the walls until his knuckles bled. His refuge from the world but also his cell.

He rang once. Hamilton buzzed him up, greeting him in the doorway with an outstretched hand. Their relationship had always been a little awkward. Hamilton had married briefly but then had divorced before he'd had kids of his own, which probably accounted for his occasional discomfort in the role of surrogate father. They never hugged. 'Ed, dear boy! Welcome back. How are things?' He was wearing his customary corduroys and checked shirt. His hair was neatly parted and smelled of the dye he used to disguise his age.

'Pretty good,' Strachan lied. 'And you? You look surprised to see me.'

'Not at all. I'm fine, fine. Come on in.' Hamilton spoke like an Edwardian schoolmaster. Slow and deliberate, as though actively checking the pace of modern life. He had been an antiques dealer since retiring from the army, and now ran a gallery, warehouse and auction room, a mile up the road in Sloane Street.

'I can't stay long. I've got work to do.'

'At this time of night?'

'It's only eight.'

'Yes, indeed. Eight o'clock. High time for a malt.' Hamilton ushered Strachan into the living room then disappeared to the kitchen to fix their drinks. He only ever bought Glenrothes, from Berry Brothers & Rudd, and Strachan had developed a taste for it over the years.

Strachan cast an eye round the room while he waited for his godfather to return. He never ceased to be amazed by Hamilton's taste. The flat was an Aladdin's cave of mahogany furniture, Vietnamese art, and bone-china coronation mugs. Persian carpets from Tabriz and Esfahan covered the floors, and a high-baroque mirror hung over the fireplace. His old bedroom now housed a Sébastien Erard piano. Hamilton's pride and joy – a three-foot marble statue of Achilles by Giambologna – stood guard in the hall. Although the collection hailed from three continents and countless different periods, the whole ensemble was perfectly balanced. There was scarcely room to swing a cat but it was all arranged with military precision.

'So how was Curaçao?' Hamilton appeared behind him, holding a crystal tumbler.

'Same old,' Strachan said. 'How's the business?'

'Not so good at the moment. It's been a quiet summer. Sales are down.'

'I'm sorry to hear that.' Strachan noticed his godfather looking at the cuff link round his neck. 'What?' he asked.

'Tell me,' Hamilton replied, 'do you wear that thing when you're diving?' They sat down in a couple of armchairs.

'Always. I never take it off.'

'That's good.'

'Why do you ask?'

'No reason. I was just toying with a new theory about your inheritance.'

'God, not another one! Let's hear it.' Strachan gave his godfather a weary smile. Speculating over what the inheritance might be and where it might lie hidden had become a regular topic of conversation over the years. It would crop up every six months, sometimes seriously, sometimes as a game. They'd even tried hiring a private investigator to find the babysitter but had been laughed out of every meeting they'd arranged. With nothing more concrete to go on than a false name and a twenty-year-old description, no one was interested in taking the case.

'Do you think it could be a work of art?'

'Haven't we had that one?'

'Specifically a statue.'

'Why a statue?' They'd been through the list of sixteen countries many times and had agreed that Malaysia and Singapore were the most likely locations since that was where Strachan's grandfather had served in the war. As to *what* it might be, their guesses ranged from the sublime to the ridiculous. A statue was about par.

'Your grandfather was a tough old bugger but he had a passion for sculpture. I don't know why I didn't think of it before.'

'Could be,' Strachan said. He wasn't really in the mood for this. His mind was on the calendar. Hamilton

70

was still looking at him for a reaction, nervously almost. 'I don't know,' Strachan said. 'What do you expect me to do? Leap out of my chair and tell you you're right?'

'"*Ed will see.*" What do you think your father meant by that?'

'I don't know. You were there, not me.'

'Is there something you should be telling me?'

Strachan looked at his godfather blankly. This was strange. They'd been over it a thousand times before. 'Not that I know of.' He took a large mouthful of whisky and looked away, signalling that the subject was dropped.

They made small talk for another few minutes before Strachan drained his glass and stood up. The deadline was getting closer all the time. He felt guilty about not staying longer and made a silent vow to spend more time with Hamilton at the next opportunity. Hamilton had made a valiant effort at keeping him on the straight and narrow throughout his childhood, and deserved more than this breezing in and out. 'Is the warehouse job still there for me?' Strachan asked.

'Yes. For a little while.'

Strachan nodded. 'Thanks for the drink. I'll see myself out.' He turned along the hall and narrowly missed tripping over a stack of paintings on the floor. There were six of them. They looked Renaissance and were probably worth a fortune. Only they weren't, not any more. Each one had a big hole in the canvas. It looked like someone had put their foot through them. No wonder it had been a bad summer at the gallery.

13

The lab was located in a basement flat, opposite the Peabody Trust estate. Strachan paid two hundred pounds a month, which gave him a set of keys and unlimited access. Use of the equipment was included in his membership. Raw materials were paid for on a pro-rata basis.

It was owned by a Latvian wedding photographer called Dimitri Spelovski. He'd come to Britain in the 1980s for his sister's marriage to an English lawyer. Finding that the money in Britain was six times better than in Latvia, he'd stayed ever since. Spelovski was a jovial man with a clown's face. He enjoyed vodka and pornography, often at the same time, and had always wanted to be better friends with Strachan than Strachan had allowed. Strachan had nothing against him; it was just they had nothing in common.

The lab was deserted. At this time of night Strachan wasn't surprised. He was one of only three regulars who'd been coming to this basement over the last five years. He got on well enough with the other two. Toby Bachop was the same age as he was, more or less. Strachan took pictures of fish; Bachop took pictures of fish fingers. And of plates of peas, microwave dumplings, and boil-in-the-bag broccoli for clients like Bird's Eye and Findus. It must have been hellishly boring work but at least his subjects stayed still. Tammy Summers was the other. Her breasts were as fake as her name. So far as Strachan knew, she was still struggling to make it onto page three of *The Sun*. Strachan had a weakness for pretty girls in labs, and they'd been lovers on more than one occasion – which was more than could be said for Tammy and old Spelovski. Strachan had twice caught him going through the cuttings bin after Tammy had been in to develop her latest set of topless films.

He flicked on the lights, entered Spelovski's office and tuned the radio until he found one of Brixton's pirate reggae stations. His mood soared as the DJ introduced *Pressure Drop* by Toots and The Maytalls. Right now he could use a drop in pressure. The last twenty-four hours had been tumultuous. It would do him good to get back to something as routine as developing film. Strachan set to work, confident that everything would be ready for a dawn collection by FedEx.

By midnight he'd developed and enlarged seven of the fourteen rolls, including the two of the barracuda. It was obvious which shot Gilchrist would use but Strachan nonetheless enlarged fifteen possibilities to give his editor a choice. He stacked the photographs on the desk next to a pile of Tammy's. He glanced at the top picture. In this series she was somewhere out in the country, sitting nude on a white horse. When he saw the shots, he immediately thought of the nursery rhyme his father had drummed into his head as a child.

To see a fine lady upon a white horse.

The word *horse* had always been followed by a bang from his father's knee, and his butt had stayed bruised until he was six. He'd hated horses ever since. As usual, Tammy hadn't got it quite right. She had the looks and figure to be a glamour model but her photographer

73

didn't have the skill. He always got the light wrong or used the wrong sort of film. The pictures looked seedy, not erotic. Strachan put them down with a shake of the head.

He paused for a cigarette while he waited for the kettle to boil. As he made coffee, his mind wandered back to Christine Molyneux. Piet Zeeman was friends with Koopmans so he might be able to find out her real name. Strachan wasn't sure what he would do with the information if he had it, but the fact that he didn't know pricked his curiosity. If he could find out who she was, it might explain why she had tried to drug him. That might help prove his innocence to Verhoeven, which in turn would lead to his ban from going back to Curaçao being lifted. It had to be worth a shot.

Spelovski's office was supposedly out of bounds but the regulars used it anyway. Strachan booted up the PC. He logged on to Hotmail and fired off a quick e-mail to The Coral Kraal. Unless Piet was doing a night dive, he and Maggie would be packing up about now. They always checked e-mail before they left. Strachan typed quickly, not bothering to correct his mistakes.

He thanked Piet for paying the fine and supplying Koopmans with the character reference, and then apologised again for commandeering the jeep. Then he asked the favour: find the girl's real name. He suggested that Piet talk to the Chief Inspector next time they played cards – casually, of course, without revealing who really wanted to know. He signed off by sending his love to Maggie, and said he'd try to find a way of seeing them next year, ban or no ban.

By four o'clock he'd developed the remaining images from his week in the Caribbean. He selected a portfolio of the best twenty-five shots. Gilchrist would choose two of them. Next he ran two extra copies of the barracuda for Ronald Groote, and found one of a reef shark for his son. Strachan had a hunch that Verhoeven had been right when he'd said they would meet again, and he figured it wouldn't hurt to maintain his rapport with Groote. It just might come in handy. He threw in a stingray and a hammerhead for good measure.

Another hour and four Camels later, he initialled the raw-materials ledger on the wall. He turned the machines off and went to the study to package the prints and negatives. The computer was still on so he checked the Internet in case Piet had replied.

He was in luck. Monday night was clearly poker night in Willemstad. Now he thought about it, Koopmans had said as much at the end of their second interview. Piet had already written back. It was midnight in Curaçao, and the e-mail had only been sent in the last ten minutes.

You hopeless bastard. Can't you stay out of trouble for more than a week at a time? The girl's real name was Molly Newchris. Not exactly subtle. Maggie sends her love. Don't wait till next year, come at Christmas. And bring a damn big present.

That was it. Piet Zeeman: short and to the point. He was no more a man of letters than Strachan was.

Strachan looked at the words on the screen, clearing a path through the dust with his finger. How many times had she used that alibi? A simple juggling of her forename and surname. He couldn't blame her: Christine Molyneux sounded a lot more glamorous than Molly Newchris, even if it didn't meet Piet's definition of subtle. It was more Home Counties, less East End.

He reached for the phone directory. His arm sent a spider plant crashing to the floor. He hurried through the pages. His fingers picked up traces of ink as he thumbed.

There were several listings under *Newcross* but only one under *Newchris*, and he thanked her aloud for having an unusual name.

Molly had lived in Bermondsey Street. Strachan jotted down the address on a piece of paper. The fact that she was listed suggested she wasn't part of a criminal organisation. If she'd been a gang member then the pack she ran with wasn't one to be feared. Ridiculous as it seemed, he experienced a sense of relief. He hadn't been the target of a sophisticated mob of East End villains. Sophisticated villains tended to be ex-directory. Even ones with no apparent motive for wanting you dead.

He turned off the PC, then packaged the photographs and negatives into a shallow cardboard box, which he left open for the time being. The pictures from Scotland and the Galapagos were still in his filing cabinet at home and needed to be included. He addressed the box to McCauley Gilchrist and then called FedEx. The girl in the call centre told him that his package would be collected between eight and half-past. Same-day urgent delivery to Washington would cost forty-nine pounds. Strachan swore, apologised, and said okay. Then he went home.

The man from FedEx collected the package at exactly 8:15 a.m. Strachan told him that he was holding him personally responsible for its safe arrival in Washington. The courier looked at him doubtfully and began to protest, so Strachan sent him on his way with a reassuring smile.

Then he went upstairs and looked up Bermondsey Street in his *A to Z*.

14

Bermondsey Street ran through the heart of Borough.

South of the river, it stretched from London Bridge Station across Long Lane and down towards Great Dover Street and the Old Kent Road. It was central enough for a short commute to the City, and its warehouses had all been converted into modern apartment blocks. When he woke at six in the evening, Strachan had slept for nine hours. He felt fresh and invigorated. He walked to Bermondsey Street from Pimlico. It only took an hour.

Molly's flat was in an old brick warehouse. The outside of the building had been restored to its original design but it wasn't fooling anyone. Inside the flats would be expensive: owned by Paisley-tied lawyers, pinstriped bankers and overpaid management consultants. It was a building that had elevated itself from an insalubrious past. A building that had escaped its roots and was now enjoying a new lease of life. A glance in an estate agent's window told Strachan that properties in this street started at four hundred thousand and he noted it down as another reason to leave this crazy city at the first opportunity.

There was no security guard in the building's lobby. The mailboxes told him that Molly Newchris had lived on the third of four floors. Strachan climbed the stairs at a brisk pace as though he had legitimate business in the place. There was no one around but he didn't want to arouse suspicion. The bankers would be home soon. The lawyers would be next; the consultants wouldn't get back until after nine.

A terracotta urn stood sentinel outside her door. It was home to a bushy green plant that was neither yucca nor fern. The door was light brown with a chrome handle. It had a spy hole that reminded Strachan of the camera on the video machine at Schiphol. He put his eye to it and got a distorted view of the hall inside. It seemed to stretch away for miles. It was like looking through a telescope the wrong way round. He saw no sign of movement.

Strachan knocked. There was no answer so he tried the door and found that it was locked. He knocked again, louder this time. Still nothing. Satisfied there was no one home, he crouched down and inspected the lock. It was robust enough to seal a bank. His foot would break long before the door did, but at least he'd seen what was required and he could return another time with the right tools for the job.

He was halfway down the stairs again before he checked himself. The chances of finding a key were close to zero but it would be foolish not to look. He jogged back up. There was nothing under the doormat but when he rolled the terracotta plant-pot to one side it revealed a shining brass prize. There was only one lock. The key turned it smoothly.

Strachan slipped inside and pushed the door to. Behind him the latch kissed the door frame, lingered for a second, then rebounded off the metal catch. Strachan was already moving inside the flat. He didn't know it, but the door was still ajar.

A wooden hall led to a large open-plan kitchen. The floorboards were stripped pine and were partially

78

covered with an ethnic rug in rustic colours. There was a three-piece suite in cream leather complementing the exposed brickwork. Six black-and-white prints of the Manhattan skyline adorned one wall. It was tastefully done. Strachan felt another ache of remorse at the girl's death. She intrigued him, and he regretted that he didn't know more about her.

An arched window offered a view of the rooftops stretching away towards London Bridge. It was dark but the city's rusty glow meant that he could still see the satellite dishes waiting for the rain to rinse them clean. But this was funeral weather and the wrong sort of rain. All it did was stain and corrode, distancing him further from the sunny Caribbean island on which he'd once hoped to live. He studied the view for a minute, sulking over his ban. Then he told himself to snap out of it. *Don't just stand there. Do something about it.*

When Strachan returned to his inspection of the flat it was the shin-high coffee table that first caught his eye.

It was home to a large pile of diving magazines. He recognised the top one instantly. It was the edition of *Underwater World* that featured his series on the Mimic Octopus. He took it from the pile. He was about to flick it open when he recognised the next magazine as well. It was a back issue of *On-The-Edge* in which he'd been given the centre spread for his pictures of bull sharks in the waters off Zanzibar. The third magazine was even easier. There on the cover of *Scuba Times* were Itchy and Scratchy, his award-winning sea otters. They were floating on their backs, shelling oysters. The peaks of the Vancouver coastline burned amber in the background. He had taken it half underwater, half above, and he had to admit that it was one hell of a shot.

Strachan rummaged through the rest of the pile. It only contained magazines in which his pictures had been published: his life's work bundled into one heap. He felt a prickle of pride and returned his attention to the copy of *Underwater World*. He flicked through it until he found the piece on the Mimic.

What he saw there caused him to sit down in the cream sofa and say 'Shit.'

15

There was a black-and-white pen-pic at the start of the
article. *Photographs by Ed Strachan*. He was leaning back
in a deckchair with his hands behind his head. He
remembered it well. One of the boat-boys had taken it.
The silver cuff link hanging on the chain round his neck
was clearly visible even if its inscription was not. And
Molly Newchris had circled it in red pen.

A hurried search through the other magazines
revealed that he'd left a similar trail over the years. Not
all the articles featured pictures of him, and of those that
did the majority showed passport images of his face only.
But by the time he'd thumbed through the pile, he
counted five pictures in which his neck was visible. All
five had received the same treatment. The cuff link had
been circled, and his name underlined with the red pen.

It was one part of the mystery solved. Strachan still
had no idea who Molly was but at least he now knew
what she'd wanted. She'd wanted his cuff link.

It struck him then that she'd had the other. His cuff
link was useless unless she knew it was one of a pair, and
the circled photographs of his neck suggested she'd
figured that out. It was just as he suspected: together the
two cuff links led to something extremely valuable.
Something worth drugging for. Something worth killing
for.

He instinctively began a more thorough search of her

apartment. The second cuff link was close. He could feel it in the crawling of his flesh.

For years Strachan had amused himself with the prospect of hidden treasure. Then, as he'd grown older, the fantasy had lost its appeal. His cuff link was useless without the other. Eventually he'd resigned himself to the fact that its whereabouts would remain a mystery. If he ever had a child of his own, he would simply pass the remaining cuff link on just as his father had done. But now it all came flooding back. He began scrabbling through Molly's drawers like a pig rooting for truffles.

He was in her bedroom when he heard it. A noise behind him, but he was too slow.

'Freeze.'

Strachan's heart missed a beat. It was a woman's voice, shaky but aggressive and as East End as Molly's.

'Put your hands up.'

He obeyed the order. Something in the voice now. She sounded older than he'd first realised.

'Who are you? Don't turn round or I'll shoot.'

'I'm a friend of Chr— Molly's.'

'What's your name?'

'John Smith.' The first and only name he could think of.

'What do you want?' She was crying now.

'I heard about Molly's death. I couldn't believe she'd gone. I just needed to be near her.' He was amazed at how easily the lies came.

'Turn around. Keep your hands in the air.'

Strachan turned round slowly, his arms still held high. The woman stood in the doorway. She wasn't a cop and she didn't have a gun. She held a mobile phone in her right hand. In her left she carried a small canister — pepper spray, perhaps.

'I've dialled 999. All I have to do is press OK and the

82

call will go through.' Her tone was curt as she issued the warning. She'd waited until she was sure she was safe before she'd allowed him to turn.

They stood twelve feet apart on either side of the room. The woman was in her late fifties. Her hair was a jackdaw's nest of unkempt strands. She looked harrowed and stern. Eyeshadow ran down her cheeks as she cried. She tightened her grip on the phone while she wiped her face with her sleeve. The make-up smudged. Now she looked like a gaunt and wasting panda.

She wore simple, inexpensive clothes. BHS or Debenhams. A grey woollen skirt, black tights, and an old blue Puffa. She had removed her shoes at the front door so that she could creep up unheard. Even through the streaming make-up it was clear who she was. She was Molly's mother, and Strachan was going to have to play it just right.

And then something very strange happened. Molly's mother raised her hand to cover her mouth. The blood drained from her face, and she turned pale as a ghost. Her whole body shook. Strachan was sure that she was going to faint. He took an instinctive step towards her in case she fell, but she recoiled in horror at his approach. 'My God!' she said, shaking her head. 'It's you.'

He recognised her instantly then. The way the skin round her eyes wrinkled into crow's-feet as she examined him. Even with the passage of twenty-one years, there was no mistaking who she was. She was Molly's mother – but she was also the woman who'd slapped him the night his parents died. The mean-looking babysitter he'd disliked the moment she'd walked through the door.

16

'Where's the cuff link?' Strachan took another step towards the woman. Hamilton's theory was right. She had stolen it.

'Stay where you are or I'll call the police.' She must have seen the look in his eye. She backed out of the bedroom into the hall.

Strachan had no intention of hurting her. Even when he'd run with the emerald thieves in Malaysia, violence against women had been strictly off limits unless you were Pili Parang, the gang leader. Besides, in the telephone and pepper spray she had weapons not to be messed with. He would have to tread softly. She had just lost a daughter, after all. 'Where's the cuff link?' he repeated. Softer this time. Sympathetic almost, but not quite. Like his conversation, Strachan ran his compassion on a pretty tight budget. He didn't have much to spare for the thieving mother of a woman who'd tried to drug him.

What Mrs Newchris said next surprised him. She didn't say 'What cuff link?' She didn't say 'I don't know what you're talking about.' What she said was, 'I ain't got it. I gave it away.'

And with those words she told him far more than she probably intended. It was an admission of guilt. Strachan was gambling with Hamilton's theory but the gamble had paid off. This woman had stolen the second cuff link the night his parents died. Twenty-one years later, her daughter had tried to match the pair.

A volley of emotions shot through Strachan, heavy as bolts from a crossbow. Anger, relief, confusion. Anger because if she hadn't stolen the cuff link, he wouldn't be in this mess and, more importantly, Molly would still be alive. Relief because here was someone who could clear him from any suspicion of deliberately causing Molly's death. Mrs Newchris could give him an alibi. She was his ticket back to Curaçao. If he could persuade her to talk to Koopmans or Verhoeven, she could explain why Molly had tried to drug him. But it was the confusion he tackled first. It was like playing *Mastermind*. He had the right coloured pegs but he hadn't yet arranged them in the correct order.

'When did you give it away?'

'This morning.'

'This morning?'

'Yes.'

'Who to?'

'A copper. A Dutch copper.'

'Did he have a name?' Strachan asked unnecessarily. He knew damn well who it was. For the first time he realised what a risk he'd taken in coming here. Verhoeven had been assigned to follow up the case so the first people he would speak to were Molly's next of kin. He might even have been the one to break the news of Molly's death to Mrs Newchris. Although Molly had been dead for seventy-two hours the grief in her mother's eyes was still fresh. Her tears weren't those of someone weeping for a missed loved one, they were the visible signs of an aching despair over a loss she didn't understand. Raw, inconsolable grief. It was possible she'd only heard the news this morning, and Strachan could think of better people to break it than Rutger Verhoeven.

She sobbed as she answered his question. 'Verhoffen or something. He said it foreign, like.' She paused. 'You're Ed Strachan.'

He nodded. 'And you gave him the cuff link?'

'Yes.'

'Why?'

'He told me he was investigating Molly's death. There were suspicious circumstances. He said she might of been murdered. Anything I could tell him might help catch the person who done it.' She looked at Strachan accusingly. They were in the living room. Her eyes narrowed, then flashed with rage.

Mrs Newchris came at him suddenly like a banshee. A hysterical gorgon with bared teeth and wild hair. She led with the pepper spray, aiming for his eyes. Strachan took a step back and caught her wrists, forcing her arms high as she pressed the valve. He dug his thumbs into her wrists until she dropped the can, then moved her away from the falling cloud of spray. He had avoided a direct hit, but already he could feel the sting in his eyes and the acid burn at the back of his throat. All the while Molly's mother writhed and fought. She kicked his shins. He winced as he felt the skin break and the flesh beneath it bruise. She was screaming at him.

'You killed Molly! You bastard! You killed her! Who's going to look after the boy?'

'What boy?'

His answer came from further down the hall. A short cry followed by a longer one, and then the prolonged wail of a distressed baby. Strachan felt his strength leak away. He couldn't see it but he could hear it. Molly had a child. By switching those glasses he had inadvertently killed its mother. 'Where's the father?' he asked, more for comfort than information. He felt sick.

'The father's run off! The father's a bastard just like

you! I'll kill you! I'll kill you, you murdering bastard!'
She spat in his face. Once theatrically, and then for real
when she realised how good it felt. The saliva caught on
his eyelid and slid down his cheek. Still he held her
wrists. He didn't dare let go.

Mrs Newchris was hysterical. There was no point
reasoning with her so Strachan concentrated on
holding her instead. They danced a horrific dance: she
swinging her feet, he dodging the kicks as best he
could. He had her at arm's length. He locked his biceps
so she couldn't twist his wrists and bite him. It lasted a
couple of minutes before she began to tire. Her screams
became sobs again. She was exhausted; physically and
emotionally drained. So was Strachan. He pushed her
backwards and guided her onto the sofa. She collapsed
into the cushions. Then she put her head in her hands
and wept.

The fight had gone out of her. Strachan had to say
something. She would hear him even if she didn't listen.
'Mrs Newchris, I didn't murder Molly. Her death was an
accident. She tried to drug me. All I did was switch our
glasses. I would never have done it if I'd known mine
was drugged so heavily.'

'I know.' She nodded, sniffled, and sobbed, all at the
same time.

'You know?'

'The inspector told me. He said you'd told him you'd
switched glasses but he didn't believe it.'

'*You* believe it, though, don't you?' The way she had
said '*I know*': heavy with resignation. As though she
knew it was an accident. As though she knew she
couldn't pin her daughter's death on him. As though
she'd known all along.

She didn't answer but sobbed at him through her
hands. 'What else did the inspector say?' He had to raise

his voice to make himself heard over the cries of the screaming child.

'He asked me if I'd ever heard the names Banbury or Ed Strachan. Whether Molly had ever mentioned them. So I told him "*No, who's Ed Strachan?*" and he said it was the man Molly was last seen with.' Mrs Newchris spoke through her fingers. They were like the bars of a grille: hopelessly inadequate for stemming the river of anguish that poured in torrents from the depths of her soul. Her voice lurched as she swallowed her sobs. 'Then he starts asking me if she ever took drugs or was in any trouble, and what was she doing in Curaçao, and he wouldn't stop. He asked me so many questions. So many bleeding questions. He was like a terrier.'

Strachan needed her to calm down. He needed her to think clearly. He needed her on his side. 'Mrs Newchris.'

'Michelle.'

'Mrs Newchris.' He didn't want to call her by her first name. It implied a level of familiarity that didn't seem appropriate. 'I'm going to make some coffee. Then you're going to tell me everything you know about that cuff link. Molly's gone now. You can't bring her back. The best thing you can do is get it all out and set the record straight.'

It was a long shot but he couldn't think of any other way to keep her talking. His only alternative was to threaten to have her arrested for the theft of the second cuff link twenty-one years ago. But he reckoned a wizened old thief like Michelle Newchris had spent most of her life helping the police with their inquiries. A trip to the magistrates' court would be no more terrifying than a trip to Poundstretcher. Besides, he had no way of proving it. That was why he needed her to talk.

Strachan got to his feet. He explored the jars in

Molly's kitchen while he boiled the kettle. Over his shoulder he watched as Mrs Newchris went to collect Molly's child from where she'd left it by the front door. She'd found a tissue up her sleeve and was doing her best to wipe up the mess on her face. Then she picked up the boy. He had black hair and blue eyes like Molly. He stopped crying. He looked at his grandmother and smiled.

There was no milk in the fridge, so Strachan made the coffee black with sugar: strong and sweet, just the way he liked it. By the time he returned to the sofa, Mrs Newchris looked the most composed he'd yet seen her. He sat back and cupped the coffee in his hands. He could tell that she was ready to talk.

'You stole the cuff link from my father? When? Why?'

'I've been stealing all my life. Never anything much, mind. Just the odd bitta jewellery here and there. Stuff out of people's handbags and wallets.'

'And safes.'

'Yes. Combination locks were always a speciality.' Mrs Newchris managed a smile through the tears. 'Your dad's was a hard one. It took me nearly an hour.'

'Why did you only steal one cuff link?'

'I only found one. Most of the stuff in the safe wasn't worth nicking. It was just legal documents. Premium bonds, share certificates and the like. Then on the top shelf there's this blue velvet pouch next to an old piece of newspaper. I could tell straight away it was something valuable so I stuck my hand in and helped myself.'

Mrs Newchris looked at Strachan apologetically. Her guard was down. She wasn't the battleaxe he'd taken her for. She was a forlorn petty thief who'd struggled through life only to bring about her daughter's death. There was no mention of a Mr Newchris nor of any other children. Strachan imagined her raising Molly on her own, stealing and shoplifting to make ends meet. And now Molly was dead. The punishment far outweighed the crime. The enormity of it was reflected in her uncomprehending eyes.

'The second one was in the newspaper. Right next to the first,' he said.

'Ha! I should've known. Keep them separate. Very clever.'

'Hardly. Keep going.'

'It's about ten o'clock and the phone rings. It's the police. They tell me something terrible's happened. They say they're coming over with your godfather but I'm not to wake you up. I'm sorry, Mr Strachan. Really, I am.'

He wasn't sure if she was apologising for the theft or offering condolences for his parents' deaths. If it was the latter she needn't have bothered. He didn't want her sympathy, and he'd had twenty-one years to come to terms with it.

His parents had gone out for dinner and had never come home. A drunken joyrider had hit them at forty-three miles an hour on a pedestrian crossing. The car was a VW Sirocco, low enough to the ground to strike them mid-thigh. They'd cartwheeled over the vehicle's roof like cricket stumps ripped from the ground by a fast delivery. Hamilton had quoted from *King Lear* to help him understand. *As flies to wanton boys, are we to the gods; They kill us for their sport.* Strachan had been eight at the time, and Shakespeare had been no help whatsoever. But over the years he had revisited the lines. Slowly, like a long course of antibiotics, the words had tackled the malignant cells of his grief until eventually he came to look at his parents' deaths as a cruel twist of fate: something unpredictable and inexplicable. And in that he now found explanation enough. *As flies to wanton boys.* To strangers at least he could talk about his loss with the indifference of concrete.

'I thought about putting the pouch back and waiting for the police to arrive, but they were hardly going to search me, were they? Besides, when I looked inside there was a note in there as well.'

'What note?' Strachan moved to the edge of his seat, hanging on the woman's every word, coiled and eager as a sprinter on the blocks.

Michelle Newchris stood up and walked down the hall to Molly's bedroom. She returned a minute later with a folded white postcard. Strachan could see that it was old. It had lost its rigidity and was turning brown along the edges. She held it out and his hand snatched it like the beak of a pecking bird.

> Worth their weight in silver
> Until they're sixty years old.
> Then put the two together
> They'll be worth their weight in gold.

Arthur Strachan, October 1945

The postcard wouldn't stay still in Strachan's hands. He looked at his arms and realised that they were shaking. So it was true. Together the cuff links led to a valuable inheritance. And this postcard was the best clue yet as to what that inheritance might be. Strachan reread the verse. His grandfather's handwriting was neat yet bold. He'd signed his name with a flourish that bordered on calligraphy. It was sixty years since 1945, which might explain why Molly and her mother had made their move now.

He noticed Michelle Newchris staring at his own cuff link. It was clearly visible in the V-neck of his shirt. She was Gollum to his Frodo. He half expected her to lunge for it and start calling it her *precious*. He rocked back out of range. This was proving a highly propitious meeting and he was keen to see what other gems Mrs Newchris and her story had to offer. 'What happened next?' he asked.

'Well, now that I knew the two cuff links were valuable I searched the rest of the house for the other one but I never found it, and I had to stop looking when the police arrived with your godfather. I tried again the day of your parents' funeral because I knew the house would be empty but I didn't have any luck. I was still desperate for the other one so I watch the house and it soon becomes obvious that if anyone has it, it's that Mr Hamilton. I followed him home one day so I knew where he lived. I even had a look round his house a few times, but I still couldn't find it.'

'No,' said Strachan. 'You wouldn't have done. It spent the next ten years in a safety deposit box in the bank.'

Michelle Newchris almost laughed. 'Typical! I knew I was wasting my time. In the end I gave up. I knew if I pushed my luck I'd get caught. I took the one I'd stolen down the pawnbroker the next day, but he weren't going to give me more than five quid for it, so I gave it to Molly instead.'

Strachan shook his head ruefully. Hamilton had spent the best part of two years looking for Michelle Newchris and she'd walked right into his house twice.

'Molly loved that cuff link straight away as soon as she saw it. You know what little girls are like with jewellery. She slept with it under her pillow.'

'How did she find me?'

'She'd got herself into trouble. She'd been working in a bank and was earning God knows what, but then she got made redundant. She was a spender, not a saver and she was up to her ears in debt before she knew it. After a while she was asking me for money and I didn't have a penny. That's when I remembered the postcard. It was all I could offer her. That and the story of how I found the cuff link.'

'So how did she find me?' Strachan repeated the question for the second time. The woman hadn't given him a straight answer. Maybe she didn't know.

'Those magazines.' She pointed at the pile on the coffee table. 'I told her where your godfather used to live, and she said she was going to have a look for it herself. I told her not to be so daft. It was over twenty years ago and Mr Hamilton had probably moved. Besides, I didn't want her going because I thought she'd get caught. I'd looked twice and hadn't found it, so I told her she was wasting her time. Anyway, she was having none of it. I don't know how much she owed, but she must have been desperate. The next day she turns up with those magazines. Mr Hamilton hadn't moved in all that time. She didn't find the cuff link but she found the man who had it. You.'

Strachan nodded. He'd given Hamilton numerous photographs in the past, but his godfather had always preferred the magazines. Hamilton was his number one fan and had copies of all his published work. He kept them in a big pile in his study.

'Molly was so excited. She said the two cuff links were the clue to buried treasure and now she knew that you had the second one she was going to get it back. She points out the cuff link round your neck, and tells me right there that she's going to get it, and one day we're going to be rich. That's when she started planning to rob you.' Michelle Newchris picked up the baby and settled him in her lap. He had calmed down. He snuggled against her and fell asleep.

'*Rob* me? She tried to *kill* me.'

'No.' She looked at Strachan defiantly. 'Molly tried to drug you. It was my idea. She never meant to kill you.

94

The drug was meant to knock you out while she stole the cuff link. But you switched glasses, and the dose was too much for someone her size. It killed her.'

'And you told all this to the inspector?' He had to say something. He had to keep the conversation going. If he didn't, he was going to crack. Koopmans had told him that the dose in the pipette was enough to floor a rhino but it was still possible that Molly had made a mistake. He'd probably never know whether she'd wanted him unconscious or dead. She'd been the only person who could have answered that question and now she was gone. Either way, Strachan still had her blood on his hands. Her child was going to grow up without a mother. Strachan knew all about that. It wasn't much fun.

'No. I told him nothing. Never told the Old Bill nothing in my whole life.'

That could be a problem. He needed Molly's mother to repeat all this to Verhoeven. It was the only way off the hook. 'Where did you meet him? Here?'

'Yes. I wanted to be with Molly's things before I flew to Curaçao. They want me to identify her body.' The tears returned thick and heavy like raindrops. Strachan could hear them landing on the floorboards.

'When did you meet him?' It was a damn sight easier conducting an interrogation than answering one. At Schiphol he'd been on the other side of the fence, the side Michelle Newchris was on. He preferred it this side.

'This morning. About eleven o'clock.'

That was good. Verhoeven was unlikely to pitch up again this evening. Strachan could afford to relax a little. He wondered if the inspector had seen the magazines. He decided to take one with him as evidence. He could always say Michelle Newchris had given it to him. There was no way Verhoeven would find out he'd broken in, and even if he did, breaking and entering was a much less serious charge than *dood door schuld*. In a way Strachan hoped Verhoeven *had* overlooked the magazines. It would be a satisfying victory, shoving evidence like that down the Dutchman's throat.

Something still wasn't quite right. 'I don't under-stand,' he said. 'You told him nothing, but you still gave him the cuff link. How come?'

Mrs Newchris's gaze darted to the window; enough to tell Strachan she was lying. Verhoeven would've shown no sympathy for her bereavement. She might have run rings round the local plod but she would have been no match for a bastard like him. Strachan could see it now. Verhoeven had turned the screw, and she'd sung like a bird.

'I might of told him a bit of the story. Just to get him off my case. He was asking so many questions. Like I told you, he was a bleeding terrier, that one. When I mentioned the cuff link, he asked if I knew where Molly kept hers so I went to fetch it for him. He asked to see it and I gave it him. When I asked for it back, he just laughed and said it was evidence.'

'It is,' Strachan told her. If she'd told Verhoeven half what she was telling him, he was in the clear. Verhoeven was most likely already back in Amsterdam, perhaps on the phone to Koopmans, telling him what he'd learned. Strachan might yet see St Michiel's Bay again. He'd almost heard enough. Almost, but not quite. He still had one more question. Now that Verhoeven had the other cuff link, it was the most important question of all. The question he'd wanted to ask for the last half-hour.

'Mrs Newchris, what were the numbers on Molly's cuff link?'

'I don't know,' she said. 'I can't remember. There was the letter E, and three sets of numbers. I think one of them was thirty-nine. Yes. Thirty-nine, because that's one of my lottery numbers I always choose.'

'And you can't remember the others?'

'No.'

It was possible that she was lying but Strachan didn't think so. The fact that she'd just opened her heart to him made him want to believe her. The way she looked at him when she mentioned his parents' deaths. Like it gave them common ground. The loss of his parents; the loss of her daughter. Their respective tragedies transcending the barriers between them. No, if she'd known those numbers she would have told him.

He drank the rest of his coffee in a single gulp. He took the top magazine from the pile and stood up. He was through. There was no point staying. He'd taken enough risks for one day. They made their way to the door. Mrs Newchris shuffled along behind in her stockings. Her big toe was poking out through one of them. Already it looked bruised and swollen from where she'd been kicking him.

'Thank you. You've been very helpful.' Strachan didn't like saying it but it was true. He had his hand on the banister and was descending the steps. She still hadn't answered his question so he turned to face her. 'How did Molly know I was in Curaçao?'

But Michelle Newchris pretended not to hear and closed the door in Strachan's face.

The rain had stopped by the time Strachan got outside. He looked up and saw the clouds being swept aside by a biting wind. A gust descended to street level where it chased leaves along the pavement into the drain at his feet. The chill forced his hands deep into his coat pockets. Strachan walked with his shoulders hunched. Half-past nine in the evening in London, mid-afternoon in St Michiel's Bay. The sun would still be shining. A good time to swim out beyond the reef and look for the dolphins. But back in the real world it was late, and he was hungry.

He made his way back over London Bridge, along Cannon Street, Queen Victoria Street and the Embankment and up to the Strand, where he knew he could find a McDonald's. Even at this time of night it was packed. The customers were squeezed in tight, fighting for space, jostling for empty seats, climbing over each other like crabs in a bucket. He ate standing up. An overflowing bin belched up a paper cup, which landed on the floor by his shoes, spraying them with banana milk shake.

Strachan usually ate well when he was diving. Most of his time was spent in warm-water countries where the currency was crippled and the fish cheap and tasty. Places like Ecuador, Thailand and Kenya. Places where he could live well on ten bucks a day. But in London he ate like a rat. He scavenged snacks, rarely cooking anything more wholesome than microwave dinners. Eating was merely a means of staying alive while he worked in the warehouse and saved for the next trip abroad. It was a dispiriting cycle. He referred to the warehouse as yin and the ocean as yang, and here he was about to start a long stretch of yin.

Not that he was complaining; it was his choice to live like this. He'd known from an early age that he wasn't cut out for a career in a suit. Similarly, the thought of following the family tradition and joining the army turned him cold. He'd sooner take orders in a drive-through than on a parade square. There wouldn't be much to choose between the uniforms but at least he could go home at the end of the day.

Strachan had never had much career advice and had stumbled on underwater photography as much by accident as by design. Uncertain of what to do, he'd taken a gap year after leaving school. Hamilton hooked him up with Carl Ryan, an ex-army friend who ran a petrol-distribution business in Malaysia. Ryan gave him a job which involved driving round the country in a big 4x4, stopping at the gas stations, noting their stock levels, and building a forecast for the fuel they needed to deliver the following month. Those were the days before e-mail had reached Europe, let alone the Third World, and the language barrier meant that they couldn't rely on phone calls. Maths was Strachan's weakest subject, but he could work a calculator and he took care not to make mistakes. He didn't want to go back to England so he worked hard. When it came to the end of the summer he sent Hamilton a postcard saying that he was binning his place at university and staying in Malaysia.

Ryan had two stations up on the north-east coast. One of them was in Kuala Besut, the gateway town for the Perhentian Islands. The islands were already famous for their diving. Strachan took a few days off and tried it for the first time. He was instantly hooked. He stopped logging his dives after he completed his Rescue qualification six months later. He'd filled two logbooks, and it was a chore with no payback. Eleven years on and he reckoned he'd probably spent around four months of his life underwater.

Malaysia had also been where he ran into Runi and Pili Parang for the first time. It had a special place in his memory. It was there that he began his career. Not only as an underwater photographer, but also as the most prolific emerald smuggler in South-East Asia.

Strachan's memories kept him company long after he finished his burger. He made his way down to Trafalgar Square, along Whitehall and past the Houses of Parliament, reaching The Morpeth Arms by Vauxhall Bridge in time for last orders.

On Tuesdays the pub was quiet, and he stopped only long enough for a pint of Guinness and to catch up on the news from behind the bar. Tammy wasn't there, which was a pity. He'd been hoping to find her. She had a special gift for helping him relax at times like these. He still had the small matter of a *National Geographic* deadline to worry about. His photographs should have arrived by now. If they hadn't, it would be Bill Tanner's that would be on their way to the printers. Strachan walked back to his flat, trying to play down the fact that his career hinged on the phone call he was about to make.

He had his key in the door when he heard it. A voice from the shadows. He hadn't noticed anyone following him, so the man it belonged to must have been waiting for him.

'*Goedenavond*, Banbury.'

Dutch. It's a throat disease.

19

Strachan didn't turn around. He didn't need this. Not now.

'Are you inviting me in? That's most kind of you.'

The odour of alcohol on Verhoeven's breath was strong. Strachan could smell it with his back turned. Maybe Verhoeven had spent the evening waiting for him in the pub. What could he do? He could hardly say no – the guy was a cop – so he shrugged and let Verhoeven follow him in. Verhoeven put a hand on his shoulder and pushed him. Not hard, but enough to make him stumble.

'You didn't call, Banbury. I missed you.'

They were at the top of the stairs. Verhoeven was right. Strachan had forgotten the daily check-in. Not that it mattered. Verhoeven was doing a pretty good job of staying on top of his movements.

'What do you want, Rutger?' Strachan turned to face him for the first time. Verhoeven was wearing black, like a Gestapo agent. Black shoes, black jeans. A black leather raincoat and black leather gloves. His skin glowed with a bar-room tan. He was flushed; eager to take Strachan down.

'I have come to see how you are doing. And to find out where you have been this evening. Where *have* you been this evening, Banbury?'

Verhoeven followed Strachan into the flat. Strachan

took his coat off and flung it on the sofa. He told him he'd been out walking, and then on to see an old friend.

But Verhoeven wasn't listening. He was looking at Strachan's pictures. Captivated, like a child visiting an aquarium for the first time. He was transfixed by one photo in particular. He couldn't move away from it, and for once Strachan admired his taste. It was the gaping mouth of a manta: one of the harmless giants that frequented the Sangalaki Marine Reserve off Kalimantan. It had been travelling straight towards him, apparently oblivious to the camera. Its mouth was wide open. Its horns funnelled plankton past gills the size of gateposts. Strachan could have swum right down its throat. The shot was all mouth except for a thin halo of blue around the edge. That was one of its appeals: it took a while to work out what you were looking at.

'So.' Verhoeven finally tore himself away. He was impressed. Perhaps now he understood Strachan's reaction to his stunt with the rolls of film. 'Why didn't you call?'

'I forgot.'

'You forgot? What if I arrested you again, and forgot to release you?'

Strachan let him talk it up, let him have his fun. If Verhoeven had something important to discuss he'd cut to the chase soon enough.

'Tell me some more about that cuff link round your neck.'

Again Strachan said nothing. Verhoeven knew all about the cuff links now. He'd spoken to Michelle Newchris. She'd given him the second one and filled in the blanks that Strachan had left at Schiphol. There was no point repeating what Verhoeven already knew.

'It's one of a pair, isn't it? Christine Molyneux had the other. That is why you drugged her.' Verhoeven was doing the maths, adding two and two and making zilch.

'Her name was Molly Newchris. And *she* tried to drug *me*, so cut the crap. She didn't have the cuff link with her in Curaçao, as you well know. That's how her mother gave it to you this morning.' Strachan tossed the magazine he'd taken from Molly's flat on the table to emphasise his point.

Verhoeven was surprised. He was trying to keep up. Christine Molyneux's real identity was still classified. 'How did you discover her real name? Did Koopmans tell you?'

'No.' Strachan could see that Verhoeven wanted him to say more so he didn't give him the pleasure. Verhoeven began to fidget. As though he couldn't decide whether to take Strachan on physically or mentally. Strachan was enjoying his discomfort.

'You found her mother? When? This afternoon?'

'Like I said, I've been visiting an old friend.'

Verhoeven wrung his hands. The stiff leather gloves creaked as he sought to control his frustration. 'I think I'd better have your cuff link now. It is important evidence in this case. I will need to confiscate it. If what you say is true, then it could eliminate you from our inquiries. Hand it over now. Please, Banbury. Be a good boy.'

Strachan grinned. He hadn't drugged Molly intentionally and Verhoeven knew it. The Dutchman already had enough evidence to close the case, and the reason for his presence here was purely personal. Maybe Verhoeven knew enough of the story to want to go after the inheritance himself. Maybe he had forgotten the coordinates he'd read out in Schiphol. Maybe he really did need the cuff link to close the case. In any event, this visit was only going to end one way. And if Verhoeven wanted to fight, well, that was fine by Strachan.

When Strachan was thirteen Hamilton had packed him off to Bradfield College, a beautiful old public school in the Berkshire countryside. His father had served twenty years by the time he died, and the army provided a generous bursary that covered most of the fees. Bradfield was pretty average academically but its sports facilities and pool were excellent. That was where Strachan had directed most of his energy. Most but not all. He'd kept some back for learning to fight.

His parents' deaths had made him withdrawn. Much of the time he was a loner: it was him against the world, and the world had better watch its step. He'd had a lot of anger back then at the way life had treated him, and he used the lunch queues, dormitories and changing rooms to take it out on his classmates. It was an expensive education, paid for with cuts and bruises. If someone insulted him, Strachan didn't bother with a slanging match, he just hit the guy. If the other guy hit back then Strachan waded in until one of them backed down. Over the next five years he developed into a strong swimmer, and there weren't many lads prepared to take him on. Most of them were happy to give him a wide berth, and those who didn't soon discovered that he fought dirty.

When people fight, they instinctively protect their heads, groins and stomachs, so Strachan quickly learned to attack elsewhere. He went for the knees, feet and fingers. He had it figured by the time he was fifteen. Fighting was all about inflicting the maximum pain in the minimum time. It was about wearing the opponents down so they couldn't defend the big finish. Strachan wasn't the biggest but he was armed with a devil-may-care attitude, and he was prepared to get hurt as long as he won. That had counted for a lot back then. Sometimes it still did now.

His housemaster saw what was happening and threatened to have Strachan expelled. He told him if he didn't learn to control his anger then he'd be out. The housemaster discussed it with Hamilton, whose solution was an idea for which Strachan was still grateful. In the holidays Hamilton paid for him to attend martial arts classes at the local gym as a means of learning control. The instructor was an Israeli who'd worked for Mossad, and he taught Strachan *Krav Maga*.

Most oriental martial arts involve a strong spiritual element of Zen Buddhism. Self-defence and unarmed combat are the by-products of body and mind working in harmony. Violence is a last resort. *Krav Maga* is different. It was spawned on the streets of Bratislava and developed later by the Israeli Defence Force in the 1950s. It emphasises simplicity and effectiveness, and teaches its practitioners to react without hesitation. Where appropriate, it also teaches them to escalate the level of violence they encounter. Law-enforcement agencies love it.

Strachan loved it too. Training in the gym was always based around real situations, and the instructors always subjected their pupils to the same levels of stress that they could expect to encounter in a genuine attack. It was pretty simple stuff: lots of elbows, knees, and fists. He went twice a week for three years' worth of school holidays. Once he'd started, he didn't fight again in school. He was too scared of inflicting a serious injury.

But that was then, and this was now. So Strachan told Verhoeven: 'You want the cuff link, you come and get it.'

'Banbury, you and I are a little too old for these games. Now, hand it over or I will have to arrest you for obstruction of justice.' Verhoeven tightened his gloves, smoothing the leather over his fingers so that they wouldn't slip. It was an ominous gesture.

Strachan doubted that a Dutch policeman had the authority to make an arrest in England but his senses came alive anyway. He was fully charged. He began working his fingers in his pockets, clenching and unclenching, easing the joints until they felt supple and loose. 'Inspector Verhoeven, the only way a shitbird like you is going to get my cuff link is to take it off my dead body.' He gave him his best smile to let him know that he meant it.

Verhoeven's right hand disappeared into the pocket of his raincoat. 'That could be arranged more easily than you imagine.' He pulled something out. A weapon. A cosh with a knuckleduster grip. It was a foot long and made of steel. It fitted his gloved hand snugly. 'Now,' he said – and the calmness with which he spoke told Strachan that he fancied his chances. 'For the last time of asking: give me the cuff link.'

Strachan shook his head. They stood two or three feet apart in the living room. His hands came out of his pockets in the same instant that Verhoeven launched his attack.

20

Verhoeven came at Strachan with the cosh held high for a downward blow to the face. Verhoeven was obviously expecting him to step back so Strachan stepped in to meet him. Surprised, Verhoeven hurried the blow. Strachan read it easily, throwing up his left arm to block him at the wrist. At the same time he gave Verhoeven a straight-arm jab to the base of the chin, catching him with the heel of his hand. The blow jerked the cop's head back, and Verhoeven must have bitten his tongue because his mouth gushed blood.

Verhoeven was armed but Strachan had the advantage and he flew in to capitalise on it. He moved lightly on his feet, his fists bunched southpaw. His next shot was a big old haymaker to Verhoeven's temple, and it put him down like a shot snipe. Strachan should have finished it there. A solid kick to the head would've taken the Dutchman out. But he hesitated. He didn't want to kill a cop, and he didn't put his full weight behind it.

Verhoeven was on his knees. He saw the kick coming and caught Strachan round the calf. He lifted his leg so Strachan had to stretch his arms to balance. Verhoeven used him like a lever to come to his feet. Strachan was expecting Verhoeven to push him backwards or twist him round to expose the back of his head for a blow with the cosh. Instead the cop dropped into a crouch. He took Strachan's right leg with him, sweeping away his left. Strachan crumpled to the floor like a demolished tower block, landing on his arse with a thump.

Verhoeven was onto him like a raging jackal, blood seeping from the corners of his mouth. His first blow broke Strachan's nose, pulverising it. Strachan's mouth filled with blood. His vision swam. One more strike like that and it would be over. Strachan had two weapons at his disposal: his forehead and his pelvis. He combined them perfectly to heave Verhoeven off. He braced his legs and pushed up, hard, fast with his hips. Verhoeven lost his balance and fell forward so that his face was an inch from Strachan's. Strachan butted him square on the nose. Verhoeven was stunned. The strength leaked out of him. Another lunge from Strachan's hips and Verhoeven was on his back, clutching his nose. The cosh fell from his grasp.

Strachan rolled to his right. He grabbed the leg of the dining table and hauled himself up. He'd taken one blow to Verhoeven's three. He beat the Dutchman to his feet by a couple of seconds. Then he escalated the level of violence.

Verhoeven was still crawling around as if he'd been thrown from a train wreck. Strachan covered the few yards between them at a run. He kicked Verhoeven in the ribs with a full swing of his right foot. Instinctively Verhoeven curled into a ball, protecting his head with his arms. Strachan's next kick was aimed at his groin, and it opened him up like a book. Strachan plunged down, driving his knees into Verhoeven's chest, and he felt the wind go out of him. Strachan retrieved the fallen cosh. He slipped his fingers through its knuckleduster grip. Then he escalated the savagery some more.

Verhoeven stopped struggling as he fought for air, giving Strachan time to pin him. The Dutchman's hand clutched at something on his hip. His raincoat fell aside and Strachan saw the holster for the first time. Coshes were one thing, revolvers were quite another. He had to end this before Verhoeven worked his gun free. Strachan knew that Verhoeven wouldn't hesitate to shoot him if he got the chance.

Strachan hit him with the knuckleduster grip, slowly and methodically. It bit like a blunt axe. The first blow cracked Verhoeven's cheekbone. A purple welt the size of a plum wept blood down the side of his face. Strachan hit him again, on top of the mouth this time. The blow snapped one of the cop's incisors at the root. It ripped through his gum and caught in the back of his throat. Seconds later Strachan was showered in spittle and blood as Verhoeven coughed it up. Verhoeven stopped screaming after the third blow. After the fourth, he stopped moving altogether.

At first Strachan was worried that he'd killed the Dutchman. He doubted whether he could convince a jury this was the second person he'd slain purely by accident. The police were especially zealous when it came to catching cop-killers, and especially brutal when punishing them. The last thing he wanted was the whole of Interpol hunting him down. It was with some relief that he found a pulse.

Verhoeven was out cold. Strachan didn't know how much time he had before the policeman came round, but he knew that he had to be as far away as possible when it happened. He guessed that he had an hour. Maybe more if Verhoeven had been drinking as heavily as the smell of his breath suggested. Strachan had to get rid of him.

He went through Verhoeven's pockets and found the second cuff link, then hoisted him onto his shoulder. He staggered to the sideboard to grab a bottle of Jack Daniel's which he wanted in case they were spotted. If necessary he could pretend that they were a couple of drunks returning from a party. He wiped the blood from his face with his sleeve. He pulled the cork from the bottle with his teeth and spat it to the floor. The whisky stung his split lip as he took a gulp but it also gave him strength. He took another hit before carting his prize down the stairs. Out into the street with Verhoeven draped over his shoulder in a fireman's lift.

Verhoeven was heavier than he looked. Strachan swayed under his weight which added to the charade. He turned left up Tachbrook Street towards the shops on Warwick Way. There was a small cul-de-sac on the right. It was home to three skips and a bottle bank. The skips were overflowing. A mound of bin-bags grew at their base. There must have been fifty of them. It was perfect.

Strachan dumped Verhoeven in the middle of the pile. The Dutchman collapsed into it. The nest of putrid cushions sagged under his weight. Strachan poured Jack Daniel's over the policeman's clothes, then wiped the bottle and tossed it in his lap. He was enjoying this. There was a certain justice to it. Only two nights ago Verhoeven had thrown his films into the rubbish at Schiphol.

It looked a comfortable enough spot to spend the night, among the Chinese takeaways, Hoover bags, nappies and fish skins. If Verhoeven was unlucky he might be nipped by rats. If he was really unlucky he might get mugged. But a rubbish heap in Pimlico was a much safer place to spend the night than a hundred other places Strachan could think of, and Verhoeven's chances of making it through the night were good. He would wake up sore but alive. He would go to hospital to fix his face and then he would come looking.

But by then Strachan would be long gone. On a quest

to find his inheritance at the crossroads of two co-ordinates.

Strachan's fist closed on the cuff link in his pocket. After twenty-one years apart, latitude and longitude were finally reunited.

PART II

═══

'Next,' said the captain, 'I learn we are going after treasure – hear it from my own hands, mind you. Now, treasure is ticklish work; I don't like treasure voyages on any account, and I don't like them, above all, when they are secret and when (begging your pardon, Mr Trelawney) the secret has been told to the parrot.'

(Robert Louis Stevenson, *Treasure Island*)

21

Strachan had never been to Singapore before. It had always been strictly off-limits for emerald smuggling. Draconian laws and stiff sentences meant that it simply wasn't worth the risk. Besides, there wasn't much demand for bootleg jewels from the law-abiding citizens of the region's wealthiest country.

It was early morning when he arrived. Through the taxi's windows, he saw that Singapore conformed to the image he'd always had of it. The highway from the airport was immaculate. A thick hedge of flowers grew in vast wooden tubs in the central reservation. Palm trees flanked the roadsides at precisely measured intervals. In most cities this stretch of road could have doubled as the botanical garden. In Singapore it doubled – allegedly – as an emergency runway.

Strachan had slept much of the way. He would get jet lag later, but there was still a spring in his step as he checked into the YMCA.

After dumping Verhoeven he had returned to his flat and called Gilchrist. Gilchrist confirmed that the photographs had arrived and had made it to the printers with fifty-six minutes to spare. The editor was thrilled with the pictures and asked Strachan how the hell he'd managed to find such an impressive barracuda. Strachan laughed and told him information like that was a trade secret, but that hunting your subjects was as much a skill as shooting them.

Had he not been in such a hurry Strachan would have bought some champagne. He would have called Tammy to see if she wanted to celebrate the pinnacle of his career thus far. But the possibility that Verhoeven might have woken up lit a rocket under his arse. He still hadn't unpacked from Curaçao, and he was gone in fifteen minutes.

It was too late to fly but Strachan still made his way out to Heathrow, where he found an atlas in a bookshop. He sat on the floor playing with the cuff links while he checked where the hell it was he was going.

The coordinates on the second cuff link read 103° 39′ 01″ E. They bisected those on the first somewhere on or around the island of Singapore. Strachan got a hit of adrenalin when he realised that the coordinates corroborated Hamilton's account of his grandfather's past. His grandfather had spent most of the war fighting in Malaya but he would have spent time in Singapore en route.

Enquiries with ticketing staff told him that his cheapest option was to fly direct with BA. He picked up a return for five hundred quid. Not that he had any intention of returning to London but he was told that Singapore Immigration wouldn't let him in on a single.

Strachan spent the night dozing in the departures hall, using his dive bag for a pillow. It wasn't the first time he'd slept in an airport and it passed quickly enough. He was gone by eight-thirty. He guessed Verhoeven was still out cold because despite his broken nose he sailed through passport control without so much as a second glance from the authorities.

At the Singapore YMCA Strachan showered and shaved.

His nose was as purple and tender as a marinated prune, but it had been broken before and it would set again. The airways didn't appear to be blocked, which was the most important thing. He changed into shorts and T-shirt, and by ten o'clock he was on Orchard Road, shopping for a hand-held GPS.

The Global Positioning System is a space-based radio navigation system. It exchanges signals with satellites, using triangulation to calculate speed, location and altitude. Advanced models can compute latitude and longitude to within one centimetre, but most are accurate to around ten feet. The atlas at Heathrow had showed only degrees and minutes, but the cuff links were accurate to the second. Once he had a GPS, Strachan could go straight to where they converged.

He found one in an electronics mall. It was a mid-range model. Now that Gilchrist had his pictures, he'd pay the calendar fee plus expenses. Strachan would recover everything he'd spent in Curaçao, the Galapagos and Scotland. Next month he'd get his first retainer. It would be the flushest he'd been in a long time so he didn't flinch when the GPS set him back a couple of hundred dollars.

Strachan stopped for lunch at a hawker stall. He ordered beef *kway-teow* and a glass of melon juice. He read the instruction booklet while he ate, and had it mastered by the time he'd finished his food. The GPS had a strong signal. It showed his location in degrees, minutes and seconds. He was a couple of miles north-east of the cuff links' coordinates so he jumped in a cab and told the driver to head south-west.

The cabbie threw him out after five minutes. His sense of humour failed when Strachan instructed him down a one-way street the wrong way. The second driver was more sympathetic. He had no idea what

Strachan was doing but he entered into the spirit of things, using his horn the whole way as though it was some kind of emergency. Strachan liked that.

His gaze was on the GPS but he still caught flashes of Singapore through the window. They drove past a cricket pitch on the edge of the financial district: an oasis in the heart of the city. The clubhouse had green bamboo shutters. It was surrounded by neo-classical colonial buildings on the right and modern bank towers behind. There was an opera house on the left. The sea glistened behind it, where a three-mile queue of container ships stretched into the distance, waiting to enter the port.

The cab drove on down palm-lined avenues, across a flyover, and out of the central business district. The surroundings became increasingly industrial as they headed towards Jurong and Tuas. As Strachan called directions from the back seat, he realised that they were following signs for the container port. That was bad news. If his inheritance was in the harbour, it was going to be a bitch to recover. They stopped in a cul-de-sac on a waterfront industrial estate. It was as far as the car could go. Strachan tipped the driver and set off for the final stretch on foot.

He walked along the quayside, controlling his urge to run. He had warehouses on his right, while yellow cranes towered above him on the left. A group of Chinese stevedores sat smoking on the railings. Traffic in the harbour was busier than it had been on the roads. Battered husbandry boats scuttled between the ships, carrying laundry, fresh food, Customs declarations and mail.

This was a far cry from what Strachan was used to. He'd done most of his diving on tropical reefs. Going underwater in the world's busiest port wasn't a welcome prospect. If that was where the inheritance lay, his grandfather had set him a near-impossible task. Aside from the danger of passing propellers, the water was too polluted. It had the visibility of ink.

Strachan continued walking. The GPS told him he was getting closer. It soon became apparent that he mightn't have to get wet after all. He'd been on the correct degrees and minutes setting since arriving in the port, but now he was on one second of longitude. If he walked a little further he would hit forty-three seconds of latitude.

Past the cranes a stinking restaurant advertised fish-head soup. A flock of gulls circled overhead, shrieking as the chefs gutted the morning's catch in the yard. A couple of fishing boats bumped the quayside, their chains clanking to the rise and fall of the swell. Strachan took a deep breath. The air was peppered with the smells of wet rope, fish scales, and kerosene from the restaurant's stoves.

His adrenalin level increased. He was about to discover the family inheritance. He was about to solve a mystery that had preoccupied him since he was eighteen years old. He smiled. It was all so easy with modern technology.

Strachan saw an old limestone fort ahead. It was no bigger than a garden shed. It sat on a grassy hillock perhaps ten metres high. It looked pre-war. As the seconds counted down on the GPS, he knew it was where he was heading. He broke into a trot. A security guard leaned on the barrier to a warehouse and threw him a disinterested look.

The hillock was the highest point on the quay. The fort held a commanding position overlooking the harbour. It was a shell from the outside but gun ports in the walls told him that it had once housed cannons. The cannons had long gone and as Strachan climbed the steps he feared that the fort would be empty.

But he was wrong. Someone was waiting for him inside.

22

Strachan recognised her instantly. The fine lady from his father's nursery rhyme. She was sitting on a white horse.

Both she and the horse were made from earthenware. They were protected by a reinforced perspex casing. An alarm flashed in one corner. There was a security camera mounted on a bracket in the limestone to provide additional protection, while a waist-high metal barricade prevented approach to the casing itself.

The statue was perhaps four feet high. It faced out to sea. It was carved from a single block of white stone and was striking in its simplicity. Although age had mottled its coat, the horse was strong. It stood proud as though on parade. It had bulging eyes, flared lips, a clipped mane and a knotted tail.

Its rider was equally graceful. She held the reins in one hand. The other was outstretched in front of her. In her palm was a gemstone. Her face was round, and her hair straight in the traditional Chinese manner. She wore flowing robes and jewellery. She had an enigmatic smile like the Mona Lisa's.

'To see a fine lady upon a white horse.' Strachan said it aloud. The connection was instant.

He checked the plaque on the wall for more information. It said she was Gong De Tian, the Chinese goddess of luck. The gem in her hand was a wish-fulfilling pearl. She was from the Han Dynasty, and the Singapore Arts Council estimated she'd been made around AD 100. She had been brought to Singapore in the eighteenth century to bring good luck to merchant sailors leaving the port. If Hamilton could have seen her, he would have fallen over. She must have been worth a fortune.

Worth a fortune. Was this his inheritance? Did he have some sort of claim over her? It seemed plausible enough. She was certainly worth travelling halfway round the world for. Strachan couldn't value her but since she was nearly two thousand years old, he figured she'd buy him his boat in the Caribbean.

But what was he supposed to do? Steal her? Had his grandfather once owned this statue? Perhaps she was a spoil of war? Maybe he'd recovered her from the Japanese, and the Singaporeans had given her to him as a token of their gratitude? Perhaps there was a piece of paper somewhere proving that the Strachan family had some right to her? Maybe his grandfather had bought her from someone who didn't know her real value? *Real value*. Hamilton had said Strachan was supposed to see the cuff links' real value, but all he saw was confusion. Strachan had a lot of questions. He didn't have any answers.

He went out in the sunshine to smoke a cigarette. He needed to think. The answer lay in the nursery rhyme; that much he was sure of. Why else had his father gone to such lengths to ensure that he learned it by heart? Why else had his father made him swear he would never repeat it to anyone?

Strachan smiled as he drew on the Camel. He'd always thought the rhyme was a bit crap. It was repetitious, and didn't seem to scan properly.

Ride a cock horse to Banbury Cross
To see a fine lady upon a white horse;
Rings on her fingers and bells on her toes,
And she shall have music wherever she goes.

Two rings on her left hand, one bell on her right,
She sits on her saddle at just the right height.
One bell on her right foot, one ring on her left,
She sits on her saddle with just the right heft.

Ride a cock horse to Banbury Cross
To see a fine lady upon a white horse;
Rings on her fingers and bells on her toes,
And she shall have music wherever she goes.

Pieces clicked slowly into place. He felt faint. Maybe it was the sun. Banbury Cross could mean *Banbury's cross*: the point at which the coordinates on his cuff links met. It was an impossible coincidence that there should be a statue of a fine lady on a white horse where they converged. Strachan didn't know what the rest of it meant, but he was sure of one thing. The rhyme was a riddle.

He'd come across the first (and last) verse in books, so he knew that it hadn't been created especially for him. But he wasn't so sure about the second. It didn't feature in the original nursery rhyme. He realised now that his grandfather had made it up. His grandfather had recited it to his father, and his father had recited it to him. The clue lay in that second verse. Strachan felt himself sweating as the excitement raced through him.

Strachan went back inside for another look, doing his best not to look suspicious in front of the camera. The horse was a fine specimen. Muscled and fearless. But what was he supposed to do with it? He couldn't just pick it up. Apart from being too heavy, the alarm would sound, and he'd be arrested before he could go two yards.

He wasn't making much progress. The heat was giving him a headache. He needed time to think, and a steady blast of air-con wouldn't hurt either. She might have been on horseback but his fine lady wasn't going anywhere in a hurry, and since it was only midday there was plenty of time to find out more about her.

Strachan walked back along the quay, contemplating the fact that he had indeed been named after a nursery rhyme. He wasn't sure how he felt about that. He guessed it could have been worse. Bo-Peep, for example. Now *there* was one to avoid.

He contemplated the fact that the first six years of his life had been geared for this moment. It would have been a hell of a lot easier if his old man had just told him the answer rather than leaving him to figure out the riddle on his own. But that was his father's insurance policy. It had to be complicated. And it had to be specific to Strachan in case the cuff links fell into the wrong hands. Hands like Molly's or Verhoeven's.

Ed will see. Maybe, maybe not. Back on the main road Strachan hailed a taxi. He ordered the driver to take him to the national library.

23

The National Library and Archives was a copper-roofed building on the edge of Fort Canning Park, on the other side of the Singapore River. It didn't look big from the outside, but once he was inside Strachan realised he was going to need help.

He took a queue ticket, then lingered fifteen minutes until his number appeared on the digital screen. It was the first time he'd been in a library since school, and he felt uncomfortable surrounded by so many books. Pictures were his medium, not words.

He temporarily swapped his passport for a reader's day-pass at the reception desk. The librarian ignored him when he explained what he wanted. 'You complete request form.'

'I don't know what to request,' Strachan replied. 'I don't have a particular author or title in mind.'

'No request form, no book.' The librarian didn't even bother to look up.

Strachan stared back at him. The ID round the librarian's neck said he'd been born in 1948 but his face suggested he was younger. A life spent in the archives of a library should have brought little stress, but this guy wasn't in any great hurry to help.

'Listen to me,' Strachan said. Jet lag was creeping up on him. His fuse was short. He signalled his impatience by drumming his fingers on the counter. 'I just want some reference books on Chinese mythology. To make it more fun, you can choose the titles.'

The librarian continued to stare at his monitor. His right hand tapped at the keyboard while his left offered Strachan a blue slip of paper. 'Request form,' he said.

'Are you having a particularly bad day, or are you always this rude?' Strachan didn't wait for an answer. 'Because if it's the former, I give you my word it's about to get a whole lot worse.'

The librarian looked up then. For a second Strachan thought he was going to continue the debate but something stopped him. Maybe he was intimidated. Strachan hoped so. That had been the general idea once common courtesy had failed. The librarian scribbled something on the blue slip and deposited it in a collection basket to his right.

'Thank you,' Strachan said. 'That was very big of you.' He returned to his seat and waited five minutes. His request slip was collected and in another twenty minutes he was invited back to the counter to sign for his books.

He took them to a quiet corner in the reading room on the second floor. The first book was useless. It was a large hardback volume on the Chinese pantheon. It focused only on the major deities such as Guan Di, the god of war, and Guan Yin, the goddess of compassion and mercy. He checked the index for his lady but she had eluded the author, and there was no sign of her when he flicked through the pages.

The second book covered the creation myths. Strachan found himself sidetracked by tales of dragons towing suns across the heavens. There was another about an archer's wife. She'd drunk a forbidden elixir, then floated to the moon where she'd morphed into a three-legged toad. It didn't say why. Molly Newchris too had drunk a forbidden elixir but she hadn't got off so lightly. The myths were colourful and vibrant. He could have read all day. But he was there to further his wealth, not his education, so he moved on to the third book.

And that was where he found her.

There was only one page of text about Gong De Tian. It was accompanied by a photograph of the statue he'd seen earlier in the limestone fort. Apparently this was one of her more famous appearances. Judging by the paucity of commentary, she was a rare and minor deity. Strachan read the entry hungrily.

The three characters of her name meant *merit, virtue* and *heaven*. Originally she had been the Hindu goddess Laksmi but she was adopted by the Chinese through Buddhism. She was shown in Chinese temples as sedate and beautiful, with a flower garland on her head, ornate clothing, and jewellery. Through the ages she'd become more dignified in dress, often clothed as an imperial consort from the Ming dynasty (1368-1644) onwards.

She was shown as having a *ru-yi* (a wish-fulfilling pearl) or string of jewels in the left hand. Usually she made a sign of fearlessness with the right. Often she appeared with seven mountains behind her. The mountains had multicoloured clouds around their summits. A six-tusked elephant stood on top of them with an agate bottle in its trunk from which it poured out precious items. Gong De Tian was often flanked by a praying mystic who usually wore white. He had a Central Asian appearance, and held a censer in one hand. His chanting ensured that the elephant's bottle maintained its supply of gems.

All of which was interesting but not as interesting as the notes in the margin. They were written in pencil next to the photograph. Two sets of coordinates bracketed by six question marks:

                         ???
                  01° 17′ 43″ N
                 103° 39′ 01″ E
                         ???

The coordinates were the same as those on Strachan's cuff links. Bile rose in his throat. He recognised the handwriting.

He flicked to the inside jacket for confirmation. The book had been swiped electronically when he borrowed it but, this being Singapore, he'd signed a library card as well. Now when Strachan checked the card he saw that only seventeen people had borrowed it in the last thirty years.

And one of them had been Adrian Hamilton.

24

Strachan flicked through the rest of the book, checking for more notes. He didn't find any, so he went outside and smoked two Camels, one after the other. Life was moving at a frenetic pace since his dive at Knife Point.

The date on the card was Tuesday, 12 October. That had been only last week. Hamilton had been in Singapore while Strachan was in Curaçao. Somehow Hamilton had found the second cuff link.

Strachan toyed briefly with the alternative. It was possible that his father had shown Hamilton both cuff links before he was killed, and his godfather had made a note of the numbers. It was possible that Hamilton had known the longitudinal coordinates all along. But if that was the case, why wait all these years to see where they led? No, it was a recent discovery. Until yesterday, that second cuff link had been hidden in Molly's flat. Strachan was sure of it.

He remembered the way Hamilton had raised the question of his inheritance. *Specifically a statue.* Those had been his words. Blasé and routine, camouflaged with innocence.

Strachan felt the anger welling within him. It fizzed in his veins like shaken soda, millions of bubbles bursting for an outlet. Hamilton was his godfather. Hamilton was his father's cousin. Hamilton was distant family, but family all the same. They shared blood. And now Hamilton had betrayed him.

There were several phone booths in the library lobby. Strachan changed a twenty-dollar note to ensure that he had enough coins for the call. He gripped the receiver tight. He was livid. He couldn't keep still. It was 2:00 p.m. in Singapore, 6:00 a.m. in London. Strachan didn't care. If the lying bastard wasn't already awake, he soon would be.

Hamilton kept a phone by the bed and answered on the third ring.

'You found the second cuff link, didn't you?'

'Ed? Is that you?'

'Who the hell else? You lied to me, Adrian – you found longitude.'

There was a long silence on the other end. It was a pretty rude awakening. Strachan pictured his godfather sitting up in bed, rubbing his eyes.

'How do you know that? Where are you?'

'Never mind where I am. Tell me what you were doing in Singapore last week.' Strachan had never used this tone of voice with his godfather before.

'You're in Singapore?'

'I didn't say that.'

'Ed, what's going on? Are you all right?'

'Okay, Adrian, listen. I *am* in Singapore. In fact, I'm in the library. I've just checked out a book that you borrowed last week. You knew, didn't you? That's why you had a hunch the inheritance might have been a work of art. You found the statue. I want to know how.'

'Yes, I did.' Hamilton's answer was pretty instant. That relaxed Strachan a little. Hamilton wasn't going to deny it. 'How did *you* find it?'

'Never mind. Come on, Adrian, start talking, and make it good.'

'Ed, dear boy! Calm down.' Hamilton was fully awake now. The surprise had gone from his voice. He was in control. 'Of course I found the statue.'

'How?'

'It was a few days before you left for Curaçao. I wasn't feeling well so I left work early. When I got home there was someone in the flat.'

'Molly Newchris.'

Another long pause. 'Ed, how do you know all this?'

'I'll tell you later. Keep talking.' Strachan fed more money into the phone. It was eating his coins at an alarming rate.

'She was in my study, going through the drawers in my desk. I think she was so engrossed that she hadn't heard me come in. It was obvious she was a thief and I managed to lock the door so she couldn't escape. Then I told her I was going to call the police unless she told me what she was doing. You'll never believe what she told me.'

'Go on.'

'She was the babysitter's daughter. She assumed I still had the other cuff link, and she'd come to try and steal it. Once I'd established that, I made her tell me the longitudinal coordinates. She told me and I let her go.'

'You let her go?'

'There didn't seem much point calling the police after that. I've got enough on my plate at work without taking time off to go to court, and we had the information we needed.'

'Not *we*, Adrian. *You*.' There was a long pause. 'Did you tell her the latitude?'

'No, of course not.'

'Did you tell her I was in Curaçao?'

'No, Ed. Of course I didn't. What are you suggesting?'

Strachan paused again. 'Okay,' he said. 'It all sounds plausible. Now, why the hell didn't you tell me any of this when I saw you two days ago?'

'I wanted it to be a surprise. There was no way of getting the cuff link back, so I wanted to have one made for you. I was going to give it to you for Christmas. In the meantime I wanted to see where the coordinates led. Naturally I was curious. You can't hold that against me. I wanted to check if there really was something valuable coming to you or whether it was all just a bit of fun.'

Strachan made a sort of grunting noise. Maybe he'd overreacted. He'd become paranoid in his excitement and automatically assumed that Hamilton had been trying to steal his inheritance. The man who had raised him after his parents' deaths. The man who had looked out for him for the last twenty-one years. His father's cousin. His own flesh and blood. 'Adrian, I've got to go. I'm sorry I was aggressive.'

'Ed, wait. Have you got the second cuff link? How did you know to go to Sing—'

But Hamilton never got to finish. Strachan was out of coins.

Strachan was tired. He wandered back to the YMCA, and his mind turned to the verse on his grandfather's postcard.

> *Worth their weight in silver*
> *Until they're sixty years old.*
> *Then put the two together*
> *They'll be worth their weight in gold.*

It had been written in 1945. Whatever the inheritance was, it was going to be more valuable sixty years on.

The statue was two thousand years old. Its value

would have increased significantly with time, but some-how the statue was too obvious. His grandfather had been wilier than that.

Strachan had never known his grandfather, and what little he did know about him had come from Hamilton. Arthur Strachan had been a silversmith before serving with the infantry in the Second World War. He'd been posted to Malaya and had learned Japanese. Sometime in March 1942 his patrol had been ambushed. After a fierce fire-fight he'd run out of ammunition and been captured. He'd been put on a POW ship bound for Japan. It had run into bad weather, struck a reef, and had sunk somewhere off the coast of peninsular Malaysia.

Arthur Strachan was the wreck's sole survivor. Washed up on the nearest island, it took a three-month raft journey across the South China Sea to reach an Australian outpost in Borneo. His escape later earned him the Military Cross. It was one of the war's great survival stories, and fast became part of military folklore. Apparently he later sold the medal and the silversmith business to raise money for an expedition back to the Far East. Now Strachan knew why. His grandfather had returned to set the whole thing up for his father before returning to England to make the cuff links.

Strachan's anger subsided as he walked. Even if Hamilton *had* been trying to steal the inheritance, he had arrived at a dead end. Strachan imagined him at the limestone fort, the same confused thoughts running riot in his head. Had he travelled to the other side of the world to be faced with a near-impossible theft? Was the statue what all the fuss was about? What claim did the Strachan family have on the statue of the Chinese goddess? And how the hell was he supposed to get his hands on her?

Hamilton had returned to England flummoxed. He

didn't have a clue what to do. *Ed will see.* The words must have been pepper under his skin. Itching, teasing, taunting. Whatever his motives, Hamilton knew that it was more complicated than simply putting the two cuff links together. That's why he'd asked the question: '*Is there something you should be telling me?*'

Not on your life, Strachan thought. He wouldn't have told Hamilton about the nursery rhyme in a million years. When something is drummed into you every day for the first six years of your life, you tend to take it seriously. His father's instruction never to repeat the rhyme was the only scripture he'd ever obeyed. Now he understood why. Between them, the statue, the postcard and the nursery rhyme held the key to the family legacy.

The penny dropped as he reached the YMCA. Gong De Tian wasn't his inheritance. She was merely pointing the way.

25

Despite his excitement, Strachan arrived back at his lodgings struggling to stay awake. Jet lag had struck. It was mid-afternoon when he collapsed into his bunk.

He woke at three, four, and five o'clock in the morning. The horse in the nursery rhyme galloped round his head like a carousel. At five-thirty he gave up trying to sleep and went outside. The YMCA had a pool. He swam a hundred lengths, doing every third length underwater. He had learned to swim aged three, and by the time he left school he'd broken every record in the book. Now it helped him relax.

The riddle and Hamilton's motives were two things on Strachan's mind at breakfast but there was also a third. Something equally serious. He couldn't stay in Singapore much longer. Verhoeven would be conscious by now, and an alert for his arrest would have been sent to every Interpol office in the world. Verhoeven had seen both cuff links – one at Schiphol, the other in London. He was a detective and it was his job to remember details. It was even possible that Ruisdael had recorded the first cuff link's coordinates as part of his inventory. Verhoeven would put the two together and home in on the limestone fort. Even if the Dutchman passed the case to the local police, Singapore wasn't going to be safe for very much longer. The heat was on. Strachan had to move.

He decided to head south to Indonesia. Bali was a good choice for several reasons. He'd never been there before, but he knew that the diving was good. It was close enough for him to return to Singapore at short notice once he'd solved the riddle, and he could make it harder for Verhoeven to find him by mingling with all the other backpackers. Best of all, tickets were cheap: the YMCA noticeboard had details of a special offer.

Twenty minutes later Strachan checked out and paid the bill. He was waiting for a taxi to take him to the airport when he noticed a jeweller's shop at the end of the road. It reminded him that he had one more chore to complete before he left.

He strolled the thirty yards to the shops, taking his time. His bags weren't heavy, but hurrying in the tropics was a bad idea. He showed the jeweller the second cuff link and asked if he could attach it to the chain on his neck so it could join the other. The jeweller told him that it would be no problem. Strachan was his first customer of the day, so he did it there and then.

Strachan watched him work. He didn't want to let the cuff links out of his sight. It was going to take a few minutes so he told himself to relax and began looking round the shop.

There was an opium pillow-box on a table by the door. It was blood red, hand-painted with gold dragons and praying monks. When Strachan opened it, the jeweller misinterpreted his laugh by promising him a special price on whatever he wanted. But Strachan was hardly listening. The box was full of rings, and in the instant he opened it he knew that he had solved the riddle.

Strachan was grinning from ear to ear as he paid the jeweller for his work; still grinning as he jumped in a cab. In twenty minutes he was back at the limestone fort. In another fifteen, he was back in the library. An hour later he was in the cool halls of Changi ferry terminal, and by eleven o'clock he'd left Singapore.

He wasn't going to Bali.

Adrian Hamilton was on his way to bed when the doorbell rang. He rarely had visitors, especially after midnight. He picked up the video entryphone. There was a man on the doorstep. It was dark but he could still make out that his visitor had been badly beaten. Whoever he was, he didn't look the sort of person you wanted in your house.

'Who is it?'

'My name is Inspector Rutger Verhoeven and I am from Interpol's office in Amsterdam.'

Hamilton's eyes glanced involuntarily at the stack of damaged paintings in the hall. 'Do you have some ID?'

Verhoeven held up his badge to the camera that was mounted in the bell panel.

'How can I help you?'

'I am looking for Banbury Strachan. May I come in?'

Hamilton paused briefly. 'I think you'd better.' He pressed the buzzer and the door clicked open.

26

The island of Pulau Tioman lies at 2° 46′ north, 104° 10′ east, forty miles off the east coast of peninsular Malaysia. It is twenty-eight miles long by nine wide. It has jungle-clad mountains, azure skies, coral-sand beaches, and reefs teeming with fish. Late October is a good time to visit. The sand is too hot to walk on barefoot after ten in the morning but the rainy season isn't far away, and most of the tourists are heading for home. *Time* magazine once proclaimed it one of the world's most beautiful islands, and years earlier Hollywood had used it as the set for Rodgers and Hammerstein's *South Pacific*.

Strachan was using it as a base from which to launch the hunt for his inheritance. It was only fifty miles south-west of the new location and there wasn't anywhere closer. Better still, there was a good chance of running into some old friends.

Tioman was the birthplace of Runi and Pili Parang, the Malaysian emerald thieves he'd run with after leaving school. He'd first met them ten years ago in a Kuala Lumpur nightclub on New Year's Eve. Runi appeared out of nowhere, bought Strachan a beer, and sat down next to him, saying that he knew his face but couldn't remember where they'd met. Strachan assured him that he was mistaken, but told him thanks for the beer all the same.

Runi had simply smiled and carried on talking.

Strachan was perplexed. Not only was Runi Parang highly charismatic, he seemed to know an awful lot about him. How he bought bootleg cigarettes from his housekeeper's son, how he drove a big 4×4 that belonged to the petrol company he was working for. How he could look after himself in a scrape. How he was learning to dive but how expensive it was for someone earning as little as he was. Strachan concluded that they really must have met for the Malaysian to know so much, so he said, '*Yeah that's right, I remember you now.*' It was a lie, but it was New Year's Eve and he was thirsty. Anything for another free beer.

The beer duly arrived, Runi got to the point, and by the time 1994 reeled drunkenly into 1995 Strachan had sold his soul and become a bandit; seduced by the smooth-talking thief and the promise of more cash than he could carry.

The Parang brothers dealt in stolen emeralds on the black market, and they needed a new courier. The last one hadn't taken sufficient care to check his rear-view mirror and was now doing time in a Melaka jail. He'd held his tongue because if he hadn't Pili would have arranged for someone to cut it off, so the operation could continue as soon as they'd filled the vacancy. Western ex-pats had the perfect cover for moving about the region, and the money on offer made leaving Carl Ryan's petrol business an easy decision. The job was low-risk. Not enough danger to lead to serious trouble, but enough to make Strachan feel like a player. He took to it like a bear to honey.

The emeralds were mined up near the Thai border by an Australian company called Matterson Blanchard. They used cheap local labour: exploited peasants who were desperate for any break they could get. When Strachan first travelled to the mines he was shocked by the miners' condition. Malnutrition, scurvy, dengue fever and tetanus were hard to treat on a weekly wage of twenty dollars, and he robbed Matterson Blanchard without losing any sleep.

The miners smuggled the ore in their mouths and rectums. Sometimes they actually swallowed the stuff and shat it out later. They were searched daily on their exit from the mines but there were no X-ray machines and Runi was bribing four of the security guards, which didn't hurt either. The good miners smuggled up to three deposits a week. Strachan met them in town at one of several secret locations. He paid them forty bucks per delivery, significantly increasing their weekly wage. For a while he even fancied himself as the Robin Hood of Malaysia, stealing from the rich to give to the poor. Once cut, the majority of stones weighed less than a carat but occasionally someone found a larger gem, for which Strachan paid anything up to a hundred dollars. Runi and Pili sold them on for ten times that, which meant there was plenty of margin for everyone, including Strachan who took twelve per cent.

His next responsibility was to drop the samples with Anwar Shahnon, the gang's lapidary in KL. A day later they would be ready for collection as gemstones: cut, polished, graded and weighed. Then he would arrange to meet Pili somewhere out in the country, where he would dip his hand into an old Liverpool FC kitbag. In with the emeralds, out with the cash, switching one kind of green for another.

For nine months Strachan lived like a king. Demand for cheap stones flourished among the jewellers, criminals and tourists of South-East Asia. He earned thirty thousand dollars, bought a 4×4 of his own and rented a beach hut in the Perhentian Islands. He began making drops all over the region as the Parang brothers took their business international. Thailand and Cambodia came first. Then Laos, Indonesia and the Philippines. Life was a blast. There were restaurants in Bangkok, KL and Jakarta, where he could get a table even if the place was packed. Pulling women was easier than shooting fish in a barrel. After the desolation of being orphaned at eight and the discipline of boarding school, Malaysia was pure release. With cash to burn, Strachan took up diving and raced through his qualifications. He bought himself some good equipment and once the novelty of chasing sharks and turtles had worn off he bought himself a camera and learned photography. He'd never felt so alive.

And then one day it all went wrong. Someone somewhere tipped off the police.

When it came, the bust was heavy-handed and bloody. Strachan had been celebrating a particularly good month with Runi, the lapidary, and two other couriers. Pili was on Tioman and unable to join them. They were in a noisy bar and Strachan had gone outside to call Hamilton on his cellphone. It was his godfather's birthday, a date Strachan never forgot. The timing was propitious, to say the least.

The police entered from the rear with their batons drawn. Runi Parang was the brains of the operation but on this occasion he chose brawn instead. It was a bad decision. When Strachan ran back inside to help, the bar was crawling with cops. Batons rained blows. Runi and Anwar the lapidary were curled on the floor, soaking them up. The two other couriers, a Dane and a Kiwi, were already in handcuffs. Strachan's assessment was instantaneous. Discretion was the better part of valour. He turned and ran.

His 4×4 had been parked in a side street and he drove north through the night, slipping over the border into

Thailand where he caught a train to Bangkok. He was out of the country four hours later. There had been no time to pack – and no time to collect his money. When he arrived back in St George's Square he had the clothes he was wearing and sixteen dollars in his wallet. Hamilton wasn't amused.

Now Strachan stood on the ferry's foredeck, smiling at the memories. It hadn't been your typical gap year, but then again he'd never been one to run with the herd.

The sun had sunk below the horizon, and Tioman's jagged peaks speared the copper sky. Palm trees rustled in the wind. A fruit bat the size of a kite flapped silently over the beach, then looped out to sea, drawing Strachan's gaze to an enormous luxury yacht moored in the deep-water channel. She had four decks and a helipad: the kind of cruiser he had only ever seen in magazines, moored in Monte Carlo or a Bahamian resort. There could only be a handful of vessels like her in the world. He shook his head and turned his attention back to the island. The captain cut the engines and the ferry slid across the water towards the pontoon. Startled by the lights, a family of crabs scuttled down the wooden struts and slipped guiltily into the sea.

Strachan was in no great hurry to see Pili Parang again, but since Runi was most likely still in jail he would take whatever help he could get. Verhoeven would be hot on his trail and time was running out. And even if he couldn't trust Pili with his secret, the Malaysian could yet prove a useful ally. Information, translation and negotiation were the services Strachan needed most, and Pili would be able to provide all three. Information on what conditions he could expect to encounter; translation for dealing with the locals; and negotiation for cheaper rates on scuba tanks and a boat.

A boat had been the first thing Strachan had thought of when he'd discovered his inheritance's real location. The key, as he'd suspected, had lain hidden in the second verse of the nursery rhyme, and it had only been when he'd seen the rings in the jeweller's box that he'd figured it out.

Gong De Tian was finely dressed. She wore earrings and a choker but she was missing rings and bells on her fingers and toes. Strachan had prayed that he was right as he'd rushed back to see her. He recited the rhyme in front of the statue, then laughed in relief when he saw his theory was correct.

> Two rings on her left hand, one bell on her right,
> She sits on her saddle at just the right height.
> One bell on her right foot, one ring on her left,
> She sits on her saddle with just the right heft.

He *was* right: her fingers and toes were bare. In order to sit at just the right height she needed rings and bells on her hands. To sit with just the right heft, she needed rings and bells on her feet. Only when the missing jewellery was added would there be music.

Strachan was sure that *height* meant latitude: the distance above or below the equator. *Heft* was therefore longitude: the distance east or west of the meridian. The rings and bells that the goddess required were actually degrees and minutes. Hell, the symbol for a degree even looked like a ring, while the symbol for a minute could be likened to the hammer of a bell. If he added the requisite number of degrees and minutes to the co-ordinates on the cuff links he would reveal the new location. It came down to elementary arithmetic.

To get the correct latitude, Strachan took the cuff-link coordinate and added two degrees for Gong De

Tian's left hand and one minute for her right. He repeated the exercise with the bells on her toes for longitude. He jotted it down on a piece of paper.

LATITUDE	
Cuff link/Fine Lady Coordinates =	01° 17′ 43″ N
Add two rings on her left hand, one bell on her right =	+ 02° 1′
Inheritance Coordinates =	**03° 18′ 43″ N**
LONGITUDE	
Cuff link/Fine Lady Coordinates =	103° 39′ 01″ E
Add one bell on her right foot, one ring on her left =	01° 1′
Inheritance Coordinates =	**104° 40′ 01″ E**

When Strachan was sure that he was right he hurried back to the library, where he found another atlas. The rhyme left no instructions for tampering with the seconds, so he assumed they were the same as those on the cuff links. The degrees led him to the east coast of Malaysia. The minutes led him to a cluster of six tiny islands in the South China Sea. They were called the Kerkullas, and they were a national park. The whole archipelago was no more than ten miles long. They were strung together like beads on a necklace. Six cowrie shells in a vast blue sea.

Pulau Tioman was the outpost of civilisation closest to the Kerkullas. The ferry was cheaper than flying and security wouldn't be so strict, which meant Verhoeven would find it harder to trace Strachan's movements. He bought a guide book at the terminal which told him that the Kerkullas were too small to be inhabited. It also told him they were surrounded by razor-sharp reefs. That was the clincher. Another piece of the puzzle clicked into place. Strachan knew then what he was looking for. No doubt about it. No doubt at all.

Coral polyps are only one to three millimetres long. Individually, they're harmless to everything except plankton, which is why they form colonies. They grow on the skeletons of their predecessors and on the skeletons of dead molluscs to form reefs. The Great Barrier Reef is 1,250 miles long, which is a hell of a lot of skeletons. The reef provides food and shelter to calcareous red algae, which are rich in calcium, just like the skeletons. Calcium compounds are brittle, but they're also hard. They're found in teeth, bones, marble and cement. They can be sharp. They can cut metal as well as flesh. They can cut ships.

Take a Japanese troop ship, for example. One sailing from Malaya to Japan in 1942 with a consignment of British POWs. It would sail right past the Kerkullas. The Kerkullas, remember, are surrounded by razor-sharp reefs. Add some bad weather like a tropical cyclone, and the ship isn't sailing *past* the Kerkullas any more, it's sailing *into* them. It's blown off course. It's under-powered in the storm. Nature is too strong. The reef is waiting and it opens the ship's hull like a tin can. Only one person survives. Years later he records the ship's location on two silver cuff links, a statue – and in a doctored nursery rhyme.

Strachan was looking for his grandfather's wreck. For that he would need a boat. And if Pili Parang was on Tioman, he would be just the man to find one.

27

Once the ferry docked, Strachan made his way to Kampung Air Batang, the nearest thing Tioman had to a capital. He'd been to the island once before. The Parang brothers used it for company away-days the way a western business uses the local country club; only instead of boardrooms and buffets they'd had beaches and barbecues.

The island was developing fast, Strachan noted. In another five years it would catch up with the likes of Ko Phi-Phi and Ko Samui. He counted five dive operators – four more than ten years ago. The main drag was littered with bars and stalls, the latter selling everything from fake Oakleys to bamboo wind-chimes. A grungy tourist offered him magic mushrooms and promised him unforgettable hallucinations but Strachan told him that the change in the island was already weird enough.

Kampung Air Batang was rough-and-ready. The honeymooners and business execs preferred the Berjaya resort, eight miles further south. Up here it was a young crowd on a tight budget. Strachan wandered through the village with his bags slung over his shoulder. At twenty-nine he felt conspicuously older than the swarm of pretty blonde girls who sauntered up and down the main drag, browsing for bric-a-brac in holiday mood and bright bikinis. He eyed them hungrily, the way a fox watches hens in a coop.

He had left his tent behind in his haste to escape London so he took a simple hut about a mile north of the village. He could live without the tub-thumping bass of the nightclubs, and he was happier out in the sticks. Some of the rooms in this area cost as little as two bucks a night. They didn't have fans, but the intrusion of roosters, rats and roaches was included in the price. He went mid-range. He had a double bed, mosquito net, fan, and salt-water shower all for six dollars a night. He'd spent enough time in the tropics to acclimatise quickly, and the thought of paying ten times that amount for a room with air-con was ridiculous. He was no more likely to suffer from heatstroke than the Pope was from sexual exhaustion.

Strachan began making his inquiries the next morning. He started with the largest bars and got lucky on his third attempt. The staff at the first two shook their heads and stared blankly when he mentioned Runi Parang's name, so he switched to asking for Pili and got a markedly different reaction from the manager of the third. Yes, he knew Pili Parang, but no, he didn't know where he was. Strachan could tell instantly that he wasn't going to get any more information: the expression on the manager's face was a blend of distaste and disapproval.

'Hey, mister.'

Strachan was on his way out when he felt a tap on his elbow. He turned. The boy who had been sweeping the bar-room floor was grinning at him. 'You are looking for Pili?'

'That's right. He's a friend of mine.'

'I don't think so.' The boy laughed and wagged his finger.

'You know where I can find him?'

The boy nodded. 'He is on *Fubuki*.'

'What's that? Another island?'

The boy laughed. 'No. *Fubuki* is a big boat.'

'Which big boat? The yacht in the channel?' The boy nodded again, then smiled as Strachan scrunched his eyebrows into a frown. 'Whose is it?' He was curious and amused. Pili Parang and luxury yachts went together like nuns and bulldozers.

'I don't know. It's from Japan.'

'Japan?' That seemed to rule out Pili being employed on board, but a social visit seemed equally unlikely.

At this point the manager marched briskly towards the boy and gave him a cuff round the ear. It was violent enough for the lad to wobble on his feet, and while Strachan wasn't going to intervene he felt guilty for the punishment that the boy had incurred. He knew he was pushing his luck by continuing what was obviously a sensitive conversation but he didn't yet have his answers. 'When is he back?'

'Twenty *rinngit*,' said the boy.

Strachan only had Singapore dollars in his wallet. The guidebook had assured him that they would be accepted on Tioman and he hadn't bothered to change any money. He peeled out a five-dollar note. It was probably overly generous but he didn't have anything smaller. Besides, the kid had earned it.

The little boy snatched the banknote and grinned at him like he'd just won the lottery. The bartender scowled at the exchange and jabbered something in their direction which Strachan didn't understand. 'Palms,' said the boy. 'The bar at the other end of the village. Two days from now.'

Strachan was delighted. He'd passed Palms last night and knew exactly how to find it. 'What about Runi? You know him too?'

The boy nodded again, leaning his chin on the broom.

148

'Where is he?'

'Runi's gone,' said the boy. 'Before I was born.'

Strachan nodded and said goodbye. He'd caused enough trouble for one day. So Runi *was* still in jail. Ten years was a long sentence, and Strachan felt a pang of anxiety for his old boss. It was too bad that Runi wasn't around. Runi was always the more likeable of the brothers: while Pili was only ever a colleague Runi had become Strachan's friend.

If Runi paid you a visit you could usually expect a joke and a smoke, but if it was Pili knocking on your door your best bet was to slip out the back and run like hell. Strachan felt the first squirt of adrenalin at the thought of seeing him again. He had never been afraid of the Malaysian, but he was well aware that the younger Parang had a streak as mean as a viper's. There was a story about a courier who'd once taken an additional fifty bucks in unauthorised commission. The rumours said that Pili had blinded him by draping jellyfish tentacles across his eyeballs. True or not, it had done wonders for his reputation as an enforcer.

Strachan had done a better job than most in staying on Pili's good side, and he was confident that there would still be some rapport between them. Like Napoleon and his generals, the only thing Pili demanded of his couriers was that they stayed lucky. Strachan had done exactly that and Pili had favoured him for it. There was even an outside chance that the passage of ten years had mellowed him. He would be forty-two now, and possibly less volatile. The demons that had haunted his past might now be swinging in hammocks, sipping cocktails in the sun. Strachan was intrigued to find out.

In the meantime there was plenty to do, and the two spare days would pass quickly enough.

★

Strachan wasted no time in calling McCauley Gilchrist to give him the number of Western Union in Kuantan, the nearest major town on the Malaysian mainland. Lost inheritances were all very well, but if there was no pot of gold at the end of the rainbow he would need to ensure that his career stayed on track.

The contract with Gilchrist was simple. Strachan was to add three hundred and sixty shots a month to *National Geographic*'s archive: a massive library of marine stills that could be licensed to other publishers and subsequently used for everything from magazines and billboards to T-shirts and place mats. His only instruction was to be original. He told his editor that he was going straight to work on the next set of shots and needed the money from the calendar to tide him over. Gilchrist said that would be no problem, so the next day Strachan took the ferry to Kuantan and collected the full amount in cash.

He spent the rest of the afternoon shopping for supplies. His first purchase was a large-scale marine chart of the South China Sea. Next, he bought films for his camera, six boxes of mosquito coils, vitamin C tablets, a pair of binoculars, and ten litres of drinking water, which was as much as he could carry.

When he returned, Strachan buried the rest of his money in a plastic bag under the bed in his hut. Crime was unheard of on Tioman but he wasn't taking any chances with that amount. He'd told Gilchrist to hold the monthly retainer for the time being. There was no need for more money at this stage. He had the best part of twelve thousand dollars, and that would last several years on the island.

If things went according to plan, Strachan would be gone in several days.

Contrary to the boy's prediction, there was still no sign of Pili on the third day, let alone the second. Strachan had spent the last two evenings in Palms and his patience was waning. It didn't take him long to realise that he'd been stung. He wasn't particularly angry with the boy – as a stranger in town, he knew that he was fair game – but he was angry at himself for falling for it. He should have trusted his instincts and known that Pili Parang was highly unlikely to have any business aboard a millionaire's yacht. Still, if he saw the little boy again he might give him some new ideas of what he could do with his broom.

There was now no guarantee that Pili would turn up at all, and no guarantee either that he would be able to source a cheap boat. Strachan figured that there was little harm in scouting out the alternatives, so on the fourth day he made his way down the main drag to ask about boat trips to the Kerkullas. He had a spring in his step as he walked. There was no sign of the local police, let alone rangy inspectors from Interpol. He was on island time and had lost track of the date. He wasn't even sure which day of the week it was. He was enjoying a healthy stretch of yang, and the yin of Hamilton's warehouse might be something he'd never suffer again.

There was a tourist-information hut next to one of the dive schools, which served as a booking-point for all kinds of expeditions around Tioman. He'd passed it the day before and seen that its walls were covered in black-boards. Game-fishing trips and tours in glass-bottomed boats were advertised next to volcano-climbing and windsurfing. Ferry transfers to Mersing were priced in green chalk next to jungle treks in blue. The live-aboard dive trip to the Kerkullas was in red near the bottom of the largest board. Strachan, carrying a beer bottle in one hand, smiled ruefully as he approached. He wasn't interested in a group jaunt round the national park. He wanted a quote for chartering the whole damn boat.

He arrived at the hut to find a small commotion brewing. A girl and her boyfriend were having a row, and it looked to be escalating fast. It appeared to be over the dates of some bookings he'd made. Strachan waited his turn in the queue and tried to stay cool. The arguing couple were American, and as far as Strachan was concerned that sort of behaviour could stay in the States. Raised voices were ludicrously out of place in this exotic environment.

The girl was unusual-looking, not classically beautiful but immediately striking. Cheekbones as smooth as pebbles arched gracefully under her eyes. Her nose was fine and angular like a chip of quartz, and her chin was just a shade too long to be perfect. She was tanned but not weathered, and her complexion was pure butter-scotch. She wore Quicksilver and O'Neill. Yellow flip-flops, a sleeveless pink T-shirt, and tight denim cut-offs. The shades were Nike and the rucksack Da Kine. Altogether she looked ready for some base-jumping in Maui. She was perhaps in her late twenties, and wore her brown hair down. It fell shoulder-length and straight. She'd tucked it behind her ears to accentuate the contours of her face. Strachan reckoned she looked good enough to eat.

Meanwhile, her companion was losing it. He was solidly built, with the shaved head and goatee of a gridiron player. He'd thrust his thick neck forward so his face was an inch from hers. Spittle sprayed from the corners of his mouth like woodchips from a chainsaw as he made his point. And then, out of nowhere, he straightened up and slapped her. *Bam*! The sound of it sickened Strachan to the core.

The American was three yards away. Strachan stepped out of the queue and tapped him on the shoulder. The guy spun round to face him. 'Help you, bud?'

'I don't think so.' Strachan stared right back at him.

'So what are you looking at?'

'I don't know,' Strachan replied. 'I've never seen one before.'

'You want me to hit you?'

Strachan took a swig of beer. 'You couldn't hit a cow's arse with a banjo.'

The American slugged at him and missed. Strachan put him down with his first punch: a straight jab to the jaw. There were a few gasps followed by a gabble of excitement from the other tourists and suddenly all eyes were on the American.

'Don't do it,' Strachan warned him.

'Or else?' His opponent was breathing hard, struggling to control his fury.

'There's no glory in coming second.'

With a gallery to play to, the American wasn't going to do what he should have done. He should have dusted himself down and apologised to the girl, but instead he got up and charged.

Strachan took another mouthful of beer and watched him lumber forward. He came in low like a linebacker, his knuckles barely off the ground. Big muscles and a shaved head aren't everything in a street fight and they count less than experience, speed, and three years of *Krav Maga*. This was an oafish attack. When the American was a metre away, Strachan stepped forward and drove his right knee into the guy's face. Bone met bone with the force of jousting bison. There was a dull thud of femur against chin, and this time the guy stayed down longer, his jaw dislocated. Strachan had won rounds one and two. There wouldn't be a third.

The girl stared open-mouthed at her boyfriend who now lay sprawled in the sand. Blood trickled from the corner of his mouth as he ran an inventory of his teeth with his tongue. Strachan was slightly embarrassed. He'd neither raised his pulse nor spilled his beer. Now he knew why defence tactics were called martial art. He'd rearranged the guy's face so that it looked like something by Picasso.

The American sat up, dazed. He almost made it to his feet when his girlfriend decided it *was* a three-round bout after all. With her mouth set firm, she stormed over the sand and punched him in the side of the head. Down he went again. It was a hell of a blow, and she clamped her fingers between her thighs to absorb the pain.

Strachan smiled at her to register his approval. It was a silly thing to do because she was still wild with rage. Without stopping to draw breath, she marched over and flat-palmed him round the ear so that it rang like a church bell. He wobbled sideways, grinning in astonishment. There was a lot of power in that slender arm. He wanted to say something witty but never got the chance. In a single second she had turned and was marching down the beach, her flip-flops kicking up the sand as she went.

Strachan entered the hut a few minutes later. The boyfriend staggered off and the crowd evaporated in the midday heat. The woman managing the stall was short and butch with a face hewn from granite. She looked Swiss and shuffled her papers as though she was still behind her desk in Zurich. When he asked her about the live-aboard trip to the Kerkullas she immediately produced a booking form. He told her that all he wanted was to speak to the captain, and did she know when the boat was due back? His answer was a look that could have withered a brick, and a curt observation that it was due back tomorrow afternoon.

Strachan said 'Thanks, relax,' and continued on to the Marine Madness dive school, where he was just in time to hitch a ride on the afternoon boat.

From the shade of a nearby palm, an old acquaintance watched him go.

29

They dived Magicienne Rock off the northern tip of the island. Rumours were flying of a sawfish sighting but Strachan ignored the hype. Usually these rumours started when a novice saw something he didn't recognise and invented a common name for it. Then the whole island jumped in the water to go looking for something that was already twenty miles away.

He let the group get on with their dive. Predictably enough, they sped off along the reef in hope of spotting large species like sharks, rays, and turtles. Strachan didn't bother. Much of the best action could be found by staying in one spot and watching what happened. On this occasion he was only fifteen metres from the drop-point when he found a pair of banded sea snakes courting in the coral.

They were reluctant subjects and difficult to shoot. Most divers know that sea snakes are many times more venomous than a king cobra, and give them a wide berth. What they don't know is that they have very short fangs. They're incapable of biting anything thicker than a table top. Handle them right, and the danger is negligible. These two were constantly disappearing into holes in the coral, forcing Strachan to pull them out by their tails.

He was about to give up when the little beauties gave him one shot that would rank among his best. The male had followed its mate under a rock but turned to threaten Strachan when he pinched its tail. The male was facing left, the female was looking right. With the rest of their bodies hidden by the rock, it looked like he had discovered a new species of two-headed snake. They held the pose just long enough for him to fire off a couple of shots but soon slithered away, startled by the flash of his strobe. Strachan grinned behind his mouth-piece. *Bill Tanner, eat your heart out.* The snakes were going to look magnificent. The blue bands on their necks contrasted richly with the purple algae coating the coral. Gilchrist would love them.

It was another satisfactory day's work, and after rinsing his equipment back at the dive school, Strachan made directly for his hammock, where he read another chapter of the novel he'd bought at the ferry terminal. It was a tough life, lounging around listening to the gentle crash of the surf. Then again, someone had to do it, and Strachan reckoned it might as well be him. He was a pro.

Later that evening Strachan walked back to the village and made his way to Palms, still clinging to the hope that he might find Pili. He didn't. There was no sign of his old employer but his insides lurched when he saw the American girl from the tourist hut sitting at the bar. She was swigging beer from a bottle, and flipping beer mats with her spare hand. She had ten of them stacked on the edge of the bar. Her hand moved through the air quicker than his eye could follow. She spun the mats through 180 degrees and caught them before they could land. It was an old trick but Strachan had never seen anyone do it so fast. She wasn't even looking. It was as natural as drawing breath.

Her boyfriend was nowhere to be seen so Strachan

figured he wouldn't be stirring things too much if he said hello. He reckoned he looked okay. Verhoeven's knuckleduster hadn't left any lasting damage. The swelling under his eyes had subsided and his nose was still more or less in the middle of his face. His tan had darkened and the residual bruising was harder to spot. Besides, he was hardly going to leave her to drink on her own.

She was sitting at the bar, watching a video about life on the reef. She was wearing a black cotton dress that hung from her shoulders on pencil-thin straps. It hugged the contours of her body and ended mid-thigh. She'd been sunbathing and her limbs blushed with a glowing tan. Her sunglasses served as a hairband, pinning her long brown hair behind her ears and exposing her face. She didn't need make-up. Strachan looked at her and felt his pulse quicken. She made him want to wrestle bears. She made him want to dodge bullets, jump canyons, juggle planets. She made him want to chop wood with his bare hands.

He strolled to the bar and took up a position four or five yards to her right. She pretended not to see him but the scowl on her face told him that she had. He ordered a beer, then walked the last few paces towards her and pulled up a stool.

'Please, go right ahead. Join me. Make yourself at home.' She was as sarcastic at night as she'd been feisty by day.

'I just wanted to say I'm sorry for what happened this afternoon. I guess I overreacted.'

'Don't worry about it. It was very gallant of you. Very chivalrous. Very English.'

Now it was impossible to tell if she was being sarcastic or serious. Strachan hoped it was the latter. 'Is your boyfriend okay?'

'He's not my boyfriend.' She began peeling the label from her bottle, avoiding his eyes.

He watched her, fascinated by her slender arms. So loose and languid that even something as mundane as peeling a label was made to look graceful.

She took a slug of beer and looked right through him. 'Not any more. He left this afternoon. That's what the argument was about. We were supposed to fly back tomorrow, but I wanted to stay another day. We could have changed our flights for fifty bucks but he was too locked into his schedule to show any interest. The guy's such an asshole. So damn serious. Only ever leads his life by the manual his parents shoved up his ass as a kid.'

'Is that the first time he's hit you?'

She lowered her eyes. Strachan apologised and told her to forget it; it was none of his business.

'Mike wanted me to be someone I'm not. He wanted a housewife. A brood mare. Someone to fit in with his family traditions. He comes from one of those big Philly families: all tradition and old-fashioned values. Big house, big lawn, big car, big ego. He was used to having things his own way. He didn't like it when I answered back to him. He wasn't used to it. Expected me to keep my mouth shut and my legs open. I dunno how I ever got involved with him.'

'And now it's over?' Banbury Strachan. Doing his damnedest to sound subtle.

'Yeah. And not before time. I shoulda aced him a long time ago. He was never my type.'

Strachan held out his hand. 'I'm Ed Strachan.'

'Shit,' she said. 'And there was me thinking you were Sir Lancelot come to rescue his damsel in distress.' She put her hand in his. 'I'm KT. KT Luker.'

'Katie or KT?' Strachan was thinking about the way she said *his* damsel, not *a* damsel. Like she already considered herself the object of his quest. He liked that.

'The latter.'

'What's it short for?'

'Sorry, hon. You gotta know me a helluva lot better before I tell you.'

'How much better?' he asked before instantly regretting it. He should have remembered KT was having a bad day. He was coming on too strong.

'Don't you listen, Lance? A helluva lot.'

'Where are you from?' It was better than nothing. Just.

'Fort Wayne, unfortunately.'

'Why unfortunately?' He'd been expecting her just to say America. Fort Wayne was going to a level of detail he didn't really need. He had no idea where it was. It sounded a cool enough place, though.

'Fort Wayne's in Indiana. It's got nothing. Just a couple of factories and a big ole freeway.'

'So what are *you* doing there, if there's nothing to do?'

'I'm not doing anything in Fort Wayne. I left home years ago. Shit Lancelot, how old you think I am?'

'Twenty-eight?'

KT laughed, punched Strachan's pecs, and said, 'Yeah, right. Thanks, man.'

There it was again. That impossible-to-read tone of voice. How the hell was he supposed to know what that meant? He had no idea whether he'd guessed right or wrong. 'So you left Indiana. Then what?'

They talked for another half-hour. KT filled Strachan in on her background. How she'd gone to Princeton to study drama and then on to New York where she'd taken minor roles in commercials and soaps. How she'd met Mike backstage at a Broadway theatre after his insurance company sponsored a production of *The*

160

Taming of the Shrew, in which she'd played Kate. Strachan's knowledge of Shakespeare was only slightly better than his knowledge of Indiana towns but he figured Kate was the one with the temper, and KT was typecast from the first audition. From this morning's performance, it didn't look as though anyone had succeeded in taming her.

Strachan had a weakness for pretty girls in street brawls, and conversation was easy. KT talked to him like he was an old friend. Now that Mike had been sent packing with his tail between his legs, she said she saw no reason to hurry home. Strachan liked her. He liked her a lot.

'You here on holiday?' she asked him.

'Kind of. Business and pleasure. I'm an underwater photographer.' He watched for her reaction and was instantly gratified as her eyes lit up. He'd once known a recruitment consultant who'd enjoyed considerable success by telling women that he trained dolphins for a living; and while Strachan's job wasn't quite as glamorous as that, he was pleased he didn't need to lie.

'Cool,' she said. 'You need any help? I'm a good diver. Qualified to Rescue status with PADI.'

Strachan sipped his beer and shook his head.

'You already got an assistant, is that it?'

'No. I work alone.' He was unusual in that respect. Most marine photographers actually did take someone with them, sometimes as a model, sometimes to hold spare equipment. But for Strachan photography was a personal pleasure, and in his experience assistants were more pain than gain.

'Come on, it'll be fun. I won't bite.'

Strachan couldn't help but laugh. It was mighty tempting. Then again, it was also asking for trouble. If he ever found him, he wasn't going to tell Pili his real reason for coming to Tioman, so he sure as hell wasn't going to tell a complete stranger. Besides, his appetite for taking pretty girls diving had lessened drastically after Curaçao. 'It's kind of you to offer, but the answer's still no. Maybe we can dive together here, but when I go to the Kerkullas I'm going alone.'

'You're going to the Kerkullas? Man, you've gotta let me come with you.'

Strachan winced. He was already letting stuff slip. Hanging out with KT Luker looked like it might be a lot of fun but right now his priorities lay with his inheritance. He changed the subject. 'So what is it you're looking for, if it's not the quiet married life?'

'Adventure. Just like everybody else.'

'Not everybody's looking for adventure.'

KT looked at him pitifully. Then she smiled. 'There are two types of people in this world, Lancelot. Those looking for adventure, and those who don't count.' He grinned at her but didn't have time to reply before she continued. 'Stop looking at me like that! You wanna 'nother beer?'

Strachan stood up and put his hands on the bar. He was trying not to smile. Miss Luker was a firecracker; the sort of challenge he loved. Sometimes life just wasn't fair. 'No, thanks,' he told her. 'And don't worry about me looking at you; you're not my type.'

30

Pili Parang watched them from the edge of the beach.

It was after nine o'clock but the sand was still warm and he lay on his belly soaking it up. He'd smoked the reefer down to the roach. Had he been less preoccupied he might have noticed that it was burning his fingers. Palms was open to the elements and although they were out of earshot he was still assimilating useful information about the flirting Westerners.

'He said he was a friend?'

'Yes.' The little boy nodded. He was afraid of the man under the tree, and was careful not to get too close. Pili Parang was a businessman. He ran his business hard, punishing mistakes with a ferocity that had earned him notoriety from Johor Bahru in the south to Kota Bahru in the north. 'He said he wanted to meet you. I thought he might be *polis*.'

Pili grunted. They were speaking in the local dialect of Bahasa Malay. 'You did well. Go now.' He held out a banknote and the boy took it gingerly, careful to avoid looking at the man's hands. Pili watched him skip down the beach, then turned his attention back to Palms. It looked like his subject was about to leave.

Pili had been entertained well on the Japanese yacht, so when he first saw the tall blond *gwailo* standing at the bar he thought his eyes were playing tricks. Then he'd recognised the laid-back swagger and all doubt disappeared. This was Ed Strachan. A ghost from the past, and a man he'd thought he would never see again. Initially he'd been so excited that he had picked his nails until his fingers bled.

Ten years had passed since Pili Parang had last seen Strachan, and his life had changed considerably in that time. The emerald ring had collapsed the night of the bust, and he hadn't dared leave Tioman for three years for fear of arrest. He'd been forced to go straight, taking bar jobs and working as a caddy on the golf course, carrying bags for the Caucasians and Chinese. Then, when he felt that the heat was off, he'd moved back to Kuantan where he'd spent six years running a small drug ring before being bought out by his current employers.

The Japanese knew more about smuggling drugs than Pili had thought possible and since their empire stretched from Tokyo to Singapore he realised quickly that competition was futile. Drug smuggling carried the death penalty in Malaysia but so did refusing to cooperate with South-East Asia's largest heroin shogun. Pili was offered a choice: work for Wakahama-san or die. To let him know they were serious one of Wakahama's men had removed both his little fingers and used them to plug his nostrils. If Pili refused, his foot was to be removed and stuffed in his mouth until he could no longer breathe. He decided against it, preferring instead to accept the offer of becoming their representative on the east coast of Malaysia. Pili didn't hold their tactics against them. After all, he had much to learn.

Wakahama was one of the region's most powerful men. He had avoided suspicion by spending most of his time aboard his yacht, only leaving international waters to refuel. If meetings were required, people would come to him, flown in on the helicopter. There was less chance of an ambush on board the *Fubuki*, and those who needed to disappear could be disposed of much more easily at sea. Now he was here for his annual check-up on his affairs in Malaysia. Pili and his colleagues had done well, and his suggestion that Wakahama should sample the marine delights of Tioman had been well received. Such was Pili's success that he'd been invited to stay on board for an extra day.

The reefer extinguished itself on the hard skin of his fingers. Pili was thinking about what the boy had told him. Strachan didn't appear to be on holiday. He had made himself at home and was evidently on some sort of mission. He was diving twice a day, but the time he spent studying his map and playing with his GPS in the evenings suggested photography wasn't his only pursuit. He hadn't changed much, either: still chasing women, and apparently he'd already been in a fight.

Pili closed his eyes and smiled. He rolled on his back and stared at the stars. Ed Strachan was back in Malaysia. How could anyone not believe in the will of God?

One hundred and fifty miles south-west, two Europeans waited for their bags to arrive on the carousel at Changi airport in Singapore. The flight from London took longer these days because of dog-legs to avoid Iraqi and Afghan airspace. The men were tired and numb. Their faces were red and puffy as though they'd been wiped with nettles rather than a stewardess's steaming towel. They would start their search tonight, though. The trail was almost a week old and there was no time to lose.

Strachan didn't know it, but the net was closing fast.

31

The boat from the Kerkullas appeared on the horizon the next day. Strachan stood in the water, raising one hand to shield his eyes from the sun. He watched her come in, her sails billowing and white. She was making twelve, maybe thirteen knots in a light breeze, racing up the deep-water channel between Pulau Tulai and Pulau Tioman like a thoroughbred in the final furlong. Then, half a mile out, she dropped sail and her pace slowed as she let the motor do the rest.

She was a beautiful old thing. A gaff-rigged ketch with a gleaming white hull and decks of polished teak. The sun glinted in the brass on her helm. Even from this distance Strachan could see the neatly pressed uniforms of the crew as they prepared to moor her. The plate on her stern, visible as she slid across the current, told him that her name was *Ariadne*. His heart sank when he saw her. He'd assumed that she would be a small and affordable motor cruiser. Instead she was a hundred-foot floating antique. Chartering her would leave him with little change from his twelve thousand bucks.

The *Ariadne*'s guests were soon climbing down a rope ladder into a waiting dive boat that had chugged out to meet them. The crew handed luggage over the rail amid a buzz of goodbyes, tipping and last-minute photographs. Five days aboard the *Ariadne* in a national park would have been the holiday of a lifetime for most people. But not this lot. They would arrive back at their banks and insurance companies with renewed vigour, their batteries fully charged, ready to earn even more so that they could improve on the experience next year. That was their game: the holiday of a lifetime every year of their lives. Strachan viewed them with distaste. He tried to reassure himself that he wasn't like them, that his cycle of yin and yang was somehow nobler.

'You need a boat?' The voice behind him was high-pitched and nasal. Strachan recognised it instantly. He turned in the shallows and there was Pili Parang, sitting on the edge of the beach and drawing patterns in the sand with a stick.

'Pili! I've been looking for you!' Strachan's face lit up. They had shared too many experiences for him to be anything other than pleased. He jogged through the surf and held out his hand, looking at his former employer to take in the ten years of change.

Pili hadn't aged. He was just heavier, healthier-looking, and more obviously Malaysian. His skin was darker than Strachan remembered, and his bones less prominent. Life was obviously treating him well. He still had a 1970s haircut: wet-look ringlets in deference to Kevin Keegan, his hero at Liverpool.

Along with emerald smuggling and violence, Liverpool FC was Pili's other great passion. Pick any year from 1970 to 1980, and he could tell you what honours the club had won, where it had finished in the league, who'd been in the team, and who'd scored the goals in the big games. His rendition of 'You'll Never Walk Alone' was truly awful. He took Strachan's hand in an arm-wrestler's grip and returned the smile.

'Jeez, Pili, what happened?' Strachan felt the missing finger on Pili's hand instantly. When he looked, he saw that although the wound had been healed for a long time it was still grotesque.

'Another time,' Pili replied. 'You need a boat?'

Strachan returned his gaze to Pili's smile and caught a flashback to how it had been before: the good times, when the world was his oyster, and Pili Parang one of the two men who had brought it to him on a plate. Late nights in KL. Full-moon beach parties in the Perhentian Islands. Pili and Runi toasting his success, telling him that they were going international. Strachan remembered the exhilaration of putting his hand in that Liverpool kitbag, and the pleasure he'd derived from the smiles of the miners as he'd rewarded their thieving.

'You look well, my friend.'

'And you've put on weight,' Strachan said. 'That canvas is stretching.' He pointed a finger at Pili's naked torso, which was adorned with tattoos. Blue-black flames curled round his forearms as though they were burning logs, while his chest seemed to roar like an open fire. Pili's back was an elaborate pattern of swirls and concentric circles that covered the skin from his neck to the line of his shorts. No people; no symbols or animals. No slogans. Just a riot of blue and black ink. A maelstrom of spirals applied with a needle. Strachan had always thought that it looked like warpaint.

'You need a boat?' Pili repeated.

'Yes – how did you know?'

'I know you well, Ed. The way you were looking at the *Ariadne*. You want to go diving, yes?'

'Yeah, in the Kerkullas, but I need privacy.'

'Why?' Pili asked. *Need* was a strong word and his English was good enough for him to appreciate its significance. Strachan was up to something. He had marine charts and a GPS; now he *needed* a boat. To Pili the whole thing smacked of opportunity.

'Some special photographs. I'll tell you later.' Strachan was pretty sure he wouldn't, but now that the *Ariadne* was out of his league he needed Pili's help more than ever. 'You know any boats I could hire?'

'I know a fishing boat,' Pili replied. 'Very fast, very beautiful.'

'Yours?'

'No. Not mine. I know the skipper. His name is Sumo.'

'Sumo?'

'You will see why when you meet him. I can arrange it – if you like?' Pili was fidgeting and he took a step back.

'Sure. When can I meet him?'

'This evening, in Palms.'

'And he'll do a private charter?'

'Yes.'

'And you can get me a good price?'

'I can try.' Pili forced a laugh. 'What time do you want to meet him?'

'Eight?' Strachan suggested.

'Make it seven,' Pili replied. 'We have many years to catch up on.' Then, as an afterthought he added: 'Maybe I could come with you? It's been a long time. We can talk about the old days.'

Strachan pulled his shades back over his eyes. This was the second time that someone had asked to join him and turning them down wasn't getting any easier. He still had no idea how valuable his inheritance was, assuming it actually existed, but at this stage it was better to be safe than sorry. It was a fair assumption that another pair of hands could make the workload lighter, but he would need to spend more time with Pili to re-establish their former rapport. And even then, trusting the wily Malaysian would require a significant leap of faith. 'No, thanks, Pili. You know me. I work better alone.'

'Okay, we will see. I catch you later.' And with that, Pili turned and jogged up the beach.

'Pili!' Strachan called him back. The Malaysian slowed. He was five metres away and flicked his stick against his thigh like a jockey's whip. 'How's Runi?'

Pili stopped dead in his tracks. He kept his back turned. He didn't dare reveal the emotion that twisted his face and made his fingers itch. He bit his lip and the pain snapped him back to the moment. Over his shoulder he said, 'It's good to see you again, Ed.'

32

Strachan arrived back at Palms at a quarter to seven. He ordered beer and a chicken satay and sat down to wait.

The crew from the *Ariadne* was having dinner at a nearby table. The skipper was easy to identify. He wore a short-sleeved polo shirt and white slacks rolled up to the knees. His skin was the colour of roasted chestnuts, his shins bruised and gnarled from a lifetime at sea. He was older than the rest of his crew by at least ten years, and while they fussed and gabbled he moved among them with the graceful dignity of a swan among geese. Like many of the locals, he was thin and wiry but the sinew in his arm as he raised his glass was as strong as industrial cable. He drank his beer two-handed, with his eyes closed.

Strachan felt a pang of envy as he watched this simple man enjoying one of life's simple pleasures. Strachan wasn't saddled with a conventional career but he still had his future to think about. He was still on a journey. He didn't yet have the beach shack in St Michiel's Bay nor the safari boat for the trips to Aruba and Bonaire. And until he did, he wouldn't find the same level of contentment as the man he now watched. The skipper's journey was over. The skipper had *arrived*.

Pili was late and only emerged from the shadows after Strachan had finished his third beer. He pulled up a chair and ordered two more bottles. He had showered and now wore a white T-shirt over his shorts. Strachan was amazed to see that it looked ironed. 'Did you find Sumo?'

'Yes,' Pili replied. 'He is coming, but he's not happy.'

'Oh?'

'He won't take just one person. His boat sleeps four and he will make more money if he waits for a full charter.'

'How much is the full amount?'

'On a two-day fishing trip with four guests, he can make 1,600 dollars plus tips.'

Strachan whistled. 'US or Singapore dollars?'

'American.'

'Shit.' Strachan had been planning a four-day trip. One day there, two days exploring the site, and one day back. On the rate card that Pili had quoted that was going to set him back over three grand: a quarter of what he'd stashed under his bed. It was way too much for the initial recce. He would need to keep plenty in reserve in case he needed to go back. Tioman was turning out to be far more expensive than he'd anticipated. No doubt its proximity to Singapore was keeping prices high. 'And you can't get me a special deal?'

'I don't think so. Sumo doesn't like me very much.'

'No one likes you very much, Pili. Present company excluded. So I'm screwed, then?'

'No.' Pili took a gulp of beer, pursed his lips and sucked air through his mouth so that the beer bubbled. 'I can help you. I will come with you and share the cost.'

Strachan was left momentarily speechless. He wasn't sure if Pili was serious, and if he was whether it meant good news or bad. A fishing boat would give Strachan the perfect cover he needed to snoop round the Kerkullas, but if he found the wreck it would be hard to keep it a secret. Then again, he was pretty sure that Pili didn't dive, so maybe it was possible the Malaysian could come along and still remain in the dark. 'Can you afford it?'

Pili's eyes narrowed. 'Don't forget I was your boss, Ed.'

Strachan grinned. He had earned thirty grand in his first nine months as a courier; Pili had probably made ten times that. Maybe he'd invested it wisely and still had some left. 'It's a kind offer, and it sounds good. Let me think about it for a while.'

'Okay,' said Pili. 'You have twenty seconds. Here comes Sumo.'

Strachan turned in his chair. One look at Sumo was enough to explain his nickname. He was unmistakable: a great barrel of a man with the face of a laughing Buddha. His navy-blue T-shirt was stretched tight over a massive chest while legs like beer kegs protruded from his yellow shorts. His centre of gravity must have been slightly lower than a bull hippo's. It was easy to imagine him leaning over the rail of his boat, gaffing a hundred-pound tuna and hoisting it lazily onto the deck. Strachan liked him immediately.

Sumo smiled as Pili introduced them. He had arrived with a day-pack and a wicker urn, which he placed at their feet under the table. Strachan said hi, then, not knowing any other way of going about it, he launched straight in. 'I need a boat. Private charter.'

Sumo nodded. 'I know. Pili told me. How many people?'

'One,' Strachan said. 'Just me.'

'One person. Very expensive.' Sumo looked at him with a twinkle in his eye. 'Fishing?'

'Diving.'

'Where do you want to go?' Sumo's voice was deep

173

and his accent strong, but, like Pili, he spoke good English. Those running tourist businesses couldn't afford not to.

'Kerkullas. For four days.'

Sumo chuckled and winked at him before producing a pocket calculator from his shorts. He muttered under his breath as he punched in the numbers.

'How much?' Strachan asked, as he lit a Camel.

A smile appeared out of the folds of Sumo's face. His eyes shone as he wiped a huge paw over his balding brown pate. He handed Strachan the calculator while he lit a smoke of his own.

'Two thousand dollars! Mate, you've been eating those mushrooms they sell on the beach.' Strachan rocked back in his chair and grinned.

Sumo laughed a great belly laugh in return. His breasts shook uncontrollably under the T-shirt. He wasn't in the least bit offended. Bargaining was a part of everyday life on Tioman. 'Three meals a day included, and my nephew to help with your equipment.'

'Uh-uh. Still too much.'

'So I cannot help you.' Sumo tried to push his chair back so he could stand up, but such was his weight that the legs had sunk too deep in the sand. 'I have a German client arriving tomorrow. Banker. Very rich.'

It might have been a bluff, but Strachan felt the opportunity slipping away. He didn't have much time. Verhoeven might be in Singapore by now. It could take days to find another boat. 'Pili, you still want to come?'

'Yes. It's no problem. I will pay half. You can pay me back another time.'

Sumo grunted and spat in the sand. Evidently he didn't like the idea of Pili Parang on his boat. Strachan's pulse was racing. The thrill of the chase was with him again, and he wanted to close the deal. At the same time

174

he knew damn well that Sumo had still gone in higher than he would accept. It was time for the second round. 'Fifteen hundred,' he said. 'Me and Pili. Half up front.'

Sumo chuckled again. This was what he did best. 'She is a nice boat. You pay more when you see her.'

'When can I see her?'

'Come, come.' Out of nowhere, Sumo took Strachan's arm in his enormous hand. Strachan was a big guy in good shape but Sumo dragged him down the beach like a piece of carry-on luggage. They reached the water. The sea sat heavy as mercury in the dark. Sumo pointed towards the *Ariadne* moored in the deep-water channel. From the bowsprit he drew a line with his finger across the bay, a hundred yards to the right. Strachan followed with his eyes. A sleek white sport-fisher convertible sat moored in the shallows, glistening under a full moon. 'My boat.'

Strachan smiled. He'd seen this boat on his way back from Kuantan. From his seat on the ferry he'd admired her lines as her bows came up on the plane and she sped for the open ocean in search of sport. She was a 1989 Viking 57 Convertible, with three decks plus observation tower. Well-worn but not shabby, and powered by two enormous inboard diesel engines. Strachan had seen the adverts boasting hundred-pound marlin, tuna and wahoo at the tourist-information hut, and he knew she was more than adequate for four days on the heavy swell of the South China Sea. She was seaworthy and strong; exactly the kind of boat he would one day buy to run his safaris in the south Caribbean. 'What's her name?'

'*Esprit Bleu.*' Sumo smiled proudly, his French accent curiously better than his English.

'*Esprit Bleu.*' Strachan mulled it over. It was somehow appropriate. *Blue Spirit.* Like Curaçao's most famous export. He was getting a good feeling from this boat and decided to give Sumo the charter there and then. 'How much really?' he asked, trying to downplay his interest.

'No, no, no. How much do you *want* to pay?' Sumo was having none of it, so Strachan paused to think it through. It was the same on the markets in Kuantan and Mersing. Their technique was to coerce you into putting the first stake in the ground. They knew you would go in lower than you could afford, and from there they would bump you up in a ruthless game of double bluff. He looked once more at Pili, his eyes pleading for a clue, but Pili just shrugged his shoulders as if to say '*What can I do?*'

Strachan scratched his head. He blew out his cheeks like a grouper as if to emphasise the difficulty of the decision. 'Fifteen hundred.'

'Eighteen.'

'Fifteen. It's my final offer.' Hardball. It was a zero-sum game. You had to be prepared to lose.

'Ed, leave it. I know another boat.' Pili pushed between them and looked Sumo straight in the eye. 'You want the job, you take the job now. This man is my friend.'

There was thunder in Sumo's face as he looked at his compatriot. He didn't like Pili's tone of voice. Nor did he understand why a native of Tioman was siding with a *gwailo*. What he *did* know was that Pili Parang wasn't the sort of man you upset. He sighed heavily. 'Fifteen hundred if he beats the snake.'

'What does that mean?' Strachan asked.

'Beat the snake, win a special price.'

'What snake?' said Strachan. 'I don't understand.'

'Come, come.' Again Sumo took his arm in that vice-like grip, and marched him back to Palms. Pili followed, an amused expression on his face. Strachan looked at him for reassurance and the Malaysian nodded encouragingly. Whatever was about to happen was clearly something he approved of.

Sumo leaned under the table and retrieved the woven-reed urn. It was perhaps a foot high, simple and elegant with a flat lid. He shook it several times.

Strachan edged backwards, already dreading what was coming next.

33

Sumo waited until Strachan had retreated before squatting on his haunches. He removed the basket's lid and poured the contents onto the sand.

The snake landed in a knot of black coils. Strachan was no herpetologist but as its head appeared from the tangle he had no problem identifying the species. It was a cobra, instantly recognisable from the hood that flared round its neck.

Sumo tapped it on the back of the head to rouse it further. Immediately the snake reared two feet in the air. Half its body was still flat on the sand. Strachan was frozen to the spot, fascinated by its heavy beauty but wary of the damage that it could inflict. It was after dark and he wasn't wearing shades. There was a good chance that the snake was a spitter, and he didn't want venom in his eyes.

A few tourists saw what was happening. Taking Sumo to be a street performer, they stopped to watch. Strachan recognised KT Luker instantly. He watched as she squeezed through the group until she had a front-row view. She was looking at him with a goading look, enjoying his discomfort as though it were no less than he deserved for his rebuff the previous night. He caught her eye and smiled, but the snake was moving and he quickly turned his attention back to his feet. The restaurant staff meanwhile simply exchanged knowing grins as if this was Sumo's party-piece.

Sumo ignored the attention and placed the basket's lid a yard in front of the snake. He stretched his hand behind him to retrieve something from the day-pack, but he never took his eyes off the cobra. Strachan's stomach turned when he saw what the skipper now held. Sumo tossed it onto the lid. It landed in a ball of grey fur, righted itself, then blinked rapidly as its brown eyes adjusted to the restaurant's lights.

The rat turned a few circles. Its feet scraped the wicker. Immediately the cobra rocked back, arching its body in the classic S-shape that preceded a strike. Its lidless black eyes stared at the meal. Its forked tongue flicked back and forth. And then it hissed. A seething, slithering sound, like gas escaping a shaken bottle.

The rat froze. It was rooted to the spot in abject terror. It couldn't see over the lid of the basket. It had no idea where the snake was but it knew it was there. It could hear it. Strachan saw the palpitations of its chest as the heart pumped adrenalin round its body. Then it splayed its rear legs, and the fear leaked from its bladder.

The snake rocked to and fro, measuring the distance to the rat while Sumo explained the rules. 'You take the rat when you are ready. But be very quick. Snake hungry.' Then he started to chuckle. 'If you are too slow, it's hospital. I'll show you.'

Tioman didn't have a hospital, but Strachan figured Sumo knew that already. He was driving a hard bargain, and Strachan shook his head ruefully.

Sumo knelt. He extended his right hand and began waving his fingers. He fluttered them like leaves in a breeze. His arm came up, shoulder high. The snake turned its attention away from the rat, distracted by the dance of his fingers. Its tongue flicked in and out, silent and black. Death licking its lipless mouth.

Sumo stopped. Instantly the cobra turned its attention

back to the rat. Sumo waggled his fingers again and the snake turned an eighth of an inch towards him. His hand came down in a perfect arc of speed, a sword-swipe carving the air. It snatched the rat and swung up over his left shoulder in the same instant that the cobra's head crashed into the wicker. The lid rattled and rolled with the force of the strike. But Sumo had taken the rat, and the snake had missed.

Now Sumo looked at Strachan, his face a mask of expectation, his eyes as dark and unblinking as the cobra's. 'Try.'

It was a direct challenge to Strachan's courage. Sumo was testing him. The snake was making for the beach but the Malaysian caught its tail and dragged it back.

'Go on, Lance, I dare you.' From the ring of onlookers, KT was challenging him too. Strachan felt the skin of his neck flush with anger. Who the hell did she think she was, calling him Lance the whole time? He looked at Pili, who stood to one side, his face taut with anticipation. Everyone, it seemed, wanted him to accept the challenge.

'Eighteen hundred dollars. Fifteen if you beat the snake.' Sumo reiterated the deal. He was smiling that infectious Buddha smile. It was impossible not to like the man. He was the sort you wanted on your side. Strong as a bull, weathered as a walnut, faster than a striking snake.

Strachan smiled back. He'd drunk four beers and there was no way he would win. His mind was made up: Sumo was skipper of the expedition boat. 'Eighteen hundred. It's a deal. I'll meet you here tomorrow, an hour before sunset.' He raised a hand to say goodbye then headed up the track towards his hut.

He had gone no more than ten or fifteen paces when he noticed something strange. The chattering and excitement in the restaurant had stopped. The crunch of the waves was amplified in the silence. When he turned round he understood why. KT Luker was kneeling in front of the basket with her right hand outstretched. She was waggling her fingers, and the snake had reared up to accept her challenge. The crowd had closed in behind her, and there was no room for her to retreat. Strachan started to run. What the hell was she trying to prove? Flipping beer mats didn't qualify her for a stunt like this. Beer mats didn't bite. Beer mats weren't venomous. Beer mats didn't have a strike range of over six feet.

'KT. Don't.' He pushed through the crowd and arrived beside her. He was watching her hand and watching the snake. Sumo looked amused as he placed the rat back in the lid. Strachan was hoping that it was a joke. Maybe the snake wasn't venomous. Maybe it had been milked. Maybe its fangs had been removed. Then he looked at the boatman's face, and the expression told him this was real.

KT's hand rose to shoulder height. She was copying Sumo's technique, wiggling her fingers as though playing a frantic piano scale. The snake turned its attention towards her hand. She barely noticed. All her concentration was on the rat. On its twists and turns in the wicker lid. On the scratch of its feet. On the twitch of its nose. On the blink of its eyes. She was measuring the distance from her hand to its body, visualising success in her mind's eye.

She paused. If Strachan distracted her now she would be bitten. She'd passed the point of no return. The snake's head shifted back to the rat. The rat paused. It saw the snake towering above it, and froze once more. KT waggled her fingers. The cobra's ebony head turned towards her hand, and she let it fly.

Strachan never saw her arm because he was watching

the snake. It struck in a blur of speed, quicker than he could follow. He saw its start position and its end position but none of the movement in between. He heard the thwack of its head as it crashed into the lid. Then the rattle of the wicker as it sought to free its fangs.

The lid was empty. With its attention on her hand, the snake had struck at an angle. It had lost a fraction of its power and speed. But a fraction was all that KT had needed. She stood up, holding the rat in the air like a prize. She took a step backwards, out of range of the angry snake, and grinned triumphantly at Sumo.

Strachan saw then that the cobra had come much closer than he had initially realised. KT's shirt was torn at the wrist. The fangs had snagged her sleeve, missing her flesh by millimetres. But the only thing that mattered was that the snake had missed.

KT handed the rat to Pili for safe keeping but safe keeping wasn't what he had in mind, and she was too slow to stop him. She'd turned to face Strachan, and only saw Pili from the corner of her eye, by which time it was too late. Without thinking, Pili tossed the rat back into the lid. The snake struck a second later. It had been tricked twice and it wasn't going to make the same mistake again. Its jaws smashed into the hapless rodent, knocking the air from its lungs. The cobra rolled its head. It threw a coil round the rat's body to hold it steady while it died. The rat quivered and gaped for air in a silent scream of pain. Venom ran riot in its veins, the poison pumping deeper with every beat of its heart.

With its attention on the rat, Sumo calmly forced the cobra's head to the sand. When it was still, he changed his grip, pinching its neck between his thumb and forefinger. He gathered it up and slid it back in the basket. Its tail flicked his wrist on its way in: a final act of defiance before the lid was replaced and it was consigned to the dark to eat its prize.

Sumo was grinning at KT as though he'd just discovered the eighth wonder of the world. He was smiling his toothless smile, bobbing his head up and down as he bowed to her. Malaysian boatmen had little respect for women, but he was acting like he was about to revolt against centuries of cultural conditioning. He held up his hand in triumph. KT took the hint and gave him a high-five. She slapped his palm with a resounding crack. Sumo howled with delight. Then he returned the favour, mindful not to hit his new favourite too hard. It released her tension and banished her shock. Relief flooded her face. The rat was forgotten, and she and Sumo were the best of friends.

Strachan had seen enough. He turned and stomped up the beach, his hands thrust deep in the pockets of his swimming shorts. KT had made him look a coward. She'd nearly poisoned herself in the process. His credibility with Sumo had been shot to shit. He'd been publicly humiliated.

But at least he had a boat.

Later that night a small launch motored out to the Japanese yacht. The *Fubuki* was moored in deep water a mile from shore and it took the smaller boat fifteen minutes to reach her. Employees of Wakahama-san didn't just disappear on four-day boat trips to the Kerkullas without first asking permission. And they needed a very good reason to get it.

Pili Parang's, it turned out, was better than most.

34

They left the following evening: a jolly crew intoxicated
with the promise of adventure. Strachan, Pili, Sumo, and
Sumo's nephew, whose name Strachan couldn't pro-
nounce. In the end he settled on calling him Shleppy. It
was close enough to get a response, and being a cross
between Shorty and Sleepy it suited his diminutive
stature and laid-back manner.

Like his uncle, Shleppy was rotund and jovial, the
happy gene clearly visible in the broad smile with which
he welcomed Strachan to the fishing cockpit, the low
open deck at the back of the boat. On a good day's sport,
it would be awash with brine and blood, but tonight it
gleamed. Sumo took pride in his operation, and that was
another reason for Strachan to like him.

There was a large swivel chair in the centre of the
deck. Strachan thought its straps and buckles looked
more like accessories for torture than for sport. There
were storage lockers for big catches, a sink with an
adjacent cutting table, and a tank for live bait. Both sides
of the deck were lined with benches for spectators to
watch whoever was in the chair. But the chair wasn't
going to get much use on this trip. When Strachan
looked round the cockpit, it was to assess its suitability
for diving.

The stern rail was low on the water, making it easier
to land big game. Getting in and out of the sea would be

straightforward. There was a transom door and a set of submersible steps, which meant there would be no need to go rolling off the side. There was even a freshwater shower to rinse his kit. Strachan was pleased about that. He didn't cut corners maintaining his equipment. His main camera was a Nikonos Pro90 which came with a range of interchangeable lenses, off-camera strobes, and waterproof housings. At a cost of well over two thousand pounds, he did his best to take care of it. Cameras don't like water. They especially don't like sea water because salt is highly corrosive. The housings would spend longer in the shower than he did.

Shleppy took Strachan's bags, and descended to the lower deck, while Sumo began a quick tour of the boat's facilities and equipment. The spectators' benches were covered in blue cushions. Sumo placed them on the deck, revealing a number of deep lockers underneath. The first locker held life-vests. The second, rope and fenders. The third had torches, gloves and a toolbox.

They crossed to the starboard side. Here the first locker was home to a rack of brightly coloured lures. They looked like an accident waiting to happen. The next locker held two harpoons, and Sumo told him it was out of bounds. Strachan wasn't surprised. There was something else in there, far more dangerous than the harpoons. It was a pistol, lurking in the shadows at the far end of the locker. He guessed a flare gun would be kept on the flybridge, which meant that this thing fired bullets.

The *Esprit Bleu* was in excellent condition. From the beach she had looked sleek and fast but once on board Strachan realised she must have been state-of-the-art when new. She was sixteen years old but at today's prices he guessed she was still worth half a million bucks. Not for the first time he wondered where the hell a Malaysian fisherman had found the money to buy her.

Sumo ushered him inside to the main saloon. It was cool and spacious and simply furnished. It had sofas, an entertainment system, a drinks cabinet, and a dinette with seats for six. But it was the decorations that gave Strachan the answer to his question.

Like his abandoned living room in Tachbrook Street, the walls were adorned with photographs. The first was of Mika Hakkinen, the Finnish racing driver, standing next to a grey torpedo. Strachan recognised the scythe-like tail as that of a young thresher shark. Hakkinen had signed the photo in black pen. The scales read seventy pounds. Next to Hakkinen, Tom Selleck grinned at the camera from under his walrus moustache. A three-metre marlin lay at his feet. Two to the right Jean-Marie Le Pen held a skipjack tuna by the tail, his bicep straining to support twenty pounds of pelagic meat. Strachan knew how much Sumo charged his regular clients for a full day's fishing, and presumably he extracted more from celebrities. The tips alone would quickly add up.

'So whereabouts in the Kerkullas are we going?' Sumo stood in the middle of the saloon with his hands on his hips. Shleppy squeezed past him with a gin and tonic and a bowl of pistachios for his guest. Pili had climbed the observation tower, wholly uninterested in being sociable.

Strachan pulled the marine chart out of his rucksack. He'd used the new coordinates to estimate the position of the wreck and had checked his theory every morning and night. If he was right, it lay two miles north-east of the furthest island. He pointed it out to Sumo, tapping the map with his finger.

'Kerkulla Ketam,' said Sumo.

'That's right. What does it mean?'

'Ketam is crab. What are you looking for?'

'A fish. I'm a photographer.'

Sumo furrowed his brow. 'What kind of fish?'

'The rabbit fish. Rare and elusive.' Strachan tried to say it deadpan but he knew he'd blown it before the words had left his mouth. Rabbit fish did exist but his cover story was still flakier than an athlete's foot.

Sumo chuckled. Then he spat through an open window. 'Maybe your rabbit fish has swum off by now.'

'Maybe,' Strachan said.

'You shouldn't stay so long in the sun, Ed. Fries your brain.' Sumo roared with laughter and nudged Strachan in the ribs. Then he put a finger to his lips, indicating that Strachan could trust him to tell his real reason for chartering the boat.

Strachan didn't trust him, though. Not yet. He would have to work on that before they reached the wreck. 'In which case,' he said, 'why don't you get this thing moving, and find us a nice shady beach to moor in?'

Sumo left the saloon and shot up the ladder to the flybridge. He would be able to monitor the whole boat from the driver's seat. It was reassuring, Strachan thought, to know that Sumo and Pili would be up there. They would keep an eye out while he was underwater. Strachan wasn't expecting trouble but he didn't want company, and the sight of the pistol had reminded him that the South China Sea was notorious for pirates. Then again, with Pili and Sumo on board, the pirates would be picking the wrong boat to attack.

Shleppy untied the fenders. Sumo nudged the throttles forward and the big inboards gunned into life. There was a surge from the stern. The propellers churned the sea into meringue-shaped swirls, and suddenly they were on their way.

187

Sumo turned on the bow lights. They burned red and green in the night. Port and starboard; ruby and emerald, leading them on to the Kerkullas.

35

The *Esprit Bleu* flew for the ocean like a tern.

Strachan took his drink outside. Pili had descended from the tower and was dozing on a bench. Strachan settled on one of the cushions opposite and watched as the sun disappeared behind Tioman's saw-blade peaks. He thought briefly of KT, and smiled as he remembered her complexion, her finely chiselled nose and the green eyes that sparkled brighter than any of the emeralds he'd ever smuggled.

But it wasn't just her looks that intrigued him. The undercoat of a comfortable bourgeois childhood had still been visible beneath her tomboy veneer. He guessed that her aspirations to become an actress didn't meet with her parents' approval. He imagined they would prefer it if she traded her Quicksilver shorts for a Donna Karan suit. They would prefer it if she joined ranks with the lawyers, accountants and brokers Strachan had watched disembarking from the *Ariadne* yesterday morning. They probably thought Mike was the mutt's nuts: an Ivy League superstar from a wealthy Philadelphia family who would keep their daughter on the straight and narrow. Only Mike had hit her, so there she was, mocking cobras and looking for adventure on Tioman. One thing was clear: she didn't just talk the talk. Too bad she couldn't have joined him. But with Pili Parang on board, Strachan already had one more accomplice than he'd originally planned; and until he knew what his inheritance was, it was better to keep numbers to a minimum.

Sumo put the throttle down, and the bows came up on the plane. He and Shleppy were up on the flybridge, sharing a joke. The skipper's big-belly chuckle rolled round the boat like thunder. The *Esprit Bleu* soon found her rhythm. The engines emitted a drowsy hum and the mood in the cockpit turned soporific. Pili stretched and announced that he was going to bed. Strachan drained his glass, alone at last with his thoughts.

They should have been happy thoughts. A school of dolphins surfed the bow wave, and the stars of another equatorial night shone above him like diamonds in a coalface. With the mystery of his inheritance soon to be solved, he should've been infused with the same excitement that had coursed through him in Molly's flat. But the significance of the moment had got to him. This was a departure all right. He was going to put an end to something that had preoccupied him since he'd been eighteen years old. And, for some inexplicable reason, he was nervous.

He'd worn the first cuff link around his neck for the last eleven years. It was as much a part of him as the hair on his head or the scar on his forearm. But having a second one there changed the load. Strachan wasn't used to the extra weight yet. It gave him an eerie feeling that this trip wouldn't be all plain sailing. There was left and right, latitude and longitude, yin and yang. There was good and evil.

He had several other things on his mind, none of them as attractive as KT. His first concern was the fact that he didn't know what to do if the search revealed nothing. There was no back-up plan for when Verhoeven remembered his connection to *National*

Geographic. Sooner or later the Dutchman would follow up that lead. Even the slightest suggestion that Strachan was in trouble would be enough to get him fired. *National Geographic* was the world's largest non-profit science organisation and it had a considerable reputation to protect. Once Gilchrist got wind of what had happened in Curaçao he would drop Strachan faster than a sack of snakes. Strachan couldn't go back to Hamilton's warehouse, either. Interpol would be waiting for him at Heathrow, like they'd been waiting for him at Schiphol. This expedition was make or break.

It got worse.

The second thought was more persistent. Parasitic, even. It had followed Strachan from London, clinging to his conscience like a remora to a shark. It had black hair and blue eyes. Molly's baby. Strachan didn't even know the boy's name. He looked as though he might have been eighteen months old. His father had disappeared and his mother wasn't coming back. Strachan had accidentally killed her. He couldn't unkill her.

There was still no way of knowing whether Molly had tried to drug him or kill him. Michelle Newchris had insisted that it was the former, but Strachan now knew that the woman's word was to be taken with a fistful of salt. In a way he hoped it was the latter. That would somehow justify the fact that Molly had paid for her crime with her life. An eye for an eye. It *had* been a large dose; maybe too large even for a man his size. But then again, there had been no need to kill him: knocking him out would have served her purpose just as well. He guessed he would never know.

But these thoughts, serious enough though they were, were trivial compared to the last one. It was like a fish caught in a net. The more it struggled to escape, the more enmeshed it became. It was the answer to a question which Michelle Newchris had twice avoided answering. How had she and Molly known that Strachan had been in Curaçao?

There was only one answer. Hamilton had told them. Hamilton had caught Molly red-handed and had black-mailed her into telling him the longitudinal coordinates. Why else hadn't he called the police? Maybe he'd been telling the truth when he'd claimed he'd never told her the latitudinal digits, but that didn't mean he hadn't told her where she could find them. There had been no danger in pointing Molly towards Curaçao. Even if she was successful in finding the other cuff link, Hamilton still had a week's head start.

Strachan sat there seething at his godfather's treachery. It was a long time before he eventually went to bed.

36

Strachan woke the next morning to the sound of a woman screaming. It cut through him like a garrotte wire. He banged his head hard on the underside of the bunk as he rushed to get out of bed. He pulled on his shorts, grabbed his knife from his dive bag, and was out of the door in seconds. He charged up the steps to the living area, out through the sliding glass doors, and onto the main deck where he ground to a halt and groaned in disbelief. 'You've got to be kidding.'

KT Luker was treading water beside the boat. There was a second scream – exhilaration not fear – as Shleppy leapt from the tower and flew past his ear. Shleppy plunged twenty feet, hugging his knees as he landed, bombing KT and drenching the cockpit. KT greeted him with a barrage of splashes to the face before turning her attention to Strachan. 'Sorry, Lance. I earned my passage fair and square.' She swam to the side of the boat and looked up at him with her big green eyes.

'This is a private charter. *Private*. You know what that means?'

'Sure, but I beat the snake, and you never even tried. You know what *that* means?'

'Sumo.' Strachan raised his voice, not bothering to conceal his anger. 'I want to talk to you. Now.'

Sumo was smiling as he descended the ladder from the flybridge.

'Listen, Lance, it's nothing personal, but you kinda pissed me off the other night.' Now KT pushed back in the water. She wore a simple black swimsuit and floated on her back like a seal. 'I could care less if I'm your type or not. That wasn't the point. I was just trying to be friendly and you had to turn into some sort of sexual pissing contest. Have you any idea how arrogant you were? If I wanted a pretty little hunk to make me feel better, I would have gone down to the Berjaya and helped myself to one ten years younger than you.'

Strachan laughed. 'And *I'm* the one who's arrogant?'

'I want to dive the Kerkullas. Sumo's cool with it. And don't worry about the money, I'm paying my own way. Listen, honey, I'll stay outta your way if it makes you feel any better.'

Strachan didn't say it, but if there was one thing likely to make him feel better it was KT Luker squeezed into that one-piece and calling him honey. He smiled inwardly at his own weakness and felt his antagonism towards her soften. 'I'm on business,' he said. 'That's all there is to it.'

Sumo was listening to the exchange, trying not to laugh. Strachan turned to face him. 'Okay,' he said. 'What the hell is she doing here?'

'If you don't like it, you can get off the boat. Tioman is that way.' Sumo laughed until tears appeared in the corners of his eyes.

'This was supposed to be a private charter.'

'But you brought your friend, who is a bad man.' Sumo indicated Pili in the observation tower with a jerk of his chin. 'So now I bring a friend too. And whose boat is it?'

Despite his anger Strachan felt himself smiling. Sumo's mirth was contagious. And it was clear which of his passengers he liked best. Strachan was on a hiding to nothing. Sumo had obviously concealed KT in the spare cabin and now they were thick as thieves. He thought about continuing the argument but decided against it, choosing instead to curse and dismiss his skipper with a wave of his hand. There wasn't much else he could do. It was sixty miles back to Tioman. Taking KT back would mean an extra day of cost. And until he knew what his inheritance was, extra cost was out of the question.

Strachan replaced his knife in its scabbard and tossed it back inside the main cabin. He didn't know what he'd been expecting, and now he was embarrassed by his overreaction. The knife was a serious bit of kit: an Ocean Master with a six-inch serrated titanium blade, rustproof all the way into the handle. It was chunky and perfectly weighted for all uses including throwing. Mostly he used it for peeling fruit, cracking coconuts and cutting rope. The only time he'd used it as a weapon had been in self-defence against an angry titan trigger fish. He'd been on a reef in the Seychelles. She'd been a large female, ready to defend her eggs with her life, and he'd made the error of finning right over her nest. Strachan reckoned you could keep your great whites, tigers, and bull sharks. If you wanted to know what it was like to be attacked by a fish, try going face to face with a titan trigger when she's spawning. Teeth like a horse's in a fury of muscle. For starters she'd bitten a chunk out of his left fin. Then she'd proceeded to the main course, ripping a strip of flesh from his right forearm. He still had the scar to prove it.

Strachan had overslept the others by at least an hour and there was one place still set for breakfast. He poured coffee and spooned down the kiwi fruit and mango. He walked to the rail where he raised his spoon at Shleppy to register his thanks. Shleppy and KT had resumed their game, and were shrieking as they took turns to duck-dive under the water. Shleppy hadn't yet lost his puppy fat but he would grow up to be a beautiful boy. He was maybe twelve or thirteen, with hazel eyes that shone in a round cherubic face.

The sea was turquoise. A shoal of fish nibbled at the minerals on the anchor chain. Staring into the sea, Strachan yearned for the feel of the air tank on his back. He yearned for the serenity of the underwater world. Underwater was a magical place. No noise, no stress. The waters around the Kerkullas were a marine national park. Their diving was among the best in the world, but because of their distance from the mainland they were seldom visited. He couldn't wait. Already his anger at KT's trickery was disappearing.

He stretched, pumped out a series of press-ups and walked to the bow pulpit to take in their surroundings. Sumo had moored them in a small cove on Kerkulla Ketam. These islands were more arid than Tioman. There was hardly any breeze and the heat smothered their small strip of beach so that the air shimmered like burning paraffin. The palm trees wilted under the onslaught, their fronds as brittle as tinder.

The terrain was volcanic. A wall of scrub-covered slopes rose steeply from the water's edge. Strachan spotted three aquatic monitor lizards at the end of the beach. They were ambling through the scrub. Their black tongues flicked in and out as they smelled for food. Relatives of the bigger Komodo dragon, these beasts were still the size of dogs. He wondered if KT had seen them. The Kerkullas were a lost world compared to Tioman. These dinosaurs had more right to be here than humans did, so Strachan left them to it and turned his attention back to his dive.

He shielded his eyes against the sun. The dive site

waited two miles offshore. He had checked on the map and it lay far enough out to be beyond the boundaries of the national park, which meant he wouldn't need a permit to dive. Being a sportfisher, the *Esprit Bleu* would provide perfect cover in the event of any unsolicited visits from the park's police. Depending on the depth, there might still be a big old swell out there, and as he wandered along the deck he hoped that KT didn't get seasick.

She and Shleppy had finished their game. Strachan followed her with his gaze as she skipped up the submersible steps into the cockpit. Drops of water clung to her limbs like dew. She crossed the deck to the shower where she tilted back her head to rinse the salt from her hair. As she arched her spine he couldn't help but notice the vulnerability of her throat and the thrust of her breasts. He turned away quickly before she caught him staring.

Strachan descended to the lower deck where he took a long hot shower, gleefully ignoring Sumo's instructions on water conservation. He re-emerged ten minutes later, refreshed, invigorated and ready to go. He twisted the cuff links round his neck for reassurance. Immediately he felt the jolt of adrenalin in the pit of his stomach. Conditions were perfect. It was one hell of a day for a treasure hunt.

37

'Sumo, let's go!' Strachan lit a cigarette. He whistled down to his skipper and tapped his watch. Sumo might have been captain of the ship but Strachan was paying his wages so he quickly joined his client on the flybridge.

'Okay. This is what we're going to do.' Strachan laid the marine chart on the map table. Back in Kampung Air Batang he'd drawn a square round the search area in red pen. Each of the square's sides was the equivalent of one nautical mile. Its centre was the point at which 03° 18′ 43″ north bisected 104° 40′ 01″ east. He was using the seconds as they appeared on the cuff links. If that turned out to be a false assumption, it wouldn't necessarily mean failure. At the equator, a minute of latitude translates into approximately one nautical mile. Since they were only three hundred miles north of the equator, he reckoned a search area of one square mile was plenty. If his grandfather had been off by more than that, Strachan would be going home empty-handed.

'Sumo, I want you to search this area in ever-decreasing squares. Start on the outer circumference and work inwards.'

It looked a small enough area on paper but as they motored out to sea Strachan realised they were talking about a hell of a lot of water. Sumo was thinking the same. 'Big place to find a little fish.'

'I know. Too bad. You can go at a steady speed so it

doesn't take all day but keep your eyes peeled on the sonar. We're looking for anything large or unusual.'

'How big is this fish?'

'It's big, Sumo. About the size of a sunken ship.' There; he had said it. What the hell. The *Esprit Bleu* was a small boat and they were miles from civilisation. It was an impossible secret to keep, and since Strachan didn't know how to work the boat's sonar equipment he needed Sumo's full cooperation. Besides, even if he had to tell the others he was looking for a wreck he would still be the only one who knew what was on board. That much he promised himself.

Sumo's eyes lit up in a mixture of mirth, comprehension and pity. Clearly he thought Strachan had no more chance of finding a wreck than he had of finding a rabbit fish. Sumo studied the chart again, squinting and scratching his head. Then he frowned his bulldog frown. He tapped the map in the centre of the red square. 'Very dangerous. The sea runs fast between those reefs.'

Strachan nodded. 'That's right. Good place for a shipwreck.'

This time Sumo just grunted and opened the throttle. Strachan noted it down as a minor victory.

The map showed a dramatic change of depth in the middle of the square. Here the seabed rose to form two parallel reefs. They were three hundred metres long by sixty wide and ran perpendicular to the north shore of Kerkulla Ketam. The area of water between the reefs varied in depth from sixty metres to as little as fifteen. The surrounding seas averaged over a kilometre, so the current in the channel would be much stronger. There would be a strong rip as the tide dragged it back and forth twice a day. It was a plausible site for a wreck. The reefs rose from nowhere. Any vessel caught in a storm could easily find itself swept into the coral ramparts.

It was an obvious place to conduct his search but with so much at stake Strachan wasn't taking any chances. He had two days ahead of him. He had air enough for eight dives. There was no point in not being thorough. They would search the surrounding area as well.

'How do you know Pili?' The merriment had disappeared from Sumo's face as he relaxed back in his seat. His eyes warned Strachan that he needed to be careful with his answer.

'I was a friend of his brother's.'

'Runi?'

'Yes. Runi.'

The change in Sumo's expression was visible. Strachan clearly wasn't the only one who preferred the elder Parang. 'Runi was a good man. The money he made —' he looked at Strachan to check that he understood, '— he always shared with people from the village.'

Strachan nodded '*Was* a good man? Isn't he *still* a good man?'

Sumo engaged the autopilot, then put a hand on Strachan's shoulder. 'You don't know?'

'No. What happened?' Strachan felt himself flush. Bad news was coming.

Sumo looked down at Pili in the cockpit. He was out of earshot, but Sumo lowered his voice anyway. 'Runi is dead. The police killed him. When he was arrested they beat him so badly that he went into a deep sleep.'

'You mean a coma?'

'Yes, coma. After a week a judge ordered the doctors to switch off his life machine.'

Strachan felt his stomach tighten and his legs go weak. 'Shit.' He sat down, surprised at the strength of his reaction. It might have been ten years since he last saw Runi, but he remembered his face as clearly as if it had been yesterday. 'Shit,' he said again. More surprising than his remorse was his instant sympathy for Pili. Pili had adored his elder brother. He'd modelled himself on Runi any way he could. He'd dressed the same, he'd smoked the same brand of cigarettes, he'd drunk the same beer. He'd driven the same make of motorcycle. When Runi had finished with one of his girls, Pili had always been next in line to ensure that he remained on equal terms. No one takes the loss of a brother well, but Pili would have taken it worse than most. 'Shit.'

Somewhere among the remorse and sympathy Strachan also felt the pangs of guilt. He could picture it now. A hot evening in downtown KL. A crowded bar. Runi in a T-shirt and Levis, talking to the lapidary and two other couriers. They'd been drinking beer and eating *popiah*. Strachan had left the bar to call Hamilton. A minute later the police had stormed the building, entering via the fire exit at the rear. Strachan had come back inside but by then the beating had begun. Blow after blow after blow. And he had turned his back and had run.

He glanced sheepishly towards the cockpit. Shleppy was giving Pili and KT a fishing lesson. He was teaching them how to cast the lines and play them out without snagging them round the outriggers. At fifteen knots it was harder than it looked. Pili's face was a study in concentration. Strachan's heart went out to him. He would pick his moment carefully and then offer his condolences.

Realising the conversation was over Sumo grunted and turned his attention back to driving the boat.

A few minutes later KT joined them on the flybridge. There was a curved sofa behind Sumo's chair, and she put towels down because the cushions were too hot without them. 'What are we doing all the way out here? Diving's better close in.'

Strachan sighed. The secret that he'd tried so hard to protect was going to be shared again. And the chances of KT's reaction being as passive as Sumo's were hopelessly slim. 'I'm looking for a wreck.'

'Bullshit.'

'Okay, you're right, it's bullshit.'

'A wreck? Are you serious?'

Strachan looked around the boat. He tapped Sumo on the shoulder, then beckoned Pili and Shleppy to come up and join them. They were a team now, and he might as well tell them everything. Right now he wanted to talk about something – anything – to take his mind off Runi.

It made sense to tell them. What if he found it? If the wreck was there, it would be impossible to hide it from them. He could still be economical with the truth. They didn't need to know he was on the run, and they didn't need to know that there was something valuable on board. He didn't need to use the word *inheritance*.

No one interrupted him.

Strachan watched their faces as he spoke. Three of them smiled, unsure whether or not to believe him. The fourth gave nothing away.

38

After Strachan had finished his self-censored account, Shleppy and Pili returned to their fishing, leaving Strachan with KT and Sumo on the flybridge. KT passed him a bottle of sun cream and turned her back without saying a word.

Glad of the distraction, Strachan spent a blissful five minutes covering her in sun lotion – much to Sumo's disapproval. Strachan had a good base tan of his own from Curaçao and didn't need any cream but when he'd finished he turned his back and told her to lay it on thick. He closed his eyes as her hands massaged his flesh. 'Okay,' he said. 'We got off on the wrong foot. I'm sorry for that. I think we should compromise.'

'I'm listening.'

'Did you bring any tanks?'

'Four.'

That was two more than he'd been expecting her to say. There was no compressor on the *Esprit Bleu* and Strachan had brought eight air tanks of his own. He'd bought them from Marine Madness the day before, negotiating a special rate in exchange for some photos for their dive shop-wall. 'We'll do four dives together. Two today, two tomorrow. But if I have to go deep, you're staying on the boat.'

'What do you mean? Why?'

'I can't let you go deeper than thirty metres.' If KT

was qualified to Rescue status with PADI, the Professional Association of Dive Instructors, she would have some idea of what to do in an emergency. Strachan was confident that she could hold her own in warm seas at recreational depth, but he was equally sure he wasn't taking her deeper than thirty metres. Below thirty, recreational diving fast becomes another kind of sport. The effects can be devastating if due respect isn't shown.

'Give me a break. I can handle the depth.'

'I don't think so.'

'Lance, if we find this wreck, I'm coming with you. Stop being such a mother hen.'

Strachan didn't want to argue so he offered KT another compromise. 'Maybe, but you'll have to stick to the upper slopes.'

'Oh, for Christ's sake! I'll show you my logbooks – you can see the qualification! Who the hell are you to tell me what I can and can't do, anyway? And if you're such a responsible diver, why are you diving without a buddy in the first place? That's pretty much rule number one.'

'Rule number one is never hold your breath.'

'Pedant.'

Strachan smiled. 'You ever get the bends?' he asked her.

'Nope. You?'

'Once.'

'Bad?'

'Worse than bad.'

'You gonna tell me about it?' KT was smiling again, telling Strachan that he was on the right track.

'It was two years ago on HaHa Reef in Curaçao. My tank got stuck against the roof of a cave.'

'Serves you right.' She laughed. 'What were doing in a cave, anyway?'

'Chasing a lobster. *Panulirus Argus*. It was a monster.'

'Yeah? Sounds like it was a lot smarter than *Homo sapiens*, too.'

Strachan smiled. 'I tried to dislodge myself but ten minutes later I was still stuck. I had no choice. I had to ditch the tank.'

'How deep were you?'

'Forty-three metres. I'd been down there for twenty minutes.'

'What happened?'

'Even after I'd taken my BCD off there was still no way I could dislodge the tank so I broke for the surface. I did everything right: exhaled all the way to the top. I thought I'd got away with it.'

'And then?'

'Then Piet appeared. We'd got separated so he came to look for me on the surface. I was waiting for him in the boat. I'd come up so quickly that the nitrogen in my blood'd had no chance to escape. First thing I felt was pins and needles in my joints. Piet drove us back to shore and threw me in the back of his jeep. By now my lips had turned blue, my stomach was heaving, and my head felt like it was being crushed in a vice.'

'Sounds pretty bad.'

'It was ecstasy compared to what came next.'

'What came next?'

Strachan leaned back against KT, purring as her thumbs worked the lotion deep into his shoulders. 'My blood started to fizz. Literally. I lay there howling with pain, doubled up in the back of the jeep while the nitrogen bubbled in my joints. My elbows were the worst. I scratched them raw. It took twenty minutes to reach the decompression chamber in Willemstad, then four more hours of excruciating pain for my body to readjust.'

'Shit.'

'Shit is right,' he said, borrowing an expression he'd learned from Koopmans. 'So now you know why.'

'Now I know why what?'

'Why you're not coming below thirty.'

KT didn't reply. Sensible girl.

Sumo interrupted to say they'd reached the edge of the square. They leapt from their seats, crowding round him like a couple of eager kids. His instrument panel was pretty sophisticated. There was an autopilot system, a VHF radio, a sea-temperature gauge. Next to those was a Furuno 72-mile radar, and a Datamarine 3000 digital depth sounder. The jewel in the crown was a Furuno FCV 600L Fishfinder: a colour LCD screen for finding fish at depths of up to 2,500 feet. Sumo patted it fondly before switching it on. He reduced speed to five knots to ensure that they didn't miss anything then slipped the *Esprit Bleu* into autopilot on a pre-programmed setting.

The first square revealed nothing, which was probably just as well. The average depth was well over a thousand metres. If they'd found something, they wouldn't have been able to do anything about it without a submarine. As they approached their starting point, Sumo took them in towards the centre of the square by a hundred metres and they began again.

It was a pleasant enough way to spend the morning. They sunbathed and smoked and cheered the flying fish as they skimmed the waves. Thirty metres was the record. At one stage a school of eight bottle-nosed dolphins appeared off the starboard rail but they'd disappeared before Strachan could fetch his camera.

An hour later, they'd completed the second square. Still nothing. Strachan wasn't bothered. You needed infinite patience to be an underwater photographer. His supply wasn't infinite but it could cope with this. KT had climbed the observation tower and was engrossed in a book. Pili was sleeping in the cockpit. Sumo wasn't a great talker, so Strachan amused himself by fetching a coconut husk from the galley. He carved a pendant for KT with his knife. Fifty minutes and another circuit later, it had taken shape. He held it up, admiring his handiwork, which bore more than a passing resemblance to a dolphin.

But the pendant wasn't the only thing he saw. They were no longer alone.

They had been joined by another cruiser. Slightly smaller than the *Esprit Bleu,* it sailed serenely over the waves some six hundred yards across their bows. It was running parallel to the Kerkullas in the direction of Tioman. It didn't look like a fishing boat. Strachan saw no sign of divers either so he concluded that it was the pleasure craft of a rich tourist, perhaps hired for a day trip round the islands. He could just make out two figures on board. They were both male, both Caucasian.

By now it was midday. The heat was as heavy as a steamroller and forced Strachan to retreat inside. KT followed him. He gave her the dolphin, telling her that it was a peace offering. She gave him a peck on the cheek in return. Excitement hatched in his gut and wriggled round his stomach like a giant beetle. She made him feel like a teenager.

After lunch the squares grew smaller but the Fishfinder remained as silent as before. The minutes dragged as they conducted their search. They circled the reefs like the hands on a clock, the boredom only alleviated by two cans of iced tea and a packet of Camels. But at least they were homing in on the parallel reefs.

Strachan took the steps up to the flybridge. He stared at the Fishfinder, willing it to find something. It registered the underwater topography with a series of peaks and troughs, drawing a jagged line across the screen like a heart monitor attached to a patient in ventricular fibrillation.

He tried to remain upbeat. On the one hand life was pretty good. Shleppy had just brought him another iced tea, and they would reach the reefs on the square after next. On the other hand, Strachan had begun to realise just what a long shot this was. If there *was* a ship here, it would have been discovered long before now. He was crazy to think he could discover a virgin wreck. Micronesia threw up the occasional Second World War fighter plane, but to find a new site so close to a national park was inconceivable. He stared at the screen, and shook his head.

The Fishfinder beeped in response.

39

The machine beeped again. It had found something.

When Strachan saw the monitor he was forced into a double take. It showed a large shiplike object directly under the hull. He shook with excitement as he whistled to KT. 'We've found it!' he yelled. 'We've only gone and bloody found it!'

Sumo was the first to reach the flybridge. Shleppy and KT followed. Pili was asleep in the cockpit, soaking up the sun's rays like a reptile on a rock. Sumo instantly cut the motors and the boat sank back in the swell. For a minute it was silent except for the gentle lap–slap–tap of the waves on the hull. Sumo and Shleppy studied the sonar while Strachan drew on his cigarette. There was something there, all right.

'*Ikan yu paus?*' Shleppy looked at his uncle.

'*Ikan yu paus,*' Sumo confirmed. And then the two of them roared with laughter, their chests heaving in unison as they shared the joke.

'What's so damned funny?'

'Look, Strachan! Your ship is moving. Maybe your ship is a submarine.' This time Sumo almost fell off his chair. Even the folds in the back of his neck were wobbling with mirth.

'A submarine? Really?' Strachan didn't get it but when he looked at the panel again he realised that they were right. Whatever was down there, it was no longer under the hull. It had overtaken them by about twenty metres and the beeps had grown softer.

'No, Lancelot, honey. Not really. I think it's a whale.'

'Not a whale, Miss. A whale shark. Biggest fish in the sea.' Sumo looked at her kindly. His big brown eyes shone with excitement.

If Strachan had ever bothered to keep a logbook, it would have read like a *Who's Who* of the world's best dive sites; an encyclopaedia of the ocean's most fabulous scenes. He'd photographed the thousand-strong shoals of hammerhead sharks off Sipidan, the dancing mantas in Palau, the Orcas in Puget Sound, and the sardine shoals off California. He'd dived in the Seychelles, the Maldives, the Philippines, the Caribbean, the Hebrides and the Galapagos. He'd been everywhere except under the ice caps. For ten years he'd grown to know the thousands of species that frequented the reefs, coastlines, and open seas of the planet. But in all that time, he'd never seen a whale shark.

Strachan didn't care if they laughed at him. He'd waited his whole life to find one, and he wasn't going to let the opportunity slip. Shipwrecks, inheritances, the mystery of Gong De Tian and the silver cuff links could all wait. He leaned over the windshield. There it was, dead ahead, moving like a Zeppelin. It was so big that it might have been the shadow of a passing cloud. It was a magnificent creature, at least fifteen metres long and weighing all of eighteen tonnes.

Strachan was down the ladder in seconds, ignoring KT's cries to wait for her. He hurried to retrieve his fins, mask, snorkel and camera. He was worried that the shark would be gone before he could change films. He usually used Fujichrome Velvia for close-ups of the reef because it was so good with colours, but now he switched to

Provia 100. The Provia was better for situations like this that required a medium shutter speed.

'You are going for a swim, Ed?' Pili grinned at Strachan, revealing gleaming white teeth. The shouting had woken him up. He stretched and rubbed his eyes.

'It's a whale shark, Pili. Biggest fish in the sea.' Strachan smiled as he repeated Sumo's accolade. It was a fact that he'd learned as a kid. Several species of whale were bigger but they were mammals, not fish. Pili smiled back. There was a buzz about the boat. Despite having just woken up, he seemed to catch the mood.

The whale shark was still there. It was moving slowly, coming to the surface to feed. Sumo cut the motors so as not to scare it as the *Esprit Bleu* drifted in behind its tail. Strachan and KT perched on the stern rail, ready to slip into the sea. Strachan's adrenalin was on free-flow. His heart drum-rolled. Whale sharks were harmless but eighteen tonnes was still a lot of fish. A friend of Piet's had got too close to one in Costa Rica. It had broken six of his ribs with a single flick of its tail. KT was nervous too. She gripped Strachan's hand like she was trying to crush it.

Sumo bought them alongside the monster on reduced power. It lurked seven metres below the surface. Its back was an enormous cobalt slate dappled with white spots the size of saucers. Its dorsal fin was as big as a wind-surfer's sail. The tip broke the surface as they eased themselves into the water. Then they put their faces down and swam.

The big blue.

There was no better term for it. Snorkelling in the open ocean on a sunny day is like floating in space. You can't see the bottom. There are no walls. No sides. There is nothing in your peripheral vision. You have no point of reference. You have no idea what is below you

211

or behind you. It is just blue. A rich, deep, impenetrable void. It is humbling, terrifying; it is without beginning or end. Infinite blue. It is utterly beautiful.

The whale shark was travelling at around two knots. They swam fast to catch it up. Strachan's breath sounded like a snorting bull in his snorkel. Suddenly the shark's tail was below them. It was even bigger than it had looked from the boat. The tail alone was the size of a double-decker bus, making it a mighty effective paddle. They stayed on the surface, minimising the water's resistance until they'd overtaken the danger.

The shark seemed oblivious to their presence. Docile and harmless, it had opened its enormous mouth and was straining plankton through gills the size of railway sleepers. It was time to go to work. Strachan took a deep breath and dived below the surface. He could hold his first breath for around three minutes. That was pretty good. If he didn't smoke it might have been nearer four. The world record was eight minutes, six seconds. It was a skill like everything else. It could be learned. Strachan had started as a kid in the bath.

He came down on the whale shark's head. For a while he simply kept pace with it as he thought through the shots he wanted. The conditions weren't great. Particles in water reflect the light, and down here there was a thick band of plankton: a tranquil blizzard of life, supporting an entire food chain. It played in the sunlight like midges in a torch beam.

Strachan kicked to the side, trying to find a suitable position that was neither too near nor too far from the enormous fish. Judging the correct distance from which to take pictures is a key skill in underwater photography. The refractive index of water is greater than that of air so most objects appear to be twenty-five per cent closer than they would on land. Even with a 16mm full-frame fish-eye lens it was impossible to get the whole thing in his viewfinder. He had used twenty seconds of breath.

Since he wasn't in the market for ordinary shots he gave up trying to frame the whole shark and swam underneath it instead. Its skin was white. Its bulk blotted out the sun. It was like walking under the fuselage of a 747. Two pilot fish lay protected under its massive belly, waiting for scraps. Strachan took six shots looking along the shark's abdomen from the perspective of the pilot fish. Then he broke for the surface to gulp more air.

On the next dive Strachan was bolder. So was KT. She went down with him. They finned hard to get in front of the shark's head. Strachan wanted a shot similar to the one of the manta that had distracted Verhoeven: a head-on shot that would demonstrate the sheer size of the fish's mouth and gullet.

When they turned, the shark was coming right at them. Its mouth opened like the entrance to a cave, a black hole moving with unstoppable power. Now Strachan knew how Jonah must have felt. KT could have stood on his shoulders, and still it could have swallowed them whole. Either it was all too much for her or she ran out of breath because she released his hand and shot for the surface. Strachan stayed put. His pulse thumped in his ears.

He reeled off the shots as fast as the automatic reload allowed. Unlike the manta this beast had no intention of stopping. If it hit him, it might kill him. Even at two knots, you don't want to be hit by eighteen tonnes of muscle. His ribs would break like matchsticks. His internal organs would be squashed like overripe fruit. At the last minute the shark veered to its left. The pressure wave from the displaced water pushed Strachan aside as if he was a strand of kelp. It was a magical experience. The sheer size of this fish created a tide. He kicked for the surface, propelling himself past its unblinking eye.

They followed the whale shark for another three minutes. KT was getting closer and closer. Strachan had taken almost an entire film when at last she dared to reach out her hand. He was underwater at the time and couldn't tell her to stop. The shark gave a flick of its massive tail and headed into the deep. Unable to follow, they watched it go until its long body melted into the blue.

Only after it had gone did Strachan realise it wasn't the only shark in the water.

40

There are three types of shark attack, and as a diver you have to be spectacularly unlucky to experience any of them. Strachan was familiar with the statistics. You've got more chance of being struck by lightning back on the boat. Or of being killed by a falling coconut in your resort. On average eighty-five people are reportedly bitten by sharks every year. That's a worldwide figure. In New York alone there's an average of 1,600 cases of people biting other people every year. Unfortunately, Strachan and KT weren't diving, they were snorkelling. The odds were shorter.

The sneak attack is the least common. It's also the most deadly. The shark attacks from below. You don't see it. It comes up fast, mistaking you for a seal or turtle. The bite is designed to bring instant death. Great whites and makos are masters of the art. Generally speaking, you don't survive a sneak.

Then there's the hit–and–run. These normally occur in the surf zone where visibility is poor. Again, it's a case of mistaken identity. Your chances of survival are higher because the great thing about the hit–and–run is that the shark doesn't return.

Finally, there's the bump–and–bite. This one is a real bitch. It's a more cautious approach so you know all about it. The shark swims in lazily. It's curious. It nudges you with its snout to see how you react. If you show signs of fear it grows bolder and nudges you again. If you don't show signs of fear, it nudges you anyway. It takes a lazy, experimental bite. Apologetic, almost. Then it comes back for another go. And another. A protective membrane covers its eye as it bites. Bulls, tigers and oceanic white-tips favour this approach.

And that was exactly what Strachan and KT had now: an oceanic white-tip. Immediately recognisable from the rounded dorsal fin, with its splash of white paint. Forget white-tip reef sharks; this is a totally different species. *Carcharhinus Longimanus*. There have only been five known attacks since records began but this species has probably killed more humans than any other type of shark. It is thought to have been responsible for the deaths of over six hundred sailors from the torpedoed USS *Indianapolis* in 1945. Over sixty per cent of the crew was taken during two nights of terror. Quint tells the story in *Jaws*. He tells it well. Strachan reckoned it was probably the finest monologue in cinema history. Two years earlier, hundreds of Italian POWs were taken from the shipwrecked *Nova Scotia* after the Germans torpedoed her off the coast of Africa. Again, eyewitness accounts implicated the oceanic white-tip.

Strachan knew all about it. A large pelagic shark. Record weight of 369 lbs, caught by Reid Hodges off the coast of San Salvador in the Bahamas in 1998. Preferred diet: squid, turtle, threadfins, stingray – and garbage.

He and KT didn't look like squid and they didn't smell like garbage but Strachan wasn't taking any chances. He'd tagged tiger sharks, he'd cut bronze whalers out of tuna nets, and once he'd hand-fed an injured grouper to a bull shark, which – apart from switching the occasional wineglass – was probably still the most irresponsible thing he'd ever done in his life.

He respected all sharks, but there was only one in the ocean he was actually afraid of: *Carcharhinus Longimanus*. It's an opportunistic feeder. It's pretty much the only shark that will attack out of curiosity, no questions asked. It will bite anything once just to see if it's palatable. It's the most unpredictable of all sharks.

This one was five metres below KT, and already it was circling her. Strachan was twenty metres away. KT had been by the whale shark's tail while he was photographing its mouth. The white-tip was moving fast. KT had seen it. Strachan saw the fear in her eyes, her terror magnified through her mask. Her head came out of the water and she gesticulated wildly at the boat, waving her hands above her head in the universal distress signal.

Strachan swam towards her. The shark was excited. The circling had been abandoned in favour of fly-bys. It was like a jet inspecting an enemy tank. It streaked past, turned, and flashed across her for a second time. It was swimming the criss-cross patterns that preceded a strike.

The most important thing for KT was to stay calm. To float with her face in the water so that she could keep her eye on the shark. Not to kick her legs or flail her arms. Staying calm wasn't easy. An oceanic white-tip can exert a biting pressure of one tonne per square inch. Strachan reckoned KT's waist measured twenty-eight inches.

He kicked hard to attract the shark's attention as he closed the gap with KT. She scrambled behind him as it launched its first attack. It came in slow, a metre below the surface. The lightning darts were for inspection only. Now it was more cautious. Bump-and-bite.

He held the camera in front of him and swam to meet it. You had to show these bastards you weren't afraid. You had to show them who was boss. Strachan was scared stiff but he did it anyway. The shark was three metres away. Strachan saw rows of teeth as its grin widened. He was ready to bump it with the camera housing. Hopefully it would get the message that injection-moulded plastic didn't smell or taste like tuna. He braced himself for the impact.

Which never came. The *Esprit Bleu* roared in bang on cue. The Detroit 12V92TA engines had 1,080 horse-power each. Strachan knew; Sumo had told him. The water throbbed. The oceanic white-tip feared for its life, and vanished with a shimmy of its tail.

Strachan turned to give KT the okay sign. Sumo already had her by the hands and was hauling her out of the water. He lifted her clean out, as though she was a baby in a bathtub. Strachan joined them a minute later. KT was shaking but grinning. *She's got spirit,* Strachan told himself. *She's got it in spades.* Then he collapsed laughing on the deck, absurdly pleased with himself, and high as a kite on adrenalin.

They were soon busy telling the others all about it. Strachan was still feeling ten feet tall and bulletproof. It was moments like that which made life worth living. Reflexively he glanced towards the islands. The other cruiser was still with them. It was back on its original course. It wasn't circling the islands, he realised. It was circling *them*.

41

Strachan didn't like it. These were dangerous seas. He'd read about pirates in the local press. Modern pirates didn't board you with a cutlass in their teeth and a parrot on their shoulder. They boarded you carrying an Uzi. They shot you between the eyes. Then they looted your boat and set fire to it.

But pirates weren't the only villains to frequent these waters. Pirates were saints compared to Abu Sayaff, the Islamic terrorist group from the Philippines. In April 2000 Abu Sayaff had sneaked into the Malaysian dive resort of Sipidan. Strachan had been there the week before. They'd abducted twenty-one tourists and a couple of staff. They'd demanded ransom. When the money had been slow in coming, they'd beheaded the Malaysian staff to let the world know that they were serious.

Strachan fetched his binoculars from his cabin and instructed Sumo and Pili to follow him up to the flybridge. He wanted their opinion before he voiced his concerns in front of KT and Shleppy. He rolled his finger over the binos' focus adjuster until the other cruiser's image grew sharp. Boats, like racehorses, are often owned by people with a cruel taste in names, and this one was no exception. She was called *Ping-Pong Taboo*. He handed Sumo the glasses with a grimace.

'Take a look. She's been circling us for the last few hours. What do you make of her?'

'She's slower than Sumo.' At first Strachan thought he was bragging. Then he realised that Sumo was reassuring him. If the other boat belonged to pirates, the *Esprit Bleu* could outrun her.

'Anything else?'

'She's trailing a sonar buoy.'

'She's what?' Strachan snatched the binoculars back. He raised them to his eyes again. Sumo was right. With the chop of the sea Strachan had missed it the first time because he'd been concentrating on the boat and its driver. He hadn't spotted the cable that snaked off its stern, nor the orange ball that bobbed in the troughs between the waves.

So they weren't pirates after all. Nor terrorists, for that matter. They were something much worse. They were two guys searching the seabed, and they were equipped with some serious kit. 'Sumo, let's go and introduce ourselves to our new friends.'

'Good idea. Maybe they already found that rabbit fish.' Sumo opened the *Esprit Bleu's* throttle. Down in the cockpit KT was flung back in the chair as they accelerated towards a top speed of thirty-two knots.

The whale shark had drawn them towards the open sea. They were some distance from the islands. There was at least a mile and a half between the two boats. As they closed the gap, Strachan saw the second man appear at the stern of the *Ping-Pong Taboo*. He began pulling in the sonar buoy. He was Caucasian. He was tall and sunburnt, wearing a baseball cap and shades. It was impossible to tell anything else about him, except of course that he had seen the *Esprit Bleu* coming and was getting the hell out of there. He and his buddy must have been looking back at them, thinking the same thing: that they were the police, pirates, or Abu Sayaff.

Strachan urged Sumo to go faster as he watched the *Ping-Pong Taboo* pick up speed. A puff of diesel smoke escaped her exhaust. Then she was up on the plane, leaving a lathery wake as she raced along the shoreline. With a head start like that, it didn't look like Sumo would catch her. He couldn't take a short cut through the channel. There was no choice but to go the long way around the parallel reefs. In less than two minutes the other cruiser had disappeared round the nearest island and was hightailing it back to Tioman.

They let her go. Pursuing her until they were able to exploit their speed advantage would have been a waste of fuel. Strachan's good mood disappeared with the *Ping-Pong Taboo*. He had caught a glimpse of the man at the wheel, and was desperate to see him up close.

It was half-four in the afternoon. The moon had already risen. Now that the other cruiser had given them the slip Strachan was keen to resume their search, but Sumo was adamant that they couldn't approach the reef at this time of day. Even with electronic depth gauges, there was still no substitute for spotting coral with the naked eye. He had no intention of exposing the *Esprit Bleu* to the rip in a fading light.

Strachan pleaded with him, but Sumo didn't want to know. KT took Sumo's side in the argument, leaving Strachan with no choice but to call it a day. And it hadn't been a bad day at all. He'd taken thirty shots of a champion whale shark. Then he'd survived the grace, speed and beauty of one of the ocean's top predators in full assault mode. He wished he'd taken some pictures of the white-tip, but he'd been too preoccupied with KT's safety.

In the evening they ate raw tuna. Shleppy caught it,

and gutted it over the rail. He skinned it, rinsed it, diced it, and put it straight on their plates. It was the freshest food that Strachan had ever tasted. His enjoyment of it was tempered only by the nagging memory of the man at the wheel of the *Ping-Pong Taboo*.

Had Strachan not known that Adrian Hamilton hardly ever left his gallery in Sloane Street, he would have sworn that it was none other than him. His godfather.

42

Day two. Reef day.

Strachan was out of bed at dawn. Shleppy and Sumo were preparing breakfast. Pili appeared soon afterwards, and even though she was last up, KT was on deck by seven o'clock. For breakfast they ate fresh fruit salad. By seven-fifteen the *Esprit Bleu* was gliding over a glass sea towards the reef.

There was no sign of the other cruiser. They'd scared it off, and Strachan doubted that they would see it again. The crew were probably a couple of scientists, trailing the buoy for research purposes. He couldn't blame them for fleeing when they'd turned to confront them. The fact that the man at the wheel had looked like Hamilton was a coincidence. Hamilton was the world's greatest landlubber. To him, a dive was a seedy nightclub in Soho. He wouldn't know a sonobuoy if one was dropped on his foot. Strachan chided himself. It was the strain of the last few days getting to him. With Hamilton at the front of his mind, it was easy to understand how he'd made the mistake.

Sumo drove them to the spot where they'd seen the whale shark. He reprogrammed the autopilot, putting them back on their course of ever-decreasing squares. The first lap of the morning took less than half an hour. The circumference of their circuits was shortening as they closed in on the parallel reefs. Strachan was excited.

He was optimistic. The search was reaching its climax. The parallel reefs were hiding something. He was sure of it.

He left Sumo to monitor the Fishfinder and descended to the cockpit with KT to prepare their tanks. He figured that she might as well come with him on the first dive. He was keen to use up as much of her air as possible so that when it came to exploring the wreck itself he would be on his own. Pili had offered to help with the equipment, but Strachan had told him no, thanks. Shleppy, meanwhile, had stowed the rods, reels, and lures in the lockers, and the cockpit was all theirs.

Strachan had brought two wetsuits with him. A 3mm shortie and a 5mm bodysuit. Given the warmth of the water, he opted for the former. It was black with a simple white logo on the chest. Not wanting to look like a German tourist, he avoided the garish colours that were popular among the students at The Coral Kraal. He was relieved to see that KT's was equally modest. Like much of her clothing it was by O'Neill. Black, with blue chevrons on the shoulders. It looked warm and well-worn. Further evidence that she was an experienced diver.

Strachan had bought a new BCD a couple of years ago. BCD stood for Buoyancy Control Device: the inflatable jacket that held the tank. The pockets of his were full. An underwater slate to write on, a pocket torch, a pair of gloves. On the other side, a piece of cord, an inflatable buoy, and a small Tupperware box of breadcrumbs. He replenished the breadcrumbs regularly. More than once they'd encouraged bashful subjects to stick around.

They were closing in on the reefs. They sailed past the channel between them. Sumo accelerated to cut across the faster water. The reef walls created a natural flume, and the water rushed down it like a flash flood. The draw was phenomenal. The big diesel engines growled. Sumo called Strachan back up to the flybridge as they came alongside the left-hand reef.

The depth gauge showed that it fell away steeply from fifteen metres to over a kilometre down. The seabed was as rugged as Tioman's hills. What they were circling had certainly once been a volcano. They weren't far from the junction of the Asian and Australian continental plates, which had shifted over time, leaving a seabed that varied greatly in depth. Changes in depth meant changes in temperature, and Strachan reckoned their channel had a big old thermocline running right through it. It would make for a chilly dive. He decided to swap the shortie for the bodysuit.

'The channel's too dangerous. The current is too fast.' Sumo shook his head and spat over the rail.

Strachan's gaze followed where the skipper's outstretched arm was pointing. Waves rippled down the channel. It didn't look so bad. 'I think it'll be all right. She'll be fine if you keep her in the middle.'

'No. It's too shallow. The water's too fast.'

They hadn't come all this way to fall at the final hurdle, so Strachan told him: 'It'll be okay. You've got over a thousand horses.'

'Horsepower isn't the problem. Coral is the problem.'

'Come on, Sumo.' But the skipper wasn't budging, so Strachan tried another tack. 'We have to explore that channel. How much extra do you want?'

KT had joined them on the flybridge. She was listening intently, biding her time, waiting for the appropriate moment to take control of the conversation. She was welcome to it as far as Strachan was concerned. She had the better relationship with Sumo, and she also had more chance of persuading the old bull than he did.

'No extra money. We're not going. It's too dangerous.' Sumo jabbed Strachan hard in the chest with his index finger. Strachan rocked back. It felt like a punch. Sumo's face was flushed with anger. He brought the *Esprit Bleu* to a near-standstill. He wanted both hands free, in case his client pushed his luck.

Strachan didn't. It was a ridiculous situation. A stalemate. The look in Sumo's eye said hell would freeze over before he put his boat down that channel.

He was right, of course. If it was Strachan's boat he'd probably have refused as well. Coral was sharp. Some of it lay as shallow as two metres below the surface. Whether they went with the current or against it, they would have to motor at a steady speed to ensure they had sufficient traction against the flow. The deepest part of the channel was sixty metres. The depth of the surrounding seas was several thousand. The water rushed down the flume at around twelve knots an hour. If they went any slower than that, the boat would career sideways. Dodging coral under those conditions would be risky as hell.

And for the same reason Strachan realised now that a dive was unlikely to work either. Underwater currents kill more divers than anything else. Three or four people die in Lake Geneva every year. There the flow of the Rhône is as gentle as a Sunday stroll. Here it was like an Olympic sprint. This was a prime spot for a fatality. The current would drown him in minutes. Once underwater he might never come up, except perhaps in Peru; his half-eaten body, bloated and rotting.

He announced his conclusion to the others, but suggested there were still grounds for optimism. The very fact that it was such a difficult location convinced him that the channel harboured his grandfather's secret. The reef's outer walls would have been visited many times, but no one would have been crazy enough to dive the channel itself. If there *was* a wreck down there, it might not have been discovered.

An idea was already forming at the back of Strachan's mind. 'Sumo, have you got any other sonar equipment on board?'

Sumo patted the Fishfinder with his huge brown paw. 'This is the best there is.'

'Yeah, I'm sure it is. But I need another one. Do you have a loose one? One that isn't attached to the bottom of your boat?'

Sumo looked at Strachan as if he had spat in his food. Then his eyes disappeared into the folds of his face as he smiled. 'Of course. Sumo has everything.' He growled a command to Shleppy. Two minutes later his fat little nephew reappeared with a white plastic briefcase. He laid the case flat on the deck. In the middle, slotted into two Styrofoam grooves, were a small sonar and a hand-held computer. A length of hose was coiled round the edge of the case. Shleppy assembled the parts quickly. The sonar was attached to one end of the hose. The computer was plugged into the other.

'What's that?' KT asked.

'Sonar. Sound Navigation and Ranging.' Sumo stumbled over the words with his heavy accent. 'Normally we attach it to a buoy, and drag it behind a boat. Like the one we saw yesterday.'

'A towed array,' Strachan said. 'Perfect.'

It was just what they needed. Submarines used bigger versions to hunt for enemy vessels. The sonar emits an ultrasonic pulse. Then it listens. The pulse reflects off large objects, and in this instance the computer would register the signal. In Sumo's case, the large object would be a black marlin, sailfish or swordfish. In Strachan's, it would be his grandfather's wreck.

'What's its range?' he asked.

'Fifty metres.'

Strachan glanced at the channel. It was as long as a sprint track, and three times as wide. They would have to make several runs.

'Sumo, I want you to drop us at the entrance to the channel. We'll float down it in our BCDs. We'll trawl the sonar behind us. If there's anything there, it'll pick it up.'

The others looked at him as though he'd lost the plot. Strachan didn't care. This just might work. In the absence of any better ideas, there was nothing to lose. 'Once we get caught in the current, drive round the outer side of the reef. Pick us up at the other end. We should slow down about fifty yards from the exit. Wait for us there and throw us a line as we come past.'

He didn't stick around to discuss it. He slid down the ladder to the cockpit. His BCD was waiting on one of the benches. He slipped it over his shoulders and tightened the straps. He blew in the valve. KT decided it was worth a shot, and he watched as her shapely legs made their way down the ladder. She joined him in the cockpit. She passed him the sonar and suited up. Sumo swung the *Esprit Bleu* towards the channel.

Game on.

43

As they drew nearer, Sumo threw the boat through a hundred and eighty degrees. He backed towards the fast water. The current bit, and he fought to maintain her on a straight line. Strachan could see him spinning the wheel. The further they drifted, the more power he sent to the engines. They crawled backwards an inch at a time.

'Go! Go! Go!' Sumo bellowed the command.

Holding hands, Strachan and KT ran across the cockpit. They didn't bother opening the gate – they just jumped over the stern rail. Sumo opened the throttles while they were still in the air. The engines gave it everything they had. Strachan and KT surfaced in a cloud of diesel fumes but they weren't in it for long. Strachan barely had time to let the sonar drop below him before they were swept away by the current.

KT loved it. She shrieked with delight. She spun circles, and splashed Strachan's face. The tide was on its way out. They raced towards the open ocean at twelve knots an hour. He caught her, and held her hand but his gaze never left the computer. Sumo had dropped them on the left-hand side of the channel. Already they were halfway down it. The sonar emitted pulses in a fifty-metre arc. Three evenly spaced journeys would be enough.

A minute later they were spat out into slacker water.

The sonar had registered nothing, but it was impossible to be down after an experience like that. They exchanged high-fives with the crew once they were reunited with the boat.

'Anything?' Shleppy asked, as Strachan collapsed into the fighting chair.

'No,' he said. 'Nothing.'

'Try again?'

'Try again.'

Shleppy rushed up to the flybridge to give Sumo the news. Strachan yelled at him to take his time. He lit a cigarette and drank a glass of iced tea. Ten minutes later they were ready to go again.

This time Sumo dropped them in the middle. The water was slightly faster here, and he didn't wait so long before ordering them over the stern. They experienced the same elation as the current caught them. They accelerated, hurtling down the channel like flotsam.

The *Esprit Bleu* kept pace with them on the other side of the reef wall. Strachan kept his eyes fixed on the computer. Suppose they did find something? What then? Sumo was adamant that he wasn't going to bring the boat in. It was a significant problem, but there was no choice but to cross that bridge when they came to it. But on the second run, as on the first, they did not.

Tired and disappointed, they opted for a longer rest to regain their strength. After a late lunch and a siesta they repeated the ride for a third and final time. They went down the right-hand side of the channel. It was slower this time. The tide was turning, and since it was on its way in they started at the other end. By now the novelty was wearing thin, and Strachan was desperate for the sonar to sound.

Gliding towards Kerkulla Ketam, he realised that the channel was directly opposite a headland. He recognised it from the map. It was called Dragon Point, and now he could see why. The boulders emerged from the sea in a long line. They grew gradually denser as they crept up the beach. The effect from distance was of a lizard's tail. As the rocks increased in number, it was possible to make out a body and head. It was unmistakable.

Suddenly Strachan understood how his grandfather had been able to be so exact with his coordinates. If the ship had sunk in the channel, it would have gone down opposite Dragon Point. He concentrated on the computer, and willed it to find his ship.

It didn't.

They sat turning circles in their BCDs while they waited for the *Esprit Bleu* to pick them up. They exchanged dark looks. Neither of them spoke. Sensing this wasn't a good time to try and cheer Strachan up, KT did the sensible thing. She closed her eyes to enjoy the sun on her face.

Exhausted, they clambered back up the steps into the cockpit. Shleppy took the sonar, and returned with green tea and chunks of coconut. The moon had risen. There were only two hours of daylight left. Strachan sat in the cockpit, wondering what to do next. The boat was chartered for another full day. There wasn't much point in sticking around. If they left tonight they'd save themselves a significant amount of cash. The sonar had found nothing. Three passes down the channel had proved that there was nothing there. The site that had promised so much had delivered zilch. The whole trip was beginning to feel like a total waste of time.

Strachan would have been better off saving his money. He would have been better off getting on with his photography. Instead he'd embarked on a wild-goose chase. There was no wreck. No treasure. No pot of gold at the end of the rainbow. Just a lethal channel of sand

and brine. Its emptiness filled his soul. His last hope of setting up his Caribbean safari had vanished without trace.

Like everything on board, Sumo's hand-held sonar was in good working condition. There was no chance it hadn't been working properly. If there was something large lying in that channel, the sonar would've detected it. Similarly, it seemed unlikely that his grandfather had made a mistake. Hamilton had confirmed that the ship had sunk somewhere off the coast of Malaysia, and Strachan couldn't imagine his grandfather screwing up.

Strachan remembered the book on Molly's shelf. *Wrecks of the Second World War*. Perhaps if he'd consulted it he would've discovered that the wreck had been discovered and salvaged years ago. It was certainly possible. The Japanese and British governments would have known about the ship's disappearance. Both would have been as keen to find it as he was. British Intelligence would have questioned his grandfather.

Had his grandfather told them where it was? Highly unlikely, Strachan decided. Why bother to make the cuff links? Why bother with the riddle if the game was already up? No, Strachan figured his grandfather had convinced his superiors that he didn't know where the ship was. It would have been easy. *'It was dark, sir. I drifted for miles before I was washed up. I couldn't say, sir. There was an island, but it was all on its own.'*

There had to be another explanation. Maybe the coordinates didn't record the site of the wreck? Maybe they commemorated some other event in his grand-father's past? Maybe the coordinates recorded the site correctly, but it was something other than a wreck he was supposed to be looking for? Maybe they weren't geographic coordinates at all, but rather some other code he'd utterly failed to spot?

Utterly failed. The words thudded into Strachan like bullets.

Slowly it sank in. He'd screwed up. His solution to the riddle was elegant but wrong. He was back to square one. He would have to start again. He would have to dissect the rhyme again, line by bloody line.

Strachan lit a cigarette. He didn't know what else to do. For half an hour he just sat there and smoked. Had he not been so preoccupied, the sound of Pili Parang using the VHF radio might have struck him as odd.

44

Strachan sat there brooding.

KT walked out from the main cabin. She wore a simple blue sarong. The thin material caught in the breeze and flapped against her leg like a flag on a pole. She tightened the tuck, giving him a glimpse of her impossibly slender legs. His heart skipped a beat. She'd never looked more beautiful.

KT fascinated him. Even allowing for the fact that she might be on the rebound from Mike, she still seemed perfectly relaxed around Strachan. Like she had nothing to hide and nothing to prove. A woman entirely at ease in her skin. She was delicate yet strong. Her default setting was feisty, but she could also act soft and demure. Looking at her now, he felt he'd known her all his life.

The last two days had brought them closer together. Strachan liked the direction in which things were now going, but having been reprimanded for his initial behaviour he was damned if he was going to make the first move. He had smiled at her enough to convey the message that contrary to his initial claim she absolutely *was* his type, and she had responded by becoming increasingly bold. When she sat down next to him their thighs touched, and neither made any effort to move away.

They'd stayed up late last night and talked about Curaçao. Strachan told her about his plan for a simple shack on the beach at St Michiel's Bay. His plan for a boat and a photographic safari business around Aruba and Bonaire. KT didn't know yet about Molly Newchris or his ban, and for a while he pretended none of it had happened. He didn't want to spoil the evening.

'Cheer up, Lancelot. Let's at least get a dive in.' It was four o'clock in the afternoon of the second day. So far they'd spent nearly a thousand bucks and hadn't even donned a tank. She had a point, Strachan realised. It would do him good and help him relax.

He called up to Sumo and asked him to bring them in on the outer shoulder of the left-hand reef, on the safe side of the channel wall. He peered over the rail. The reef sloped away steeply. It would make an interesting dive. Strachan didn't want the boat dropping anchor and damaging the corals so he instructed Sumo to follow their bubbles. They would drift along twenty metres below the surface. Forty minutes would be plenty.

Still thoroughly pissed off, he suited up and stepped through the stern gate. KT, as usual, was one step ahead.

They followed the reef down. It was a stunning dive. Visibility was close on thirty-five metres. The corals grew thick. The seabed was littered with starfish, sea cucumbers and empty conch shells. Shoals of butterfly fish surrounded them like falling leaves. A pipefish sheltered in a shoal of translucent fry. Away from the reef slope, larger shapes flashed silver, then melted into the shadows.

It was silent except for the sound of their breathing. Strachan felt himself relaxing. No one here gave a shit about his predicament. Inheritances, accusations of date rape, *National Geographic* editors, deceitful godfathers and Interpol inspectors were all meaningless in this under-water Eden. The reef was doing its best to lift his spirits. If he gave it another few minutes, it just might work.

An octopus shot past using invisible jet-propulsion. Strachan stuck out a hand to touch it, and it darted away to a boulder field, ten metres below. Eager to see it again, KT finned towards the rocks. Strachan followed, buoyed by the excitement in her eyes.

The octopus was hiding in the boulders so Strachan retrieved his torch from the pouch on his BCD. The rocks covered an area the size of a football field. At some stage in the last hundred years there had been a landslide here as the ocean floor stirred in its sleep. He had his camera ready in his other hand. Octopi have vibrant hues in their skin, and they make colourful subjects. Strachan peered into the fissure. The torch's beam made little headway into the black, so he pushed his hand in the hole to encourage the octopus to reappear.

Even by Strachan's impulsive standards it was a silly thing to do. Terrified, the octopus released a cloud of blank ink before shooting past him, jamming his hand against the side of the rock and forcing him to drop the torch. *Ungrateful sod,* he thought. *I could have made you famous.*

Strachan put his hand back in the hole. He felt nothing. He began to work the boulder loose in the hope of retrieving the torch. The boulder was the size of a beach ball. It took all his strength to shift it. Eventually it started to wobble, and the coral cementing it to its neighbours began to crack. He wasn't setting KT a good example, but it was an expensive torch and he was damned if he was going to leave it there. Not with the *National Geographic* contract in such a perilous state. Verhoeven had almost certainly introduced himself to McCauley Gilchrist by now. Strachan's future income, not to mention his reputation, would be hanging by a thread.

KT tapped him on the shoulder and wagged her

finger at him. Strachan bristled. He'd done more than his fair share of conservation. He didn't need a lecture to know that damaging the reef was wrong. In the meantime, the lost torch was threatening to damage his wallet. Besides, if it wasn't for his pictures, people wouldn't know what the hell to conserve anyway. He'd earned the right to move a boulder or two. There was no way of explaining all this to KT, so he scrawled the words *Just help me* on the slate.

She didn't.

Not that it mattered. The boulder finally ceased its resistance. It came loose in a swirl of coral sand. Things are much lighter underwater and once Strachan had it rocking, he was able to topple it down the landslide. It accelerated away, charging down the scree like a loose toboggan, and disappeared into the void. Neither of them was prepared for what they discovered in its place.

Dive instructors call them Closed Overhead Environments. Strachan called them caves.

45

It was like rolling away the stone from the entrance to a tomb. A gaping black hole had opened below them. They stared at it. Crumbs of dislodged coral fell like snowflakes into the abyss. Strachan and KT looked from the hole to each other. From each other back to the hole.

There was no sign of Strachan's torch. It had dropped so deep that its light was no longer visible. Evidently the bottom was a long way down. It was as though they'd lifted a manhole cover and discovered the entrance to the old volcano. Strachan rubbed the slate clean, and wrote KT another message.

New torch please. In my bag. Tie and drop on weight belt. Will be up in 5.

She gave him a look that said she wasn't there to run errands, so he added a few kisses and flashed her his best spaniel eyes. She grabbed the slate from his hand and printed her reply.

OK. DON'T BE LONG. DON'T GO IN CAVE.

He nodded. It was one of the first rules of diving. Don't go into confined spaces unless you're properly trained. Unless you have the right equipment. Unless you have at least one other person with you.

There was a second rule. It was equally important as far as he was concerned. Don't disobey KT Luker, unless you want to be severely punished. Already he could imagine her fury if she discovered he'd explored the cave without her. But his speculation was redundant anyway. He was in no hurry to get stuck again. All he wanted was more light, to see if the first torch was retrievable.

KT swam off. Strachan caught her ankle, hauling her back down. They'd been under for fifteen minutes. He pointed at his watch. He showed her five fingers, followed by three. Three minutes at five metres: the standard safety-stop, and an essential procedure after every dive over eighteen metres. Without it, the body can't release its nitrogen. An excess of nitrogen in the blood leads to decompression sickness, a.k.a. the bends.

KT rolled her eyes to tell him she hadn't forgotten. Then, with a flick of her fins that grazed Strachan's ear, she was off. He blew a few air-rings to chase her on her way, then sat down to wait. There was little life down there in the boulder field but if he looked hard enough he knew that he would find something worth photographing.

He lifted another, smaller rock, and found a juvenile stonefish, camouflaged on the seabed. It was perhaps four inches long, but even at that size it was still more deadly than yesterday's white-tip. Stonefish have thirteen dorsal spines along their back and each one is equipped with a venom gland, which releases its poison when pressure is applied. Strachan had no intention of applying any pressure. He set the exposure to f/16 and took three shots. With all the particles in the water the light wasn't great. His little stonefish wouldn't be making the big time. That was a pity because it was a very willing model. It was absolutely still and showed no reaction to the strobe.

Meanwhile the temptation to explore the cave swelled inside him. Like the stonefish, it was armed with a series of sharp needles. The needles pricked him. *Just a little look*. They pricked him again. A quick peek wouldn't hurt. He'd travelled halfway round the world to make this dive and here he was, farting around, playing it by the book.

KT would still be on her safety stop. The spare torch wouldn't be here for another few minutes. Besides, now that Strachan measured it, the gap was plenty wide enough. There was no danger of his tank snagging like it had on HaHa Reef. *Just a little look*. KT would never know.

He waited until he was sure that she was out of the water before positioning himself above the hole. Then he exhaled, and sank between the boulders.

It was like passing through to another world. There was just enough light from the hole for him to make out the roof of a vast chamber. It sloped away on all sides: the cupola of a coral cathedral. Deprived of the sun's rays, the water was several degrees colder. For the same reason it was wonderfully clear. Shielded from sunlight, there'd been no chance for algae or plankton to grow. It was like diving in liquid crystal.

Responsible divers use the law of thirds. One third of your tank to get where you're going; one third to get back; one third left over for emergencies. Strachan had two-thirds of his air left, and he reckoned that was plenty. Air consumption is determined by several factors. Technique and lung capacity are two of them. Fear, cold and depth are the others. Strachan wasn't worried about the first two; it was the next three that were the problem. He would get through his air that much quicker. It really would have to be a quick look only.

He finned down, eager to see how deep the chamber

went. His heart pecked his chest. There was still no sign of his torch. He guessed that it had disappeared into the sand at the bottom. He was onto something here, he knew it. He checked his depth gauge. Forty metres. Forty-five. Above him the exit hole shone like a halo. He swam down the shaft of sunlight. It too was exploring the cave for the first time. Down he went, as though entering the cathedral's crypt.

As Strachan swam deeper, the sun's power faded. The beam eventually petered out at fifty metres. Undeterred, he pressed on into the black. He kept his fear in check by reassuring himself that he could find his way out. Any time he wanted, he could simply ascend until he found the beam of sunlight. It worked for another three metres. Then he got scared.

The cave wasn't just dark, it was black. Pitch black. Abandoned-mine-shaft black. He was in space. He was weightless. He was about as far removed from man's natural habitat as it was possible to be. His arms were outstretched in self-defence. He didn't know what against. He could have been inches from anything. From rocks or thermoclines. He could have been inches from teeth. He could have been swimming down a crevasse: a dead end with no room to turn around.

Strachan couldn't see his hand in front of him. Or for that matter, the dials on his SPG. He counted off the depth in his head. One metre for every kick of his fins. Fifty-three, fifty-four metres. Nothing. All around him solid black. He'd go to sixty metres.

For all he knew, he'd just discovered a canyon to rival the Mariana Trench. Lying off the south-west coast of Guam, the Mariana wasn't so far from here. It dropped to an estimated eleven thousand metres. Strachan reached fifty-seven. He had a way to go before he broke any records. Still black, still groping. Still his breathing, like gusts of wind in the night. The sound of his fear, his only reference.

The dark was absolute. He was taking far too many risks. Fifty-eight metres. They could come back with specialist equipment. Fifty-nine. Torches, flares. Sixty metres. Not least a decent wetsuit to keep him warm. Sixty-one. He was beginning to shiver. It was time to go. Sixty-two metres. The dive had been a partial success. He'd found an underwater chamber that merited further investigation. Sixty-three. No disgrace in calling it a day. Sixty-four. *Okay, enough.*

And then, at what Strachan estimated to be a depth of sixty-five metres, his hand struck something hard. His arm jarred at the shoulder. He wasn't finning hard, but the jolt came as a total surprise, and he recoiled in terror. He sucked on the regulator, his breathing as loud as that of Darth Vader on a ventilator.

When you stumble to the bathroom in the night, your hands are outstretched as a precaution only. If you bump into something, you know what it is. You swear, but you don't feel sick with adrenalin. You don't gasp for air as those these are your last breaths. You don't flail your arms to right yourself. Strachan did all of these things, and it cost him valuable air.

He groped in the dark with his fingers. There it was again. It was rough. A rock, perhaps. He had reached the bottom. He ran his hand over the surface for a third time. Now his heart turned back-flips inside him. Whatever was under his hand, it didn't feel natural. It seemed to go on for ever.

Strachan finned a couple of metres to his left, trailing his hand as he went. He had a pretty good idea what the surface was made of. It wasn't rock. He bunched his knuckles and knocked against it. The sound was eerily loud. A metallic clunk. It reverberated around the chamber's walls like the toll of a funeral bell. The object that he'd hit was a plate of steel.

A sense of elation surged through him as his imagination ran riot. He wanted to investigate further, but he was low on air. He had no light. Without light, further exploration was futile. He would have to go up. He was already on his way when he remembered his camera. When Strachan wasn't taking pictures, it was simply an extension of his body. He knew how to work it with his eyes shut. He knew how to work it in the dark.

He set the strobe to maximum brilliance. Pointing the camera along the length of steel, he pressed the shutter. The surrounding area was instantly flooded with brilliant white light. Lightning on a dark and stormy night.

The steel plate was enormous. It was covered in rust. Strachan could see the rivets that held it together. The plate was broad. It sloped away to his left, signalling that he hadn't yet reached the chamber floor. And then it was gone. The darkness returned. More impenetrable than before because now he'd lost what little night-vision he'd developed during his descent.

Strachan finned down to his left. He kept his hand on the plate as he followed it round. The curve grew increasingly convex, then came to an abrupt end. His hand closed round the lip of an edge. By now he was sure what it was. He steadied himself. He held the camera in front of him at arm's length and pressed the shutter again.

The chamber was illuminated in another explosion of white light. For a split second only. $1/2500^{th}$ of a second. But it was enough. Enough to confirm that his theory was right. Enough for him to know what it was that he had found. There, in the corner of his vision, thirty metres to his right. A snapshot of history. The twin barrels of an anti-aircraft cannon, rusting on the deck of a Japanese ship.

Ed Strachan had found his inheritance.

46

It took Pili Parang a shade over forty-five seconds to take the *Esprit Bleu*. With Strachan and the girl underwater, the numbers were instantly more manageable. The element of surprise and Sumo's revolver were all the help he needed.

He'd retrieved the revolver from the cockpit locker earlier in the day, and then had hidden it in the saloon so that he would be ready when the time came. He gave the divers ten minutes before he made his move. Once they'd descended deeper than eighteen metres he knew they would need a safety stop before they could return to the surface. That guaranteed him at least five minutes to prepare for their return.

Revenge is a dish best served cold, and Pili Parang was ravenous. His hatred for Strachan was chemical. It seeped through his blood like ink, turning it black. Ed Strachan. The man who had sold them out. The man responsible for Runi's death.

The lapidary had seen it with his own eyes, and sworn it on the life of his child. Pili had corresponded with him while he'd been in jail, making him tell the story over and over until he knew every detail. Until he could picture it as clearly as if he had been there himself.

A hot evening in downtown KL. A crowded bar. His brother Runi in a T-shirt and Levis, talking to Strachan, Anwar and two other couriers. They were drinking beer and eating *popiah*. Strachan left the bar and made a call on his cellphone. A minute later the police stormed the bar, entering via the fire exit at the rear. Strachan came back inside to check that his signal had been received. Then he'd turned and run like the coward he was. Runi put up a brave fight, Anwar said. He took out several policemen, but was eventually overpowered. The police had continued striking long after he was unconscious, and when they'd dragged him away he was as limp as a rag doll. Pili didn't receive the news until a few days later, by which time a High Court judge had authorised the switching off of his brother's life-support machine.

And Strachan was responsible.

Ed Strachan. A man Pili had thought he would never see again was now a man delivered to him by God. What other explanation could there be? Strachan had appeared from the other side of the world. He had come to Tioman and sought him out, claiming to be his friend. It was a gift. God wanted Pili to avenge his brother.

Pili had wanted to do it straight away but knew that it was better to wait. Strachan would beat him in a fair fight, but it was the *un*fair fight in which Pili excelled and, if he was patient, he would be in a strong position to engineer one. The chances of being caught were higher in a small island community. People would talk. People would ask difficult questions. So when he'd seen Strachan looking at the *Ariadne*, the idea of killing him at sea seemed beautiful in its logic. If he confronted Strachan on Tioman it would be over too quickly. His hatred had festered for ten years; it could fester another few days.

Once Pili knew that Strachan needed a boat, getting on board was easier than he anticipated. Revenge was a concept that the Japanese understood well, and

Wakahama had been swift to grant him leave. Meanwhile Sumo's love of US dollars was stronger than his dislike of unwanted guests. But even then Pili had waited, employing unknown reserves of restraint until he discovered what Strachan was up to. When he finally knew, there was no reason for the charade to continue. Pili knew the Kerkullas and, while he wasn't a diver, he had grown up among people who had fished these islands for years. There was no wreck here. Strachan's mission was a lost cause: an avarice-fuelled hallucination.

Part of Pili was disappointed. He had a grudging respect for Strachan's cavalier spirit. Briefly, and only briefly, he had been deceived by the *gwailo*'s boyish enthusiasm. He had allowed himself to believe that the trip might yield material opportunities beyond revenge. But now he knew what Strachan was doing, he let those beliefs float away on the rolling swell. There was no opportunity for gain, and that meant there was no reason to delay.

Pili smiled to himself as he set about his work. He wasn't sure where the idea had come from but it was a magnificent plan. His revenge would be visually spectacular. A two-course feast of retribution. There would be collateral damage along the way but that was acceptable, given the circumstances. He had known Sumo and Shleppy for many years, but they were from the mainland and only visited Tioman for the tourist season. They weren't friends; they were acquaintances. They were dispensable. Their lives meant little in the context of his revenge.

The giant skipper was up on the flybridge with his back turned. He heard Pili approach but addressed him without turning round. It was a mistake that would cost him dear. Pili felt vaguely absurd as he stood on the curved bench behind the captain's chair. It was the only way that he could make himself tall enough to deliver the knockout blow. The revolver's butt came down on the back of Sumo's head with massive force. Sumo collapsed obediently under it. He never made a sound. Now he lay sprawled over the dash, as inert and heavy as a game carcass. Pili grabbed him by the collar and dragged him off the dials. Then he set off to find Shleppy.

They met in the saloon. Shleppy was standing in the galley, dicing fish and preparing curry. He saw Pili with the revolver in his hand and knew instantly that this was a life-or-death situation. Pili was impressed by the boy's pluck. The fear in Shleppy's eyes lasted no more than a second before the eyes themselves narrowed and the instinct for survival kicked in. Pili saw Shleppy tighten his grip on the kitchen knife. Then he pulled the revolver's trigger.

The bullet caught Shleppy in the upper body, spinning him round so that he fell against the sink and slid to the floor on his stomach. Pili waited thirty seconds, the revolver now aimed at the boy's head. But, like his uncle, Shleppy never moved. And the pool of blood that seeped from under his left shoulder told Pili that there would be no need for a second shot.

His revenge was near now. The divers knew nothing. The boat was his. He would set fire to it later, making it look like an accident. A severed fuel pipe or a leaking gas cylinder in the galley – he hadn't decided which. There would be no evidence, and no inquiry. Afterwards he would take the life-raft back to the islands and wait for the *Fubuki* or its helicopter to pick him up. He'd radioed the Japanese yacht earlier to give his position and to tell Wakahama-san that he would be ready for collection after dark. Now there was only one thing left to do.

Pili returned to the flybridge and nudged the throttle

forward until he caught up with the divers. He eased back on the power and looked over the rail. Their bubbles were boiling to the surface at different intervals and in two different patches. Clearly Strachan and the girl were no longer together. One of them was on the way back up. Pili peered closer until he could make out a dark shape in the water. The girl was five metres deep, hovering in the lotus position as she idled through her safety stop. She was pretty, this one. Too bad for her that she was in the wrong place at the wrong time. He had no qualms about including her in his revenge. After all, he was only doing God's will.

Clutching the revolver in his fist, Pili hurried down the ladder to greet her arrival at the surface.

47

The ship was sitting on the seabed, enclosed in a tomb. There was only one explanation that Strachan could think of to account for his discovery.

This chamber must once have been a volcano's crater. Possibly a small fumarole on the side of a much larger mountain, which now formed the main slope down which they had dived. Over the ages the reef had grown across the crater. It had formed a thin coral crust, sealing the chamber shut. Hundreds, thousands, perhaps millions of years later, a Japanese ship stopped to collect a consignment of POWs from Kuantan. It set sail and ran into bad weather. The captain lost his way in the deteriorating conditions. In his haste to avoid the shallow channel between the two reefs he ploughed into their outer wall, and the coral pierced his hull.

Once breached the ship opened like a tin can. It filled with water. It sank down the reef slope until it reached the crust-covered crater. The crust caved in under its weight, and the chamber was reopened as the ship dropped through it like a stone.

Then, with the seal temporarily broken, the process had started again. The reef had grown back. In these waters it would have grown at a considerable rate. Twenty-six to twenty-seven degrees Celsius is the optimum temperature for coral growth. The sea here was spot on. Up to a metre's growth a year would be possible under those conditions. Sixty-three years was plenty of time for the ocean to hide its prize. The seabed had swallowed its prey like a giant clam, sealing itself shut from prying eyes. The wreck had lain there undiscovered since 1942. Invisible to the human eye, undetectable by sonar. Its location known only to its sole survivor.

But not any more.

Strachan could imagine the scene as panic engulfed the ship. In the confusion, his grandfather had escaped his cell. Where others had drowned, Arthur Strachan had swum or drifted the two miles to shore. There he had taken a bearing on the site of the wreck, using the headland of Dragon Point as a reference. He spoke Japanese, so he had known there was something valuable on board. Later, perhaps back in England after the war had ended, he had consulted a map of the South China Sea. He had identified the Kerkullas and Dragon Point. Then, to safeguard his secret, he had recorded the wreck's location in two silver cuff links, an ancient statue and a doctored nursery rhyme.

Whatever was on board would be more valuable in sixty years' time. Strachan still hadn't fully figured that part out, but the verse on the stolen postcard was beginning to make more sense.

> Worth their weight in silver
> Until they're sixty years old.
> Then put the two together
> They'll be worth their weight in gold.

That was why his grandfather and father had not made any effort to retrieve the bounty themselves. They were guardians of the secret but ultimately excluded from it.

And so the cuff links had come to him. One at first. Then, like a magnet, the other had sought its mate, the two chunks of metal attracting each other over time and space. Yin and yang. Left and right. Latitude and longitude.

Not knowing what else to do at such a poignant moment, Strachan took the regulator from his mouth. He tugged the chain on his neck from under his wetsuit, and kissed each of the cuff links in turn. Then he said '*Thanks, Gramps,*' and watched as the bubbles carried his words towards the surface. Expressing his gratitude seemed the least he could do so he thanked his father as well. Soon he was giggling on his mouthpiece.

Strachan recognised the symptoms immediately: nitrogen narcosis, a sure sign that it was time to go. The diving physiologists he had spoken to still weren't clear what caused this sense of euphoria but the consensus of opinion was that the nitrogen in the blood dissolves and turns into a fatty substance that coats the nerves. The fat then interferes with the transmission of nerve impulses. It isn't harmful in itself but it can lead you to do dangerous and erratic things. Like talking to dead relatives when you should be on your way up.

He flashed the strobe again, and checked his air. He was down to 70 bar. The needle was nudging the red. It was time to go. They could return in a few days' time. With torches, flares, and adrenalin glands the size of footballs. He finned back out from the deck and kicked for the shaft of sunlight.

Strachan went slowly, mindful to conserve air. Diving to sixty-five metres was a hell of a risk on a conventional mixture of oxygen and air. He would need several decompression stops on the way up. He would have been better off with a light breathing mixture, where the nitrogen was replaced with helium or hydrogen. He made a note to read up on which would be best for his next visit.

His first stop was a natural one. Thirty-five metres: back at the entrance to the cave on the shoulder of the reef. He stayed there for ten minutes. It wasn't boring because there was work to do. Like finding debris with which to conceal the entrance.

It was unlikely that anyone would be diving this spot before they returned, but Strachan was damned if he was even going to risk letting anyone else in on the game. The original boulder had run away down the slope so he searched around the surrounding reef until he found a giant clam shell. He laid it over the gap like a manhole cover. Then he camouflaged it with clumps of dead coral, small rocks, and handfuls of sand. By the time he'd finished, it was well concealed. He complimented himself. It looked pretty authentic.

He was about to ascend when he spotted the stonefish again. It still hadn't moved. When Strachan peered closer, he understood why. Something silver was lodged in one of its gills. It might have been a piece of tin foil or the ring-pull from a soda can. Either way, it looked man-made, and if it stayed there much longer it was going to kill the fish before it had a chance to grow up. Strachan shook his head in disbelief. Even in a location as remote as the Kerkullas, man's litter was still polluting the environment.

It would be a delicate operation involving thick gloves and tweezers, but the thought of leaving the stonefish to die never entered Strachan's mind. He pulled the Tupperware box from his pocket, emptied the breadcrumbs and delicately scooped the stonefish inside, mindful not to touch it. He added a few small stones to make it feel at home before closing the lid. There was little room for the stonefish to move, but it had sufficient water to keep it alive while he performed the operation back on the boat. With hands as steady and gentle as a surgeon's, he replaced the box in his pocket.

Only when he'd finished did Strachan realise that KT's weight-belt and the second torch were nowhere to be seen.

48

The hull of the *Esprit Bleu* was directly above Strachan. The weight-belt should have been close. He finned back and forth several times, combing the area for signs of the webbing. KT hadn't made the drop.

Not that it mattered. Down in that cave he needed slow-burning flares, not battery-operated torches. He thought no more of it as he idled through the next safety stop: another ten minutes at ten metres. The seconds dragged like years. Seven minutes in, he heard a dull thud from the boat above. Sound travels particularly well through water which is why sea mammals use it to communicate. A depth charge detonated in Australia can be heard by sonar in Bermuda. That thump hadn't been a depth charge but it still sounded like trouble. Sumo ran a tight ship. Things wouldn't just fall over and damage his beautiful decks. Strachan cut the stop short and hurried up to five metres.

It was warmer there. Another minute passed. Then another. Two or three more and he could get the hell up there and see what was happening. It was probably nothing, but the absence of the weight-belt and the bump on deck were a worrying combination. At least there was still only one hull above him, so Strachan knew that they hadn't received any unwelcome visitors.

He ran through a list of shark species to check that he wasn't suffering from decompression sickness or nitrogen narcosis. There are over three hundred and fifty species of shark, and Strachan reckoned he could name seventy. He had probably photographed forty-five. Since they were in the right part of the world, he started with the *Sphyrnidae*. Great hammerhead, scalloped hammerhead, smooth hammerhead, bonnethead. The names were coming fast. *Lamnidae* next. Great white, short-fin mako, long-fin mako, salmon shark, basking shark.

Strachan felt good. His brain appeared to be working fine. He decided to push himself with the *Carcharhindidae*. There were about fifty of them. He ought to get at least twenty-five. Silky shark, tiger shark, bull, oceanic white-tip, dusky, nervous, his old friend from Curaçao: the Caribbean reef shark. Suddenly the valve on his regulator clicked. He sucked again. Nothing. Ready or not, it was time to go. He was out of air. He let the regulator fall from his mouth. He exhaled and rose the last few metres to where sea met sky. If he was going to get them, the bends wouldn't be long in coming.

Strachan's head broke the surface. He squinted in the sunlight as he removed his mask. He wiped the back of his hand across his eyes to clear them of salt. Instantly he wished that he hadn't.

The first thing he saw was Sumo's revolver. It was pointing at his face. Only it wasn't Sumo who was holding it, it was Pili Parang. And Pili seemed very pleased to see him.

There's a first time for everything, and this was the first time that Strachan had seen a gun pointed at him. He didn't like it. He didn't like it one little bit. He didn't know much about guns, but he knew something. He knew enough to know that the thing in Pili's hand would take his head off. Its barrel was as black as the cave from which he'd just ascended.

His mind whirred. What the hell was going on? There was no way this could be about the inheritance. Like the other six billion people on the planet, Pili had no idea that Strachan had just discovered the wreck. It didn't make sense. Pili was a friend. He was probably just messing about. A bit of cheap one-upmanship to remind Strachan who was boss. But even as he thought it through, Strachan knew it was wishful thinking. His senses came alive with fear. Everything was suddenly clearer. The shapes, sounds and colours were sharper. The water sloshing over his shoulders; the sunlight dancing on the waves; the gentle swell of the ocean tugging at his fins.

The air in his BCD had inflated during his ascent, and there he was, floating on the surface, as easy a target as a barn door. He couldn't go anywhere. He couldn't do anything. His *Krav Maga* classes had taught him how to disarm an armed man on land, but they'd never covered doing it from five metres away in the sea. He was wearing a five-kilo weight-belt. Had he been able to ditch the BCD he would have sunk like a stone, but removing it required undoing three plastic clips and two Velcro straps. Pili would realise what Strachan was doing long before he could do it. So instead he bobbed on the water, and let Pili take his shot.

It came soon enough.

Pili wasn't much of a talker. There were no histrionics. No melodramatic speeches. He just got on with it. He closed one eye as he aimed, and Strachan saw the muscles in his forearm tighten.

There was a deafening roar in Strachan's ears. He was vaguely aware of Pili's forearm being thrown up by the recoil. And then the world went black.

Pili Parang let out a shriek of triumph: a high-pitched squeal that started somewhere deep inside his chest and scythed through the surrounding air. Everything was going to plan. Runi was watching. Runi was pleased.

Strachan's head rang with white noise. He had lost all feeling in his hands and feet. For a while he lolled on the swell, unsure if he was alive or dead. Then tiny pinpricks of light appeared in the black of his vision, telling him that it was time to find out. He opened his eyes. He was expecting to see a guy in white robes, standing outside some pearly gates. But the man he saw wasn't St Peter. He was the devil. And he was laughing.

'That was close, Ed. Maybe I try again?' Pili thought this was the funniest thing he'd ever seen. His mortal enemy entirely at his mercy. Ed Strachan, a sitting duck.

Strachan's head hurt as Pili came into focus. He raised his hand to investigate, and it came away red. The bullet had smashed into his tank. A splinter of red-hot metal had cut a furrow through his scalp. Strachan didn't know what the effects of firing a bullet into a tank of compressed air were, but he was glad his had been empty.

'Come now, Ed. You are just in time for Pili's party. You are guest of honour.' The gun was still trained on Strachan's face but he noticed that Pili was relaxing his grip. He hadn't been trying to kill him after all. Pili had something up his sleeve. And whatever it was, it was going to hurt like hell.

'What the hell's going on?' Strachan was groggy from the explosion. He was tired from the dive. He swam to the submerged ladder hanging from the stern. Pili kept the gun aimed at his face all the way. Strachan took his fins off, and threw them at the man on the boat. He knew that Pili wasn't going to kill him yet. It was a petulant gesture, but it made him feel better. What the hell *was* going on?

Pili dodged the fins and laughed. Then he fired a

round into the water by Strachan's hip. It left a white trail like a miniature torpedo before striking the reef below. Strachan felt the pressure wave as it displaced the water.

He hauled himself up the ladder and stopped on the top rung, rooted to the spot in anger and worry. KT lay face down on the cockpit floor. Her hands were bound with rope. The rope had been tied to a length of fishing line, which snaked away across the deck to one of the benches where it coiled itself around the spindle of an enormous reel. It looked like the strongest in Sumo's locker. Pili had stuffed her mouth with a handkerchief. Sensibly, she wasn't fighting the gag. She was conserving her strength for whatever was coming. There was no sign of either Sumo or Shleppy. That was bad news. Strachan figured that they were almost certainly dead. It was Pili's boat to do with as he pleased.

'Pili, you miserable gimp.' There was no point being nice to him. Strachan knew him better than that. 'What the hell are you doing?' He just had time to pull the Tupperware box from his BCD pocket and place it in the shade where the stonefish wouldn't overheat. Then Pili shoved him forward. He tripped over KT and landed on the deck in a heap. 'Pili, tell me, for Christ's sake – what's going on?'

But all he got was Pili stamping on his neck and telling him to shut up. He kept his foot there, pinning Strachan to the deck as he spoke. His voice became higher-pitched. He squealed as his excitement increased. 'I have waited a long time for this, Ed. I didn't think I would ever get the chance. But I swore to myself that if I ever saw you again I would kill you.'

'Why? What did I do?'

'What did you do? Still you pretend? You come to my country; you come to my island and you ask for me because I'm your friend. You smile at me and you ask me where my brother is.'

Strachan groaned. *Runi*. This was about Runi. It had to be.

'I'm sorry about Runi. Sumo told me what happened. I was going to say something.' Strachan looked up from the deck. Pili was pointing at the fighting chair with the barrel of the gun. Strachan realised that it wasn't pointing at his head. He considered making a move, but the idea fled as quickly as it appeared. Pili was on his feet while he was still supine. Pili was fast and agile while he still had a twenty-six-pound Pressed Steel HP-80 tank on his back.

'If you try anything, Ed, I will shoot the girl's kneecaps. Now get up, and get in the chair.'

Pili had been reading his thoughts, so Strachan did as he was told. He tried to catch KT's eye. He wanted to reassure her. He didn't know how. The skin around her eyes creased in a brave attempt at a smile. He heaved off his tank and dumped it on the deck. Then it went dark again as Pili hit him on the head with the butt of the gun.

49

Strachan came round with a headache. A belter. A big grey slab of pain. A team of tunnel workers was assaulting his frontal lobe, armed with an arsenal of drills, hammers and chisels.

KT was still on the deck at his feet. She'd been pushed up against the side of the boat. He could hear Pili somewhere behind him, fetching something from the rod locker. Strachan tried to move his hand to see if the wound on his head had stopped bleeding. It wouldn't budge. Pili had bound him to the chair. For good measure he had also strapped him into the fishing harness. The leather straps pressed on his shoulders, and the chrome buckles bit into his flesh like the teeth of that damned trigger fish. Strachan struggled against the bindings, straining like a maniac in a straitjacket. There was no give. He sank back, relaxing his muscles and conserving strength that he might need later.

Pili appeared in front of him. He held a bait knife in one hand and the pistol in the other. He pressed the gun into one of Strachan's eyes. Strachan tried to close it to protect the retina, but he was too late. The pain was intense. He had experienced both ends of what that pistol had to offer, and he loathed the sight of it.

'I saved you the best seat, Ed.' Pili laughed his nasal little laugh. He was pleased with his joke. Then he turned his attention to KT. He bent down, placed the bait knife on the deck and took a handful of her hair, using it to hoist her to her feet. She didn't need the encouragement. She sprang up like an impala, kicking at his crotch with her leg. She was a little off but still struck his inner thigh. Not for the first time, Strachan marvelled at her spirit.

Pili was less impressed. He brandished the knife in her face and then rewarded her with a backhand slap to the mouth. Strachan strained against the straps. If there was one thing he hated, it was violence against women. He had seen KT slapped once already but this time he was powerless to intervene. He felt sick with anger. There was blood on her teeth.

Her failed attack was a wake-up call. Pili worked quickly now. He walked to the bench and picked up the fishing reel. Strachan watched in horror as Pili disappeared behind him and fetched a rod. Then he attached the two together. Reel met rod with a resounding click. It sounded ominously loud. The afternoon was hot and still. The only other noise came from the waves lapping the hull. There was nothing Strachan could do except sit and watch. And wait. It was just as Pili had planned. Strachan was the one in the chair, but KT was going to be executed first. This was a nasty stunt, even by Pili Parang's standards. Strachan screamed at him to stop. 'Tell me why, Pili!'

'You killed my brother.'

'The police killed him. You know that.'

'Still you play your game with me.' Pili squatted down in front of Strachan so that their eyes were level. 'You were seen.'

'Doing what?' Strachan asked. 'By who?'

'Anwar saw you talking to Sergeant Hamid in Kota Besut.'

Strachan looked to the sky. He began to see where

this might be going. Sergeant Hamid had been a friend of Strachan's from up near the Perhentian Islands. Hamid's wife ran a T-shirt stall on the night market and Strachan had taken some pictures of the reef for her to scan onto her clothes. Anyone who saw them talking together could easily have arrived at the wrong conclusion.

'Two days later my brother was arrested,' Pili said. 'You were with him. You left to make a phone call. Then the police arrived. Don't deny it, Ed, or I will make her suffer even more.'

'So what happened to Runi?' Strachan took his captor's advice. He could plead until he was blue in the face but he had seen that look of Pili's before. The Malaysian's mind was made up. Nothing could change his conviction that Strachan was guilty. His best – and only – bet was to keep Pili talking.

Pili stood in front of him and slapped him round the face with his open hand, punctuating his words with his blows. 'They' – *whack!* – 'beat' – *whack!* – 'him' – *whack!* – 'to' – *whack!* – 'death.' *Whack! Whack! Whack!* Strachan's face bounced from side to side. He was barely conscious. He had the bitter taste of blood in his mouth.

Pili was getting increasingly excited. 'Now it is time for some fishing. We will try to attract that shark again.' He stooped and picked up the bait knife. It flashed silver in the sun as he drew it over KT's forearm. With her hands bound she could do nothing to stop him. When she jerked away the knife only cut deeper. Her blood spotted the deck.

Strachan exploded in the chair, fighting the straps until he felt a blood vessel rupture near his temple. Still the bindings held him tight.

Pili removed the gag from KT's mouth, then pushed her in the belly with his foot so that she toppled over the back of the boat. Strachan saw her open her mouth, but the only scream came from the reel. She submerged briefly before coming back up to break the surface, coughing and gasping for air. The *Esprit Bleu* drifted on the swell. Pili allowed thirty metres of line to play out behind the stern. Then he locked it so that no more could escape. He placed the rod's stock in the clasp on the harness, right on Strachan's chest. So near, yet so far. If only Strachan could get his hands on it he could let out more line to ease the pressure on KT's wrists.

She had drifted away from the big propellers. That at least was something. They would have chewed her to pieces like a soft toy. She was treading water. Her legs would be working double-time to compensate for her inability to use her arms. Strachan's mind did likewise. He struggled to think of a plan. 'Pace yourself, KT. When the boat starts to move, roll onto your back.' That was as far as he got before Pili punched him. His knuckles caught Strachan in the corner of the eye. It stung like hell.

Then, suddenly, Pili was gone. Strachan heard his feet on the ladder to the flybridge. His hurried steps made the rungs hum. A few seconds later he revved the engines and the boat lurched forward. The line slithered like an eel, then snapped tight as the slack disappeared. Immediately KT was yanked forward. She screamed but was cut short as her mouth filled with water. She started to choke.

Pili accelerated again. He was experimenting with the throttle, seeking the correct pace. Each time KT was tugged under. The boat didn't yet have the power to pull her up. On the fourth attempt he found the speed he wanted. KT began skimming the waves like a fallen water-skier, refusing to let go of the rope. The pressure on her wrists must have been unbearable. Strachan watched as she flipped on her back and tried to keep her head out of the waves. She was bleeding fast. She would last no more than a couple of minutes. Either she would pass out with pain or she would drown.

The rod was taking the strain. It arched in a perfect parabolic curve. It was the thickest of the five, capable of holding Tom Selleck's three-metre marlin. Marlin can weigh up to 1,400 lbs, so it wasn't going to break under the weight of KT's delicate frame. Strachan had to cut the line. He had to knock the rod free from its clasp. Where were Sumo and Shleppy? He'd seen neither of them since surfacing. He figured that they were lying downstairs with their brains blown out. He looked to the sky again. It was crystal. So clear that even at five o'clock the first stars were visible. A hell of a day to die.

KT was tiring fast. Already her efforts to stay on her back were weakening. She was drowning. There was nothing Strachan could do except watch. Only he had to do *something*. 'Pili! How much do you want?' he shouted at the top of his lungs. Pili didn't answer and Strachan guessed that his voice must have been lost in the wind. 'Pili! I'll pay you. Let the girl go.' He was concentrating on volume, doing his best to stay calm. If he showed Pili his fear it would only excite him to further atrocity. 'Pili! I have emeralds!'

'Emeralds?'

The Malaysian was right behind him, his breath hot and rancid on Strachan's neck. Strachan hadn't heard him come down the ladder. He must have switched the boat to autopilot because they were racing along at the same speed as before. KT had a minute at most. Her wrists would be bruised beyond recognition. And then there were the sharks.

'You have emeralds? I don't believe you.' But the

animation in Pili's voice said otherwise. It was an idea worth pursuing.

'I've found the wreck, Pili. There are emeralds on board. You can have them all if you let her go.'

'All the stones in the world would not be enough. You cannot buy back my brother, Strachan.' Pili punched him in the back of the head. 'And you cannot buy back your American bitch.'

Strachan winced. They didn't have time for this. Thirty metres off the stern KT was dying. 'There's some over there. Emeralds, Pili. In the box.' He didn't know where the plan came from. It materialised out of nowhere, and he didn't like it one little bit. It was the mother of all long shots.

'The box?' Pili eyed him suspiciously. He had seen Strachan retrieve it from his pocket and place it on the bench in the shade. 'No tricks, Strachan. Otherwise I won't kill you quickly.'

'See for yourself, Pili. Feel how heavy it is. Emeralds, Pili. And there's a whole ship of them down there. Now let the girl go.'

That was all it took. Pili crossed the deck to where the Tupperware box sat on the bench. He put the knife down and nudged it with his hand. It barely rocked. Its contents were heavy. He picked it up and shook it. The pebbles on the bottom rattled encouragingly. Pili squinted in the sun. The box certainly sounded as though it might contain jewels. Maybe Strachan was telling the truth. Maybe there *was* a wreck down there. That would explain his temerity in returning to Tioman after all these years.

Ever wary, Pili turned to face his prisoner. He had his back to the box and the gun was still trained on Strachan's torso as he groped for the lid with his spare hand. Pili Parang knew Strachan better than most, and in not taking any risks he walked headlong into the trap. He removed the lid and tossed it overboard. He bent his knees slightly as his left hand disappeared inside the box.

50

The box leapt off the bench as Pili tried to withdraw his hand. The stonefish's spines had impaled themselves so deeply into his palm that he lifted the whole thing into the air. He struggled to shake it free. It only came loose when he swung it over his head and onto the rail. The box and the stonefish both fell over the side and into the sea.

In the same instant Strachan heard the saloon door slide open. Shleppy flashed past him with the Ocean Master dive knife in his fist. His left arm was bleeding at the shoulder. He was going for Pili, not the line. He had no chance. Pili still had several minutes before paralysis struck.

'The line!' Strachan yelled at him. 'Shleppy, cut the line!'

Shleppy stopped in his tracks as he considered this new option. With Pili approaching fast, he made a desperate lunge with the knife. The line was taut. It cut with a twang. KT's body sagged and settled into the sea.

Pili's left arm jerked spasmodically as though it was plugged into the mains. He could no longer maintain his grip on the revolver and it disappeared over the side. He screamed a piercing battle-cry and launched himself at Shleppy, flailing his arms wildly in an attempt to land a blow.

Waving his arm around was a big mistake. Stonefish

have multicomponent venom: neurotoxic, myotoxic, cardiotoxic and cytotoxic. The effect is comparable to being bitten by a cobra and a rattlesnake, before being stung by a box jellyfish and a scorpion, all at the same time. Any second now the venom would attack the nerve centres responsible for controlling Pili's respiration and heart action. He was pumping a large dose deep into his body. Down his arm and towards his heart. His arm ballooned in front of Strachan's eyes. All Shleppy had to do was stay away from him for another thirty seconds and the game would be up.

But in that time the distance between KT and the boat would grow. They were still making around fifteen knots. The gap widened with every second. Strachan could see her head and shoulders, but already it was impossible to distinguish her features. 'Don't fight him, Shleppy. Cut me loose.'

Pili approached from Strachan's left. Shleppy retreated on his right. Strachan sat in the chair between them, still vulnerable, still the target for Pili's revenge. But Shleppy had the knife, and Pili was going to deal with him first. He feinted one way and darted the other. Shleppy was equal to the task. Young and agile, he was too fast for the pain-racked devil who pursued him. Wide-eyed with fear, his adrenalin gave him an edge. He sprang away from Pili's blows like a mongoose baiting a snake.

'Shleppy! Cut me loose! KT's going to drown.'

Pili slowed as the venom hit home. His knees wobbled. He was losing control. He wore an expression of intense disappointment. Pain mixed with confusion and despair; as though he couldn't fathom his bad luck. Then, suddenly, he stopped. His body was packed with pain, and he doubled over and vomited on the deck. Shleppy didn't need telling twice. He skipped behind the chair and slipped the knife between Strachan's bound hands. It was razor-sharp. It went through the heavy line like a scalpel through silk. Strachan felt the blood seep back into his hands, just as it had when Groote had released the cuffs at Schiphol. He shook the line loose and released the buckles on his chest.

Pili had reached delirium. He swung at Strachan wildly, but his punches lacked power. Strachan weathered the blows until he'd set himself free. In his desperation Pili came for him one last time, screaming a blood-curdling shriek. He clawed for Strachan's face. Strachan spun round to protect his eyes and waited until he felt Pili's nails close on his throat. Then he drove his right elbow backwards with the force of a pneumatic drill. Strachan was taller than Pili by several inches and he caught him full in the face. Pili went down in a heap, landing in his own vomit.

Shleppy ran up the ladder to the flybridge, presumably to check on what was left of Sumo. Without thinking, Strachan picked Pili up and dropped him over the stern. The Malaysian fell through the water like a sandbag. Strachan didn't wait to see if he came back up. He followed Shleppy up the ladder.

Sumo lolled unconscious in his chair. Blood ran down his bald head as thick as yolk from a cracked egg, but the rise and fall of his chest told them that he was still alive. Strachan grabbed the wheel, opening the throttle in the same instant and swinging the *Esprit Bleu* in a tight arc. The autopilot disengaged. She came around as though on rails. KT was four hundred metres away. He pushed the rev counter into the red, and closed the gap in less than thirty seconds.

As they approached, Strachan feared the worst. KT had given up the struggle. She was floating on her back. He cursed himself for coming in too fast because now the bow wave splashed over her face. It caused her to splutter but at least that showed that she too was still alive.

Strachan grabbed the nearest life-ring and dived off the flybridge. He came up beside KT and forced the life-ring under the water so that it bobbed up in the small of her back. He called her name, told her it was over, and told her she was going to be okay. The sea still lapped at her lips. He put his hand under her head to raise her mouth. Then he noticed her hands.

Still bound at the wrist, they'd swollen to the size of grapefruit. She held them palm down against her stomach. The rope had burned her badly. Meanwhile the blood pumped from the wound in her arm, leaving a cloudy trail in the water behind her. It formed a thick slick that stretched away as far as he could see. She whimpered in pain.

KT was barely conscious. Strachan cleared the strands of hair from the corners of her mouth. She caught his eye, then smiled and passed out. Taken to within an inch of her life by pain and exhaustion, it was the best thing that she could have done. He towed her gently to the submersible steps and called for Shleppy, just as the first fin appeared like a thorn some fifty yards further down the blood slick.

51

Shleppy flew down into the cockpit, his mouth set firm.

'Is Sumo okay?' Strachan asked.

'Yes. He's okay.' Shleppy was leaning over the rail, waiting for instructions.

Strachan had no doubt that Shleppy had inherited some of his uncle's strength, but with KT's hands in such critical condition he didn't want to take any risks. He told Shleppy to hold KT steady while he himself climbed the ladder. They swapped places. Strachan hooked his hands under the girl's armpits and hauled her straight up onto the deck. Once she was there he picked her up and carried her straight to her cabin. 'Shleppy. First-aid kit. Go!'

Shleppy reappeared with the red plastic briefcase in under a minute. Above him Strachan heard heavy footsteps and a deep growl. Sumo was conscious again and coming to lend a hand.

They gave KT a shot of morphine and cut the knots. Strachan pulled the rope free from her wrists. They pressed the wound on her arm with swabs to soak up the blood. After several minutes and several dressings the bleeding stopped. They bound her wrists with bandages. It was a tricky operation. They needed to wrap them tight enough to stem the bleeding, but loose enough to let the swelling go down. In the end Strachan was confident that they'd made a pretty good job of it.

KT drifted in and out of consciousness as they worked. By the time they'd finished she was shivering violently from a mixture of cold and shock. Strachan covered her with blankets and stroked her hair until she drifted into the comfort of oblivion. There wasn't time to hang about. She needed urgent medical attention. Strachan communicated this in a single look at Sumo, who registered it with a nod. Strachan followed as the skipper made his way unsteadily up the ladder.

Shleppy's wound was less serious than it looked. The bullet had grazed the underside of his armpit but hadn't penetrated his flesh. He'd gone down on the galley floor and played dead. Then, when the danger had passed, the boy had crawled through to the saloon. When he'd groped to pull himself up, the first thing that he'd touched had been the handle of Strachan's dive knife, left there since the morning of the day before. A couple of stitches would see him right. In the meantime, another dressing and some surgical tape were an adequate substitute.

Sumo sat slumped in the driver's seat. The blood had dried on the back of his head. The scab was bloated and black. Now it looked like a leech. He tried to stand but had to steady himself against the wheel. His legs had the strength of boiled spaghetti. He had severe concussion. Strachan didn't want him falling over so he took his arm and eased him back into his chair. Strachan knew that there was no way that Sumo would let him drive so he simply told him to take them home. Sumo would need to keep the *Esprit Bleu* at a steady speed to minimise the bumps but Strachan figured he knew that already. He put his hand on the skipper's shoulder to show support.

A display of affection like that would normally have caused the skin between Sumo's eyes to scrunch into one of his bulldog scowls. On this occasion he made no effort to pull away. Strachan knew what today had meant. Shleppy and the *Esprit Bleu* were the most important things in the big man's life. He'd nearly lost both of them. He was mentally and physically spent.

Sumo gripped the wheel for comfort. With his right hand, he eased the throttles forward. The engines growled in response. He drew strength from their power, as though he and the boat were one. The bows reared up. A smile skidded across his lips. They had made it, and now they were going home.

There was a small black shape in the sea. It was about half a mile ahead. When Sumo swung the boat's bows towards it, Strachan made no attempt to alter his course. Whether Pili Parang was alive or dead when they hit him, they would never know. There was a small bump but no discernible impact as Sumo drove through him at thirty knots an hour. When Strachan turned round he saw what was left of Pili's body. It bobbed in a macabre dance amidst the boiling wake. It slowed as the distance between them increased and the corpse grew heavy with water.

They sped back to Pulau Tioman under cover of dusk. *Carcharinus Longimanus* would do the rest.

52

They reached Tioman at ten o'clock. They had seen the lights of the *Fubuki* passing their starboard side en route. She was nearly a mile away but unmistakable as she ploughed a furrow through the black sea, heading north towards the Kerkullas. Strachan wondered again what business Pili Parang had had with her. There had been plenty of time to ask him but Pili had kept himself to himself, and Strachan had been more interested in finding his wreck. Now he would never know. But whatever it was, the fact that the Japanese were leaving Tioman could only be construed as good news.

Sumo refuelled while Strachan collected some cash from under his bed and then went to KT's lodgings to retrieve her belongings. Soon he was back on the boat. He and Sumo had recovered their strength, and took turns to check on their patients during their journey across the straits to Kuantan. Shleppy was exhausted and had gone below to sleep. KT was in far worse shape. The morphine was wearing off, and she had developed a fever. Perspiration ran down her forehead and dripped off her nose like rain. Despite an extra layer of blankets, she continued to shiver. Strachan was worried sick.

An hour later they pulled into the marina in Kuantan, where they bundled KT into a taxi. The driver put his foot to the floor but the journey to the hospital still took eleven minutes. KT whimpered and groaned the whole way there.

'Wait here,' Sumo told them as they arrived in the lobby.

'Wait? What the hell for? We haven't got time to wait. KT needs help. So does Shleppy.'

'I have a cousin here.' Sumo fixed Strachan with his glare. 'He is a doctor. No questions. No paperwork.'

Only then did Strachan realise what a risk it had been, coming to the hospital. He was probably still climbing the charts of Interpol's most wanted. Showing his face anywhere remotely official was a risk. A responsible doctor would take one look at their injuries and call the police. He would have no choice. Between them they had two bruised wrists, one cut forearm, two cut heads, and an armpit grazed by a bullet. No way could they pass it off as a car crash. 'Just hurry up.' Strachan held up his hands to show that he meant no offence.

Sumo beckoned them over a few minutes later. They were ushered into a private waiting room by an enormous doctor who was even larger than Sumo. His arms bulged in his sleeves like French pillows, and the buttons on his white coat were missing, presumably flung to the far corners of Malaysia by his porcine gut. He flashed them a reassuring smile. When Strachan saw it, he had no problem entrusting KT to his care. By now she was too weak to stand so she was taken away in a wheelchair. Shleppy went with her.

Sumo and Strachan sat down to wait. A nurse appeared with a metal dish containing disinfectant. When she bathed their wounds it stung like acid. They wriggled in their seats like a couple of schoolboys as she stitched their heads. Shleppy returned soon afterwards, sporting six stitches of his own. He was absurdly proud of them, and said they looked like a line of spiders.

Strachan warned him that they would soon itch like hell, and the smile fled from his face. Sumo ruffled his hair, evidently delighted that his nephew was going to be okay.

'I found it,' Strachan said. There was no point hiding it. Further exploration of the cave would be impossible without a boat, and he wasn't changing skippers at this stage. Sumo and Shleppy were part of the team. He'd even decided what he was prepared to offer in order to have them stay on.

'The wreck? Where?'

'In a cave on the edge of the reef.'

'Ah! Of course.'

'You don't believe me?'

'Tell me,' Sumo replied, dodging the question.

Strachan recounted the story as best he could. Knowing that KT was in so much pain, some of the magic disappeared from his narration but the fishermen still edged closer on their chairs as he told them about his descent into the abyss.

'What do you think is on the boat?'

'I don't know, Sumo. I really don't. Perhaps something. Perhaps nothing.' Which was true, if not particularly inspiring. 'Whatever it is, it's my inheritance, and I'm confident it's valuable. And if there *is* something there, you're welcome to ten per cent of it, on condition that I can use your boat for another week.'

Strachan watched Sumo mull it over. He could just about hear the cogs turning inside the big man's head. Sumo's face was as creased as a wet sheet. Ten per cent of nothing was nothing. Ten per cent of a lot was well worth having. It was a difficult decision.

'Come on. Think about it,' Strachan goaded him. 'The tourist season is coming to an end. The rains are just around the corner. Your fishing business is about to fall off a cliff.' He put his hand in his wallet to make it easier for him, and counted out the cash. 'Eighteen hundred dollars. Plus an extra five hundred.'

'Why extra?'

'A bonus for finding the wreck, and an apology for endangering you by having Pili on board. I misjudged him. I should have known better, and I apologise.'

Sumo grunted, and took the banknotes in his enormous fingers. He passed them directly to Shleppy, who stuffed them in the pocket of his shorts.

'So? Will you take me back next week?'

'What's been started must be finished.'

And, for once, Strachan agreed.

Some time later, the doctor knocked and let himself in. It was two o'clock in the morning. They'd been dozing but now they were wide awake, their anxious expressions pleading for good news. The doctor looked washed out. He cut straight to the point.

The rope had bruised KT's wrists severely and there was damage to several veins. She had a temporary loss of feeling in her hands and it would be days before she regained full use of her fingers. She'd lost several pints of blood but her forearm was now stitched and she was in a stable condition, asleep on a drip. She was receiving warm blood and other fluids to raise her body temperature. She still needed to have her lungs pumped to expel the remaining water, and would require a large dose of antibiotics to combat pneumonia. Sumo's cousin could supply the antibiotics but a small regional hospital like this couldn't provide the full range of preventative care that a victim of near-drowning required. 'She will need to go to ICU in Kuala Lumpur or Singapore.'

'Kuala Lumpur,' Strachan said. Singapore was too

dangerous. If Verhoeven wasn't there himself, Interpol would have assigned someone else to the case.

'No,' Sumo interjected. 'Singapore is better. You need to get out of Malaysia while I tell the police what happened to Pili.' He stood up and drew his cousin to the far side of the room. He switched to Bahasa Malay and spoke at some length, evidently recounting their ordeal. The doctor's face remained impassive throughout. Then he sighed and replied to Sumo, looking at Strachan as he spoke.

'What's he saying?' Strachan asked.

'He has a friend at Changi General Hospital. He can arrange quick and secret treatment. Singapore is better.'

Strachan still didn't like it but there were now two good reasons for returning to Singapore. His diving training had taught him all about near-drowning. It could still be fatal long after rescue. There was a nasty chain of events that needed to be prevented. Taking water into the lungs washes out the surfactant coating and can lead to pulmonary oedema. This can lead to acute respiratory distress syndrome, which in turn can affect the supply of oxygen to the brain, resulting in hypoxia. If Sumo's cousin was insisting that KT should spend a night in the intensive care unit of Changi General, then Strachan wasn't going to argue.

It wouldn't be easy, though. KT was too sick to travel unattended, but he couldn't risk joining her on a scheduled flight because his name would be on every computer in Immigration. He discussed it with Sumo, who told him not to worry. He'd sneak them into Singapore on the *Esprit Bleu*. Strachan could take KT to the hospital without having to use their passports. Strachan liked that plan. He liked it a lot.

The odds of KT suffering permanent neurological damage were increasing with every minute. Sumo's cousin was adamant that they had to get her to Singapore as fast as possible. He delivered her back to them in a wheelchair in the early hours of the morning. Strachan winced when he saw her. She looked truly sick. He wondered if she was capable of another boat trip; the seas were smooth, but it would still be a bumpy ride. Her hands were up on her chest in two slings to ensure that the blood didn't flow to her damaged wrists. They were so heavily bandaged that it looked like she was wearing mittens.

'You okay?' Strachan knelt down and put his arms around her shoulders.

'I'm fine, honey. Really, I'm fine.' But the tears in her eyes told him that Pili Parang would haunt her dreams for years to come. It had been stupid to send her back up to the boat without him. He should never have gone into the cave. He had presented her to Pili on a plate.

'KT. Listen. I'm sorry. I know it was wrong. I should never have done it. It was ridiculous.'

She looked at him with an intrigued look on her face. 'What the hell you talking about, Lance?'

'The cave. I should never have gone in. If I'd stayed outside I wouldn't have had to make such a long safety stop. I might have got up sooner. Before he got to you.' Strachan looked at the ground. He didn't know where else to look. At least she couldn't hit him.

'You went in the *cave*?' Her voice was a terrifying mixture of anger and incredulity.

'Yes, but I found—' Strachan didn't get to tell KT what he'd found – at least, not right then. Her shin came up hard into his groin. He doubled over as cold pain spread through his balls.

'I told you not to.'

'Yeah, I know, I should have listened.' His face

280

stretched tight as he winced. They breed them tough in Fort Wayne. 'At least I found the wreck.'

'You're kidding me! In the cave?'

'Right at the bottom. It must have fallen through the reef.'

'Did you check it out?' The girl's face looked jaundiced, and her eyes were heavy with drugs. The effort of kicking him had jolted her hands. Tears pooled in her eyes, but somehow she still managed to find some enthusiasm.

'No, I couldn't. I didn't have enough air. Or light, for that matter.'

'So now what?'

'So now we get you patched up. Then we go back and find out what's on board.'

'A lot of bodies, I imagine.'

She was probably right. It had crossed Strachan's mind as well. The wreck was a war grave. It wasn't going to get any easier. 'I don't think my inheritance is a bunch of Japanese corpses, do you?'

'Your inheritance? Lance, what's going on here?'

It only took him a couple of minutes to fill in the blanks he'd left when he'd given the edited version on the *Esprit Bleu*. KT looked at him as if he was a faithful old pet gone gently mad. 'So,' Strachan said. 'I'm going diving in the Kerkullas. You wanna come with me?'

She smiled and nodded her head.

'Are you sure you're up to this?'

KT was sweating. 'Of course I am.'

Out in the South China Sea, Kazuyoshi Wakahama had just ordered his captain to turn the *Fubuki* around. Pili Parang wasn't where he had said he would be. It was a wasted trip, and that made Wakahama angry. He didn't like his patience being tested, least of all by someone as low down the food chain as the tattooed Malaysian.

But Parang's absence also made him suspicious. Pili had requested leave to pursue a personal vendetta against the man who had killed his brother. Now he had disappeared, and the boat he'd been meant to destroy had sailed past the *Fubuki* several hours ago.

Wakahama hadn't reached his position by being blasé or ignoring tell-tale signs. As soon as he'd seen the *Esprit Bleu* returning from the Kerkullas, he'd ordered his captain to monitor her progress on the radar. Wherever she went, she was to be followed until they'd established what had happened to Pili.

But there was a second reason why Wakahama ordered the surveillance. Parang had radioed to say that the man who had killed his brother was now looking for a wreck. It was a snippet of information that had set Wakahama's mind whirring.

He knew his history. And that meant he knew an old story about a Japanese ship that had gone missing in the South China Sea.

53

They took a taxi back to the marina. Every bump in the road sent a shudder through KT's wrists. The next few hours would stretch her stamina to the limit. Strachan helped her into bed and made sure that she had plenty of water. She had a packet of painkillers with her: the pills were the size of blueberries.

Before they left Strachan called Gilchrist. Washington was twelve hours behind Malaysia so he called his editor's cellphone, knowing that he would have left the office long ago. 'McCauley, hi. It's Ed.'

'Hey, Ed, how you doing?'

'Pretty good,' he lied. 'Thought I'd check in and keep you up to date with progress.'

'That's good.' Gilchrist didn't say anything more, so Strachan realised that he was supposed to continue. 'Did you get my films?'

'Sure did.'

'Did you like them?'

'Sure did, Ed. You gotta lotta skill, my friend. Hell of an eye.'

'Thanks. Listen, I've got some more on the way. I ran into an old whale shark yesterday. I think you'll like him.'

'That's great, Ed.' But something in the editor's voice suggested it wasn't. It was one of the golden rules of underwater photography: you can never publish too many pictures of whale sharks. This ought to have been a small triumph, even for a seasoned old cynic like Gilchrist. The edge to his voice made Strachan uneasy.

'Everything okay there, McCauley? You sound a bit preoccupied.'

'Ever heard of a guy called Rutger Verhoeven?'

'Yeah,' Strachan said drily. 'An old mate of mine.'

'He called. Said you were in some kinda trouble. You in trouble, son?' The words were friendly but the tone wasn't. Gilchrist already knew the answer.

'It's a long story.'

'Damn right it is. Two hours after he called I got a knock on the door from a couple of Feds, wanted to know where the hell you were. That was kinda embarrassing, Ed, having the Feds in my office. Tongues are wagging here.'

'What did you tell them?'

'I told them you were in Malaysia. That you were sending me ten rolls of film a month, and for all I cared—'

'Malaysia? You weren't any more specific than that?'

'Not at first.'

'And then?' Strachan plugged more coins into the payphone's slot, and waited for Gilchrist to answer.

'Then I told them I thought you were in Kuantan, because that's where I wired your first payment.'

'Shit.' Instinctively Strachan looked around. Verhoeven could have been right there, watching him.

'Verhoeven said you were wanted for murder and assault.'

'No,' Strachan said, a hint of desperation in his voice. 'That's not true. There's a cop in Curaçao you need to speak to. He'll confirm there was never any murder charge. What happened was an accident.'

'Ed?'

284

'Yes?'

'I don't care. I don't wanna know.' Pause. 'Ed?'

'Yep?'

'You need me to wire you some more of your money, son?'

One of these days Strachan was going to buy Gilchrist a very large beer.

They motored south with the coast on their right. Sumo kept the speed up, entering the Straits of Johor shortly before noon. He dropped them on the north coast and handed Strachan a piece of paper bearing the address of a marina where he would be waiting for them tomorrow. Sumo's main task over the next twenty-four hours would be to concoct a plausible story for the disappearance of Pili Parang. Strachan didn't ask, but Sumo told him not to worry anyway. He had cousins in all the right places and guaranteed that there wouldn't be an inquiry.

It was a mile's walk to the nearest main road. By the time they reached it, KT was sweating profusely. Strachan put his hand to her forehead. It wasn't the sun's heat, it was fever. Her lungs rattled and rasped every time she drew breath. They were putting an extra toll on her condition but there was no way he was sending her to Singapore on her own. Immigration would want to know how she got her injuries, which could have led to some tricky questions. It was safer coming in through the back door. They stood at the edge of a suburb called Pasir Ris. Within ten minutes they found a taxi heading back towards town. The taxi took them straight to Changi General Hospital where KT was admitted in gloriously efficient manner.

Sumo's cousin had telephoned ahead, and the surgeon was expecting them. He wore chinos and a rugby shirt under his white coat. Chinese faces typically look younger than Caucasian ones but Strachan reckoned the surgeon was still only thirty-five. He would have preferred it if he'd been twenty years older. He wanted him to look drawn and tired. He wanted him to look overworked and underpaid. Above all he wanted the man who was going to pump KT's lungs to look experienced. Instead the surgeon looked as though he'd just walked off the set of a toothpaste ad. He introduced himself as Fraser Chan. His handshake was sashimi: limp and damp. He took a quick look at KT's hands. 'How?'

'Fishing accident,' Strachan replied.

'What kind of accident?'

'The worst possible kind. She got caught in a runaway line.'

Chan looked at them as though he thought that it was more likely she'd cut her hands on the horn of a runaway unicorn. He grunted something unintelligible and announced that he would drain KT's lungs later that afternoon. Strachan pushed his reservations to the back of his mind. He had to be trusting. He was in no position to shop around for a doctor he liked the look of. He kissed KT's forehead. 'See you when you wake up.' Seconds later a nurse arrived with a wheelchair and led her away to the ward.

With time to kill, Strachan wanted to get his latest shots to Gilchrist as soon as possible. Not only to repay the American's loyalty but to reassure his editor that he was worth persevering with. The last thing he needed was to be axed from the *National Geographic* payroll.

Chan let him use the phone in his office. Strachan found several labs listed in the phone directory. After twenty minutes of hard negotiation, he persuaded the proprietor of one in Chinatown to let him use his equipment for a reasonable fee and while KT was rolling into theatre on a hospital trolley Strachan was rolling into town in the back of a cab.

He found the lab in a side street next to a temple. It was on the first floor of an old shop-house above a tailor's, and boasted impressive views of the skyscrapers in the financial district. Across the street, hawker stalls cooked black-pepper crab, *sambal goreng* and bean curd, the aromas battling for supremacy over the incense from the temple next door. The air itself was hot and sticky.

Strachan paid the proprietor up front. The man was a freelance photojournalist who covered current affairs, and judging by the sophistication of his lab he was good at what he did. He was nervous at first but once he saw Strachan's camera he began to relax. It only took Strachan a couple of minutes to make himself at home and convince the Singaporean that he knew what he was doing. They smoked a cigarette together before the owner disappeared across the road for some food.

With such a well-equipped lab Strachan was able to work quickly. He soon had a string of thirty-six negatives, which he held up to the light for closer inspection. They looked pretty good. The whale shark had been a cooperative subject until KT had touched it. Strachan was particularly pleased with the images of the pilot fish looking along the giant fish's belly. He'd taken another four of its dorsal fin as it scythed through the plankton. It looked like an alpine peak in a snowstorm: a slab of granite dappled with spots of sleet.

He had taken thirty shots in approximately six minutes. A shot every twelve seconds. That was pretty good going. Then there were the three shots of his injured yet heroic stonefish in the boulder field. They weren't great, but they would do. The final three frames of the film were less impressive and turned out to be duffs. They were almost entirely black. He must have accidentally pressed the shutter while the lens cap was still on. He hated wasting film. He cut the first negative and threw it in the bin, cursing his carelessness.

The second negative was heading in the same direction when he noticed three white marks in its top left corner. Strachan peered closer. The lines looked like maggots or short pieces of intertwining thread. He had no idea what they were or how they'd got there. He grabbed his camera to check if he'd scratched the waterproof lens-protector.

He hadn't. Still curious, he switched on a spotlight and shone it over the negative, which he rotated in his fingers. He missed it the first time but on the second rotation he suddenly twigged what he was looking at. He grabbed a magnifying glass from a nearby shelf.

Magnification removed all doubt. Strachan remembered the three shots that he'd taken in the cave. It had never been his intention to photograph anything: he'd only used the strobe to illuminate his surroundings and his SPG. The first time the camera had been pointing at the cave's roof and had captured nothing. But the second time it had been pointed along the ship's hull towards the bows. By complete chance, he had photographed something crucial to his quest.

The squiggles weren't pieces of thread. They weren't scratches on the lens. They were Japanese characters. White paint, spelling the ship's name.

54

Strachan couldn't read the symbols but that didn't matter. It was still a significant breakthrough. Having the ship's name gave him his first real lead in discovering what was on board. He tidied up the lab as quickly as he could. He left the owner one of the more ordinary shots of the whale shark as a thank-you before putting the door on the latch. He closed it behind him with a bang and hurried into the street.

The tailor was busy telling tourists how he made the best shirts in Singapore but let Strachan go with a dismissive glance, as though the contents of this particular foreigner's wallet weren't worth his while. Strachan looked a right state. He hadn't slept very well and the back of his head was still matted with salt, stitches, and blood. He hadn't shaved for at least a week. The photographer's jacket that acted variously as his filing cabinet, tool shed and pillow hadn't been washed in the six years he'd owned it.

He cut through Chinatown, dodging a phalanx of schoolkids and narrowly avoiding a collision with a rickshaw. He had an idea for getting the Japanese characters translated and the financial district he'd seen from the lab window seemed a sensible place to start.

The skyscrapers were huddled in an impressive cluster on the bank of the mud-brown river. They shone in the early evening sunlight, reflecting the clouds, palm trees and bustle of Singapore. It was in one of these towers that Nick Leeson had inadvertently engineered the collapse of Barings Bank. Strachan strained his neck as he peered at the tinted windows. They hid the wheeling and dealing of a world that he didn't understand.

Once he was in the business district he kept his gaze fixed firmly at ground level. Where there were banks there were bankers. Where there were bankers there were restaurants. In this part of the world one of those restaurants was bound to be Japanese. And it wasn't beyond the wit of Banbury Edward Strachan to realise that a Japanese restaurant was an excellent place to find someone who could read Japanese.

He eventually found one in a mall beneath the Overseas Union Bank tower. Like the curry house beneath his flat, this place had an equally predictable name. But The Jade Garden was in a different league to The Taj Mahal.

There was a fish tank in the window. It was home to several tropical fish, one of which was a rabbit fish. Strachan smiled and thought of Sumo. He recognised a pair of kissing gourami and a betta, and wondered if they'd been bought on the black market. The hairs on his arms stood up in anticipation of a showdown with the restaurant's manager. Live-caught tropical marine stock was big business. Some two hundred million dollars' worth of fish ended up in aquaria each year. It made him mad. The betta seemed pretty upset, too. As Strachan stood in front of the tank, he must have caused the glass to reflect like a mirror because the fish suddenly charged it, apparently attacking its own image.

He peered through the doorway and saw businessmen enjoying Bento boxes of sashimi and Kobe beef. They were washing it down with Montrachet, Château Lafite and Perrier. Strachan smiled to himself as a waiter carried a plate of sushi to a group of Chinese bankers. They were probably paying thirty dollars a head for that dish and still it wouldn't taste as good as the meal Shleppy had prepared on board the *Esprit Bleu* the night before last.

A waitress spotted him loitering in the entrance and hurried to greet him. She was tall and slim. She wore a maroon silk kimono and high heels. The heels punctuated her approach across the white marble tiles. *Click-click-clack*. Her hair was pinned in a bun with a pair of chopsticks. If she let it down, it would have reached the small of her back. Strachan had developed a weakness for Asian women during his gap year, and the sight of her hips swaying beneath the silk stirred fond memories of his sexual education, before the mental image of KT on a ventilator chased them away.

Despite his ragged appearance the waitress still greeted him with a small bow. Her voice was as light and tuneful as a songbird's. He noticed the relief in her eyes as he turned down her invitation for a table and told her that he was only stopping for advice. She looked at him, intrigued, and asked how she could help.

As soon as he'd realised that the white squiggles on the penultimate negative were Japanese characters, Strachan had developed the photograph and enlarged it. It was just possible to make out the line of the hull, but the anti-aircraft cannon was nowhere to be seen. The picture needed to be studied closely before the bows of a ship could be made out. He produced it now. 'I need some help translating these characters.'

If the waitress thought he was crazy, she was polite enough not to show it. She took the print, her expression amused. She looked at it, rotated it, and then gave him his answer. '*Kagura*.'

'*Kagura*?'

'It means "music of the gods".'

'Music of the gods?'

'Yes. *Kagura* is the music of the Shinto religion. It is played at ceremonies and festivals in Japan.'

'*Kagura*.' Strachan repeated it, trying to mimic the young woman's pronunciation. She looked at him impatiently. Their conversation was over. She was eager to get back to work, and Strachan was standing in the door, blocking the stream of clients like a soiled rag in a pipe.

'Thank you very much indeed,' he told her. 'I appreciate your help.'

So, his ship was music. Another part of the mystery was solved. The nursery rhyme was explained. The final verse put it all together.

> *Ride a cock horse to Banbury Cross*
> *To see a fine lady upon a white horse;*
> *Rings on her fingers, and bells on her toes,*
> *And she shall have music wherever she goes.*

Damn right she shall.

KT would be coming round from her treatment any time now. Strachan figured she'd be so groggy that she wouldn't miss him. It wouldn't be unkind to give her another few hours to rest. Right now the only thing on his mind was the *Kagura* and what she'd been carrying when she sank two miles off the coast of Kerkulla Ketam. He shoved the photograph into his pocket, and set off for his second trip to the library. A digital thermometer on a glass skyscraper told him that the temperature was thirty-four degrees, but Singapore was going to have to try harder than that if it wanted to break the spring in his step. He was making progress, and he whistled an old Jimmy Cliff number as he went.

Strachan attracted fewer glances in the library than he

had at The Jade Garden. There were students in torn jeans, and old men in open-toed sandals. Strachan fitted right in. By now he was an old hand who knew the system. The same librarian as before advised him that if he wanted a record of every ship in the Japanese fleet then his best bet was to go to Japan and ask in a library there. Strachan didn't care for the librarian's patronising tone but he couldn't fault his logic. Nonetheless, he still managed to persuade the man to fetch some books, including one on Malaysian salvage law.

The first book was a register of every ship built in Singapore between 1850 and 1950. It didn't take long to dismiss it as irrelevant. Strachan checked the index for the word *Kagura* just in case, but it wasn't there.

The second book was a history of the Japanese navy from 1914 to 1945. The index listed a dozen references to *Kagura,* and he almost tore the pages in his hurry to get to the first paragraph. When he found it, his disappointment was intense. The mention was merely of Emperor Hirohito attending a war memorial service *riding his favourite horse Fubuki, while the orchestra played* kagura *as befitting an imperial occasion.*

That told Strachan how the luxury Japanese yacht had got her name but precious little else. Every subsequent reference to *Kagura* turned out to be about the damned music. After ten minutes Strachan knew that it was played at shrines and folk festivals. It was performed with drums, rattles and flutes, and was composed to entertain the gods. Apart from that, the most interesting thing he learned was that he had something in common with Hirohito himself. Hirohito had been a keen student of marine biology, and had even published several papers on the subject.

Big deal. That wasn't why Strachan was there. He was sitting in a quiet corner of a reading room, surrounded by bespectacled Singaporeans and bearded westerners. He'd felt more at home in the cave. The urge to roar with frustration was almost overwhelming. It took all his powers of self-control to close the book quietly. It was six o'clock in the evening. He'd wasted a lot of time getting nowhere.

He gave up. It would have been useful to know what was on board the *Kagura* so that he could plan the salvage operation accordingly. But he would find out soon enough. The wreck had been there sixty-three years. It would still be there in a few days' time.

After a cigarette, Strachan spent an hour with the book on Malaysian salvage law. Its nuances were extremely complex, but by the time he reached the end he had established two important facts. Firstly, it was now clear why neither his father nor his grandfather had attempted to salvage the wreck themselves. The *Kagura* lay in Malaysian waters, and according to local law the gains from any wreck raised within sixty years of sinking would be subject to a capital gains tax, chargeable at fifty per cent of the recovered value. Strachan had no intention of telling the authorities what he was doing, but he couldn't help but admire his grandfather's patience, generosity and ingenuity at composing the rhyme on the postcard. And by leaving the inheritance for another generation, Strachan's father had ensured that his son would benefit from the full amount, even if he had to declare it.

The second fact was simpler. Whatever the ins and outs of the small print, the large print could be summarised in two words: Finders Keepers.

55

KT looked stronger when Strachan returned to the hospital. She also looked pissed off. She sat up in bed, scowling. He slunk across the floor like a disobedient dog.

'Where the hell have you been?'

'Trying to find out what's on my boat.'

'Yeah? Great. Bully for you. I thought you said you'd be here. I extended my holiday for you. The least you could do is act like you give a shit.' Her words stung like acid.

'It's got a name.' Strachan showed her the photograph to change the subject. She peered at it until she made out the bows.

'What does it say?'

'*Kagura*. The music of the gods.'

'The music of the gods. I like it.'

'Forgiven?' Strachan stroked KT's hair. He thought it would work. It usually did. He was wrong. She was still dopey, but her eyes were riddled with hurt. He hadn't been there when she'd needed him most.

Chan stopped by and broke the news that the treatment had been a success. He'd used an endotracheal tube to introduce heated oxygen into her lungs, and then given her a small dose of Phenytoin to eliminate the risk of a delayed seizure. Her stomach had also been cleaned with warm fluids to rinse out the salt water. The swelling

of her wrists was deflating, and with gentle physio-
therapy there was every chance that she would regain full
use of her hands. They would have to remain in slings
for another few days, but in the meantime there was no
reason why she couldn't go home tomorrow.

Home. Strachan didn't think he'd ever heard such an
ugly word. It hit him between the eyes like an arrow. He
didn't dare look at KT. It had never occurred to him that
she might go back to America. Now it seemed the
logical thing to do. This wasn't a minor accident, this
was major trauma. It would leave physical and emotional
scars. The burns round her wrists would leave her with
a pair of permanent scar bracelets. Strangers would
mutter unkind comments about suicide attempts for the
rest of her life.

KT had claimed that she was in search of adventure.
In reality, she had only ever been in Asia on holiday.
Mike's departure didn't alter the fact that sooner or later
she had to go home. She had her career as an actress to
think about. *Home*. Strachan hated to admit it, but it all
made sense. He looked at Chan. 'How long before she
can use her hands again?'

'She can begin with some light exercises tomorrow.'

'Tomorrow! Fantastic! We'll have you diving in no
time.'

'No diving for at least a month. Mr Strachan, your
friend has had a very bad accident. She is very lucky that
she hasn't been damaged for life. Her lungs are sore and
her recovery will be slow. The last thing she needs is to
get back in the water. She needs to see another specialist
in a month's time to check on her progress. She has
insurance that will pay for her repatriation. I have given
her the details of a colleague in Indianapolis who will
look after her well.'

Strachan ignored Chan and turned to KT. He would

try and persuade her to stay. Just once. After that, he'd let her go. He might have slunk in like a dog, but he wasn't going to beg. 'Listen, you can sit on deck. Shleppy will serve you iced tea. You can read books. Sumo will fuss over you.'

'While you have your fun? I notice you don't include yourself in the role of caretaker.' It was the same old KT; all those tubes and drugs hadn't dulled her fighting spirit. And, as usual, she was right.

Chan's pager beeped and he said he had to go. Strachan wasn't fooled. Sensing that it was a good time to leave them alone, Chan had set it off himself. He told Strachan he had ten more minutes before KT needed to rest.

'What if the *Kagura* makes us rich?'

'Get real, Ed. I gotta go home.' She had tears in her eyes. It was the first time she'd called him by his real name. It enforced her message with brutal simplicity. She had a faraway look in her eye, and he could tell that she was thinking of home. Hanging out with Ed Strachan had been a hell of a ride but she didn't believe in treasure hunts. She didn't believe in his quest. Her split with Mike and her torture at the hands of Pili Parang were taking their toll. She no longer looked the tough cookie who'd given him a ringing ear and a bruised crotch. Nor the lightning-fast beauty who'd beaten the cobra on Pulau Tioman. She was a young girl with tears in her eyes. A young girl who needed to go home. Strachan wouldn't stand in her way.

He leaned forward, kissed her forehead, and told her it was okay. He told her he understood. He told her she should get some sleep. As he left the room, she blew him a kiss to chase him away. He trudged down the corridor, unsure how he felt.

Strachan made his way down to the reception hall. It

was quiet except for the voice of the newscaster on Channel News Asia. She was running through a list of the day's casualties on the stock exchange. The economy was contracting. Jobs were being cut. Somewhere beyond the hospital walls there was a real world. A world of redundancy and bankruptcy. A world of politics and war. A world in which fantasies of sunken treasure had no place. A world in which he didn't belong. A world that would soon reclaim KT Luker as one of its own.

Strachan found a seat in the corner and closed his eyes to sleep. It was a tortuous night. He spent it thrashing like a hooked game fish on Sumo's deck. His dreams were troubled by images of Adrian Hamilton at the helm of a fast motor cruiser. His godfather was trawling the South China Sea. Tioman's serrated peaks rose like sharks' teeth behind him. He kept hauling up paintings and statues. Every time he caught a painting, he put his foot through the canvas. Michelle and Molly Newchris applauded in the background.

56

Breakfast was a sombre affair. Strachan and KT didn't talk much. They just exchanged a few platitudes about the weather and the morning's headlines.

KT was due to have a final session with Chan at ten o'clock. That would be followed by an hour's rest, then she'd be ready to go. The hospital had made the necessary arrangements. She was booked on a United Airways flight to Chicago via Tokyo. They were flying her back business class. As she sat up in bed, it was the only thing that brought a smile to her face.

Chan came to collect her on the stroke of ten. Strachan had time to kill before they said goodbye so he asked the nurse in reception what there was to do locally. She told him that there wasn't much. There was the naval museum, but that was pretty much it. It was a fifteen-minute walk or five minutes in a cab. With no other form of distraction, Strachan said what the heck, and asked for directions.

It was a sultry day with wet, oppressive heat. The kind of day to make reptiles pant. Strachan was glad to be lightly dressed. An old pair of Nike trainers, a pair of blue swimming shorts, and a white linen shirt; three items, if you didn't count the cuff links or shades. He had pushed KT to the back of his mind, and was dealing with her departure the way he dealt with every difficult emotion. He ignored it, burying his head in the sand like an ostrich.

As he walked, he compiled a list of the equipment he needed for his return to the cave. He still didn't know what he was looking for so he needed to be prepared for anything. Powerful torches would be essential. Slow-burning underwater flares to illuminate the wreck while he worked. Plenty of rope. Metal-cutting equipment. A welder, a blowtorch, a thick wetsuit. Special breathing mixtures of helium and oxygen. Possibly even a pump and a winch. It quickly added up to an expensive list but he still had cause to smile as he added the final item. It was something that money couldn't buy, something more useful than all the other kit put together.

Pieter Zeeman was fifty-five years old and had been a dive instructor for the last thirty. During that time he'd dived an average of three times a day for up to three hundred and twenty days a year. He had logged well over nineteen thousand hours underwater. Strachan had run the maths one night in St Michiel's Bay when he'd had nothing better to do. He'd calculated that Piet had spent over two years breathing compressed air below the surface. There might have been people in the world who had dived more, but somehow Strachan doubted it.

He reached the museum in fifteen minutes, just as the nurse had predicted. Its drive had been planted with frangipani. Unlike many of Singapore's historic build-ings, this one didn't date from colonial times. It looked more like an officers' mess from the Second World War. It stood amid peaceful lawns, tended by powerful sprinklers and ageing groundsmen in straw hats. A bird he couldn't identify sucked nectar from a bed of orchids, its plumage an iridescent blue. Away to his right wisteria snaked voraciously across the face of an outbuilding. In the centre of the main lawn, a eucalyptus thrust its impressive trunk sixty feet in the air while the breeze thumbed through its leaves as if it was riffling the pages of a book. Strachan wandered up the drive, taking it all in. He was feeling unusually virtuous. Museums ranked right up there with libraries as places he didn't normally visit.

The museum was cool and dim inside. By the time Strachan reached the entrance and paid the admission, it was a relief to be out of the sun. The exhibits were arranged in historical order. There was only one corridor through them, so there was no danger of missing anything. His running shoes squeaked on the floor. The sound echoed round the building as he made his way through the halls. The display was immaculately laid out, and to his surprise he soon found himself thoroughly engrossed.

There were models of boats dating from the fifteenth century. Back then Singapore had been part of the Melakka sultanate. The boats were typically Asian: wooden sampans and single-sail junks with high poop decks, short keels, and long rudders. Further along, the storyboards became larger as Singapore grew in strategic importance.

Sir Stamford Raffles, the founding father of modern Singapore, received permission to use the port as a trading post for the British East India Company in 1819. With the opening of the Suez Canal in 1869, the place's long-term connections with Europe were secured. Strachan marvelled at the pictures of the big clippers that had sailed the spice routes, returning to England laden with exotic cargo. Coffee from Java; tea from China; rubber from the Malay peninsula.

He moved on to the next exhibit, which dealt with the growth of the harbour in the 1920s. By then, Britain had proclaimed Singapore to be its primary naval base in East Asia and significant military installations had been added to the commercial infrastructure. And so on to the

Second World War where, halfway down the exhibit, Strachan stopped dead in his tracks.

He was standing in front of a wall-mounted story-board. It had three sepia photographs and three blocks of explanatory text. The first photograph showed an immaculately groomed British general behind a desk. He wore khaki shorts and short-sleeved shirt, and was sucking vigorously on a pipe. He was flanked on either side by two impassive Japanese guards and was signing what were evidently surrender papers. There was a look of abject failure in his expression. Strachan didn't blame him for needing a smoke. He read the first block of text.

After a campaign lasting less than a week, Japanese forces captured and occupied Singapore in February 1942. Here Lieutenant General Arthur Percival, General Officer Commanding of the Combined Army and Air Force Operational Headquarters, is seen signing terms for the colony's surrender in the Ford Motor factory.

In their haste to retreat, the outnumbered British troops only partially destroyed the causeway linking Singapore to the Malay peninsula. This granted the advancing enemy easy access to the island, which boasted the region's most strategically important harbour.

British ammunition stocks had been severely depleted during the fighting in Malaya but Winston Churchill, the British Prime Minister, expected his general to fight to the death, instruct-ing him: 'There must be no thought of sparing the troops or population; commanders and senior officers *should die with their troops. The honour of the British Empire and the British Army is at stake.'*

Percival surrendered. His decision to carry the Union Jack next to a white flag borne by a staff officer was an act which Churchill never forgave.

The second photograph was more interesting. It was a shot of the harbour. Still in brown and white, and blurred somewhat after being blown up to A3 size, it showed a Japanese merchant navy ship involved in some sort of salvage operation. A crane had been mounted on the ship's aft deck and was lifting what appeared to be an iron boiler tank. Judging from the position of the crane's arm, the iron tank had been raised from the sea.

Strachan peered closer and spotted a wooden platform floating on the water in the foreground. The platform was being used by a diving team. Two men were holding tubes connected to a compressor, which was feeding air to a pair of invisible divers beneath the surface. That was how they had done it before Cousteau invented the aqualung. The platform only held his attention for a second. Something far more interesting was happening in the background.

Behind the crane-ship was a second ship. It was partially obscured from view, and only its rear half was visible. On its deck were six more of these iron tanks. They were stacked in three rows of two, like modern-day containers. Whatever the containers were, they were being raised from the harbour floor. Strachan consulted the text to see if it offered an explanation.

Despite their inability to fend off the enemy, the British Army had sufficient forethought to sabotage many of the harbour's assets before being overrun.

They destroyed the dry dock, which at the time was the largest in the world, in order to prevent the Japanese from using it to make repairs to their own fleet. In addition they burned their remaining oil supplies. Black smoke stains are still visible on some of the buildings on the left of the picture.

In a final act of desperation, General Percival ordered the colony's entire gold reserves to be thrown into the harbour to prevent it from falling into enemy hands.

The secret lasted less than ten days. It was extracted from a junior officer under torture. Here vessels from the Japanese navy can be seen raising the British safes and loading them for transportation back to Japan. Note the diving platform in the foreground, and the recently flooded dry dock on the far right.

Despite the museum's air-conditioning Strachan found himself sweating. By the time he came to study the third photograph he was so excited that he could feel his heart kicking. It was a side-on shot: the second ship leaving the harbour. This time he could see it all. It was perhaps forty metres long. It carried light defences. A twin-barrelled anti-aircraft cannon on its bows. Behind it, an Imperial Japanese rising-sun flag fluttered in the breeze. Three crew members leaned on the rail, waving goodbye to their comrades on the dock. Strachan counted twelve cast-iron boiler tanks chained to the stern deck. Only by now he knew they weren't boiler tanks at all. They were safes.

And then he realised something else. He realised this was the most beautiful photograph he had ever seen. He realised that he would gladly have traded his life's work for the discovery of this single shot. They were painted on the side of the hull, a short way down from the bows. Just visible through the mists of bromide, enlargers, and time. No doubt about it. No doubt at all. The same Japanese characters that he'd caught with his strobe at the bottom of the South China Sea.

The recovered gold left Singapore at dusk on 7th March 1942 in a convoy of eight cargo ships, bound for Osaka. The Imperial Navy did not have control of the Pacific arena so the convoy was escorted by two Shiratsuyu-class destroyers, the *Shigure* and the *Suzukaze*.

Two hours out of Singapore, one of the container ships (the *Kagura*, pictured here) was ordered to divert to Kuantan to collect a platoon of Allied commandos awaiting deportation to a POW camp in Japan, a detour of two hundred and fifty kilometres. At full speed, the *Kagura* would rejoin the convoy in ten to twelve hours. Japanese war records show she left Kuantan with her additional consignment at 05.30 a.m. on 8th March 1942. She subsequently failed to rejoin the convoy.

What happened next is still the subject of much speculation. The *Kagura* is widely believed to have sunk shortly after departing the mainland. Radio communications were severely impeded by poor weather. Captain Tameichi Hara, commanding the convoy, was unable to take a fix on her position when she disappeared from his screens.

There were no known survivors. The wreck has

never been discovered. A theory that the crew attempted to steal the gold has been discredited by Japanese historians, who believe that she sank in one of the region's many deep-water trenches. Neutral observers claim she was secretly salvaged by either the Japanese or British governments after the war.

British sources estimate ten million pounds in gold sovereigns were discarded into the harbour. Given Singapore's history as a trading post, the real figure is likely to have been very much higher. The *Kagura*'s whereabouts and the real value of her cargo remain a mystery to this day.

Real value. Strachan had heard that somewhere before. He grinned from ear to ear as he reread the final sentence.

Sometimes it was amazing how wrong people could be.

57

Strachan raced from the museum as fast as he could, bouncing off people's shoulders in his haste to escape. He didn't care if his behaviour looked odd.

The heat hit him like the breath of a blast furnace. He didn't care about that either. He didn't care whether KT was awake or not. If she wasn't, she soon would be. News like this couldn't wait. News like this could change her life for ever. News like this could help her forget what Pili Parang had done to her hands.

Strachan was so elated that it took him a minute to realise he was being followed.

He hadn't noticed the car when he'd come out of the museum, but he did now. It was a grey Range Rover Vogue. It had black-tinted windows, and black-tinted windows always made him want to know who was hiding inside. Singapore is the most expensive place in the world to own a car, so this monster belonged to someone very wealthy indeed.

He was sure that it was tailing him. It slid away from the kerb a couple of minutes after he walked past. There wasn't much traffic. He could hear its engine note. It hadn't yet pulled out of first gear.

Strachan rejoined the main road that ran towards the hospital. When he looked over his shoulder a few minutes later the Range Rover was still there. It was keeping well into the left-hand lane, maintaining a snail's pace twenty yards behind him. It let every other car overtake it. He didn't like it. Not one little bit. Interpol. It had to be. Who else would be following him in a car like that?

If it *was* Interpol then the game was up. In a country as small as Singapore, Strachan could run but he couldn't hide. His description would be posted at the airport and ferry terminals. He'd be arrested the moment he tried to escape. Strachan had to hand it to him: Verhoeven was a relentless son of a bitch. Michelle Newchris had been right when she'd called him a terrier. The hairs on the back of Strachan's neck prickled. He had no idea how Verhoeven had found him. It had been two and a half weeks since he'd left London, and two since he'd left for Tioman. Perhaps the security office at the hospital had tipped the Dutchman off. Not that it really mattered.

Verhoeven's timing was lousy, to say the least. Just when all the pieces had come together. It had been a long journey from The Lobster Pot in Willemstad. A journey that had taken Strachan from the Caribbean to the South China Sea. Via London, Amsterdam and Tioman. From a dead girl's apartment in Bermondsey Street to the halls of a museum on the other side of the world. A journey on which he'd made new friends – and killed an old one. Strachan wasn't ready for it to end. There were two more legs to go. From Singapore to the Kerkullas. From the Kerkullas back to Curaçao with something in the region of ten million pounds plus sixty years' worth of inflation. The *Kagura* meant that the photographic safari around Aruba and Bonaire no longer needed to be the stuff of dreams. Piet could talk to Koopmans and get his ban lifted. Curaçao Immigration would welcome him with open arms once they knew how much he was worth.

Strachan considered making a run for it but realised

that he wouldn't get far in heat like this. He looked instead for a side street or park; somewhere the car couldn't follow. But there was only road on his right and a wall on his left. There was no cover. If he crossed to the other side, the car would make a U-turn and follow him back in the other direction. There was nothing to do except wait.

Verhoeven. It had to be. No other cop would play a game like this. Singapore Interpol would have got the job done without any fuss. They would have clapped him in cuffs the moment he left the museum. No cat-and-mouse stuff. Strachan's anger rose within him. It burned like the lava in one of Tioman's ancient volcanoes. *Bring it on*. He was ready. He figured he might as well go out with a bang. He wasn't going to go quietly for Verhoeven; that much he promised himself. He slowed his pace and glanced over his right shoulder. The car was still there, but the gap between them had closed to fifteen yards.

He could see a crossroads a hundred metres ahead. It was controlled by traffic lights. He passed a skip of rubble and instinctively grabbed a chunk of broken concrete. It was sharp, coarse and heavy in the palm of his hand. As he walked, he counted the time it took the lights to change. They stayed green for fifteen seconds, and were red for another twenty. He adjusted his pace accordingly, timing it so that he arrived at the lights just as they turned from green to red. There were a few other cars on the road. They stopped, blocking the Range Rover.

Strachan waited until it had closed up behind the other cars. Once it reached the back of the queue, he turned and raced towards it. He crouched low and pumped his arms to build up speed. The Range Rover saw him coming. It tried to spin out of the traffic, but there was a car in front and another behind. It was wedged in tight. It had nowhere to go. Strachan reached it in seconds.

He grabbed the passenger door. It was locked. He didn't care who saw him. He didn't care about the consequences. All he cared about was giving Rutger Verhoeven the fright of his miserable life. He opened his fist and drove the concrete block through the window. The glass shattered as the lights turned green. There was a screech of tyres; fearing that it was a carjacking, the drivers of the other vehicles were slamming them into gear and fleeing the scene.

The Range Rover didn't hang around either. The glass had exploded onto the passenger seat as the window disintegrated in a blast of razor-sharp crystals. Now Strachan had a clear if fleeting view of the person at the wheel.

It was only a glimpse. The Range Rover accelerated away, forcing him to jump back onto the pavement. Strachan didn't recognise the driver but he'd spent enough time in Asia to recognise his race. The man was Japanese.

Strachan could see the hospital in the distance. He started to run.

58

The only thing that mattered now was to get KT and leave Singapore. Fast. Strachan had no idea who the Japanese man was but he didn't need to be a genius to connect him to the *Fubuki*. And that made him an associate of Pili Parang's.

He began piecing it together as he ran. Pili must have told the *Fubuki* where he was. That was why she was heading north towards the Kerkullas as the *Esprit Bleu* returned to Tioman. Then he remembered Pili on the radio, which hadn't struck him as odd at the time but now made sense. Pili had been planning his revenge for some time and had banked on the *Fubuki* collecting him. By killing him, Strachan had just made a whole new set of enemies.

And the Japanese wouldn't be the only ones who wanted to know where he was. Witnesses would report his assault on the Range Rover. The police would be looking for him too. Someone might mention the shattered glass window, and then they'd make a precautionary check of the hospitals to see if anyone had been admitted with an injured hand. Strachan's hand was fine, but Changi General wasn't going to be safe for very much longer.

However loyal Fraser Chan was to Sumo's cousin in Kuantan, he would have no choice but to confirm that Strachan had been staying there. The net would close around him. The police would arrest him and match his profile to that on the Interpol manifest. Then he would find himself flying back to Schiphol next to his old friend, Verhoeven. Verhoeven wouldn't let him slip away a second time. The game would be well and truly up. One of these days Strachan vowed he was going to leave a country in his own good time. Like normal people did.

He arrived at the hospital sweating like a stevedore. The run from the museum had taken five minutes, which had been plenty of time for his shirt to turn see-through. Plenty too for his toes to start squelching sweatily in his running shoes. The lifts were in use so he took the stairs. The air-conditioning was like a katabatic wind. By the time he reached KT's ward on the third floor he was shivering. Another unpleasant surprise was waiting for him when he got there.

KT was gone.

Her bed was empty. There was no sign of her bags. Strachan ran round the corridors, jinking left and right like a mouse in a maze. He checked the bathroom. He checked the TV room and the bookshop. He checked Chan's office, bursting in without knocking. Chan was holding a consultation, and raw panic erupted in the expression of his patient. Chan didn't seem surprised to see him. 'She left you something.' He didn't even look up.

'Where?'

'Over there.' Chan raised his chin, pointing at the computer with his nose. There was a blue envelope on the keyboard. 'Now, Mr Strachan, if you'll excuse me.'

Strachan grabbed the envelope. 'Thank you. For all you've done.' Chan was a good man. He'd worked magic with KT's lungs. He'd let Strachan use his office and let him sleep on the hospital floor. He might get away with one more favour. 'I was never here, right?'

'On condition that I never see you again.'

'Great. Thanks.' Strachan tore at the envelope as though it contained a lottery-winning cheque. It didn't. It contained a postcard. He held it in both hands and read it again. He looked at Chan accusingly. 'Her hands. How did she write this?'

'She didn't. She dictated. I wrote it.'

'When?'

'Ten minutes ago.'

Strachan felt as if someone had crept up behind him and whacked him across the back of his knees with a sledgehammer. He wasn't sure what to believe.

'Ed?' Chan saw the doubt in Strachan's eyes.

'What?'

'Trust me. I'm a doctor.'

Strachan shuffled out of the office like a prisoner at the start of a life sentence. He slumped down in the first chair outside Chan's office and put his head in his hands. The picture on the postcard was of a whale shark; the message simple.

To my gallant Sir Lancelot,

I hate goodbyes. It's easier this way. Thanks for the adventure.

KT

At least ten million pounds in gold sovereigns was sitting in an underwater cave, and they were the only people in the world who knew where it was. KT had left before he could tell her how close they were to retrieving it. He couldn't believe how cruel life could be.

Instinctively he reached into his shirt pocket for his packet of Camels. He was accosted by a porter in green overalls who pointed to a *No Smoking* sign on the wall. In his anger Strachan told the porter that he'd mistaken him for someone who gave a shit. It was a ridiculous reaction. He apologised immediately, crushing the cigarette and hating himself from the bottom of his soul.

And then Strachan was up and running. KT had left only ten minutes ago. There was still a chance of catching her at the airport. It was a risk, but a risk worth taking. He charged down the stairs like a fell runner. On the ground floor the flow of people became thicker as other corridors merged with his. Junction after junction flashed past; tributaries of a human river that would eventually spill into the delta of the main entrance. He was forced to slow down to a fast walk as he weaved in and out of patients, staff and visitors. He took a short cut through oncology and flew into a group of students on a field trip. They scattered like songbirds before a hawk, flapping wildly as he sliced a path through their middle. And suddenly, there in the distance, was KT.

She must have been riding the lift while he'd been climbing the stairs. He'd only missed her by minutes. She was saying her goodbyes, joking with the ward nurse. A taxi pulled up to collect her. 'KT, wait!' he shouted down the corridor. She turned, and he saw the smile in her eyes before it appeared on her lips.

'Gallant to the last, hey, Lance?' The cabbie had taken her bags and was loading them into the trunk.

Strachan's lungs heaved for air. The ward nurse looked at him doubtfully as she helped KT into the taxi. 'KT, wait up. You've got to stay. I promise you it's worth it.'

She looked at him searchingly. 'You promise?'

'Yes. You have to trust me.'

'What about the plane ticket?'

'Change it.'

There was an awkward silence. The taxi driver gave it fifteen seconds before he spoke. 'Airport, right?'

'Wrong,' said KT. 'Ponggol marina.' She blew a wisp of hair from the corner of her mouth, then turned her attention back to Strachan. 'Well, don't just stand there, Lance – let's go find Sumo.'

PART III

'From hence, ye beauties, undeceived,
Know, one false step is ne'er retrieved,
And be with caution bold.
Not all that tempts your wandering eyes
And heedless hearts, is lawful prize;
Nor all that glisters gold.'

(Thomas Gray, *Ode on the Death of a Favourite Cat
Drowned in a Tub of Gold Fishes*)

59

Pieter Zeeman arrived on Pulau Tioman four days after Strachan and KT. It had taken all Strachan's powers of persuasion to get him to make the trip. The telephone in the Berjaya Resort had gobbled Strachan's coins while Piet demanded proof that the wreck actually existed. Strachan didn't have any. All he had was the excitement in his voice. *Gold*. He repeated it over and over, while he force-fed the phone like a goose.

In the end his enthusiasm was enough. Piet had hung up with a promise to talk to the President – his name for Maggie when she wasn't around. Piet may have been ex-Special Forces but his wife wore the trousers in their relationship. She was the only person in the world he was scared of. When Strachan called him back the following day, Piet was full of good news. The President had said yes, he could go. After hiring an instructor from a neighbouring dive school to cover for him during his absence, he'd boarded the plane to Amsterdam at dawn.

'Pretty soon you're gonna run out of favours, Ed.' It had been a twenty-four-hour journey, but Piet still came out fighting. He greeted Strachan with a paternal slap on the back as he stepped from the ferry.

'I love you too, Piet.' Strachan took his friend's hand. 'It's good to see you.' He wasn't lying on either count. Piet Zeeman was father and elder brother rolled into one. Protective enough to pay his thousand-dollar fine, then roguish enough to turn it into a joke. He'd once been part of the 7 Netherlands Special Boat Squadron, a highly trained amphibious platoon which regularly worked in tandem with the British SBS. Nowadays it was there to protect Dutch oil rigs from terrorist attack, but back in the 1970s it had seen active service in the Dhofar, repelling Marxist guerrillas and fighting along-side the British. Piet had fought in that campaign and had taken a bullet in the hip. It had forced his early withdrawal from the forces and he'd spent the last thirty years running The Coral Kraal. Strachan thought he looked pretty good on it.

Piet was tall and broad, with a mane of silver hair that he wore swept back off his forehead, exposing chiselled Roman features. He had a healthy tan from being born and bred in Willemstad, and a ruddy athleticism from living off a diet of fish, fruit and Heineken. He also had appalling taste in shirts. Today's was no exception, and KT grimaced as Strachan introduced them. He couldn't blame her. The cartoon fish would have been more at home on a kid's duvet.

Strachan had booked his friend into a beach hut some twenty yards from his. They dumped Piet's bags, then strolled into the village for a long lunch. Strachan filled him in on events since his flight from Curaçao. That had been almost a month ago, but it felt like a lifetime. There was much to tell and Strachan told Piet everything. Much of it was new to KT as well, and the two of them listened intently, keeping their questions to a minimum. He finished with the news that Sumo had convinced the local authorities that Pili had drowned after falling over-board when drunk. Apparently their scepticism had nearly equalled their indifference. After a few hours Strachan was exhausted and drunk. 'Piet, I dunno how to say this but . . .'

'Probably best not to, then.' Piet rolled his eyes and winked at KT. He could tell immediately that Strachan was going to embarrass someone.

'The money you paid Koopmans. You didn't need to do that. I could've paid it myself.'

'You're a hopeless liar, Ed. Always have been, always will be.'

'Seriously. I would've found a way. I could've borrowed from Hamilton. He's got far more than you and—' He cut himself short. That hadn't come out right. 'What I mean is: thanks. Thanks a lot. I'll pay you back. Two days from now you'll be so rich you wouldn't miss a grand anyway.' He noticed Piet grinning from ear to ear, as though enjoying a private joke. 'Something funny?'

'No, just enjoying the sun.'

'You've got plenty of sun at home. Tell me what's so damn funny.'

Piet leaned forward and threw an arm round Strachan's shoulders. 'Ed, you really think a guy like Koopmans would just drop those charges and settle for a fine?'

'I dunno. A thousand dollars is a lot. He said he couldn't use a prisoner, but he could use the cash. What are you suggesting?'

'You think a cop's allowed to fine you that much money on the spot? It didn't strike you as odd that the fine didn't come from a court or a judge?'

Strachan stared at him blankly. Butterflies fluttered in his chest. He'd been so elated at being released that he'd never questioned the legitimacy of the process.

'Koopmans is a good man,' continued Piet. 'He's a good cop. He runs Curaçao like he runs his own home. He's harsh but he's fair. If you recklessly endanger somebody's life and run away from a crime scene, he's likely to throw you in jail.'

'So why didn't he? What does he need the money for?'

Piet started to whistle. He looked around and expressed his admiration for the scenery. Strachan flicked beer in his face to express his frustration. Zeeman was a big kid. Winding people up was typical of his sense of humour.

Piet chuckled and leaned back out of range. 'Let me tell you a secret. Just because Dirk's a cop doesn't mean he doesn't enjoy a night out with the boys.'

Strachan looked at him, blankly. He still didn't get it. 'So?'

'So, let's just say he isn't the best poker player on the island.'

'You're kidding me!'

'Uh-uh. A thousand isn't all he owes me but it's most of it. I didn't pay a thing to get you out. Just called in a few debts.'

'Are you serious?'

'As a librarian's will. Now, if you'll excuse me, I need a siesta.' Piet pushed back his chair and stood up. 'First one back gets the hammock.'

'You're on,' KT said. Her hands were out of their slings now and the stitches in her forearm would be removed in a fortnight. Her lungs were fine; her recovery fast and full. The two of them sped up the track towards the beach huts.

Strachan watched them go. He drained his beer and put his head in his hands as he thought it through. They say a friend in need is a friend indeed, and Piet Zeeman was the best a man could have. It struck him then what a lucky son of a bitch he was. Even if they never raised the gold, he was already rich in other ways. He shook his head, left some money for the beers, and ran to catch up with his friends.

*

In the evening KT invited them round to her hut, where she barbecued chicken breasts on the edge of the beach. They ate them with *bak choy* in coconut sauce. Piet interrogated Strachan about the wreck. He wanted to know how deep it lay; what the current and the visibility were like; and how the hell they were expected to raise twelve iron safes from an underwater cave.

'Fair point,' Strachan said. In fact, he'd already developed a plan for raising the safes, but since it involved blasting the reef he didn't want to mention it in front of KT. Her appetite for conservation was as big as his was for barbecued chicken. Besides, because Piet had been such a hard-arse in his twenties he assumed everybody else was hopeless when it came to underwater grunt-work, and Strachan was happy to play dumb if it meant he could give his friend the bird later on.

Piet was right to mention the weight, though. It presented a formidable challenge. Strachan had spent most of yesterday in an Internet café punching numbers into Sumo's pocket calculator and reading up on gold. It was heavy stuff.

Isaac Newton had set the price of gold in 1717 when he had been Master of the Mint. He had set it at three pounds and seventeen shillings per troy ounce. For two hundred years it didn't change, except for a brief wobble during the Napoleonic Wars. The first major revision didn't come until the outbreak of the First World War in 1914. Then it rose rapidly. By the 1940s it had reached £8.40 per troy ounce.

From there it had gone up and up. Strachan had checked on the *Financial Times* website, and the spot price on the London market was now £211.50. That meant it was worth twenty-five times more than when General Percival had dumped the safes. The ten million pounds sterling could now be worth as much as two hundred and fifty million. Strachan almost fell off his chair when he worked it out. Then he grinned. He wasn't greedy. He would have happily settled for the original ten million.

The gold's value might have increased but its weight hadn't. Assuming it was spread evenly across the eight boats, and each boat carried twelve identical safes, then the value of the gold in each safe was a little over a hundred grand in 1940s terms. Using a value of £8.40 per troy ounce, each safe would weigh around 12,400 troy ounces, which was getting on for half a tonne.

Half a tonne was the bad news. The good news was that in today's money each boat was carrying around thirty-one million pounds, and each safe was worth around two and a half million. Strachan was using some hefty assumptions but he didn't care. As far as ball-park figures went, these were good enough. It gave him a fair idea of what they were dealing with. A lot of money and a lot of dead weight.

Half a tonne was heavy, but even allowing another two hundred kilos for the safe itself it wouldn't be impossible to move. Not with Sumo, Shleppy and Piet to help. So long as they didn't have to actually lift the safes, they ought to be able to move them to a spot where they could be opened. Strachan could hardly wait.

Piet's jet lag caught up with him around eight o'clock, so he retired to his bed to ponder the challenges that lay ahead. He had a present for Strachan which he handed over as they said goodnight. He'd picked it up in Amsterdam and hadn't bothered to wrap it.

Strachan pulled it from the bag. He laughed and let out a whoop of triumph before hugging Piet hard. At last he had done something right. The calendar was A4 with a wire comb-binding along the landscape edge. The cover shot was clearly visible through the cellophane packaging. The giant barracuda grinned at him, motionless in the current. A perfect display of controlled aggression. McCauley Gilchrist had moved fast.

After washing their dishes in the surf, Strachan threw a pan of water on the fire and thanked KT for supper. He was about to follow Piet back when he noticed her looking at him with an amused expression on her face. She was standing in the doorway of her hut, leaning against the frame. She raised a hand to run her fingers through her hair and as she did so he couldn't help but notice the swell of her breasts under her T-shirt.

'Where the hell are you going?' she asked him.

'Home,' he said, blushing. The air was warm. It smelled of burning wood and pulsed with the songs of countless invisible insects.

'Home? You're not much good to me there, are you, honey? Now quit being so goddamn British and get your cute little butt in here.'

Strachan grinned. *And God bless America too*, he thought as he followed her into the hut.

60

Adrian Hamilton used to refer to sleep as the chief nourisher in life's feast. He said that the phrase came from *Macbeth*. Never having read much Shakespeare, Strachan was in no position to disagree. He and KT had eventually fallen asleep around midnight, which left eight hours for a deep and blissful rest. When he woke the next morning, he knew exactly what his godfather meant. The bruise on the back of his head had subsided and he felt the most invigorated since the day the *Esprit Bleu* had first closed in on the parallel reefs.

Today they were going back.

At nine o'clock they took Piet down the main drag to meet Sumo and Shleppy. The boat crew was already up, and Shleppy had prepared one of his special fruit salads for breakfast. Sumo struck up an instant bond with Piet, and they were soon laughing like old friends. Strachan watched them, noting the respect in their eyes as they swapped stories of big game fish. Sumo earned one of Piet's slaps on the back when he told him that his clients were no longer allowed to keep the fish, which were weighed but returned to the sea alive.

KT, meanwhile, renewed her friendship with Shleppy, and as they sailed from Tioman Strachan was left alone on the bows, glowing with thoughts of the previous night. KT made love like she did most things, and what she lacked in tenderness she made up for in energy and enthusiasm. He lit a cigarette and ran a hand down his spine. He could still feel the claw of her nails as they drenched the sheet with their sweat.

Their first port of call was a marine-supplies wholesaler in Mersing. Mersing was on the mainland, closer than Kuantan but not as big. Two days earlier Strachan had bought much of the equipment they needed and Sumo had stowed it aboard the *Esprit Bleu*. Now they were only shopping for two more items.

Piet had slept on the problem of raising the safes and had arrived at the same conclusion as Strachan. The *Esprit Bleu* wasn't equipped with a winch and Sumo had already refused to have one bolted to the cockpit floor. The only way to move the safes was to float them to the surface, then tow them to shore. That explained the first item on the shopping list: an inflatable lifting bag.

Lifting bags came in all shapes and sizes. Parachute bags the size of hot-air balloons were used to salvage downed planes and submarines. Strachan didn't need to go that far: he was only raising the safes, not the *Kagura* herself. A lift capacity of 1,000 kilograms would be plenty. It was a specialist item but Sumo assured him that the shop would have one: apparently it was the biggest dealership on the east coast.

According to the photograph in the museum, the safes were located on the *Kagura*'s aft deck. They were easily accessible, and so long as Piet could burn through the bindings with the blow-torch Strachan wasn't anticipating a problem attaching the bag. That was the easy part. The hard part would be getting the safes through the roof of the cave. From his memory of the photograph, Strachan reckoned that each safe was about the size of a large packing crate. The entrance to the cave was less than half that size. Wide enough only for him and his tank to squeeze through. Getting a safe up would

327

be like shoving Pavarotti through a cat flap. Hence the second item on his list.

None of them particularly liked the idea of blowing a hole in the reef, and KT was actively against it. She had recently joined a campaign against dynamite fishing and accused them of being irresponsible and hypocritical. It took some hard-talking capitalism from Strachan to convince her that once they'd raised the gold they could initiate all the conservation projects they liked, and in the end she'd had no choice but to agree with the logic.

Forty minutes later, they pulled into the small marina in Mersing. It was situated a quarter of a mile up a narrow estuary. The water was brown and murky. Gnarled mangrove roots slithered into the river while their leaves chattered with sparrow song.

Sumo refuelled the tanks with diesel while Piet and Strachan wandered off to find the marine-supplies store. It was on the other side of the marina, and they had to walk round three sides of a square to reach it. The wood on the jetty was still in the shade. They went slowly, enjoying the feeling of freedom that walking barefoot brings. Piet had changed shirts from last night. This morning's offence was bright pink and patterned with pineapples. As Strachan fell in with his stride he saw the scar on Piet's ankle where he'd started to amputate his foot on the day they'd met.

Piet had never been to this part of the world, and Strachan watched him absorb his new surroundings with obvious pleasure. A flotilla of wooden fishing boats spun on the current like dead leaves. Off to their left a peasant farmer drove a cart of durian along a dirt road. The cow kicked up a dust cloud, causing the farmer to hold his T-shirt over his mouth as he tapped the animal's rump with a bamboo rod. A mosque appeared in a gap between the mangroves. Its onion dome reflected the few rays of sun that had penetrated the morning haze. A handful of worshippers sat in its marble courtyard like pieces on a chessboard.

The shop turned out to be more of a junkyard than anything resembling a retail outlet. It sprawled across two floors of an open-sided barn. The roof was corrugated iron. In twenty minutes the haze would clear and the shop would be hot enough to smelt aluminium. Piet seemed to be in no rush, though. He disappeared up the creaking stairs to the mezzanine level, examining every item as he went.

A lot of it seemed to be second- or third-hand. Outboard motors stood next to pots of paint. Greasy fenders hung from the ceiling like punchbags. Bundles of oars and punt-poles stood in a corner, looking more like firewood than anything useful. There were chests full of nails and screws; buckets full of fishing hooks; and shelves laden with anchor chains, jerrycans and refillable gas cylinders.

Strachan wandered through the maze of rubbish, doubting that he would find what he needed. A mongrel dog lay in the shade, blinking occasionally to disturb the flies that had settled in its eyes. Then he reached the far end of the barn, where the shop opened up. In stark contrast to the rest of the place it was clean and full of quality gear. It housed a wide selection of modern marine equipment, hidden from the view of the casual passer-by like a temple's inner sanctum. His optimism returned as he inspected new sail bags, ropes and winches. There was even a clothing section with rain gear and wetsuits.

The mezzanine level was shorter than the ground floor. Above him Piet was inspecting a stack of lead counterweights for balancing masts. He was looking at them as though they were relics from a lost world. Piet loved boats as much as he loved diving. What he didn't know about the way they worked wasn't worth knowing.

Sumo had instructed Strachan to mention his name to the store manager who, not surprisingly, was another cousin who would secure them a decent price. More importantly, if Strachan slipped him twenty bucks Gajah wouldn't ask to see a licence for buying the explosives.

Strachan found him drinking tea behind the counter. Gajah must have been a pretty distant cousin because he was as thin as a pipe-cleaner and didn't look anything like Sumo or the doctor in Kuantan. His eyes none-theless lit up when Strachan mentioned Sumo's name, and he promised to make a very special price on what-ever it was his new customer wanted. He scuttled off with the list while Strachan thumbed through his wad of bills. When Gajah returned, Strachan negotiated an extra ten per cent discount for paying in US dollars.

The lifting bag weighed sixteen kilograms and the explosives weren't light either. Strachan was about to call up to Piet to quit messing around and give him a hand when he heard the mongrel growling behind him. He had always been fond of dogs and he wasn't bothered by the growl until it was followed by a dull thud. The thud was followed by a yelp so he turned to see what was happening.

Bad things were happening.

Suddenly he was in trouble. The kind of trouble you don't get out of. Strachan swore silently. He should have been more careful. He should have known.

There were three of them. They were Japanese, and one of them was holding a gun.

61

The Japanese were dressed in silk shirts and chinos. They had slicked-back hair and freshly shaved faces. They looked totally out of place in a marine-supplies store. Strachan recognised one of them as the driver of the Range Rover.

He'd been careful to the point of paranoia in watching his back. The Johor Straits were full of boats, but he hadn't been aware of anyone following them when Sumo had picked him up. It didn't matter. The Japanese had followed him to Tioman. They had been watching again this morning and had evidently decided that now was the time to introduce themselves.

The one with the pistol was the tallest. He fitted naturally into the role of ringleader, and he wasn't there to make small talk. He beckoned Strachan towards him with a flick of his wrist. The pistol had a silencer. A professional team. Strachan's mind raced through the possibilities. They weren't here to kill him. Once he was dead they'd have no way of finding the wreck. He had little doubt, however, that they would be expert at making him talk.

'You. Come.'

'No,' Strachan said. Right then he couldn't think of anything else to say. When he stood his ground, the ringleader fired a shot into the dirt at his feet. Blasted dust stung his ankles. The silencer did its job. The report sounded more like a sneeze than a gunshot.

Strachan was hardly making things easy by being so stubborn but there was a reason why he didn't want to join them just yet. They'd either forgotten about Piet or they'd never seen him in the first place. Out of the corner of his eye Strachan could see his friend standing directly above them, on the edge of the mezzanine floor.

You underestimated Piet Zeeman at your peril, and if Strachan could hold out for another few seconds these bastards were going to find that out the hard way. He didn't dare look at his friend for fear of betraying his position. Instead he focused on the driver of the Range Rover, who looked the next most dangerous after the one with the gun. He was wearing a black waistcoat over his green silk shirt, and something bulged in its inside pocket. The guy on the right appeared to be unarmed. He had an undulating scar which traversed his face like a sine wave. He was probably no stranger to close-quarter combat, and Strachan would be happy to leave him to Piet once the dude with the gun had been neutralised. A bead curtain rattled behind him as Gajah backed out into the sunshine. He was in no small hurry to escape the line of fire. He had his money and no intention of helping any further.

'Okay, okay,' Strachan said, putting the box of explosives back on the counter behind him. He held up his palms to show them that he wasn't going to fight. 'Relax. I'm coming.'

The tall one in the middle had the gun trained on Strachan's midriff as the gap between them closed, but despite his position of apparent superiority he still had no idea what killed him. Fifteen feet above him, Piet dropped the lead counterweight with perfect precision. The ringleader's skull made a hollow noise as the counterweight cracked it like an egg. The gun fell from his hand as he crumpled to the floor. His death was instant. It was binary. First he was a one, then he was a zero. No other outcome was possible.

His two companions were momentarily stunned. Strachan flew into action against the driver, pumping his arms forward like pistons and catching him on the chin with the heels of his hands. As his opponent reeled back, Strachan was aware of Piet jumping off the balcony. Zeeman landed on the shoulders of the man with the scar, dragging him down by the neck like a lion at the throat of its kill. Strachan's guy had his hands up to defend himself, karate-style, but with the ringleader down it was one-on-one and these two could make all the fancy moves they liked. No way was Strachan going to lose on those terms.

Piet was making short work of the man with the scar. He had taken him in a headlock and was systematically pounding him into oblivion. Momentarily distracted by Piet's efficiency, Strachan took a kick to the knee that made his patella explode in pain. He retaliated with a couple of fast jabs. They bit quicker than a striking moray and sent the driver back to the dirt.

Big mistake.

The driver landed next to the discarded revolver and instantly picked it up. He even had the sense to aim his shot. Had he aimed it at Piet, Strachan might never have left that shop alive. But in turning his back on Zeeman the driver exposed himself to brutal punishment.

Piet Zeeman was one of the most decent men that Strachan knew, but when it came to fighting the Curaçaoan would use anything to win. On this occasion it was a gleaming steel gaff. It had been hanging in a bracket with a selection of other fishing gear. A rubber cap had covered the point to make it safe but once

Zeeman had removed it safe was the very last thing it was.

Zeeman gave the gaff a full swing. It went through the driver's arm at the elbow. The force of the blow caused him to pull the gun's trigger but the round splintered harmlessly into some wooden shelving at the back of the shop. Strachan stepped in and kicked the pistol from the man's hand. The driver's forearm dangled from the elbow like a joint of meat on a butcher's hook. The gaff had gone clean through. Strachan could see bone. The driver wasn't screaming; he was in shock, staring at his elbow.

Game over. Strachan grabbed the explosives. Piet picked up the sixteen-kilogram lifting bag as though it was a picnic hamper, and they hurried from the barn. The planks groaned as they sped along the jetty. Sumo had the boat refuelled. When he saw them running, he ordered Shleppy to cast off. The big Detroit engines bubbled into life as they threw the supplies on board.

'Go, go, go!' Strachan shouted.

Sumo reversed into the estuary on full throttle. He red-lined the revs. The other boats spun on their moorings like tops. 'Where are we going?' he asked as Strachan joined him on the flybridge.

'Kerkulla Ketam,' Strachan replied. 'Where'd you think?'

62

The Japanese would follow soon enough. It would take the two surviving goons a short while to regain their senses, and the driver would need urgent medical attention if he was ever to use the Range Rover's wheel again. Still, it would be a matter of hours not days before they resumed their search. The race was on.

At twenty knots an hour, the Kerkullas were four hours away. It was only ten in the morning so Strachan and Piet would still have time for at least two dives when they arrived. All being well, they would set the charges and blow the entrance to the cave today. The debris would settle overnight, and they could begin raising the safes tomorrow morning. Strachan was keen to wrap the whole thing up in three or four days; fewer if possible.

With the Japanese searching for them, there wasn't time for the meticulous planning that the operation warranted. There was no way the *Esprit Bleu* could accommodate twelve iron safes on her decks, so they'd agreed over breakfast that they would tow them back to Kerkulla Ketam and open them there. They would have to do it one by one: twelve separate trips. Strachan had bought sixty heavy-canvas holdalls from the market in Kuantan: five for the contents of each safe. Anything left over could be stashed loose around the boat. They would ditch the empty safes into the sea, just as General Percival had done sixty-three years ago to hide them from the Japanese. Strachan grinned. History was about to repeat itself.

With Mersing shrinking in the distance, Sumo put them on autopilot and Strachan convened a meeting in the cockpit. The Japanese had followed him to Singapore. They had followed him to Mersing. Both times he'd had no idea they were there. He was sure they were using surveillance equipment and he wanted Piet's views on security. 'You okay, KT?' He was worried that the presence of the Japanese might have scared her.

'I'm fine.'

'Good.'

'Besides, the fact that you're so popular supports your story that there's something valuable on this boat of yours.'

'Not that you ever doubted me.'

'Not that I ever doubted you,' she replied, with a smile.

'The stakes have been raised,' Strachan said. 'We need to think about our security. Next time they might not be so sloppy. Any suggestions, Piet?'

'From now on, we always have one person up in the tower with a pair of binoculars. Day and night. The earlier the warning, the better. We don't want to give away the site of the wreck.'

'Damn right we don't,' Strachan said.

'No naked lights or open fires after dusk.'

The others nodded their agreement but no one interrupted as the gravity of the situation began to sink in.

'Next, we'll need an alarm signal for the divers.'

'I can bang on the boat,' Shleppy volunteered.

'Nice try, kid,' said Piet. 'Unfortunately, we're going to be too deep. We'll need a tin bucket, a spanner, and a long length of line. You got those, Sumo?'

'Sumo has everything.'

'Good. Next, two spare tanks hidden on the reef. If there's a problem at the surface, we might need to stay down longer than expected. How many tanks have we got, Ed?'

'Forty. Twenty with Trimix. Twenty with compressed air.' Strachan had done a round of the dive schools on Tioman while he'd been waiting for Piet to arrive. It was the end of the season, and many of them had been happy to flog him their old tanks in a last-ditch effort to boost their annual take. 'You can buy them back off me afterwards. Take them back to The Coral Kraal in your suitcase.' He gave his friend a wink and got the finger in return.

The Kerkullas appeared on the horizon a little after one o'clock. It took another hour to reach the parallel reefs. The skies were clear and sunny and the temperature was thirty-four degrees but the good weather wouldn't last long. In the distance Strachan could see the first storm clouds gathering to usher in the rainy season. The clouds wouldn't arrive for another day but when they did their power would be enormous. The wind would howl like a skinned wolf and the hail would strike like bullets. It was one more reason to get this show on the road.

Sumo dropped anchor. Piet was already suiting-up in the cockpit. There were a number of important tasks to complete on the first dive, not the least of which was to give Piet a chance to familiarise himself with the new conditions. The water here was richer in salt and minerals than it was in Curaçao. He would soon discover that he needed more weight to get himself neutrally buoyant.

They used one of Sumo's fishing lines to rig up the communication system. It was over two hundred metres

337

long. It would have no trouble reaching the *Kagura*. Sumo tied the loose end to the cockpit's rail, while Strachan took the end with the spanner and bucket. KT climbed the ladder to take first watch in the tower. She looked a little disappointed to be missing out on the diving, but that only made her more eager to contribute in other ways. Strachan dumped the air from his BCD, joining Piet in the azure calm of the South China Sea.

Each of them was armed with a fifteen-watt torch. They sank down with the two spare tanks. It was the calm before the storm, and visibility was excellent. The tension from the morning's skirmish dissolved in Strachan's shoulders. Finning against the gentle current felt like good therapy for his bruised knee.

The Caribbean has around seventy species of coral. The South China Sea has four hundred and fifty. This single reef was probably home to more kinds of fish than the entire expanse of water from Caracas to Key West but Piet took no notice. Right now, all that mattered was the cave. The flora and fauna could wait. Strachan was glad that his friend had his priorities right.

It took him a little while to find the clam shell. Even in the week that he'd been away, the swell had covered it with debris. Sand and dead coral had thickened the camouflage. He wrestled it free, and the entrance to the old volcano yawned open. While the dust settled, they explored the landslide for a place to hide the spare cylinders. Piet found a space the size of a dog kennel under a cluster of rocks. Strachan watched him recoil as a giant Napoleon wrasse erupted from it. It was four feet long and probably weighed over a hundred pounds. Giant wrasses were being targeted as delicacies for the Hong Kong market. Their lips alone fetched up to two hundred dollars a plate. Strachan was disappointed not to have his camera with him. This was the first time in years that he'd been diving without it, but with so much work to do there was no point carrying extra weight. If the mission was successful, he'd soon have enough leisure to take all the photographs he wanted.

With the spare cylinders stashed a hundred yards from the cave, Piet Zeeman and Ed Strachan returned for their first exploration. One after the other they dropped down through the gap. They descended slowly, equalising the pressure in their ears and sinuses and stopping every five metres to give each other the okay. They had reserve cylinders attached to their hips. They would switch to compressed air for the safety stops on the way back up. Right now they were breathing a special gas mix: 15/50/35 Trimix. Fifteen per cent oxygen, fifty per cent helium, thirty-five per cent nitrogen. Delicious stuff. Much safer than Nitrox for dives below forty. Helium has no narcotic side effects, but it's lousy for retaining body heat. Strachan had upgraded his wetsuit to something thicker. He was warm. He felt great.

The wreck's silhouette loomed in his torch beam.

63

There are strict rules governing the diving of wrecks. Many are heritage sites, and under normal circumstances divers need permission to visit. According to the rule book, they're supposed to check with the relevant local government department to see if the wreck is a national monument or war grave. The *Kagura* was certainly the latter, but these were hardly normal circumstances and Strachan had had little incentive to trouble anyone for a permit.

The *Kagura* was enormous. Rust clung to her like brown snowflakes. From a distance she even looked fluffy. They came down above the anti-aircraft cannon; its turret was as tall as Strachan. Behind him the bridge rose like a haunted house. He played his torch over the windows, half-expecting to see the face of a dead sailor glaring back at him. He was gripped by a sense of awe and anxiety. Maybe it was the depth. Maybe it was the dark. He felt as though he was trespassing. The cave was a sepulchre, the *Kagura* a vast steel sarcophagus. They were intruders. Raiders. Grave-robbers.

Strachan secured the fishing line round one of the gun barrels, creating enough resistance to make it tight all the way to the surface. He gave it an experimental tug. The spanner clattered against the inside of the bucket like a hammer striking a bell. The clang resounded round the cave and bounced off the walls. It echoed off the steel hull. With the safes on the aft deck there was no need to venture inside the wreck, but even if they did they would still be able to hear the alarm. They were in touch with the surface. They could relax. It was time to go to work.

Their torch beams panned through the water like searchlights, reflecting off the hull and creating a soft glow of ambient light. About a metre from the bows they discovered a massive tear. Evidently the *Kagura* had struck the reef head-on before scraping along its side. The scar was several metres long. The steel had peeled back like the lid of a tin of sardines.

They finned back to the aft deck and passed the bridge. A door was ajar. Something was curled round the bottom. It looked like a squid, so Strachan swam closer. Something white appeared, and suddenly he was backtracking. He was backtracking fast. He spun like he was having a fit. They weren't tentacles, they were skeletal fingers. The white thing was a man's arm. The bare bones of a man stretching for the door, stretching to escape the wreck.

Piet swam over and gripped Strachan's shoulder.

Okay?

Okay. Strachan returned the signal and pointed at the door. Piet simply nodded, and moved on.

Strachan hovered until his breathing settled. He imagined the panic engulfing the ship. The cyclone picking her up, smashing her against the reef, again and again. The crew fighting each other for space on the ladders. The POWs realising that this was their chance for escape. The captain trying to restore order over the loudspeaker. The spray like water cannon. Water everywhere; impossible to tell sea from rain, or up from down. The *Kagura* had gone down quickly, before they could launch the life-rafts. Strachan's grandfather had been the sole survivor. Maybe a sympathetic guard had released him. Maybe it had been like the *Indianapolis*, and those in the water had been taken by sharks.

When he was ready, Strachan followed Piet to the aft deck. The safes were all there. Seeing them was like discovering an eighth wonder of the world. Elation. Pure elation. His earlier hesitation disappeared in his bubbles. This was British gold. *Finders Keepers*.

The twelve safes were stacked neatly in three columns of four. They were made of wrought iron and had corroded more than the steel ship. They looked like huge cubes of beef stock. Piet slapped him enthusiastic-ally on the back and Strachan sighed with relief. It had all been worthwhile. He hadn't let anyone down. This time his life really had amounted to something. It had amounted to something in the region of twenty-two million pounds. That was after Sumo and Shleppy had taken their ten per cent. It was even after Piet and KT had taken theirs.

Despite the collision with the reef, the safes hadn't broken their bindings. When Strachan inspected them he understood why. Each was lashed to its neighbour, then to the deck itself. The Japanese Imperial Navy hadn't taken any chances. It had used industrial chain with loops the size of doughnuts. The bolt cutters would be useless, and it would be a laborious process burning through them with the blowtorch.

Piet began making notes on his slate. The cave's entrance was over the *Kagura*'s bows. They would have to manoeuvre the safes the length of the boat before they could raise them. They could render them weightless with the lifting bag, but it would still require a lot of hard swimming to drag them over. At nearly half a tonne each, it wouldn't be easy.

Piet tapped his watch. He pointed to the surface, indicating that it was time to go. They'd been at sixty metres for twenty minutes. That was plenty for a first dive. When they returned tomorrow it would be with the blowtorch. They would be down for an hour at a time, and would need to be up early if they wanted to make three dives.

They made their first safety stop just inside the mouth of the cave. They swapped regulators and started breathing compressed air. They inspected the cave's roof, playing the beams of their torches over the crusty coral to establish how thin it was. Strachan and Piet each made a series of sketches on their slates. Then they repeated the process on the other side, looking for suitable places to plant the charges. The crust was less than two feet thick. Although he'd never worked with explosives before, Strachan was confident that they would take it apart like a cardboard box.

Once back on deck, he retrieved the dynamite from his cabin. Sumo inspected a couple of sticks with a grunt of approval. None of them challenged him directly, but they didn't need to be geniuses to figure that he'd once caught fish the illegal way.

The dynamite was a gelatinised plastic mixture, manufactured by a Bulgarian company called Elovitza. It would work as well underwater as on land. The sticks could be detonated by fire or electric cord. Each was 65mm long. The instruction manual told Strachan that they would generate an explosion temperature of $3,150°C$ and a gas volume of $870 \ \mathrm{dm}^3/\mathrm{Kg}$. He looked at Piet blankly. Piet reassured him that was a lot.

'How many do we need?' he asked.

'Six should do it.' Piet looked at Sumo, who nodded.

'Six. That sounds like a lot. We don't want another landslide.'

'Relax,' said Piet. 'This stuff's designed for quarry work. The force of the blast will travel straight down.'

He and Sumo conferred some more. Then he told the others the plan. 'We'll map out a square on the seabed. It's got to be three times bigger than the top of one of those safes. One stick in each corner. Two more in the middle. There'll be a concentration of force in the centre, so any loose rubble will fall into the cave.'

'What about collateral damage?' KT asked.

'Minimal. There'll be very little sideways force. The *Kagura* might take a battering from the falling rocks but that's all.'

'And the safes?'

'Safes are built to withstand abuse.'

'Let's hope you're right,' Strachan said.

They waited a couple of hours to allow the nitrogen to escape their bodies. At five o'clock they were ready to dive again. The Japanese knew that Strachan and his colleagues were probably in the Kerkullas because Pili had told them. They would be on their way. Every second counted.

The sun was sinking below the horizon and the water was cooler. Strachan placed the four corner charges while Piet swam into the cave and jammed the two central ones against its roof. It took less than ten minutes. Soon they were back on deck, drinking one of Shleppy's fabulous mugs of coffee. They untied the alarm line from the stern rail and attached the loose end to a plastic bottle. Shleppy filled the bottle with just enough water to keep it moored at the surface. It looked like flotsam. In the morning they would haul it back up with the gaff.

Strachan had surfaced with the detonation cable and while Sumo drove them to a safe spot Piet played it through his fingers, out into the sparkling wake.

Dusk fell. They dimmed the lights on the *Esprit Bleu*. The others made room for Strachan as he walked into

344

the cockpit with the detonator. At seven-fifteen he threw the switch.

They heard the blast of the explosion somewhere out in the black. It crumped like a mortar. The sea belched and bubbled, and the *Esprit Bleu* rocked in the shock wave. Then it went quiet.

Any minute now, Strachan was expecting to see the flashing blue lights of a police patrol boat racing towards them. That was why blast fishing was becoming less popular: it was too noisy. The locals didn't use explosives any more. The conservationists were onto them. Instead, they used cyanide. Poisoning fish was cheaper and quieter than blowing them up.

He needn't have worried. When he returned to the main cabin Piet and Sumo wore expressions of quiet satisfaction. It was left to KT, of all people, to ask whether anyone else had heard that first rumble of thunder, which signalled the approaching storm.

Strachan was glad that it was night. The darkness hid them. The Kerkullas were uninhabited, but he still felt guilty about the damage he'd caused. There would be many casualties among the reef's inhabitants. He hoped the sharks would have hoovered up the mess by morning otherwise KT was going to be mighty upset by the soup of dead fish.

They motored back to the cove they'd used as an anchorage on the last visit and spent the evening in reflective mood. There was little conversation. Sumo and KT played cribbage. Strachan managed another thirty pages of his novel. Piet still had jet lag and went to bed around nine.

Day one had gone according to plan. They were well on track. Assuming they could avoid the Japanese then tomorrow they would raise the first of the safes. They would tow it to shore and break it open.

Later, Strachan collapsed exhausted into his bunk. He was too tired to dream and his sleep might have lasted ten hours had he not been awakened at three o'clock by the unmistakable *fwapfwapfwap* of a helicopter's rotor blades.

64

Strachan had gone to bed exhausted and had forgotten to post a sentry. Another big mistake. He rushed on deck and shinned up the ladder to the flybridge. Piet was already there, holding the binoculars. The empty coffee mugs on the dash told Strachan that his friend had been up all night. Piet had assumed responsibility for the watch, his military instinct still keen after thirty years.

'No point running,' he said as Strachan joined him at the wheel. 'They're more likely to spot movement.'

Strachan didn't argue. Pieter Zeeman had shot communist guerrillas with an early version of the .762 Fn–FAL rifle. Strachan had shot fish with a Nikonos Pro90. Right now, that made Piet the boss.

The helicopter was only half a mile away. It was getting louder, heading straight for them. They saw a cabin light reflecting in the water. Piet yelled at KT to turn it off. It must have been an instinctive reaction to turn it on when she woke up. Even as the darkness returned, Strachan knew that it was too late.

The helicopter came in low. They'd been spotted, but there was no point making it any easier. They hurried back into the main saloon. The others were waiting. No one was sure who lay down first, but it seemed like a good idea. They pressed their faces into the carpet so that they couldn't be seen through the windows.

The helicopter passed overhead. Strachan turned his

head to look at it. It had a winking red light on its tail rotor. The pilot swung the helicopter along the beach. He made a sharp turn to the left, lining himself up for another pass. He'd seen the boat and wanted to confirm its identity.

This time he stopped directly above them. He descended to fifty feet. The helicopter hovered over the boat like a giant dragonfly. It looked close enough to touch. They could feel the beat of its blades as their down draught thwacked the sea like a big leather belt. The turbulence played havoc with the palms on the beach. It played havoc with the boat. The surrounding water was churned to a milky broth. The *Esprit Bleu* teetered like a newborn foal steadying herself on unfamiliar ground.

Then the helicopter was climbing again. The engine note changed. It was heading off, its mission accomplished.

'Just like old times,' Piet said.

'What do we do now?' KT asked, once it was safe to stand up.

Strachan had been asking himself the same question. They settled into the sofas. They all looked pale. They were coming down from a big adrenalin rush. Far from being a pleasure cruise, this expedition was spiralling out of control.

'Well,' Strachan replied, 'we could run, but I'm not sure where to. We can't go back to Tioman, Mersing or Kuantan without running into a big old reception committee. Alternatively, we could try and hide out for a few days. But now they know we're here it won't be long before they return. Hiding a boat from a helicopter is a lot harder than hiding it from another boat.'

'So what we do?' asked Sumo. He didn't bother to conceal his anger. He glanced guiltily at Shleppy.

348

Strachan realised he was admonishing himself for bringing his nephew along.

'We go and get one of those safes. Right now.'

'You serious?' asked Piet.

'As a heart attack, my friend. Listen, whoever those guys are they want that gold as badly as we do. They're more than capable of getting us to tell them where the wreck is. They could return later tonight or first thing tomorrow. If they capture us, there's no telling what they might . . .' His voice tailed off. There was no need to spell it out. The expressions on the faces opposite told him that they understood exactly what he was saying. 'Anyway,' he resumed, eager to put a positive spin on things, 'we owe it to ourselves to find out what's in those safes. We've got three hours until dawn. That should be enough to get one up and have a look. If it *is* gold inside, we can always come back another time to get the rest.'

'And if it isn't?' KT snuggled into his shoulder.

'If it isn't, we all go home. We save everyone a whole lot of hassle.'

'What if they turn up when we're over the dive site?' KT continued, testing his plan.

'That's a risk we have to take. The helicopter's going back to the *Fubuki*. It's going to report our position. It may come back, but I doubt it so we've got some sort of window before the boat gets here. Anyway, that's not the point. They don't need to find the dive site. They just need to get their hands on one of us. It amounts to the same thing.'

'I won't talk.' Sumo pushed out his lower lip in an act of defiance.

'Thirty-one million pounds is a lot of money, Sumo, but it's not worth getting killed for.' Strachan didn't tell him that once anyone had a knife to Shleppy's throat the big man would sing like a diva on speed. Strachan was pretty sure he'd do the same if there was any chance of harm coming to KT. 'Besides,' he added optimistically, 'there's always a chance that the helicopter wasn't the Japanese.'

'Who else?' asked Shleppy.

'The park warden, perhaps. Looking for whoever blasted the reef. Which is just as bad, and doesn't alter the fact that we owe it to ourselves to see this through.'

'Ed's right,' Piet said after a short while. 'No harm in trying to raise at least one of those safes. You get us there in the dark, Sumo?'

Sumo looked at Piet as though he'd insulted the skipper's mother. He took Shleppy by the arm and disappeared into the cockpit. The soles of their feet rasped on the aluminium rungs as they climbed to the flybridge.

'Well, I guess that's that,' Strachan said. 'Let's get some gear together and go diving.'

By now the storm was almost on them. The clouds had blanketed the moon and stars, providing plenty of cover. It was the first dark night in a long time, and it added unnecessary extra drama to their situation. Strachan and Piet suited up in silence. Sumo brought them in over the drop site. Shleppy stood on the bows and raised his hand to indicate that he'd found the almost submerged plastic bottle. They reattached their crude alarm system to the stern rail.

As Strachan stepped into the water, he had an uneasy feeling that they were going to need it.

65

Strachan and Piet dropped ten metres into the black before turning on their torches. Even underwater the light was blindingly bright. Had the helicopter been around it would have spotted them a mile off.

It took a few minutes for their eyes to adjust. When the seabed appeared it was unrecognisable. A crater the size of a tennis court had opened beneath them. There was debris everywhere. It looked more like a battlefield than a coral reef. The deteriorating weather had generated a gusting wind, and the chop at the surface was now complemented by a strong drag at the bottom. The seabed whipped into a wet sandstorm around them.

The rubble had settled in the eight hours since the blast, but some evidence of the carnage that the explosion had created still remained. A pack of twenty black-tip reef sharks was scavenging for scraps among the boulders. They thrust their bodies into every nook and cranny, tearing at the dead fish that were still stuck there. A feeding frenzy broke out away to Strachan's left. Steel-grey knots writhed and convulsed in his torch beam as the three-foot sharks wrestled each other for the larger mouthfuls.

Strachan gave them a wide berth and sank down into the cave. The gap was now wide enough for the safes and the inflated dome of the lift-bag. He led the way with the inflatable bag. Piet followed with the blowtorch and bag of underwater flares. Something huge and grey shot out of the dark and flew past Strachan like a Scud missile. Sandpaper skin grazed his face. It bumped the top of his cylinder, and the regulator fell from his mouth. He turned to identify it with his torch, and glimpsed the flank of a much bigger fish disappearing into the black.

Exposed to the sea for the first time in sixty years, the cave had filled with plankton and dislodged sand. Conditions were difficult for working but the incident with the helicopter worked wonders in concentrating their minds. They set to it with measured haste. Strachan lit three flares, bathing the *Kagura* in purple light. Piet lit the blowtorch and began tackling the chains on the nearest safe. The aft-deck soon looked like a welder's yard.

The chains had rusted onto the safe itself, and it took all Strachan's strength to tear them free. They came away with a satisfying rip. It was like peeling ivy from a tree trunk. He let them fall to the deck, glad of the protective gloves he'd bought in Kuantan.

It took twenty minutes to free the safe from its bindings, and another twenty to weld four reinforced steel rings to its roof. Once the rings were in place, Strachan used a short metal cable and a carabineer to attach the safe to the lift-bag's load-restraining harness. The harness was made from heavy-duty polyester webbing, and fabricated into the skin of the bag: plenty strong enough for the job in hand.

The bag had a lift capacity of one metric tonne. It was the size of a parachute and was inflated by a push-button high-flow dump valve and a canister of air. Strachan opened the valve. Immediately the crumpled orange skirt burst into life. The rush of air caused it to spasm and billow like a hot-air balloon at the start of its flight. The safe rocked. Strips of rust tore like bark. The safe rocked again. Then it began to rise.

It was a tremendous moment, and Strachan felt sick with relief. His plan was going to work. The rust crackled and the safe came free, moving for the first time in over sixty years. It clanged against its neighbour.

He had to play the valve on the lift-bag just right. Too much gas and the safe would rise uncontrollably, jamming against the roof of the cave. Too little, and it would sink back down to the deck. They raised it twenty metres off the deck so that it was well above the cross-hairs protruding from the bridge. Then he closed the valve.

It took another five minutes to get the safe neutrally buoyant, the point at which it neither rose nor sank. Trial and error. A lot of trial. A lot of error. Once it was static, they pushed against it, swimming hard to manoeuvre it towards the bows. They were like ants pushing a brick. They kicked as though their lives depended on it, inching their way under the hole in the cave roof.

Once the safe was directly beneath the gap, Strachan played the valve on the lift-bag while Piet steered. They came up slowly. Five metres a minute. The safe sailed through the entrance hole, not even touching the sides.

They completed their safety stops without incident. They spun in continuous circles, keeping their eyes firmly on the dark shapes that slid menacingly across their torch beams. When they broke the surface, the top of the safe leapt into the night like a submarine at the end of its dive. Water as black as oil drained down its sides. Above it, the lift-bag danced in the wind.

The others appeared in the cockpit to welcome the safe's arrival. Sumo's surprise was almost tangible. Until

353

now he'd still doubted Strachan's story. Shleppy was grinning like a Cheshire cat. He clapped his hands in delight, whereupon Sumo cuffed him and shooed him back up the ladder to maintain his watch.

They ditched their air tanks on deck, then Piet and Strachan returned to the water with just their masks and fins. Six plastic barrels followed them in. Originally they had been water vats that Strachan had sourced in Kuantan, but now they found employment as buoyancy aids to keep the safe at the surface. They were good at their job. Even with Piet pushing, Strachan found it impossible to force just one of the barrels below the surface. Meanwhile the air had expanded in the lift-bag and it now looked ready to burst. Strachan wasn't too concerned. With the swell growing larger all the time, they needed the safe as high out of the water as possible. They left the valve as it was. Strachan put his face in the water. There were only two inches of metal below the surface, so the resistance would be minimal. He attached the tow rope with a bowline so that the safe was at last connected to the *Esprit Bleu*.

Back in the cockpit KT helped him out of his wetsuit. The first drops of rain fell on his shoulders, big and heavy as swollen berries. For two minutes it just spotted. Then a sudden thunderclap announced the arrival of the storm in all its glory. A crack of lightning tore the sky. More thunder ripped above them. It was a massive peal. It crackled away for several seconds. Hailstones the size of chestnuts battered the decks. The sea looked as though it was being riddled by gunfire.

Sumo started the engines and they began the delicate operation of towing the safe towards the Kerkullas. It was slow progress through increasingly rough seas. After half an hour Strachan asked Sumo to stop and went to check the bindings. Having done the hard part of raising the safe, he was damned if he was going to lose it in water over a kilometre deep.

The storm raged around them. It fought, growled and spat like a rabid dog on a chain.

66

The two-mile journey back to the islands took almost an hour. Strachan and his colleagues spent it studying the map for a suitable hideout. The hailstorm would ensure that the helicopter was temporarily grounded, but they couldn't risk returning to their original mooring. Strachan doubted whether they could stay hidden for long. They could expect another visit from the chopper as soon as the storm passed. In the meantime there were enough bays and coves to offer shelter while they opened the safe and decided what to do next.

In the end it was Sumo who chose their destination. The third island in the chain was the biggest. It was square in shape: a mile long by a mile wide. The map showed a steep gully running through its middle where the sea had eroded a passage between the cliffs. In fact, this third island was actually two separate land masses, but the gully was only ten metres wide, and the map still referred to it as Kerkulla Besar, meaning Big Kerkulla.

Dense rainforest grew on both banks of the gully. A quarter of a mile up it, the channel made two hairpins as it carved round a mangrove thicket, providing them with cover from any boat that sailed past on the open sea. They wouldn't be invisible from the air, but it was probably as good a spot as they were likely to find.

Sumo's expression grew increasingly pained as the water grew shallower. The *Esprit Bleu* drew four feet, and if they went much further they would add a number of go-faster stripes to her keel. He began looking for a mooring immediately beyond the mangrove thicket and found a thin strip of brown beach where the cliffs on one side were set back from the water's edge.

The next challenge was how to get the safe out of the water and onto dry land. The group didn't have a crane, and they couldn't put the boat in reverse and shunt it up the beach because the metal cable wasn't strong enough and the water was too shallow.

Sumo took them in as close as he dared. They cast the safe off and floated it to the beach by hand. There was no surf to help drive it up the shore, and although the gradient was gentle the safe soon became wedged in the sand, still two metres short of dry land. They unfastened the barrels and lift-bag and wondered what the hell to do next.

They were tantalisingly close. So near, yet so far from discovering what was inside. It was certainly heavy enough to be gold. The five of them were unable to shift it. Either Strachan had underestimated its weight or had overestimated their strength.

Brute-force straining produced nothing but exhaustion, so they took a well-earned break. They gave their arms a rest and put their minds to the task instead. Above them the lightning flashed behind the clouds: a celestial disco display of purple, orange and white. The rain fell hard and pressed their hair flat against their heads. The drops ran down their faces. The thunder was constant now.

'Levers!' Shleppy tapped Strachan on the shoulder. 'Levers!'

'What levers? We don't have any.' Strachan had to shout to make himself heard above the noise of the storm.

'Bamboo.' Shleppy pointed to a nearby thicket. He ran to the boat and came back with a machete. Then he disappeared into the jungle. Five minutes later he returned with three poles and a grin that spread from ear to ear. The bamboo was green and strong. It didn't bend.

Strachan, Piet and Shleppy took a pole each and jammed them under the safe's base, leaning down on them with all their strength. At the same time, Sumo heaved on a mooring line that they'd lashed round the safe's sides. KT wanted to help with the physical work but Strachan wouldn't let her, so she assumed the role of foreman instead. On the count of three, the base at last began to lift.

They quickly changed their positions so that they were now pushing up on the poles. The safe rolled forward and they gained two metres of ground. They rolled it three more times, and after half an hour it was sitting in the middle of the beach.

They didn't have the key to the safe, but it would have been useless anyway. The lock had been filled with molten iron, which meant that the only way in was to remove the entire door. Piet attacked the hinges with the blowtorch, which burned with a pastel-blue light.

Dawn was approaching fast. It was torture sitting on the sand watching Piet work. In true Zeeman style he whistled, winked and generally wound them up; taking his time but making a thorough job of it. At last the lower hinge sheared through. Strachan wedged a jemmy bar into the space behind. The rust had formed an additional seal around the door and he began chiselling through it, using a hammer from the boat's tool kit.

Eventually the fourth side was prised free, and they jumped back as the door slid from the front of the safe. It landed on the sand with a thump. Strachan felt four pairs of eyes on him. Acknowledging his role as leader, the others were hanging back, allowing him the honour of investigating further.

The safe had remained air- and watertight. It had been fitted with two columns of metal trays. Strachan knelt in front of it and pulled gently on one of the trays. Every fibre in his body quivered. The tray was mounted on runners, and as it slid into view the contents glistened in the torchlight.

Sovereigns. Gold sovereigns. Hundreds, perhaps thousands of them. They were stacked in ten rows across the tray. They were so densely packed that they looked like solid bars. The tray stretched deep into the back of the safe. Awe turned to euphoria, and Strachan collapsed on the sand in a reverse roll. He began waving his arms, kicking his legs like a dog scratching its back. As well as being wildly excited, he was also mighty relieved. He released the tension with a roar of triumph. The dream had come true. The cuff links had worked their magic. His grandfather and father had left him an inheritance as valuable as it was beautiful.

The others crowded forward to see the fruits of their labour. KT counted fifty trays and then began counting the number of coins in each row. Strachan pulled one out and held it up for inspection. It was a sovereign that bore the face of Queen Victoria and it was dated 1887, the year of her golden jubilee.

'What are they worth?' Piet asked.

'A coin like this can sell for a hundred pounds,' Strachan replied. After reading the storyboards in the museum he had spent some of his time in the Internet café reading up on sovereigns. There was a big international collectors' market for this kind of stuff.

'Well, there's a hundred of them in each row, and ten rows per tray.' KT was still counting over his shoulder. 'With fifty trays, that's fifty thousand sovereigns per safe,

359

and if you reckon they're each worth a hundred pounds then we're looking at five million.'

'And with eleven more safes still lashed to the *Kagura*, we're talking about a total of sixty million quid.' Strachan tried not to laugh. It sounded just too ridiculous to be true. Thanks to the museum's conservative estimates, he now realised that all his calculations had been ludicrously low. 'Happy?' he asked.

'I guess it'll do,' Piet said.

They no longer cared about making noise or shining lights. All thoughts of helicopters and Japanese gangsters disappeared. They danced and sang in the rain like a lost tribe in a primitive celebration ritual. Shleppy lobbed them cans of beer from the galley window and they shook them up, spraying them all over the place like racing drivers on the podium. Sumo nearly crushed Strachan's spine as they embraced, and Strachan realised that the tension that had occasionally existed between them was now a thing of the past.

Their joy lasted twenty minutes before the enormity of their discovery began to sink in. They'd been up for half the night, and had now breakfasted on several cans of strong lager. The babble of conversation was eventually replaced by a chorus of yawns.

There was still much to be done, however, and while KT and Shleppy went back to bed, Sumo, Piet and Strachan went back to work.

67

The view from the hill was spectacular but not in the way that Strachan would have liked.

His desire to see the rest of the gold secure had neutralised his fatigue, and he'd taken the binoculars from the bridge of the *Esprit Bleu* before setting off to find a vantage point from where he could look out over the parallel reefs. Now that it was daylight there was no point taking unnecessary risks. He didn't want to return to the *Kagura* until he was sure they had the sea to themselves. They couldn't give her location away. Not now. If necessary, they would salvage the remaining eleven safes under cover of darkness. It might take three nights, but with so much at stake it would be worth the effort.

The trek up had been arduous. The slopes were almost vertical in places. They were overgrown with thick, unforgiving jungle, and were slippery from the rain. Vines and roots covered the hill like ropes. Without them, Strachan might never have made it to the top. He arrived dehydrated and bloody. His torso was streaked with lacerations.

The peak he'd chosen wasn't the highest, but he figured that it would give him an uninterrupted view of the sea. He was right. The helicopter was clearly visible. Not in the sky this time, but parked on the *Fubuki*'s helipad. She was moored directly over the hole that they'd blown in the reef. A radar dish rotated silently on the yacht's bridge. A huge white golf-ball dome sat beside it, an electronic nest housing navigation systems, communication devices and surveillance equipment, some of which had no doubt been tracking them for the last twenty-four hours.

It was too late. The Japanese had been watching them all the time. Strachan had led them directly to the prize. He'd even made it easier for them by opening a hole in the seabed. He felt sick with anger as he took it all in.

He spotted a man, who was clearly the yacht's owner, in a heart-shaped swimming pool towards the rear of the lower deck. He was maybe forty-five with the kind of physique you get from pumping too much iron. Right now he was pumping something else. Strachan finally understood why they built swimming pools on yachts: the other three bathers couldn't do what they were doing if they were out of their depths. They were young girls, perhaps in their early twenties, and without a stitch of clothing between them. They say money can't buy you happiness, but this guy was giving it his best shot.

Movement caught Strachan's eye. Activity in the water at the front of the boat. He swung the binoculars away from the stern. The man in the pool was already rich, but now he was about to get a whole lot richer as the first of the remaining eleven safes broke the surface.

The dive team were using a similar method to Strachan's to float the safe to the surface but they had a more elegant solution for the next stage in the operation. One of the yacht's two lifeboats had been lowered to the foredeck. It had been disconnected from the small crane which was designed to winch it down to the sea in an emergency. As Strachan watched, the crane's cable was fed down to the divers on the surface. One of them attached it to a net of industrial webbing wrapped round the safe. In a few minutes the safe was easing through the air, up towards the foredeck.

The storm had moved on, and the sun was behind him. There was no danger of the binoculars catching the light. He re-examined the yacht from end to end. This time he spotted four armed guards patrolling the decks. One on each level. Each carried a Kalashnikov AK-47, the world's most popular automatic rifle, unmistakable with its curved magazine. Judging by the relaxed manner in which the rifles were slung over their shoulders the guards weren't expecting trouble. They looked professional and eminently capable of handling any threats to their boss. Strachan felt sick, weak and numb. Waking up to what he was up against was like waking from an operation. His hopes sank as the next safe rose from the sea.

The yacht slewed in a shift of current. The starboard side, which had been hidden from view, was now visible for the first time. So too was a second boat. It was the *Ping-Pong Taboo*: the cruiser from the previous week. It didn't look like a social visit. She was moored alongside the *Fubuki*, and the men whom Strachan had assumed were marine scientists were being ordered aboard the larger vessel. Their backs were turned, and their hands were tied. Strachan and his crew weren't the only ones the Japanese had been tracking.

He had seen enough. The Japs were stealing his gold. Unless he came up with a plan it would all be over by this time tomorrow. He ignored the leeches and thorns, tumbling down the mountain like a loose rock, crashing through everything in his path.

In the distance the storm clouds billowed in the November sky. They swirled angrily, morphing from one form to the next. As their shape evolved, so too did

Strachan's plan. Slowly at first, then faster until its outline and body were clear.

The Japanese had a helicopter, assault rifles and a yacht the size of Texas. Strachan had Piet Zeeman. That made them even.

68

The top speed of a Viking 57 Sportfisher Convertible is thirty-two knots per hour. Pushed to the limit, it will top out at around thirty-four. The *Esprit Bleu* hit thirty-five a mile out from the *Fubuki*.

Strachan was hidden under an awning in the cockpit, bracing himself against the transom door. Piet Zeeman was by his side. Strachan lifted the canvas for a quick look at their objective. A Japanese guard was running to the bridge to report the incoming craft. Two more appeared a few seconds later and took up firing positions on the upper deck.

The *Esprit Bleu* charged on unperturbed, eating up the sea to her target. She was like a missile: sleek, fast, and deadly. The wave pattern changed and she slammed into a trough with bone-jarring force. Then her bows came up and she was flying again.

Piet had monitored the Japanese throughout the day, and despite their superior equipment they seemed to be making heavy work of raising the safes. By five-thirty in the afternoon they had retrieved only eight, and he watched with considerable relief as the dive team apparently called it a day. Night fell at six o'clock; by seven it was dark. There was still significant cloud cover and Strachan waited until it drifted across the moon before instructing Sumo to drive them out of the gully and hit the gas.

The Japanese fired their first shots when the *Esprit Bleu* was still three hundred yards out. A couple of bullets struck the windscreen on the flybridge and flew out the other side. The cracks they left looked like spiders' webs crystallised in the glass. Sumo was lying on the deck with the boat on autopilot. He gave Strachan a thumbs-up to let him know he was unharmed.

The air around them screamed as more bullets whistled through it. Strachan stole another look at the Japanese. There was panic on board their boat. Two suited figures appeared on the main deck to see what all the noise was about. Strachan recognised one of them as the man from the pool. He didn't look afraid – he looked irritated.

Things started to happen very quickly after that. Thinking that he was going to be rammed, the man from the pool shouted a command at his bodyguards. They responded by changing the setting on their rifles to automatic fire, and a hail of bullets thudded into the *Esprit Bleu*'s hull. One of her engines made a noise like a lawnmower chewing a stone but she never faltered. She never slowed. Soon the engine note corrected.

She was fifty yards from the *Fubuki* and still travelling at thirty-five knots. The guards were directly in front of her. They thought they were going to get smashed so they lowered their aim and ran. Impact was seconds away when Sumo jumped to his feet and threw the *Esprit Bleu* into a sharp U-turn. The G-force was phenomenal. It pinned Strachan to the cockpit floor, stretching the skin round his face like cling film on a salad bowl.

A wave of spray crashed over the rail of the enormous yacht, soaking the men in suits so that they instinctively turned their backs. In that instant Strachan and Zeeman rolled through the transom door. They were hidden by the wall of water and the sleek flank of the *Esprit Bleu*.

366

They had doubled the lead on their weight-belts and they sank like stones, disappearing beneath the frothing wake in the blink of an eye. The shooting had stopped but there was chaos above. Strachan was confident that no one had seen them.

They came up directly under the *Fubuki*'s hull. Their air bubbles were invisible in the churn and most burst harmlessly against the underside of the boat. The Japanese had no idea they were there.

The *Fubuki* might have been capable of sailing from Key West to Cairns in less than a fortnight but she was never going to be a match for the *Esprit Bleu*. After a few minutes Strachan heard the thump of the helicopter's rotor blades as it scrambled to pursue his friends.

Piet had anticipated that, and they had planned accordingly. Sumo was heading directly to the park warden's outpost. It was ten miles away on the furthest of the Kerkullas. If they wanted to attack there, the Japanese would have to do it in full view of the national park's police. Even if the post was unmanned it would still be a foolish thing to do. It would also give Sumo a chance to repair the boat before the next phase of the plan rolled into action.

They had used six sticks of Gelex to blast the reef. The explosive came in a case of twenty-four so there was plenty left over to tape to the *Fubuki*'s hull. Strachan and Piet worked swiftly. Eight of the eleven remaining safes were already on board. Although they appeared to be waiting for morning, there was no guarantee that the Japanese wouldn't descend for the last three safes that night. If they did, there were safer places for Strachan and Zeeman to be than in the water above the dive site. Once discovered they would be quickly overpowered, and their deaths would follow as sure as night follows day.

After fifteen minutes they had attached ten sticks of dynamite to the keel. They exchanged signals of good luck, then went their separate ways. Zeeman had further work underwater while Strachan went topside, and as the former Dutch Special Forces man made his way to the *Fubuki*'s stern Strachan swam to the bows.

When he got there, the anchor chain looked bent due to the refractive power of the water. He ditched his BCD and tank, shedding everything except his wetsuit, knife and the satchel containing the last eight sticks of Gelex. He paused to muster his strength. Then he began hauling himself up the chain.

It was like being on an assault course. The sheer size of the yacht meant that the point of the bows sat eight metres off the sea. The bad weather meant the moon was mostly hidden and Strachan's progress was slowed by the inexorable fetch-and-carry of the surge. As he came up over the rail he immediately rolled onto his back, lying still while his outline dissolved in the black.

Now he heard the throb of the helicopter's engines as it returned to the *Fubuki*. Evidently it had called off the pursuit. He could see several crew on the bridge above him. They were drinking coffee and seemed relaxed. Order had been restored. The captain was talking into a radio, perhaps clearing the returning helicopter to land. Strachan watched it come in. He waited until it had settled on its pad before making his move. The pilot was completing a flight report. The engines were still running and their whine provided additional cover.

His first stop was the anchor well. He lifted the trap-door and dropped three sticks of Gelex inside before darting along the deck. The lifeboat had been lowered from its cradle to free up the crane. Two more sticks went under its tarpaulin. Strachan barely stopped. He was moving in a crouch, moving fast. Get in, get it done, get out. The final three went in a ski locker on the stern.

On his way back Strachan paused for cover behind one of the eight safes. He could see a guard patrolling the bridge deck above him, his assault rifle still slung over his shoulder. He was staring out to sea with his back turned. He wasn't expecting trouble now that the *Esprit Bleu* had vanished. And Strachan wasn't going to start any. Not yet, anyway.

It was strange being so close to the gold. Strachan had discussed it with Piet and they'd concluded that they were unlikely to recover the rest. There was a small army on board the *Fubuki* and they couldn't take them on directly. But if Strachan couldn't have it, he was damned if he was going to let these bastards walk in and help themselves. The Japanese had shot at him in Mersing and shot at him again tonight. Now they were fair game.

With his mission successfully completed, Strachan should have dropped over the side. He should have swum down to collect one of the two spare cylinders they'd cached in the landslide the day before. Then he should have followed Piet on the long swim back to shore. Instead he was stopped in his tracks by a conversation taking place in the cabin below. There was a skylight in the deck floor. Voices were coming through it and they fixed him to the spot.

Three men were locked in heated debate. Strachan recognised two of the voices. Their accents were unmistakable. The first was Dutch. It belonged to the man whose face he'd broken; the man he'd doused in Jack Daniel's and left bleeding in a pile of Pimlico rubbish. The other — and it shocked him to the core when he heard it — was the educated rasp of his godfather.

69

Strachan lay flat on the deck with his brain working overtime. So it *had* been Hamilton at the helm of the *Ping-Pong Taboo* after all. And the man in the cap had been Verhoeven. Verhoeven hadn't been in Singapore when Strachan was there. On the contrary, he had been one step ahead, closer than Strachan had ever known.

Yet Verhoeven hadn't come to arrest him. He'd chosen instead to team up with Hamilton and trawl the parallel reefs with a sonar buoy. There was only one explanation that Strachan could think of. Verhoeven had tracked down Hamilton after coming round in the rubbish tip. The two of them had talked. Verhoeven had put two and two together and this time made four. Michelle Newchris had already told him part of the story and Hamilton had finished the job. Hamilton had told him that the cuff links would lead to a fortune and Verhoeven had wanted in. He was an opportunist. First he'd take what Strachan was looking for, then he'd take Strachan himself. The man was as crooked as they came.

Hamilton knew that Strachan had gone straight to Singapore once he had secured the second cuff link. Gilchrist had told the investigation that he had wired money to Kuantan. Enquiries there would have confirmed Strachan's association with the *Esprit Bleu*, and that had led them to Pulau Tioman.

Tioman was a big enough island for Strachan not to

have spotted them. They'd probably spent most of their time away from Kampung Air Batang, perhaps in the Berjaya Beach resort. They'd followed them to the Kerkullas, at which point they'd been on level terms. Then they'd started searching the same area.

Two groups of people had followed Strachan without his knowing. He wouldn't make the same mistake again. He held his breath so that he could listen better.

'Please,' Hamilton was saying. 'We don't have it.' He was barely in control of his voice. The breathless sobs suggested that he was being subjected to some old-fashioned coercion.

'Then you are no use to me.' The third voice belonged to a Japanese man. The man from the pool. The man they'd soaked twenty minutes ago. He spoke with measured calm. Matter-of-fact rather than hostile. Determined rather than aggressive.

'You can't just kill us.'

'Why not?'

'For one good reason.' This time it was Verhoeven who spoke. Unlike Hamilton he seemed unflustered by the mess he was in.

Strachan strained his senses. Air-conditioning systems whirred. Pans rattled in the galley. Someone was running a shower away to his right. He commanded his brain to block out the background noise of the yacht.

'Interpol knows where I am. I filed an update on Strachan before you captured us.'

The Japanese man didn't need to ask who Strachan was. He already knew. It must have come out during an earlier interrogation. Maybe Pili or Hamilton had told him. Maybe their fly-by in the *Esprit Bleu* had prompted this second round of questions. Either way, Verhoeven was full of answers.

'I reported that I had found him. Since he is not alone

and is considered dangerous, I requested back-up from Kuala Lumpur. If they are not already on their way they will be soon.'

'You are bluffing, Inspector. But I must say you do it rather well. Yes.' The voice of the Japanese man grew weaker, then stronger as he moved round the cabin. Strachan envisaged him prowling round his prisoners like a lion.

Strachan was desperate to look inside but he knew that he couldn't risk it. He was learning too much. If he sat tight he might learn more. It might increase their chances of escape with the safe they'd already raised.

'Check the fax machine on the boat,' continued Verhoeven. 'It will display the last number called. If you like, you can call the number. I am sure that Kuala Lumpur Interpol would be delighted to hear from you. Tell me, Wakahama, how is the Japanese heroin market performing these days? Better than the stock market, I hope?'

The man called Wakahama jabbered something in rapid Japanese. For the first time Strachan realised that there was a fourth man in the room. He heard a door slide open, then light footsteps as someone walked across the deck towards the rear of the boat. At this point he could bear it no longer. He edged his face to the lip of the skylight window and peered into the cabin.

The room was a bar. Bottles of gin, vodka and sake lined a row of glass shelves on the far wall. A cocktail shaker and a bowl of olives occupied the counter-top, along with a simple bone-china ashtray. Soft spotlights were embedded in the wooden panelling, singling out the artwork that hung on the walls. Hamilton and Verhoeven were perched on bar stools, facing the paintings. Their hands were cuffed with plastic bindings. Strachan recognised the cuffs from news reports on

CNN. They were the kind that the military used for prisoners of war.

Verhoeven's face was sunburnt, and his eyes were still black from Strachan's blows with the knuckleduster. When he spoke, Strachan saw the hole left by the missing incisor. But Verhoeven still had that familiar air of defiance. Strachan had to hand it to him: the Dutchman was as impenetrable as Kevlar.

Wakahama had changed into a white linen suit. He sat on the edge of a table with his arms folded across his chest. He had the hook-jaw of a salmon and a boxer's nose. His shoulders bulged from too much time spent in the gym. The suit looked expensive. A pair of Gucci sunglasses perched on his head like a tiara. He was surrounded by an invisible aura of power and his presence dominated the bar. One of the bodyguards who had jumped them in Mersing stood to one side.

'I wish you had not said that,' Wakahama said. 'Now I will have to punish you. It is not good for you to know about my business affairs. Nor is it good for you to try and bluff me.' He said something in Japanese. It sounded as though he was calling a name. The door opened and an older man walked in. He was perhaps sixty years old. He wore blue jeans and a white T-shirt. A few white hairs dangled from an arrow-shaped chin. His skin was pallid. He moved with an air of remarkable strength for a man his age. He had something in his hand. It looked like a truncheon.

Strachan turned his attention back to Verhoeven who had spotted the truncheon in the old boy's hand. Verhoeven didn't look afraid. He looked intrigued. He looked like he was about to learn something. The other bodyguard disappeared behind the stools. He embraced Verhoeven in a bear hug, pinning his cuffed arms to his sides. The older man took Verhoeven's jaw in his left hand and squeezed. Verhoeven's lips pursed in a kiss shape. The old man squeezed harder. Verhoeven's eyes began to water. The hand is stronger than the jaw. Slowly his mouth eased open. At first the baton stuck against Verhoeven's teeth. The sixty-year-old wiggled it, then pushed it deep into Verhoeven's mouth. As soon as it was stuck fast, his thumb pressed a button on the handle.

The mouth and tongue are highly sensitive. They're bright pink, which means that the blood vessels and nerve endings are close to the surface. The pain must have been unbearable, especially with the roots of a broken tooth exposed. Verhoeven bucked like a rodeo bull. The stool rocked on two legs. Hamilton screamed and turned away. Saliva foamed round the edges of the baton. It was an electronic device usually used for riot control. Verhoeven's body shook as it absorbed the kick of 3,000 volts. Anarchy took over his face muscles. His eyes rolled in his head. Mucus bubbled in his nostrils. The stool skidded from under him and he crumpled to the floor. Then he vomited.

Strachan pressed his face to the deck. He didn't want to look. He couldn't look. Verhoeven was wheezing like a donkey. Hamilton was saying 'Oh, God' over and over again. As a result, Strachan never heard the guard from the upper deck approach from behind. The first he knew of his presence was the cool muzzle of an assault rifle pressing against the bone behind his ear.

70

Strachan didn't resist when the guard instructed him to put his hands on his head.

The muzzle of the gun knocked against his spine as he was prodded around the deck to a side door. They descended some stairs, then retraced their steps along the lower level. The yacht was as big as a palace and decorated like one, too. They arrived at a tinted-glass door. The guard jabbed Strachan with the gun barrel as if he was a reluctant bullock at the entrance to an abattoir.

Strachan slid the door open and stumbled into the softly lit bar. The look of surprise on the faces inside was priceless. If he came out of this alive he would remember it for the rest of his life.

He was pushed towards the only spare chair and told to sit down. The knife was removed from where it was strapped to his calf. They didn't cuff him but the goon who'd caught him kept his rifle aimed at him all the time. The safety was off.

Strachan stared hard at Hamilton. They had a lot of catching up to do. A wave of guilt spread across his godfather's face. Hamilton looked like a beaten man in every sense of the word. Maybe he'd been made to suck the baton earlier.

Verhoeven was a mess. He stank of vomit and his face was red. But despite the torture he was his usual self.

'Banbury! What a pleasant surprise. Have you met Wakahama–san? He has been wanted by Interpol for—' He never got any further. Revealing the man's name was mistake enough and he was silenced by the butt of an AK-47.

'Mr Strachan.' Wakahama sighed and lit a cigar. 'There were twelve safes on the *Kagura* when it sank. Twelve. Yes. We have recovered eight. Tomorrow we will recover three more.' His accent was strong. 'Eight plus three is eleven. Yes. The twelfth safe . . .' He paused for dramatic effect. 'Well. Yes. Let us just say, it is not with these two gentlemen.'

'No,' Strachan replied. 'It's not. I have it, and . . .' This time it was his turn to pause. 'Well, let's just say I've hidden it somewhere safe. Pun intended.'

Wakahama held out his hand. The man with the arrow chin handed him the electric baton. They weren't wasting any time. 'Pain, Mr Strachan. How much can you take?'

Verhoeven looked at Strachan expectantly. Strachan blew him a kiss. 'I think I can hold out long enough for Interpol.' In truth Strachan doubted whether he could hold out for more than a few seconds. He'd seen what that thing could do and he was in no hurry to try it. But at this stage they were still in the first round of betting. His hand was sufficiently strong not to fold. 'If you kill me you'll never find that safe. And if you piss me off you won't find it either. So,' he said, 'I suggest you be nice to me.'

The bodyguard who'd inspected the fax machine on the *Ping-Pong Taboo* reappeared through the glass doors. He was better dressed than the other guards, and Strachan guessed that made him head of security. He duly shot Strachan a worried look. Strachan had climbed aboard the yacht that the man was supposed to be

protecting. If Strachan was right, the guard could probably expect a tonsillectomy from Wakahama's baton.

Strachan watched as the head of security handed his
boss a slip of paper. He glimpsed a telephone number
handwritten in blue biro. Verhoeven wasn't folding
either. His hand seemed at least as strong. If it was a bluff
it was a very good one. Verhoeven knew it and upped
the ante. 'I will make a deal with you, Wakahama.'

'You are in no position to make deals, Inspector.'

'I disagree. It is you who are in trouble. You let me
have the twelfth safe and I will let you keep the other
eleven. I know the Japanese are men of honour. If you
agree, I will call off Interpol.'

Wakahama conferred with his men. The nods from
the head of security suggested that the fax number was
possibly the one Verhoeven claimed it was. 'When can
you make the call?' Wakahama, it seemed, had fallen for
it.

'What assurance can you give me that you will let me
keep the gold?'

'You have my word. Yes. You can have two men to
help you load the safe onto your boat.'

The look on Verhoeven's face suggested that he was
looking for something a little more concrete than the
word of a heroin shogun but he nodded all the same.
'Good,' he said. 'Then we have a deal.'

'Yes. A deal.' Then, almost as an afterthought,
Wakahama asked the question that most interested
Strachan. 'How will you persuade Strachan to tell you
where the gold is?'

'That could be a problem. Banbury and I do not get
on very well. I do not think he will tell me. He would
prefer to die, I think.'

'That's the first sensible thing you've said all day,'
Strachan said.

'Mr Strachan, please be quiet. Inspector, I think, yes, I can help you.' Wakahama took a hit on his cigar. He blew the smoke at the fan in the ceiling. 'I went sight-seeing yesterday. I made a movie. It is very interesting. Tomorrow morning Mr Strachan will have the opportunity to become a movie star. We will make another movie. In the movie Mr Strachan will tell you where the gold is. He will also tell us what happened to Pili Parang.'

Fear burst in Strachan's stomach. His mind reeled as he considered the possibilities. The baton would be nothing compared to what lay in store the next day. He was probably better off telling them where the safe was now. But that wasn't a very Strachan thing to do. He thought of his grandfather. His grandfather had fought the Japanese. Against all the odds, he'd managed to escape after he was captured. He'd waited for the right opportunity. If Strachan was patient, he might get his chance. He'd never known his grandfather but he knew that he would turn in his grave if Strachan threw in the towel now. 'Pili got his facts wrong. Then he got greedy. As for your movie, I'm very difficult to work with. Ask Spielberg.'

Wakahama ignored him. He continued to address Verhoeven through a veil of Cuban exhaust. 'And your friend? Yes. What about him?' He indicated Hamilton with a nod of his head.

'He is not my friend. He is not a man of honour. You should let Strachan deal with him.'

Strachan twisted in his seat so that he could see Verhoeven better. A hand came down on his shoulder to restrain him. 'What do you mean?'

'Your godfather made some interesting confessions before you arrived.'

'What do you mean?' he asked again, looking at Hamilton's sweaty face. He didn't doubt that he would have confessed to the murder of JFK with that baton in his mouth.

'Mr Wakahama has been asking how we found the gold. It has a long history, you see. He believes it belongs to Japan. He was asking how we found it. How *you* found it.' Verhoeven paused. Wakahama showed no sign of interrupting. 'Mr Hamilton was not very helpful at first but with a little persuasion he told us everything.'

'Like what?' Strachan asked.

'Like the significance of the cuff links. I must say, Banbury, I did not believe you at Schiphol. I really did not. I honestly thought you meant to rape that girl.'

'And now?'

'Now I know she tried to drug you. Maybe she even tried to kill you.'

'So where does he fit in?' Strachan asked, looking at Hamilton.

'He told her where she could find you. He made a deal with the Newchris woman.'

'A deal?'

'Shut up, Verhoeven!' Hamilton spoke for the first time. There was panic in his voice.

'That is correct. He tracked them down. He persuaded them to tell him the second map reference in exchange for telling them where they could find the other cuff link.'

'Shut up, Verhoeven! Shut up! Shut up! Shut up!' Hamilton screamed.

Strachan looked at him. It was written all over his godfather's face. Verhoeven was telling the truth. 'Molly had a son, Adrian. Did you know that?' Strachan stared hard at Hamilton whose eyes were welling with tears. 'Now she's dead. That kid has lost his mother. How do you feel about *that*?'

Hamilton turned his head, avoiding Strachan's glare.

Wakahama was sitting back with his arms folded again. He was intrigued, more than happy to watch this sideshow play itself out.

'He is trying to steal it, Banbury. He is trying to steal your inheritance. He betrayed you.' Verhoeven was enjoying himself too.

Verhoeven's words were sparks. They touched a fuse that had been a little over three weeks in the laying: a series of suspicions and conclusions, snaking through Strachan's consciousness like a trail of gunpowder. At the end of the fuse was a man who still had blood on his hands. Molly's blood. The whole thing could have been avoided. Hamilton was as much to blame for her death as Strachan was.

'He told us, Banbury. He betrayed you.' Verhoeven said it again. A red mist descended over Strachan's eyes and he exploded like a keg of gunpowder. He charged at Hamilton's chair. Blind with fury, the last thing he felt before he was knocked unconscious were his fingers closing on his godfather's throat.

71

Strachan came round in a brig.

It was a sparse, narrow room that tapered at the front. No carpets here. Just a bulkhead and several steel ribs stretching down to the keel. They were right in the point of the bows. Hamilton was next to him, his beloved brogues still polished and shining as if in defiance of the damp conditions. Strachan doubted whether a brig was standard on a boat like this but, then again, the whole yacht was probably custom-built.

He was shackled like a medieval criminal in the stocks. Now he knew what it had been like for his grandfather. History was indeed repeating itself. His hands and feet were locked in iron clamps. The clamps were bolted to the wall and floor. There was no point struggling. He wasn't going anywhere.

'Start talking,' Strachan said to his godfather. They had plenty of time to kill, and he wanted to hear it all again. From Hamilton himself this time.

'Dear boy, I can explain everything.' Hamilton wasn't being patronising. He'd called Strachan that for as long as Strachan could remember.

'I'm all ears.'

'What Verhoeven told you is true. The business is in terrible trouble. I have huge debts. I needed money. I needed cash otherwise I was going to be ruined.'

'Why? I always thought that business was a licence to print money.'

'It *was* until six months ago.' Hamilton shook his head. He looked at the floor, embarrassed. 'Then I bought some paintings. Six of them. I thought they were Verrocchios.'

'Verrocchio?'

'Andrea del Verrocchio. He was the leading Florentine painter in the 1460s. Leonardo Da Vinci was his apprentice.'

'What happened?'

'I was approached by an Italian businessman in London. He told me he had some special paintings. They'd been in his family for over five hundred years. He wanted to sell them but didn't want a big public auction. That's why he came to me rather than Sotheby's or Christie's. He knew I would be discreet.'

'Only they were fakes?' Strachan prompted.

'Yes. But not just any fakes. They were the best. I had them authenticated by Swift—'

'Who's Swift?'

'He's the expert I use. He's the best in the country. But the Italian had bribed him. His report said the paintings were authentic when they weren't. I found a buyer, a collector in the States. He used another expert to authenticate them. It took him a long time but eventually he exposed them as fakes. The whole thing was a massive scam. I got burned. I got burned really badly.'

'How much?' Strachan almost felt sorry for Hamilton. His earlier rage had subsided. Here was the man who had raised him for ten years. The man who had educated him, fed him, and housed him. His father's cousin. Hamilton's honesty was making amends.

'I bought them for three million dollars. Half a million

each. I had to borrow most of it. The business only turns over half that.'

'Three million.' Strachan whistled. 'Presumably those were the damaged paintings in your flat? You put your foot through them when you realised they were fakes?'

'Actually it was my fist – but it had much the same effect.'

'Tell me again about your meeting with Molly Newchris.'

'It was like I told you on the phone, only I made a deal with her. I had managed to lock her in the study so there was no escape, but when I told her I was going to call the police unless she told me the longitude, she just laughed. She told me to go ahead if I never wanted to find out the coordinates. In the end I had no choice but to tell her where she could find you.'

'Why didn't you just tell her my coordinates? You've known the numbers ever since you gave me the cuff link. You could have saved Molly a trip to Curaçao.' Strachan didn't add that he could have saved her life. He'd made that point earlier.

'Guilt, dear boy. Guilt. I didn't feel proud of what I was doing. It was a desperate time which called for desperate measures but I couldn't bring myself to tell them your coordinates. I had to make it harder for them. Not to mention the fact that I wanted to get to the inheritance before they did.'

'How did Molly know what I looked like?'

'I gave her a pile of your diving magazines. The ones with your pictures in. She must have left for Curaçao the same night and done a round of all the dive schools as soon as she arrived.'

Good old Molly, Strachan thought. That fitted with what little he knew of her. He'd said it before: she knew what she wanted from life and she wasn't afraid to go and help herself. 'Meanwhile you went to Singapore and found the statue.'

'Yes, but I couldn't work out if it was the inheritance. I thought about trying to steal it but an operation like that would take months to plan.' Hamilton twisted in his bindings.

'Then what?'

'Verhoeven contacted me. He was looking for you. I made a deal with him too.'

'Christ, Adrian! *What* deal?'

'Dear boy, I was going to be ruined. I needed the money. The banks were closing me down.'

'What deal?' Strachan repeated. His sympathy was waning and he wanted to wrap this up. There were more pressing matters to deal with. Like getting off the boat. Like saving their lives.

'He wanted to know where you were. I knew you were in Singapore so I agreed to tell him on condition that he used his authority to ensure we bagged the inheritance. Whatever it was, we were going to split it fifty-fifty.'

Strachan was suddenly exhausted but there was relief mixed with his fatigue. There were no more mysteries. They sat in silence for perhaps twenty minutes. When Hamilton spoke again there was fear in his voice. 'What do you think they'll do to us?'

'I don't know. But the sooner we go to sleep the sooner we can wake up and find out.'

'Sleep? Dear boy, how on Earth are you going to sleep at a time like this?'

'By closing my eyes and thinking of nothing. I suggest you do the same. You're going to need all your strength tomorrow if you're going to come out of this alive. It'll do you good. Chief nourisher in life's feast.'

Strachan closed his eyes. Their conversation was over.

72

Strachan and Hamilton didn't see Wakahama in the morning. He was a professional criminal who didn't need to be there when the really dirty work was done. If yesterday's exhibition was anything to go by, he was probably already enjoying the benefits of a jacuzzi full of concubines.

The brig was opened by two guards. One was armed with an AK-47; the second had two bottles of Evian. The bottles were placed on the floor while the guard unlocked the clamps. Strachan eased out of them gingerly. He was sore and cramped. His buttocks were numb. When he tried to stand he fell against the wall. Hamilton was having similar problems.

They took a bottle of water each. Strachan drank his greedily, unsure where the next drink would come from. There was a chance that today would be his last day and he wanted as much strength as possible to prevent that from being the case.

They were given a minute to go to the bathroom, then were handcuffed again on their return. The guards escorted them along a series of carpeted passages. Strachan caught a glimpse of the main saloon as they passed a glass door. It was furnished in the traditional minimalist style: silk cushions, bonsai trees, and rice-paper screens; lacquered scholars' chests and polished parquet in rich mahogany. Modern fine art shared the walls with a collection of samurai swords. He thought he even saw a tiger's pelt before a shove in the back forced him on.

They emerged on deck, squinting in the sunlight. The diving team were drinking tea on the deck below. They were checking their gear. Soon they would descend for the final three safes. Within a couple of hours the yacht would be setting sail and Strachan doubted that he would ever see her again.

He was frogmarched to a side-gate in the rail. The *Ping-Pong Taboo* was moored alongside. She was over ten metres below him. He wobbled down the aluminium steps. He was precariously balanced. It wasn't easy, descending a ladder with his hands tied. A fall from this height would have serious consequences. Eventually he reached the solid footing of the deck. Hamilton followed. They were prodded into a seat by the muzzle of another rifle. The pushing and shoving were unnecessary: Strachan couldn't leave fast enough with all that Gelex on board. Wakahama didn't know it but his yacht was a floating bomb.

Strachan and Hamilton weren't the only ones on board. There was another prisoner. His head was hung in shame. He never looked up, but Strachan knew who it was. It was the man in the dark suit. The one who had gone to check the fax machine. Strachan had guessed right: Wakahama's head of security had screwed up and now he was paying the price.

Verhoeven was next on board. He hadn't been cuffed, but with three minders to watch him he posed little threat. It was highly likely that the *Ping-Pong Taboo* had been searched. Whatever weapons the Interpol man might have cached would have been confiscated long ago. As Verhoeven walked past he caught Strachan's eye. He never said a word but

Strachan understood what he was trying to say.

It was obvious what was going to happen. Wakahama was no more a man of honour than Verhoeven was. Wakahama would renege on their deal at the first opportunity. The bodyguards would force Strachan to talk, and once they knew the location of the final safe they would execute the lot of them. Strachan knew it, Verhoeven knew it, and even Hamilton knew it. As soon as Strachan talked, their time was up. With that look, Verhoeven was trying to broker some camaraderie between them.

They would have to work together if they wanted to live. Bizarrely, Strachan was in the strongest position. If they killed him too soon, no one was going to get their hands on the twelfth safe. Verhoeven needed Strachan as much as Strachan needed him. The unlikeliest of allies, thrown together because life was a more valuable commodity than gold. Strachan gave the slightest nod of his head. He would be ready when the time came.

Verhoeven covered the two miles to shore at a fast pace. One of the bodyguards gave him directions. Hamilton and Strachan required little supervision. The former head of security stared out to sea. His face gave nothing away. If he knew what was coming to him, he was confronting it with stoic indifference. The remaining two goons smoked and joked as they went. One of them was holding two wooden stakes and a sledge-hammer. Wakahama would have a perverse sense of entertainment. Any movie he made was unlikely to get a general release.

For a while they seemed to be heading directly for the gully where they'd buried the safe. Then the boat turned right. They pulled up at the fourth island. Strachan's map said it was called Kerkulla Cicak. Shleppy had told him what *cicak* meant. It meant lizard.

There was the narrowest of beaches. The scrub grew down to the water's edge. As the anchor bit and they swung around, Strachan noticed that a small path had been hacked through the foliage. The three guards became more alert. One of them was the man with the sidewinder scar: the one whom Piet had pummelled in Mersing. It looked like he'd been hit in the face with a sheet of corrugated iron. The second was the guy who had held Verhoeven's arms in the bar. He was tall and rangy, not unlike Verhoeven himself. The third was the sixty-year-old master of torture who'd wielded the electric baton.

The guards ordered them off the boat. Hamilton went first, followed by Strachan, then Verhoeven, then the former head of security. They still maintained the charade that Verhoeven was a free man but the assault rifles tracked his every move. There was plenty of cover and the temptation to run was strong. But Strachan doubted he'd get very far, given the density of the jungle. By bolting he'd only invite more unpleasantness than was already coming. Piet might well be watching and planning a rescue. Strachan stayed alert. He was waiting for an opportunity. All he had to do was remain calm and patient. He could do that. Patience was one of his strengths.

They pushed on in silence for another twenty minutes, watched by the jungle's many hidden eyes. The path had been cut by machete and the trail was still fresh. It became increasingly clear that Wakahama had gone to no small trouble to make his movie.

Gibbons whooped alarm calls. Parrots flashed red and blue in the jungle's canopy. Strachan's shorts and T-shirt were soon wet through. There had been more rain in the night and even at this early hour the jungle was steaming like a Turkish bath. The undergrowth licked his ankles as he walked. Sweat ran into his eyes, blurring his vision. He stumbled regularly. He noticed a leech on his shin. His hands were tied so he couldn't brush it off. Ten minutes later it had doubled in size. A mosquito fed on Hamilton's neck.

They walked up a gentle incline. Strachan picked up the scent of something rotten. The further they penetrated inland, the stronger the odour became. He recognised it now. The stench of carrion and maggots: pungent and sharp as ammonia. Wherever they were heading, something else had got there first. Then it had died.

Eventually they came to a small clearing where the jungle had failed to conquer an outcrop of rocks. The ground was muddy from the storm. Roots snaked through the sludge like varicose veins. A troop of black frogs leapt from the moisture, bouncing into the undergrowth at the sound of the men's approach.

The source of the stench lay on the far side of the clearing.

73

It was the half-eaten carcass of a goat. Its ribcage had been stripped of flesh. Its bones stuck into the air and flies buzzed in its eye sockets. Its hide crawled with maggots. There was no sign of its hindquarters.

Movement in the scrub behind it caught Strachan's eye. The jungle floor rustled. An enormous brown tail flicked through the leaves. Bushes crashed, branches shuddered. Then the rainforest fell silent once more except for the background chirp of the cicadas.

'What the hell was that?' Hamilton asked.

The question was superfluous. They all knew what it was. You couldn't visit the Kerkullas and not notice them. The giant monitor lizards patrolled the beaches like denizens of hell. Some of them were two metres long. Strachan guessed that Wakahama had bought the goat from a village on the mainland, then sacrificed it for his camera.

The former head of security was ordered to the middle of the clearing. He was moon-faced. He looked younger now that he had lost his air of invincibility. He refused to move. The man with the sidewinder scar hit him in the small of the back. The head of security stumbled forward and fell to his knees. When he picked himself up there were tears in his eyes. He was a long way from home. His natural habitat was the plush velvet sofas of Wakahama's yacht. He was coming apart at the seams. He waved his wrists around as he tried to tear off the plastic cuffs.

He was ordered to sit down with his back to one of the rocks. Now it became clear what the wooden stakes were for. The second guard threaded one of them between their prisoner's arms and back. He pounded it into the earth with the sledgehammer. Somewhere behind him the rainforest floor rustled again. The giant lizard was curious. It wanted to know what the intruders had brought it this time.

They had brought it blood.

The guard pulled a switchblade from his back pocket. He opened the flesh of his colleague's right arm as if he was opening a carton of mince. As if he'd done it before. It was a deep cut, but the prisoner never felt it. He was in shock. The blood ran down his arm into the mud. The guard drew a trench through the damp soil with a stick, and the blood rushed along it like molten lava.

The third guard – the old man with the arrow-shaped chin – put down his rifle. He produced a camcorder from his backpack and started to film. Verhoeven and Strachan exchanged the subtlest of looks. The unattended rifle was a lifeline. A short one, but a lifeline all the same.

In front of them, the security man panicked. He managed to stand but could only slide his hands halfway up the pole. Lifting them over the top required double joints. His were the ordinary kind, and he was staying where he was.

'You. Come here.' Sidewinder grabbed Strachan by the hair and dragged him to the edge of the clearing. Once again, Strachan was going to have the best seat in the house. 'You watch. When you have had enough, you tell us where the gold is, and we will shoot him. If you do not talk, you will be next.' And he held up the second stake to emphasise the point.

Strachan nodded. He wondered how much of this he could take. He searched hard for a plan. Where the hell was Piet? *Just be patient.*

The second bodyguard covered them with his rifle while Sidewinder disappeared into the jungle. They heard him moments later, crashing through the foliage. He gave the clearing a wide berth. He worked his way behind the goat's carcass and stopped fifty yards beyond it. Then he began beating the undergrowth. He was driving whatever was lurking there in a straight line towards them. The cameraman zoomed in on the man at the stake.

The security man was going nuts. He rocked back and forth, trying to shear through the plastic cuffs, rubbing his hands raw on the pole. He screamed until his lungs were void of air. When he drew breath, he choked on his own saliva.

Four of them appeared together. Monsters from a bygone age. They stood on the edge of the clearing. Their tongues flickered from their mouths. They were tasting the air, tasting the fear. Their skin looked as rough as bark: armour-plating that had changed little in the last million years. One lizard was much larger than the others. Its body bore the scars of combat. It was the alpha male. It was bigger than Strachan was, comfortably over two metres long from head to tail. Thick yellow drool, rife with bacteria, swung from the corner of its mouth.

The prisoner's struggling was unlike anything that the lizards had seen before. His panic whipped them into a frenzy of thrashing tails and darting tongues. Gradually they grew bolder. They entered the clearing together. They paused when they saw the other guards, assessing the level of threat they posed.

The horror of the situation rooted Strachan to the

spot. He couldn't turn away. He watched as the security man lost control of his bladder and piss spread silently across his lap. The lizards reacted to the smell and broke into a lumbering trot. They bounced off each other's shoulders in their haste to examine its source. As they drew closer they found the blood in the mud. They stopped. They tasted it with black forked tongues. Something clicked in their tiny brains and suddenly they recognised the man at the stake as prey.

When it reached him, the first lizard reared up on its hind legs. It planted its claws in his shoulder and licked his face. Not yet sure if this was food, it slid to the ground. It raked its claws the length of his arm. His shirt ripped and the flesh of his arm split like an overripe peach. Tissue and torn triceps meat oozed through the slits. The lizard blinked. Its tongue slid in and out. It clambered up again, this time locking its jaws on the man's ear.

'Shoot them,' Strachan screamed. 'For God's sake!' But no one was listening. They were too engrossed.

The other lizards joined the attack, lowering their heads like raptors. They tackled the security man's groin and legs. The flesh came away in strips. His blood ran in torrents through the mud. His adrenalin kept him alive long enough for him to see the largest lizard open its jaws and seize him by the throat. Then his screams died with him.

Sidewinder appeared on the far side of the clearing. 'So, where is the gold?'

Strachan said nothing. Sidewinder nodded at the second guard, the rangy one, who duly picked up the wooden stake.

Strachan was pushed in the back and stumbled forward towards the middle of the clearing. The largest lizard turned. It eyed him warily. It thought he was coming to steal its food. Its snout was covered in blood and a string of human flesh hung from its lower jaw. Thinking Strachan was a threat, it inflated its throat. It turned sideways-on to show him its size. Strachan stood his ground. He figured that lizards were similar to sharks. Both had been around for millions of years. Both reacted to displays of fear. The trick was not to show any.

The monitor lizard hissed at him. When that didn't work, it lowered its head and charged. For an animal over ten feet long, its acceleration was startling. Its tail came up off the mud for balance, and its legs worked like pistons. Strachan didn't move. He figured it would draw up just short of him. Wild animals often threaten but rarely do they attack without issuing a warning first. That was Strachan's theory. He had about three seconds before he found out if it was right.

Behind him, the Japanese guards laughed. The cameraman hurried round the side of the clearing to get a better view. The lizard latched onto the movement. Strachan was stock-still. Maybe he was a tree. The thing on the edge of the lizard's vision wasn't. It was an old man, and he was moving. That must mean he was afraid. The lizard altered its course.

The cameraman realised what was happening but it took him a while to react. He stopped laughing and ran back towards the others, drawing the lizard towards them. Panic broke out. Hamilton and the second guard leaped off the path, out of the way.

It was the distraction that Verhoeven and Strachan had been waiting for. They reacted together. Strachan ran back towards the group, arriving at the same time as the cameraman. As he came past Strachan stuck out his foot. He caught him, and sent him crashing to the ground. In the same instant Verhoeven made a dive for the spare rifle. He snatched it from against the rocks, coming to his feet in a roll. The lizard was confused by this sudden flurry of activity, and stopped to reassess its options.

Two bursts of gunfire were all it took.

The cameraman was shot in the back. Puffs of smoke erupted from bullet holes in his shirt. The second guard had turned to fire his rifle but he was poorly trained. In his haste he hadn't bothered to take proper aim. Verhoeven dropped him with a single round. It smashed through his teeth and on through his brain into the jungle, taking the back of his skull with it. Startled by the gunfire, the lizard retreated to join its mates, who were already fleeing into the rainforest.

Two down, one to go. Sidewinder was still on the loose, and had the advantage of cover. Strachan spun round, looking for him. He was on the far side of the clearing, kneeling down with the rifle butt tucked into his shoulder. It looked pretty textbook. He had Strachan in his sights. Strachan was a dead man.

'Ed! Get down!'

A second in time. The sound of pounding feet on his left. The crack of the rifle. A blur as Hamilton threw himself in front of him. The *whoosh* of the air being driven from his lungs as he hit the ground. Another burst of automatic fire. The shriek of birds.

Then quiet.

Strachan could smell cordite.

74

When Strachan looked up Verhoeven was standing over him. The rifle was pointing between his eyes. Hamilton lay a few yards to his left. He'd been shot in the stomach. Strachan ignored Verhoeven and slid through the mud to his godfather.

Hamilton was lying on his back. His face was ghostly white, and his breathing didn't sound right. Sidewinder had only managed a single shot before Verhoeven killed him, but it had been enough. This was a mortal wound. Strachan remembered what Piet had once said about stomach shots. They were the worst. There was very little you could do.

'Free my hands!'

Verhoeven hesitated. He didn't like the idea of setting Strachan loose.

'Release the cuffs, damn it!' Strachan turned his back to Verhoeven so that he could reach the clasp. Verhoeven pushed the gun into his back with one hand but sprung the catch on the plastic cuffs with the other.

Strachan shook them off. He wasn't thinking of escape. He pulled off his T-shirt and pressed it over the hole in Hamilton's gut. His godfather's blood spilled over his fingers. He pushed his thumb into the hole to plug the wound. It was warm and wet.

Hamilton tried to speak but the effort was too much. Death was very close. The life was leaking from him.

There was nothing more that Strachan could do and his only hope was that Hamilton would soon pass out. His godfather tried to smile. There was a look in his eye. It was a look of peace. Strachan understood what he was thinking. He nodded and smiled back. The wrong he had done by trying to steal the inheritance had been put right. More than.

Hamilton closed his eyes. Strachan held his godfather's head in his hands until his breathing stopped.

'The gold,' said Verhoeven after it was over. 'Are you going to tell me where it is or shall I just kill you now and go home? That would be a pity but I promise you I will do it if I have to.'

'We're not leaving until I've buried him.'

'We do not have time for that, Banbury. Wakahama will be suspicious.'

'Hamilton saved my life. He was my godfather. I'm burying him.' It was a statement of fact.

Verhoeven knew Strachan well enough by now. He knew Strachan was stubborn enough to get himself shot so he reluctantly agreed. 'Be quick.'

They retraced their steps to the *Ping-Pong Taboo*. It was slow going. Strachan had hoisted Hamilton over his shoulder in a fireman's carry, exactly as he'd carted Verhoeven out of his flat two weeks earlier. It was gruelling work. Hamilton's blood ran down his back and spotted his calves.

Strachan chose a coconut grove at the far end of the thin beach. The ground was elevated. The *Fubuki* was out of sight around the headland of Dragon Point. Strachan didn't believe it was purely to ease his conscience when he told himself that Hamilton would have approved of this spot. The palms provided shade. The higher ground provided a magnificent view of the sapphire sea, where the marlin leaped in sport, and the tuna shot through the blue like rounds of silver tracer.

Strachan dug his godfather's grave with his hands. The last thing he did was to wipe the mud from Hamilton's shoes.

It was nearly two miles from their mooring to the small gully where they'd buried the safe. Verhoeven was in a considerable hurry to get there. Strachan couldn't blame him. The horror of what they'd witnessed was fresh in their minds. And then there was still Wakahama to consider. Although they were invisible from his yacht, it wouldn't take him long to realise that something was wrong. He'd be expecting his men to return. If they didn't appear soon, he would send the helicopter to look for them.

Verhoeven made Strachan take the controls so that he could cover him with the rifle. Strachan's wrists hurt like hell from the plastic cuffs and his night in the stocks, but if the rest of their plan had been a success then leading Verhoeven to the gully was his best chance of escape. They reached its entrance. Strachan eased back on the power and made the turn upstream.

It had been their plan all along to rendezvous in the gully. They knew the helicopter would be scrambled to follow the *Esprit Bleu*, so they decided the safest thing was for Sumo to drive to the warden's outpost. He would reach its tiny marina before the helicopter could catch up and launch an aerial attack. Sometimes the outpost was manned, sometimes it wasn't. They'd seen no sign of the national park authorities so far, but the presence of the liveried patrol boat in the marina would be deterrent enough for the Japanese.

Sumo and Shleppy would patch up the bullet holes in the *Esprit Bleu* and check the engines. At two in the morning she would slip silently from the marina. All lights on board would be switched off. She would travel at one or two knots to keep the noise down. Once clear of the outpost, Sumo would drive her back to the gully, hugging the coastline. Shleppy would perch on the bows, signalling left or right with his arms as he plotted a course through the corals.

Piet, meanwhile, would have finished his work on the *Fubuki*'s hull. He would have finned down to the fissure in the landslide to collect one of the two spare tanks where he would have waited five minutes. Then, realising that Strachan was running late, he would have headed back to shore as per their agreement. There was no point in them both being captured.

Once Strachan had appeared in their bar, the Japanese would have relaxed their vigil, allowing Piet to fin close to the surface as he swam back to land. With his years of experience, he would have enough air to last at least ninety minutes. That was plenty for the two-mile journey back to Dragon Point.

Once Piet hit the rocks, he would have ditched his scuba gear and returned to Kerkulla Besar on foot. There would have been many headlands to swim around and many beaches to cross, but the furthest distance between the two islands was half a mile and Piet would have swum that in no time. His total journey would have taken a couple of hours. He would have arrived at the gully in time to welcome the *Esprit Bleu* and begin planning Strachan's rescue.

Strachan stole a glance at Verhoeven to see if he suspected a trap. The gully was his territory. His odds of survival were shortening with every metre. So long as they heard the approaching boat there was a healthy chance that Piet and Sumo could prepare an ambush. Since he hadn't yet revealed himself, Strachan was confident that Piet was biding his time. Had they launched a rescue party in the *Esprit Bleu* they would have been gunned down by the helicopter in no time. Maybe he'd seen Strachan leaving the *Fubuki* and had attempted to reach Kerkulla Cicak by foot.

Ideally they would have recovered all twelve safes, but there was money enough in the first to last a lifetime, and the other eleven weren't worth dying for. If they could overpower Verhoeven, Strachan would happily settle for enough to build his beach shack in St Michiel's Bay, and Wakahama could die with the rest.

Strachan steered them round the hairpins. There was no sign of the *Esprit Bleu*. He guessed Sumo had heard their approach and motored upstream. Strachan was exhausted from the emotional impact of Hamilton's death but the thought of being rescued brought a welcome surge of energy.

It didn't last long. He should have known better than to count his chickens at a time like this.

Shleppy.

Sumo's nephew was in the middle of the gully, catching breakfast. Having heard them too late, he was only now fleeing for the beach. He wore mask, snorkel and fins. His chubby brown arms thrashed the water as he swam. When he threw away his harpoon to gain more speed, Strachan saw that he'd skewered three mullet. One of them was still writhing in its death throes.

For a brief second he thought Shleppy was going to make it, but he was wrong. Fins are designed for displacing water, not sprinting over beaches. Shleppy fell with his first steps on land. Verhoeven charged down the boat, leaping off the bows like a leopard. He landed in knee-deep water and charged up the beach. He was onto Shleppy in seconds.

Strachan opened the throttle and rammed the boat up

the beach. He carved a trench in the sand with the keel. Verhoeven had Shleppy by the hair, marching him up the beach so forcefully that the poor boy's feet scarcely touched the ground. Then he stopped. There was a wild look in his eye: a mixture of excitement, desperation and greed. He pressed the rifle under the boy's chin. 'Listen to me!' he yelled. 'All of you. Wherever you are.'

Strachan didn't like the look of this. Whatever rescue plans Piet might have drawn up were suddenly redundant. He slid over the rail onto the beach. The edge in Verhoeven's voice told him that the man from Interpol meant what he said.

'I am going to count to four,' Verhoeven was calling out, addressing the beach, the jungle and the surrounding hills. 'I know you are there. If you do not show yourselves, I will shoot the boy child in the head.'

Strachan ran towards them. He had no idea what he was going to do but he had to do something. Verhoeven was only fifteen yards away. The Dutchman spun and fired a single shot. It nicked Strachan just above the hip, grazing his flesh. The shock of it brought him up cold. He stopped where he was. The next shot would kill him. Another charge would be suicide. He peered gingerly at his hip. There was a lot of blood but the wound wasn't deep. It was nothing more than a scratch. If Verhoeven had been aiming for that it was a peach of a shot.

'Stay where you are, Strachan.' Verhoeven was breathing heavily, high on adrenalin, sweating like a junkie in the morning heat. He started to count. 'One.'

Strachan knelt in the sand and surveyed the surrounding jungle. There was no sign of life. Even the cicadas had fallen silent.

'Two.'

Still no sign of movement. Where the hell were they? Strachan couldn't believe they would call Verhoeven's bluff. Even if Piet wanted to tough it out, Sumo wouldn't stand for it.

On 'Three' Verhoeven released his grip on Shleppy. He shouldered the rifle and took aim against the boy's head. Shleppy froze. He was like the rat in the wicker lid. He stared at Strachan in wide-eyed terror, those beautiful brown eyes imploring him to do something – anything – to make this man go away. Strachan's vision swam with pain as he hauled himself to his feet.

'Four.'

75

The others emerged from the edge of the jungle. They'd been hiding in the same bamboo thicket that had provided the lever poles. They walked onto the beach, Sumo leading the way. His fists were clubbed at his sides and his eyes burned. He never blinked. His face was set firm. It was hard and brown like teak. Strachan thought that Verhoeven had better make damned sure he knew what he was doing otherwise Sumo would inflict untold suffering on him when he got the chance.

'Excellent.' Verhoeven sighed with relief when he saw them. 'Now then, where is the safe?' Verhoeven held Shleppy by the hair again. He backed up a few paces until the others joined Strachan and he could cover them all with his gun.

'I'm standing right on top of it,' Strachan told him through gritted teeth.

'No tricks, Strachan. Otherwise the kid dies.'

'Go to hell, Verhoeven.' Strachan hardly cared if Verhoeven shot him again. Especially if it gave Piet a chance to go for the gun. He turned to his friend. 'Where were you earlier?'

'Waiting. I knew you'd come back.'

Verhoeven was getting impatient. 'Shut up and dig. All of you.'

They were in no position to argue so they fell to their knees, and set to work with their hands. Half an hour ago

Strachan had buried his godfather. Now he was exhuming his safe.

They'd buried it a foot deep, but the rain had moistened the sand, which meant that the walls of their hole stayed firm. After a few minutes the safe's top was exposed to view but it still took the best part of an hour to clear the sides. Strachan was in dire need of water. His hip burned. The wound became caked in sand. It stung like hell but at least it stopped the blood.

Verhoeven sat in the middle of the beach. He was still holding the rifle to Shleppy's head. He allowed them to catch their breath, then sauntered over to inspect their work, dragging Shleppy behind him. Strachan noted the look of surprise on the Dutchman's face. Verhoeven had been expecting a trick. He even seemed disappointed that he didn't need to punish anyone, but his disappointment rapidly turned to anticipation. The safe was almost his. All he had to do was to get it on deck, then he would be a rich man. He indicated KT with the muzzle of the AK-47. 'You.'

KT walked forward reluctantly. Verhoeven made no attempt to conceal his approval of her curves. She replied with a look that would have petrified Medusa.

'There are some ropes in the forepeak. Get them out, and bring them here.'

KT did as she was told and clambered aboard the *Ping-Pong Taboo*. She burrowed in the forepeak until she found the lines. There were three ropes. Sumo and Piet lashed them round the safe. Verhoeven instructed KT to lower a gangplank to the beach before returning to the *Ping-Pong Taboo*, taking Shleppy with him. 'Now, pull it on board.'

'It's too heavy,' Strachan said.

'Not for three strong boys like you. I will not tell you again.' He hit Shleppy on the head with the barrel of the AK-47 to emphasise his point. *Tonk!* Shleppy winced.

The three of them strained like pack mules. The rope bit into their shoulders and hands. Their skin blistered but inch by inch they heaved the safe from the hole: the spoils of an earlier war.

Moving the safe was easier than it had been before for a number of reasons, not the least of which was the fact that this time they were pulling downhill. Once they had some momentum, they rolled it onto the gangplank with surprisingly little effort. Next they climbed on board and took the strain for the final five yards. The gangplank bent in the middle under the weight. Strachan thought it was going to snap but the wood was highly polished and offered little resistance to the safe's iron base. The sight of Verhoeven with a gun to Shleppy's head gave them hidden strength. Sumo pulled like a man possessed, and eventually they hauled the safe on deck.

They stood with their hands on their knees, gulping for breath. It was a sultry morning. Strachan felt bile rising in his throat. The air was damp in his lungs, and he knew that he was dehydrating. The litre of Evian had been quickly absorbed. Now, with the loss of blood and the physical exertion, he was beginning to suffer. Somehow he still found the strength to call Verhoeven a miserable bastard. 'Let him go now. You've got the safe.'

Piet joined in with a few expletives of his own. Verhoeven raised his eyebrows, surprised at hearing his native tongue so far from home. He smiled at them. He was a professional. He wasn't going to be riled at this stage. 'Back up. All of you.' He waved the rifle at them one-handed like a wand. Then he returned the muzzle to its resting point against Shleppy's temple. They saw the sinews in his arm tighten. They moved back as one. Verhoeven's finger was on the trigger. Even if they'd been able to get at him, any aggressive movement would have caused the gun to fire. 'Off the boat.'

Verhoeven watched their every move. He waited until they'd completed the command before issuing the next. One by one they walked down the gangplank into the shallows and onto the beach. 'Now. Very slowly. Back up the beach.'

They obeyed silently, each of them thinking the same thing.

'Don't do it, Sumo.' Piet could see him fighting the temptation to charge. 'Not yet, big guy. The time will come. Stay alive. Shleppy will be fine.'

He was right, of course. Shleppy's best chance was for them all to cooperate. Strachan repeated it to himself as they retreated up the burning sand. They reached the edge of the bamboo thicket and paused. None of them knew what to do. Verhoeven had the safe, and there were thirty yards between them. Strachan was unarmed. The ball was firmly in Verhoeven's court. So long as he had Shleppy, there wasn't a darn thing anyone could do to get it back. They stood there, powerless.

'Strachan?' Verhoeven called to him. As at Schiphol, he mispronounced his name.

'What?'

'I don't want to see your ugly face ever again. I am going to have to kill you now.' And he raised the rifle to make his shot.

Strachan didn't wait for another invitation. He threw himself sideways behind a cluster of rocks. The crack of the rifle came at the same moment, the bullet searing the air where his head had been. Verhoeven needed two hands to fire the gun. It was the break Shleppy needed. He ran the length of the boat and leaped from the stern, disappearing into the deeper water behind.

Verhoeven let him go. It was Strachan he wanted.

The shots came quickly. The jungle shuddered with the crack, whistle, and thud of high-velocity rounds. Verhoeven was emptying his magazine into the rocks and undergrowth, seemingly at random. It pinned Strachan down while the others bolted for the depths of the bamboo thicket. He watched as they took cover. They lay in the prone position with their hands over their heads. Shleppy had crossed the gully underwater and now he too had found some rocks behind which to shelter.

Verhoeven paused. He scanned the thicket for movement. He looked annoyed. He should have killed Strachan while he had the chance. Hauling the safe on board had dislodged his boat, and it had slid back off the beach. It was drifting towards the faster water in the middle of the gully. When the gangplank slipped off the side and into the water, he made no attempt to retrieve it.

Although the others were still alive, Verhoeven had an opportunity to make his escape. He wasn't going to blow it. He fired the remaining shots in the weapon's magazine into the air, then threw the rifle on the deck. He turned and ran to start the engines.

There was a primeval bellow as Sumo charged from the thicket like an enraged bull. The jungle flattened around him as he burst onto the beach. He held a machete high in his hand. He lumbered towards the boat, eating up the ground in strides that shook the earth.

There was no need for this. It was over, Shleppy was safe. Strachan yelled at Sumo to stop but his words fell on deaf ears. Rage consumed the big man. Fury boiled in his brain. The trauma that Verhoeven had inflicted on Sumo's nephew could not be forgiven. He reached the water and threw the machete. It spun through the air, glinting in the sun as the light caught its blade. It was a hell of a shot. It thwacked into the door frame of the main cabin where it quivered like an arrow.

Sumo was five metres from the back of the boat when the propellers suddenly burst to life, churning the water like a jacuzzi. The stern swerved left and right, fishtailing as Verhoeven fought to bring it under control. Sumo was losing ground. He punched the water in frustration. It was an uneven match. The *Ping-Pong Taboo* increased its lead with every second. Then it rounded the bend and disappeared from sight. The drone of its engines mocked them. The safe was gone.

76

The *Esprit Bleu* was a hundred yards further up the gully. The banks were so steep and the jungle so thick that it took a while to reach her.

Rutger Verhoeven had a fifteen-minute head start. The *Esprit Bleu* was the faster of the two boats but as they burst out onto the open sea the Interpol agent was nowhere to be seen. He would be weaving in and out of the islands until he could make a clean break for it. It was unlikely that they would ever catch him.

Flying the safe home would be a non-starter for him. It was prohibitively heavy. It would invite a series of unwelcome questions from Customs. Strachan figured that Verhoeven would probably sail the *Ping-Pong Taboo* all the way back to Holland, and he had better things to do than chase his enemy across six thousand miles of ocean.

The *Fubuki,* meanwhile, stuck out like a sore thumb. As they rounded Dragon Point they spotted her on the same mooring above the wreck. Wakahama had given up waiting for the return of his three guards. Maybe he had heard the gunfire and assumed the worst. Bodyguards were as disposable as razor blades to a man in his position, and he was preparing to leave without them. Strachan could see that the final three safes had joined the others on the yacht's foredeck. Eleven was enough. Wakahama wasn't going to wait for the twelfth. Verhoeven could keep it.

The *Fubuki* raised anchor when she saw the sport-fisher coming but she was too late. The big yacht was slow by comparison. The *Esprit Bleu* was onto her in minutes, hunting her down like an orca pursuing a bigger whale. The *Fubuki* had travelled no more than a hundred metres from her mooring when Piet instructed KT and Shleppy to go below. Then he joined Sumo and Strachan on the flybridge for the final act.

The alarm had been raised. Through the binoculars Strachan saw Wakahama and three of his bodyguards taking up defensive positions on the upper deck. He recognised one of them as the man who'd caught him. The bodyguard raised his rifle to his shoulder but Wakahama swatted it down.

Wakahama wore an expression of profound annoyance. Strachan wasn't supposed to be alive. He was supposed to be in small pieces. He was supposed to be in the belly of a large lizard. Strachan watched him with an air of detached amusement. Wakahama was wondering what was going to happen next. If he stayed where he was, he would find out soon enough.

Piet opened the locker in front of his knees. Sumo's flare gun had never been used. It was a twelve-gauge aerial alerter, still in its box. The box said it was *For Marine Safety Only*. The gun was bright orange. It looked like a child's toy. It had a short barrel with a bore the size of an exhaust pipe. It had three cartridges. Piet loaded one, then handed the pistol to Strachan.

Wakahama snatched a rifle from the nearest goon. There was a hint of panic as he fed a round to the chamber. The two boats were fifty yards apart and closing fast. Wakahama was armed with an assault rifle, lethal at over a mile. Strachan had a flare gun with a range of three hundred feet. Strachan fired first.

Sumo cut the throttle at the same instant. The *Esprit*

Bleu settled into the sea. The flare flew into the water behind the *Fubuki*. Wakahama lowered his rifle. His earlier annoyance turned to amusement.

They all knew what he was thinking. He was thinking that Strachan had been aiming for him. He was thinking that Strachan had missed. He was thinking that he was safe.

He was wrong on all three counts.

They'd picked up the fuel trail while they were still a minute out. It snaked over the surface in a black and blue slick, a highly combustible mixture of diesel and oil.

Piet had continued to work on the underside of the yacht long after Strachan had climbed up the anchor chain to plant Gelex along its deck. The manufacturers had made it easy for him. They'd marked the engines' maintenance hatches in English. He had drilled five small holes in the fuel tanks, and another five in the oil sump. Sufficient for both to leak at a steady trickle but insufficient for the gauge on the captain's dash to register anything out of the ordinary. The sea was flat. The oil hadn't yet dissipated. It sat on the surface a metre wide. The flare fell into the water five metres off their stern. Sumo put the *Esprit Bleu* into reverse.

For a second Strachan thought it had all gone horribly wrong. The flare fizzed on the surface. It burned itself out in a bright red flame. Then it flickered back to life like a firework on a rainy night. Some of the guards were laughing when the diesel finally ignited. *For Marine Safety Only*. Strachan grinned at the irony.

The fuel slick caught with a brief but audible *whoosh*. Then the flames spread across it. The oil went up with a roar. Oxygen was sucked from the surrounding air to feed the fireball. At less than ten knots, the *Fubuki* had a beautifully smooth wake. There were no waves to douse the flames which accelerated voraciously towards the boat.

The bodyguards' smiles disappeared. The flames reached the leaking fuel pipe and the engines exploded with a blast that forced them to duck. When Strachan looked again, the aft section of the boat was on fire. There was a flurry of activity. Wakahama marched backwards and forwards, screaming at his men to extinguish the flames. But they had no chance. No chance – and no idea that Piet had taped the hull with eight sticks of dynamite. That Strachan had concealed three more in the anchor well. That there were two more in the lifeboat, and another three in the ski-locker.

The sticks in the ski-locker were the first to go. They seemed to suck in the air from miles around. Then they threw it back in a blast that knocked Strachan off his feet. The shock wave reverberated off the sea and rumbled back at them from the Kerkulla hills.

One after the other, the remaining sticks exploded. The dynamite detonated along the length of the keel in neatly punctuated intervals. Wakahama's yacht went up like a tinder box. Debris was thrown a hundred metres into the sky. It rained down in a lethal storm of serrated edges. The safes came down undamaged, striking the sea like big iron bombs. Water was thrown fifteen metres in the air as they landed.

What was left was unrecognisable as a yacht. The larger sections of wreckage sank below the surface now ablaze with diesel. Sumo motored in closer but had to stop at the edge of the flames. Most of the infrastructure had already sunk but the surface was still awash with junk that hadn't been dragged under by the yacht's sinking carcass. Planks of torn wood hissed as the *Esprit Bleu*'s bow wave washed over them, extinguishing the flames that curled round their edges. A charred body spun in a slow circle with a chair, life ring and water-ski. Further away, a leather suitcase bobbed over the water like an upturned coracle. Elsewhere washing-up bowls, deckchair covers, Coke bottles and fenders gathered in clusters that would eventually wash up on the Kerkullas, giving the national park's police their biggest-ever case.

The sea still burned. Thick black smoke rose into the sky. It was time for Strachan and his friends to go.

They were on the open ocean. The *Fubuki* had only travelled two hundred yards from her mooring before she'd sunk. In that distance the depth had changed significantly. Strachan glanced at the instrument panel on Sumo's dash. The digital depth sounder read 1,820.7m. That was deep. Very deep. There was no way that gold was coming back up without the help of a submarine.

Piet and Sumo went below to check on KT and Shleppy. Strachan was left alone on the bridge with his thoughts. As calm returned, he heard Sumo working the radio, making contact with his cousin in Kuantan.

Strachan scanned the horizon and picked up a black speck away to his left. Rutger Verhoeven was three miles away. Chasing him down would be a waste of time. The final safe was making its way back to Holland.

And Strachan wasn't going to stop it.

77

Verhoeven's journey home would be about as long as Strachan's. While the *Esprit Bleu* took a short cut through the Panama Canal, the *Ping-Pong Taboo* would be shooting the Suez. Verhoeven might decide to cruise the Mediterranean for a while: to enjoy the warmth of the North African coast before heading back to November in Amsterdam. He would spend his time contemplating how much better bounty hunting paid than police work. If he hadn't already been fired for going A.W.O.L. he might even resign.

Having been an international cop for ten years, Verhoeven would have a good idea of how to sell a safe of gold sovereigns on the black market. Within a couple of weeks the *Ping-Pong Taboo* might be moored in the marinas of Tripoli or Palermo while he went ashore to make his enquiries.

But first he would need to open the safe.

He would stop to buy an oxyacetylene torch or some plastic explosive. He would choose a sunny afternoon and sail far out to sea. The anticipation would be delicious as he cut the motor. He would kneel in front of the safe. In total privacy and absolute silence he would set to work on the hinges. In his excitement he would hardly consider it significant that the solder sealing the door looked newer than the rest of the safe. The door would fall to the deck with a heavy thump and he would congratulate himself on making such light work of it.

Then the contents would come spilling onto the deck. Pouring from the safe like a landslide, they would bruise Verhoeven's knees and batter his hands. Miles out to sea there would be no one to witness the expression on his face, nor anyone to hear his roar of fury. But somewhere on the other side of the world Ed Strachan would sense it. And if there was life after death, Adrian Hamilton and Molly Newchris would smile with him as rock after rock tumbled onto the deck of the *Ping-Pong Taboo*.

It had been hard work emptying the gold into the holdalls. Harder still carrying it on board the *Esprit Bleu*. But their caution had paid off. Strachan had insisted on loading the safe so full of stones that it didn't rattle. After Piet had soldered the door back in its place they'd used the last of their strength to bury it.

One day Verhoeven would come looking for Strachan. They would meet again; Strachan was quite sure of that. In the meantime he would enjoy this victory. He stood on the bridge and watched until the black splinter of Verhoeven's boat became indistinguishable from the flat line of the horizon. Strachan was glad to be leaving Malaysia with its snakes and lizards. As he took the wheel, he felt his two silver cuff links burning his chest in the sun. Left and right. Longitude and latitude. Yin and Yang.

They had done their job, but they had brought bad luck as well as good. It was time for them to go. His determination to fulfil their prophecy had caused him to kill Molly Newchris, Pili Parang, Wakahama, and an unknown number of the Japanese gangster's crew. Michelle Newchris and Rutger Verhoeven had fallen under their spell and both had lost heavily. Adrian Hamilton had been touched by their magic and had paid the ultimate price. And back in London a young boy was growing up without his mother.

The cuff links were useless now. Their magic was spent. Without giving it a second thought, Strachan took the chain from around his neck. He coiled it in his fist and launched it spiralling over the rail. The cuff links melted into the sun. He never saw them land.

They sailed back to Tioman where Strachan collected the calendar and the rest of his money. They settled their bills for the beach huts, then motored across the straits to Kuantan. On the way Strachan called a short meeting to discuss his plans for the rest of the gold. He knew exactly what he wanted to do with it, and within a few minutes the others had all bought into his idea.

Sumo's cousin was waiting for them with a needle and thread. He bathed Strachan's hip in disinfectant, and Piet chuckled gleefully as his friend was stitched up without an anaesthetic.

'How are you going to get your gold home?' Sumo put a hand on Strachan's shoulder.

'We'll hire a boat. Hell, we'll even buy one.'

'I have one that you can buy.'

'Excellent,' Strachan told him. 'When can we see it?'

'Now.'

Strachan scanned the marina. It was mostly full of local fishing boats. The *Esprit Bleu* was the only vessel not made from wood. 'Er, I don't think so, Sumo. I'm not sure any of this lot would make it across the Pacific.'

Sumo laughed his big belly laugh. His eyes twinkled and his breasts wobbled. Then he stamped his foot on the cockpit floor. 'No, Strachan. The *Esprit Bleu*. She's all yours.'

Strachan didn't think he'd heard him right. The *Esprit Bleu* was the only woman in Sumo's life. She was his love. His pride and joy. 'You're kidding me!'

'No. She's junk. You can buy her. I'm going to get something faster.'

Strachan laughed like a child. He threw his arms round Sumo's shoulders and hugged him. It was a terrible error. Sumo squeezed back.

Sumo and Shleppy spent a couple of hours removing their belongings. They had a garage at the end of the marina where they stored their stuff. Strachan counted out their share of the gold and added some more for the *Esprit Bleu*. They loaded it into the back of the doctor's car. The suspension creaked and the wheel arches came dangerously close to the tyres. Then they sat on the quay and drank iced tea. It was time to say goodbye.

'Promise me you won't go back for that gold.' Strachan looked Sumo in the eye.

'I promise. We have enough. I can afford a boat but I cannot afford a submarine. You're doing the right thing.' The big man shook Strachan's hand. The secret was safe.

KT embraced Shleppy and gave him a huge kiss on the cheek. He wriggled like an eel before Piet and Strachan cuffed him playfully round the ears.

They climbed into the doctor's car, and Sumo wound down the window. '*Ada air adalah ikan.*'

'Say that again.' Strachan hadn't got it.

'*Ada air adalah ikan.*'

'What does it mean?'

'Old Malaysian proverb. It means *where there is water, there are fish*. "Que sera, sera," if you prefer.'

Strachan didn't. *Ada air adalah ikan* sounded much better. 'Where there's water, there're fish. I like that.'

The car pulled away in a cloud of dust.

They left at eight o'clock that evening. Sumo had a cousin who worked in Customs and there were no questions about the export of the *Esprit Bleu*. Strachan did his best to maintain a straight face as he told him they had nothing to declare.

En route to Singapore Strachan discussed arrangements for wiring KT her share of the gold to America. Her torture by Pili Parang meant she had earned her quota as much as anyone. It would take considerable time and legal advice to convert the sovereigns into cash, but when it was done Strachan insisted that she should come to Curaçao to collect her cheque personally.

He briefly suggested that she join him on their journey across the Pacific, but she just laughed and told him to get real. A week ago she had been on a diving holiday with her boyfriend. Now she'd been used as shark bait and shot at with an automatic rifle. Come hell or high water she was going home.

They dropped her at the Changi marina in Singapore. Strachan followed her down the jetty to the taxi rank. The lights of the container ships were strung out over the sea like lanterns. There was a question Strachan had to ask. It had been eating away at him since they'd first met. Since she'd flipped ten beer mats and caught them without looking. Since she'd first called him Lance. It was a test. He needed to know if he'd passed. He took her hand and looked her in the eye. 'What does KT stand for?'

Her face lit up in unexpected pleasure and Strachan knew that this time he'd got it right. She rolled her eyes. Then she leaned over and whispered in his ear.

'Nice,' he said. 'It's pretty.'

'You think?'

'I've heard worse.'

'What about you? I looked at your passport the other day and it says your real name is Banbury.'

'That's right.'
'Banbury? As in Banbury Cross?'
'Exactly.'
'It's classy.'
'You think?'
'I've heard worse.'
Strachan kissed KT full on the mouth. Now that they'd introduced themselves, it was time to say good-bye. They kissed again. She climbed into the taxi and was gone.

Heavy with gold and extra barrels of diesel, the *Esprit Bleu* sat low in the water. They would have to be wary of strong seas as they made the eight-thousand-mile journey across the Pacific. Towering waves would crash over the rails in a storm. It would be a battle just to stay afloat. But, like its previous owner, the *Esprit Bleu* was strong and steady, and she wouldn't let them down on their journey from east to west.

They would refuel in Micronesia. Then they would drive carefully towards South America. Slow enough to conserve fuel, fast enough to keep her on an even keel. Once they hit the Galapagos they would bear north-east to Panama. They would cut through the canal and emerge into the calmer seas of the south Caribbean. From there it would be a straight run home, around the north coast of Venezuela to St Michiel's Bay in Curaçao.

Piet was on the radio to Koopmans, smoothing their arrival. Strachan had enough money to satisfy Curaçao Immigration. St Michiel's Bay was no longer out of bounds. St Michiel's Bay was home.

Strachan closed his eyes. He pictured himself lying in a hammock. He pictured the horizon blushing from the sun's last kiss. He pictured the dolphins leaping in the lagoon. He had a barbecue going. The smell of char-grilled lobster drifted over on a breeze that rustled the palms above his head. Somewhere in the distance a band played calypso.

EPILOGUE

One month later.

Michelle Newchris sat on the sofa in her London flat. Her grandson was asleep in the room next door. He was growing up fast.

In her hands she held a parcel. It had been delivered that morning by air express. It bore a Curaçao postmark and she was reluctant to open it. The word *Curaçao* brought back painful memories. She looked at the parcel again. It didn't look official. Her address was handwritten.

Michelle Newchris took a mouthful of coffee. She went to the kitchen and returned with a knife. Carefully, nervously, she opened the package.

Inside was a book. It was a collection of nursery rhymes. Something was wedged between the pages like a bookmark. She took it out. It was a silver cross on a chain. It was engraved with Molly's initials, but it was also engraved with a map reference. Two sets of coordinates. Latitude and longitude. Simple, elegant, priceless.

Michelle Newchris put the cross down. She walked through to the bedroom. She picked up the baby boy and carried him back to the sofa. He began to cry.

She gave him the cross. She put it round his neck and held it up for him to see. He took it in his podgy little fingers. He stopped crying, and smiled.

Very gently, Michelle Newchris moved the infant onto her knee. The man who had sent the book had added a second verse to the nursery rhyme on the bookmarked page. She recognised the rhyme but not this second verse. He had also added a short paragraph in the margin: a mixture of explanation and instruction. She looked again at the silver cross with its two engraved coordinates, and the penny dropped.

Her grandson squealed, then gurgled with delight. She bounced him on her knee, and began reciting the rhyme.

Ride a cock horse to Banbury Cross ...

ACKNOWLEDGEMENTS

John Capron read the first draft with a lawyer's scrutiny. He suggested several ideas that later became central to the plot, and was an enormous help throughout. Elizabeth Wright, my agent at the Darley Anderson Literary Agency, receives over 250 manuscripts a week. She was a fan of *Double Cross* from the start, and her advice, enthusiasm and encouragement have been invaluable. Oliver Johnson, my editor at Random House was patient, rigorous and great fun to work with as we tightened the screws on the final draft. Thank you.

I would also like to thank the following for their advice, help and encouragement: Darley Anderson, Nick Austin, Giles Bryan, Warren Chester, Julia Churchill, Joffy Conolly, Kevin and Victoria Dowd, Catrine Gapper, Allan Gasson and the staff at Burlington Consultants, JP McManus, Nathalie O'Dwyer, Don Starr, Boris Starling, James Taylor, Erich Zielinksi, my parents, and my sister Kate.

ALSO AVAILABLE IN ARROW

HMS Unseen

The deadliest ship in the world has fallen into the hands of a terrorist enemy – the submariner believed to be behind the destruction of the *Thomas Jefferson*, has returned to seek his revenge on
his Iraqi paymasters and the country that betrayed him.

He defects to Iran, where he is helped in his plan to transform a
stolen submarine into a unique weapon capable of causing the
most shocking air strikes in an American history. His vengeance
on the US is devastating, H.M.S. Unseen is lost, and the blame
appears to lie with Iraq.

It is up to Admiral Arnold Morgan to prove his suspicions that Iraq
isn't responsible, and that Ben Adnam is the only man skilful
enough to orchestrate such an attack, and he must stop him,
whatever the cost . . .

'A brilliantly conceived and breathlessly executed thriller'
Kirkus Reviews

'Patrick Robinson's best book yet. *HMS Unseen*, the third volume
of his brilliant naval series . . . is a dazzling, page-turning yarn that
establishes its author as a master craftsman of the techno-
thriller. No one does it better – not even Tom Clancy . . . Highly
recommended.' Carol D'Este, author of *Patton: A Genius for
War*

'Watch out for Robinson. He is in the same league as Clancy'
Birmingham Post

arrow books

Scimitar SL-2

Patrick Robinson's latest novel

A world-renowned vulcanologist mysteriously disappears after a lecture on geophysical catastrophes. Two policemen are found brutally executed nearby. Then, Mount St Helen's suddenly and inexplicably erupts in Washington State, leaving a wake of death and destruction. The new, liberal administration in the White House speaks of coincidences, but the retired Admiral Morgan and Lt Cdr Jimmy Ramshawe suspect an old nemesis: Major Ray Kerman, the fabled Hamas terrorist. Their suspicions are quickly confirmed by a sinister Hamas threat: to launch a brand-new, state-of-the-art Scimitar SL-2 missile straight at the heart of the volcano Cumbre Vieja in the Canary Islands. The impact would explode the mountain into the Atlantic and send the greatest tidal wave in history towards the East Coast of the United States.

Shocked into action, Admiral Morgan returns to the White House to run *Operation High Tide* – a desperate race to evacuate the East Coast and locate the nuclear submarine before it launches its deadly weapon.

'An absolutely marvellous thriller writer' Jack Higgins

'Watch out for Robinson. He is in the same league as Clancy'
Birmingham Post

'The new Frederick Forsyth' *Guardian*

arrow books

Greed

Greed is an explosive story of what happens when terrorism, money, love and jealously combust.

Five Men. One Robbery. A deadly game of greed, revenge and betrayal is about to begin.

Fresh out of the SAS, Matt Browning is down on his luck. He owes £500,000. If he doesn't get the money soon, he dies. From nowhere, he is offered a lifeline. A hit on al-Qaeda, sanctioned and helped by MI5. Matt gathers a small team of former SAS men to steal $10 million in gold and diamonds from the world's most deadly terrorist organisation. MI5 will give them all the equipment and information they need. No charges will ever be pressed.

Matt thinks it's the perfect crime. Safe, quick, and patriotic. But after the money is stolen, the killing starts.

Someone is taking down the members of the team one by one. A silent, expert assassin is stalking the team, gruesomely murdering both them and their families. And Matt knows that he's next.

"lean prose delivers all the action with the usual trenchant force . . . The plot moves like the proverbial express train"
The Good Books Guide

'Hard as nails' Mirror

arrow books

Land of Fire

1982. The Falklands War. Young SAS trooper, Mark Black, risks his life to capture an Argentine girl spy. To knock out enemy bombers a daring mission is planned against a fortified airbase on Tierra del Fuego. Black and his fellow SAS are sent ahead to reconnoitre. Detected by the enemy, they must fight their way out . . .

Twenty years on, now a senior NCO, Black is back in the South Atlantic, haunted by memories he thought he had buried. Once again Argentine forces are being secretly readied for an assault on the islands. A team from the crack SAS Mountain Troop is inserted by submarine. But has the mission been compromised from the start? When fate throws Black together with the girl from his past, he is faced with a conflict of loyalties. Can he trust her now? And can they escape in time to destroy the enemy bombers and prevent all-out war?

Praise for Land of Fire:

'A rampaging boombuster'
Mirror

'Tough, high-testosterone stuff, gripping'
Herald

'Takes your breath away'
Northern Echo

arrow books